# PRAISE FOR *HER NAME IS KNIGHT*

"A crackerjack story with truly memorable characters. I can't wait to see what Yasmin Angoe comes up with next."

—David Baldacci, #1 *New York Times* bestselling author

"Yasmin Angoe's debut novel, *Her Name Is Knight*, is an amazing action packed international thriller full of suspense, danger, and even romance. It's like a John Wick prequel except John is a beautiful African woman with a particular set of skills."

—S. A. Cosby, award-winning author of *Blacktop Wasteland*

"It's hard to believe that *Her Name Is Knight* is Yasmin Angoe's debut novel. This dual timeline story about a highly trained Miami-based assassin who learns to reclaim her power after having her entire life ripped from her as a teenager in Ghana is equal parts love story, social commentary, and action thriller. Nena Knight will stay with you long after you've read the last word, and this is a must-read for fans of Lee Child and S. A. Cosby. I found myself crying in one chapter and cheering in the next. I couldn't put it down!"

—Kellye Garrett, Anthony, Agatha, and Lefty Award–winning author

"This was a book I couldn't put down. Yasmin Angoe does a brilliant job of inviting you into a world of espionage and revenge while giving her characters depth and backstory that pull the reader in even more. This story has depth, excitement, and heartbreaking loss all intertwined into an awesome debut. The spy thriller genre has a new name to look out for!"

—Matthew Farrell, bestselling author of *Don't Ever Forget*

# HER
# NAME
## IS
# KNIGHT

# HER NAME IS KNIGHT

### YASMIN ANGOE

THOMAS & MERCER

Text copyright © 2021 by Yasmin Angoe

Published by Thomas & Mercer, Seattle

www.apub.com

Amazon, the Amazon logo, and Thomas & Mercer are trademarks of Amazon.com, Inc., or its affiliates.

ISBN-13: 9781542029957 (hardcover)
ISBN-10: 1542029953 (hardcover)

ISBN-13: 9781542029940 (paperback)
ISBN-10: 1542029945 (paperback)

Cover design by Anna Laytham

Printed in the United States of America

First edition

*To my dad, Herbert Nana Angoe, chief of our tribe.*
*Rest in peace, Dad.*

Memory is both a gift and a curse.

# AUTHOR'S NOTE

Please note this novel depicts issues of emotional, sexual, and physical abuse; parental death; human trafficking; and both physical and sexual violence. The descriptions of violence are vivid, and I have worked to approach these topics with the utmost sensitivity and respect; I wanted you to be aware in case any of the content is triggering. Please use the resources below if you need any support.

One other thing: This novel is about one fictional woman's story, told concurrently during two different times of her life. During her childhood her story is in first person present tense so that you see the world and her journey through her eyes. As an adult, her story is in third person past tense to give you a panoramic view and scope of what this kick-ass assassin can do.

Thanks,
Yasmin

**Suggested Resources for Victims of Human Trafficking and Abuse:**

- RAINN National Sexual Assault Telephone Hotline: 800-656-HOPE (4673)
- Department of Defense Safe Helpline: 1-877-995-5247
- National Human Trafficking Hotline: 1-888-373-7888

- National Domestic Violence Hotline: 1-800-799-7233
- National Suicide Prevention Lifeline: 1-800-273-8255
- National Alliance on Mental Illness Helpline: 1-800-950-6264
- Crisis Text Line: Text HOME to 741741

# LANGUAGE NOTES

Wudini (pronounced *WHOA-dih-knee*)—a noun.

Twi, one of the Ghanaian dialects from the Fanti region of the Ashanti.

Translated, "wudini" means *murderer, killer,* or, as it relates to Nena Knight, *assassin.*

# 1

## AFTER

Echo cast one more look at herself, making sure the swim cap was securely on her head, the waterproof earpiece embedded in the diamond stud earrings she wore. She bent down, grabbing the fluffy white towel next to her, making sure her tool was nestled within its folds. Nigerian businessman and fixer Adam Mofour liked to take a swim early in the morning, before the community pool began to fill with patrons preparing for classes or practicing on Nigeria's Olympic team.

She padded out of the locker room toward the inside pool. She could hear the mark's splashes echoing in the hallway as he took his laps. Smelled the chlorine before spying the blue of the water with the black painted lines on the pool floor. She stopped at the entrance, scanning in case anyone was there and she'd have to take them out too. The place, as she'd anticipated, was empty.

A disembodied voice said through her comms, "Security is doing rounds. You're clear."

She laid her towel on the tiled floor next to the edge of the pool as Mofour approached, slicing through the water with the grace of an athlete. From the intel she'd received, Echo knew swimming was a passion of his. He should have stuck to that, rather than selling out the

Tribe and passing state secrets to their enemies for his financial benefit. Wasn't her concern if he was truly guilty or not. The Tribe had marked Mofour for dispatch, and she was there to see it through.

His strong arms cut through the water in a breaststroke. She readied herself. When his fingers were about to touch the pool's edge, she struck out, yanking him toward her so she could wrap her arm around his neck. She lifted his head above water, using one hand to prop herself along the edge as she brought him in thrashing and choking with surprise. She used that surprise to pull him up farther while she plucked the syringe from the towel and injected the needle into his neck. She adjusted, leaning her weight on him as she plunged his head below the surface. His arms shot out, beating at her in weak attempts to get her off. She could hear his garbled yells as his body convulsed. She held on with a viselike grip until her mark's thrashing began to wane, till the gurgles stopped bubbling to the surface, till the stimulant took effect, stopping his heart. Then Echo let him float away.

She got out of the water, wrapped the emptied hypodermic back in the towel, and returned to the locker room, where she changed her clothes and dumped the towel, her suit and cap, and the empty syringe in her duffel to dispose of elsewhere. She waited until Mofour's security team passed the locker room on their way back to the pool to check on their boss. When she was clear, she slipped out and walked the opposite direction up the stairs and out the front entrance. She was approaching the car she'd lifted when Witt, head of the Dispatch division of the Tribe, spoke through her comms.

"Nicely done. As usual."

"Thanks." She buckled her seat belt.

Her mouth twitched with pleasure at the rare compliment from her mentor. Then she turned the ignition and drove off amid the blare of sirens as paramedics and police raced to the scene.

# 2

## AFTER

"Is there a problem, Dad?" Nena asked, watching her older sister pace the floor of Nena's quaint little home. Elin rarely came to this part of Miami, but today was an exception. She must have been pretty upset to make the trek from Coconut Grove to Citrus—"slumming it," as Nena's upper-crust sister liked to say. In the next breath, after the insult, Elin would comment that Nena's home was the calmest place she knew. It was peaceful because Nena made it so. When she walked through her front door, she was no longer Echo, only Nena.

From their secure line, Noble Knight's smooth voice, laced with an edge of irritation, came through the speaker so both his daughters could hear. "The problem is that this is the job you've been given, and it needs to be done," he said. "Handling the attorney now will be a show of good faith to our incoming Council member. We need the deal he's bringing us to go through with no complications."

Elin glared at Nena but said nothing. *But the mark's a federal attorney,* Nena was thinking. And what did Dad mean by "show of good faith"? Since when did the Tribe dispatch people as a "show of good faith"? She didn't like it one bit, but who was she to question their father? He'd never given her a reason to doubt him, not since she was fifteen and he and her mum had adopted her off the streets. Still, the thought niggled in her mind.

"This mark seems out of the norm, no?" Nena asked when they'd ended the call. "Out of the norm for us. I mean, we're not mercenaries."

"Why the second-guessing?" Elin countered, rifling through her bag. "Do you have something better to do than the job? Sit out in the hot-ass sun in your backyard? Or go play with your best bud with the crude name."

"Keigel," Nena supplied helpfully. He was her neighbor three doors down and also the head of a large local gang. "I ask because this guy isn't our typical mark."

Elin let out a burst of exasperated air. "I could use a smoke. You're stressing me the hell out." Elin produced her pack of cigarettes and a lighter. "Honestly, I don't know. Maybe the guy's a perv or crooked. That seems to be the standard to get the—" She completed the sentence by slicing a well-manicured finger across her throat.

Nena leaned forward from her perch on the couch, resting her elbows on her knees. "You're quite rude. You know that?"

"You wouldn't have me any other way." Elin broke out into a magnificent grin and wouldn't stop until her sister shook her head in defeat.

"Is this guy really more crooked than the man he's prosecuting?" It had been all over the news. Alleged money launderer Dennis Smith was to be tried on RICO charges and witness intimidation.

"You know how it all goes down," Elin said. "Council makes the decree and sends up the names; I work the intel at Network; Dispatch carries out their orders. We never question the Council's reasons." She shook her head in concession. "Anyway, Smith's dealings are questionable at best, and while the Tribe wouldn't normally get involved, they're doing it to secure our new Council member. Politics."

"Politics isn't what the Tribe is supposed to be about," Nena griped.

"Yes, well, plot twist, this member happens to be the father of the man I'm screwing, so there's that."

Nena scoffed. "Screwing? Is this an arrangement? A traditional pairing like back home? Did the man's father present goats and liquor to Dad?"

Elin shot her a middle finger. "No. He brought a country." She deflated, suddenly looking tired. Or perhaps annoyed. "The Council wants Lucien Douglas, and Douglas wants Smith—for whatever reason—to remain prison-free. It's easier to take the lawyer out and keep the man happy. And it's cheaper and less time consuming than buying off a jury."

The words were cold and callous coming from Elin's lips. To be killed just because it was the easier choice. It didn't make the Tribe sound inspirational when the advancement of the African diaspora was supposed to be their ultimate goal. It made them sound selfish, greedy . . . wicked.

"Dispatching this federal attorney, this Cortland Baxter, sounds a bit self-serving, yeah?" Nena ventured.

Elin gazed at the cigarettes longingly, then gave her sister a pouting look, but Nena shook her head. Elin released a frustrated sigh and shoved them back in her bag. "Douglas has close ties with one of the countries that have been hard to bring on the team. So if making the new guy happy means the African Tribal Council secures this country so we can shore up imports and exports from the coast, then yeah, the Tribe is self-serving."

She twirled her ponytail of long box braids around her fingers, studying Nena for the first time since she'd arrived. "Are you all right? Real talk."

Nena shrugged. It was the only answer she could give at the moment because she didn't know how she felt. She was thinking about how the attorney's dispatch felt like a break from the Tribe's norm. It wasn't her job to like or dislike any dispatch. It was her job to carry it out as commanded, and doubting the organization she'd pledged her life and loyalty to was what made her uncomfortable.

"Anyway," Elin said, "don't think too much on it. It's just another job. Focus on the Cuban dispatch coming up in a couple nights. I can't make the dignitary party that night, so you need to attend that, too—as yourself."

"Elin." Nena felt her anxiety heighten a notch at the thought of having to attend a pretentious party as the Knights' youngest daughter. "You know I don't care for those people. The party plus the Cuban is double duty." Nena paused, thinking some more. "I can go alone, right?"

Elin ignored her. "We'll call in the rest of the local team." She ticked off the jobs on her fingers. "You just completed the Nigerian dispatch; the Cuban is next, and then the attorney. After that, little sis, you need to lie low for a few months. Witt's on board with it. He's hated having to assign you these back-to-back jobs, but it's been difficult trying to square all these different factions away."

"And the party? I prefer to go without a date."

Elin wouldn't answer, but her face said it all. She clomped in her thick-heeled sandals to the front door, throwing it open just as Keigel's fist rose to knock, his other hand bearing a container of lemon-pepper wings. It was Nena and Keigel's thing, their shared love of this wing flavor. Nena saw the hopeful look on his face, the puppy dog way he looked at Elin, on whom he had a major crush. He'd likely seen Elin's car and thought to use the wings as an excuse for coming over, rather than waiting for Nena to pop up at his home like she normally did.

Nena didn't have the heart to tell him he and Elin would never happen.

"Oh, look," Elin said wryly, "the cavalry's here."

Keigel was handsome—even Nena thought so—with a headful of long locs, an immaculate beard, and brown eyes that betrayed how much of a softy he was. "What I just walk in on?" he asked.

"Nothing, lovie," Elin cooed, trailing her long nails lightly along the angle of his jaw. He visibly melted from her touch. Stuff like that tickled her.

Nena barely heard their exchange, deep in her own thoughts—about the attorney, about her two upcoming jobs, about this party she didn't want to go to. "Do I have to take a date?" She didn't like surprises.

Elin slid past an openmouthed Keigel, gracing him with a heart-stopping smile. She called over her shoulder, "Naturally. But better pick one out before I do."

# 3

## AFTER

Up until this point, dispatch jobs were no different than clocking in at a nine-to-five. Her kills didn't get a second thought. However, tonight, when the Miami sky looked like the inside of an African diamond mine, the thought of leading another mission zapped the strength from her. For a second, she'd rather have been navigating the perils of Miami's elite than running through the upcoming dispatch of the Cuban cartel's second-in-command for the millionth time.

A sense of unfulfillment sneaked up on her, making her wonder where this sudden ache welling up in the middle of her chest was coming from. What was she thinking? She chastised herself, swallowing down the wretched feeling as quickly as it had come upon her. Joining Dispatch had given her purpose and a blessed reprieve from a lifetime of cursed memories. Yet as Nena looked down at the rifle in her hands, she couldn't help wondering if there was more to life than taking lives.

Her watch read 11:00 p.m.

"It's time," Witt announced through their imperceptible ear comms. He was holed up with Network, their all-seeing mission control, in the undisclosed location in Europe from which all their successful missions spooled.

"Echo, you copy?"

"Copy," Nena said, tamping down her unease and shedding the rest of who she was. It was time, as Witt said, and that meant it was time to be the other half of her, time to be Echo. Just one name from her long, sordid history of names.

"The security system?" she asked.

Nena and Alpha, second-in-command of their five-person team, watched together as the red lights on Alpha's handheld device flashed twice, then emitted a long flash before changing to green, confirming that the mansion's security-and-surveillance system was off line and now running on Network's feed. Anyone watching the cameras would see only a loop of the empty house and grounds.

Witt's crackly voice always provided Nena a sense of calm. "Keep it clean, family. In and out."

She, Alpha, Charlie, and Sierra pulled on the rest of their gear: night vision goggles, black ski masks, thin gloves to hide any identifying marks or their racial makeup.

The team slipped out of the black nondescript van, leaving X-ray behind in the driver's seat. Covered in darkness, they crouched low, pausing before beginning their hustle toward the entry point. They moved in snakelike tandem through the ornate statues of naked women and cherubs lining the walkways. Each member swept the perimeter with their weapons, checking for guards.

The layout of the mansion and its grounds was burned in Nena's memory as if she'd lived there all her life. It took them three minutes to cross the lawn using the bushes and palm trees for cover. They were coming up to the house when Nena spied two guards standing atop the low-slung shingled roof. She leveled her semi at her target and squeezed off a shot. Before the man was down, she aimed and shot again, dropping his partner. She'd been dispatching for so long that taking lives, even corrupt ones, elicited no more emotion from her than firing off an email. She didn't relish killing. Killing just . . . was. It was keeping order and advancing the Tribe's cause.

The Cuban's new foray—peddling immigrants through their black-market transit system—jeopardized the Tribe's business partnership with the organization. The Council wouldn't allow their funds to support human trafficking. After all, was it not from their lands that so many Africans had been stolen, sold, and shipped to America to be enslaved? They'd never sanction that dark part of their history being revitalized. But Juarez, the Cuban, wasn't the one who made the decisions. Juarez was only the face of their drug empire. It was his number two, Esteban Ruiz, who was the brains behind the face, marking Ruiz for dispatch. With him gone, the organization would be under the Tribe's control and their wrongs set right by the Tribe's standards.

She gave another signal, and her team split up, the other three branching off to their preplanned locations while she located the mark.

She found Ruiz where she'd known he'd be, behind his massive oak desk in his office. His executive chair was turned away, facing a wall of TV monitors, his head back, and at first, Nena thought he might be asleep. Even better.

She shouldered the strap of her rifle, pulling her sidearm and aiming it as she neared him. Her steps faltered when a deep groan emanated from him. That was when she noticed movement beneath him. He had one hand resting on the arm of the chair, the other . . .

She craned her neck, unable to tell where the hand was, only that it was moving. She didn't even want to guess.

She pushed away the unwanted thoughts and closed in. She put the gun to the back of his head and squeezed the trigger. He was so engrossed he hadn't noticed her. His head jerked forward, then dropped, chin to chest.

She was leaning over to make sure he was really dead when a dark head of hair popped up from below, in front of Ruiz, like a prairie dog on one of those National Geographic documentaries. She recognized the uniform. He was one of the guards. Couldn't be more than twenty, if that. She swallowed her surprise with a blink. This information was *not* in the intel. And she hated surprises.

He looked up, but before the young guard could make sense of his slack-jawed lover, the exit wound between his eyes, or the thick rope of blood forking down both sides of Ruiz's nose, Nena repositioned her gun and put a bullet in him too. The guard's head plopped back into the lap he was intimately, and quite recently, familiar with.

———

Nena swept the room, ensuring there were no more playthings who would pop out at her. Her eyes landed on the array of TV monitors and narrowed, zeroing in on one screen that looked different from all the others. It was a black-and-white video feed of Juarez in his bedroom—and she could see he wasn't alone. She swallowed, visions of what could have gone very badly running through her mind. How Network had missed this feed, she had no idea. They'd been lucky.

"Dispatch is complete. There's a separate feed running," she muttered into her comm device. "Looks like the mark's been watching number one's bedroom."

"We see it," was the response she received. This time it wasn't Witt but some member of the Network team she didn't care to know. "Leave him. Use the flash drive to burn their system and return home."

"But what if it's in the cloud?"

A pause. "It's not. They're old school."

She didn't register the last part because the screen held her attention hostage, her jaw tightening as she made sense of what she was watching. Through her earpiece, Nena heard the team engaging more guards, clearing the home, readying to return to the van—each soft grunt, each *pewt* of the silencers, each *padda padda pat-pat* of the semiautomatics.

She forced herself to move on her new orders. She found the computer and slipped in a small flash drive Network would use to fry the system.

Then she hustled, leaving the room to head downstairs. But she paused at the top of the carpeted steps. Time was winding down, but what she'd seen on the screen made her turn around and run up the next flight of stairs instead of down. She had to do one last thing. People thought slavery was long dead, but they only had to look at the recording of the Cuban's master suite to see that slavery did indeed still exist, and right in this very home. It was something of which Nena knew all too well. That was, *before* she became Echo.

She recalled the mansion's layout, finding the master suite quickly. Ignoring the chatter of her team and Network communicating in her ear, she grabbed the doorknob and twisted silently. The door opened on a slight creak, making her pause. She listened in case anyone inside had heard. No one had.

"Echo, switching to a private channel," Witt said in her ear. A second later he asked, "What are you doing?" She grimaced. Witt never went off script during missions. But then again, neither did she. Her straying from the playbook must have worried him enough to break protocol. "You're off course. Get where you need to be."

But Nena was where she needed to be. She pushed the door open wide enough to enter a suite bathed in burgundy and gold and furnished with a massive four-poster bed that would fit six grown men. The room felt bigger than her little home in Citrus Grove, bigger than any room she'd imagined when she was a girl living in Ghana. This ugly, dark room reminded her of *Fifty Shades*, but in it was the stuff of nightmares—and the Cuban, the boogeyman.

The girl Nena saw was nothing more than a waif. It was difficult to tell her ethnicity from behind the veil of long stringy hair obscuring her face like something out of a horror movie. The straps of the inappropriately adult negligee slid off her young shoulders. She trembled so violently the massive satin-covered bed shuddered beneath her. Her whimpers struck a nerve-jarring chord in Nena. Memories of barbed wire, the Hot Box where she'd been kept, and the bodies—so many bodies—flashed through her mind and nearly brought her to her knees.

His back to where Nena stood in the shadows, the Cuban carefully selected a collar with an attached leash, smiling lecherously. He did it as if he were choosing an engagement ring. He lurched toward the girl while shrugging off his robe, revealing he was naked as the day he was born.

The girl, now on her knees, whimpered louder. Her eyes were wide as she stared from behind the curtain of hair and whispered, "Por favor, señor. No."

Nena wasn't sure why she was hesitating. Why she watched as he fastened the choker around the girl's bone-thin neck and clicked the lock. The girl winced when he cinched the collar too tight. Every time he touched her, she jerked as if branded with a white-hot poker.

Nena holstered her sidearm and, from the sheath strapped to her back, pulled out her blade.

"Time," Witt warned.

"You gonna love it, mami," the Cuban said.

Nena's muscles grew taut as she readied herself.

"I'm gonna give it to you good." The Cuban slapped the girl hard, so hard Nena felt its sting. He pulled his hand back, up behind his head. His fingers curled into a tight fist.

It was the girl's high-pitched whinny of terror that finally spurred Nena to action. She moved swiftly, ignoring the thick, wiry carpet covering the Cuban's back or how he smelled of body odor and stale cigar smoke.

The girl was no longer looking at him. She was staring open-mouthed at the creature behind him. Nena held her fingers to her lips in a silent communiqué.

Ignoring Witt calling time in her ear again, she raised her arm, grasping the Cuban's face and jerking it back against her chin. With her opposite hand, she dragged the blade across his neck, separating the soft, quivering folds of skin as if she were cutting through softened butter.

He gurgled, blood bubbling out of the gaping wound. His hands flew to his neck in a futile effort to seal his skin back together.

She released him, his body falling with a heavy thud on the floor. Nena and the girl watched as his life spilled out in a growing pool around his body.

"What. The bloody. Hell?" Witt growled through Nena's earpiece, snapping her back to attention. The team was waiting for her. Nena had deviated from the plan long enough.

A rustling from the bed drew Nena's gaze to the girl, who she considered carefully. What to do with her? Nena couldn't leave her like that. She couldn't take her either.

The girl's tiny hands picked at the collar around her neck, and without another thought, Nena stepped to the Cuban's bureau of sex paraphernalia and the little key dangling on a hook inside it.

She could hear the team checking in with Network as they returned to the van. She'd skew the mission time if she was late, possibly compromise the safety of the whole team if more of the Cuban's men arrived on-site. She had to move. She tugged the key off the hook. The girl would need to figure out how to survive, or not, on her own.

Witt growled, "For God's sake, you need to leave now."

"On the way." Nena gave the room one final sweep, her eyes pausing briefly at the bed, before she slipped through the doorway. Behind her, the girl scrambled toward the little silver key that had landed among the satin sheets and pillows. As Nena raced through the hallways and down the stairs, away from the girl in the bed who'd reminded Nena of a past she wished she could forget, she felt like she was running right back to the beginning of it all.

# 4

## BEFORE

Before I became Echo, before I was Nena, I was Aninyeh. And this is my story, my recounting.

Of who I was.

Of how I came to be.

My journey begins in my small village, nestled among the plush, vibrant green forests and cocooned on Aburi Mountain. If one is looking for me, they will often find me on the cliffs, overlooking the world below. My favorite time of day is early morning, when everything is still dewy and the fog is low lying and heavy but burns away as the sun comes up. It's hot in Ghana, not uncommon for the late summer. This year has been a good year with a fair amount of rain, which allowed crops and our animals to grow well enough to sell at market and feed the village. We are prospering.

Here on the mountain, the temperature is cooler, perfect. On a clear day, I can stand on the cliff, look out through the dissipating fog, and see Accra, only twenty-five miles away but seeming so much farther from where I stand. The deep valleys below constantly remind me of how beautiful my home is. Of its richness. Of how lucky I am to be an African, a Ghanaian, a N'nkakuwean.

"Papa says to mind our business and do not covet—"

"—what our brother or sister has. Yes, I know, Aninyeh." Ofori, my brother, rolls his eyes. "Does not mean I cannot worry about what happens to me after Wisdom assumes leadership and Josiah becomes his counsel."

When Ofori gets this way, jealous over things our older brothers have and he does not, I strain from not slapping him senseless. Wisdom—tall, fierce, brave Wisdom, who not only inherited Papa's Christian name but has a name that reflects his demeanor—will assume the title of chief as firstborn when Papa steps down. Josiah is three minutes Wisdom's junior and will become Wisdom's chief advisor.

"You should be glad there are no responsibilities binding you to N'nkakuwe like them," I tell Ofori. Why he does not see his luck, I do not know.

The kitchen of our family home is a warm blend of cooking spices and sweetened pastry. Auntie, Mama's closest cousin, who stepped in when Mama passed, glistens as she stands over a cast-iron pot of bubbling bean stew laden with bits of salted codfish. In a minute, Auntie will heat a pan of oil to fry the ripened sweet plantains. Bean stew and fried plantains are Papa's and my favorite.

I consider all of this as Ofori steals a bofrot, a small round ball of sweetened fried dough. In the background, Auntie complains he will ruin his dinner. Diligently, I count bofrots in my head, dividing them by the six of us. I grimace because Ofori has already had more than his share.

Auntie says, "Ofori, you should be with your papa and the twins, seeing to the end of the day."

"Why?" he asks, popping the last of his stolen goods in his mouth.

"Why what?" she asks.

"Why should I follow them around when I will never govern? They do not need me."

"You will be on the council of elders, Ofori. That is important work because a chief cannot rule well without his council," our auntie says as she flaps her free hand at him. "Now leave this women's work and see to your father at the village center."

My shoulders jerk as if pierced with a sharp stick. That Auntie delegates where the place of women and men should be is archaic, and I have no plans to adhere to it. My fifteenth birthday will come in days, and when I am eighteen, I will attend university abroad, not in Ghana like Auntie thinks. I will travel the world as Papa did, learn even more languages than the ones Papa has taught me. No one will tell me what a woman can or cannot do. But I say none of this aloud. I value my head too much and would rather not be thumped on it with the heavy wooden ladle she wields or have my ears boxed.

My father is the village chieftain, so technically I am a princess. But there are lines even modern-day princesses dare not cross.

Ofori deftly dances beyond my grasp when I catch him stealing yet another of the bofrots. "Ey!" I yell, about to charge after him, but Auntie grabs me by the neckline of my school uniform, preventing me from leaving her side.

"These do not count!" Ofori laughs as he scampers away.

"Mind the snakes!" Auntie calls at his retreating figure. She says this at morning and at dusk, when the many snakes that share this mountain with us are the most active. There are other animals, bugs—no lions or predators, but still harmful things. However, snakes bother Auntie the most.

"Auntie!" I protest. "Ofori has eaten too many."

"Hush, child." She smooths her furrowed brows. "There are enough, and all will be well."

Will it? What is it like to run the nightly village perimeter checks with Papa and my brothers? They check with the other men to ensure everyone's made it back safely, that there is no outstanding business between villagers that may result in conflict. My chest tightens and my eyes blur with unwanted tears, as I know Ofori is off with Papa and the twins. He bemoans the privilege while I remain trapped in this sticky, boiling kitchen doing "women's work." The resentment burns in my chest, making me lose focus, and I nearly slice off a fingertip with the knife I am using to cut ripened plantains into diagonals.

Ofori is not considerate of others, not like Papa, who is fair, honorable, and the hardest worker. Papa never asks others to do what he would not do first. He is a leader, a big man, loved by most, and would never take more than his share of bofrots. Not like Ofori—

A burst of staccato noise cuts through Auntie's chatter.

She waves it away as if shooing buzzing flies. "Boys practicing drums or whacking sticks in swordplay," she says after clearing her throat of its slight tremor. "Maybe a hyena or other animal has wandered too close to the village perimeters."

I nod, but I know better. And when screams begin piercing the walls of our kitchen, Auntie knows better too.

I freeze, the knife like an extension of my hand hovering over the cut pieces of fruit, all thoughts of frying plantains and bubbling bean stew vanishing.

Auntie reaches a hand—skin weathered and leathery from years of plunging them in hot water, churning banku and beating cassava leaves—out to me. "Aninyeh, wait!"

But I dash out the door, ignoring her increasingly frantic calls. I quicken my pace down the walk, through our high wrought iron fenced gates, and out into the unknown, moving farther from our compound, which is larger than most in the village because of our family lineage.

N'nkakuwe sits on the cusp between the old world and the booming cities of Accra and Kumasi. It is not Papa's family land. He is from a tiny village in Fanti land, low-lying valleys nearly four hours from here. The history of my father's people goes back hundreds of years to when the Ashanti and Fanti peoples warred among themselves for dominance and to trade with the Europeans who sought out African goods—*goods* being slaves.

But after years of war, the two tribes came together and began to blend their peoples. That is how my father came to be of both peoples. But when he was younger and newly returned from studying overseas, he met Mama at an open market in Accra. And because he loved her, he left his home to marry her. Mama was the chieftain's only daughter, and by law, when Grandfather died, Papa became chieftain.

Mama was one-fourth Yoruba, Nigerian, on her grandmother's side. The rest of her was Ewe, from her father's side. Thus making me and my brothers a blend of all three great regions of Ghana: Ashanti, Fanti, and Ewe.

Of all things I will remember, this I know to be the truest of all: my father is an honorable man.

But even the most honorable of men have an enemy or two.

Tonight, those enemies have arrived with guns. With machetes. And with bloodlust as ravenous and destructive as a wildfire that will consume us all.

# 5

## AFTER

When Nena finally made it to the van, she tried her best to ignore the probing glances from her team members. Yes, she was late. But it had all worked out, hadn't it? She hurriedly shed her gear as if speed could shed her guilt at putting the team behind and possibly in jeopardy. She changed back into her flowing melon-colored evening gown, which had been chosen by her sister, not her. But Nena supposed Elin had done all right this time.

The van coasted away from the base of the long, winding drive of the Cuban's estate. Five miles away, Miami's upper echelon was drinking and dancing and likely hadn't missed her at all.

The job was complete, minus a few hiccups, but the night was not yet over.

Charlie handed forward her gold clutch. It looked comical in his big, burly hands, hands that not twenty minutes ago had been shooting people to death.

"Thanks." She opened it to pull out a mirrored compact to assess herself. She removed wipes from the go bag containing her clothing and proceeded to clean the sweat from her face, glad to be rid of the mask. The air-conditioning felt glorious on her skin.

She had to get through the rest of the party. She had to focus and get back to her regular self, whichever self that was. Oftentimes, she found it hard to distinguish which was the real her, the socialite or the wudini. But she guessed, for now, she was the socialite, forced to attend this pretentious soiree because Elin was handling the Tribal Council's business abroad. Plus, the party had served as a perfect alibi—be the face of her family and eliminate the Cuban on the same night. What luck.

Alpha watched X-ray maneuver the van onto the main road, increasing the speed to put more distance between them and the Cuban's home. Through the mirror she saw him raise an eyebrow. "Maybe clue your team in the next time you decide to go off-roading?" he said.

She applied a few dots of lotion, then smoothed it into her skin. Lastly, her tinted lip gloss. "You're right," she said. "My fault." She pulled her hair up so it sat in a lush mound atop her head, held in place by a gold hair band. She brushed her edges smooth.

"You know," Sierra chimed in from beside Charlie. They were also in various stages of undress, exchanging their work gear for their normal attire to dispose of when they split up later. "We always got you, fam; just let us know what's up."

Nena offered Sierra an apologetic nod through the mirror, applying another coat of deodorant and then perfume. She stole a glance through the window, checking their location. Ten yards ahead was a set of security gates flanked by tall palm trees. "Drop me here, please."

As the van door slid open, Sierra said, "Behave in there, boss."

Nena gave a nod. "Always."

Sierra grinned lasciviously, still talking as the door closed: "'Cause I sure wouldn't."

The team wouldn't see each other again until they were assigned their next job. For now, they'd go back to their respective homes scattered along the eastern front. None knew the others' real names, and none were exactly sure where the others lived, though Nena suspected Sierra lived somewhere in Florida, as she did.

In heels she despised, she carefully trudged up the drive toward the grandiose mansion in which the party was being held, its strobing white lights illuminating the night sky as if it were New Year's Eve. She took in the high gates, swaying palms, perfectly cultivated bushes, and brightly lit windows. The sprawling, manicured lawn stretched out before her looked more like a football field.

She passed the valets, clad in crimson vests, who busily squeezed high-end cars into makeshift parking spaces as attendees arrived and left the party. She walked past a college-aged kid determined to be curbside before an approaching Bentley slowed to a complete stop.

"I'm in," she murmured, knowing the high-tech comms embedded in the onyx earrings snaking around her ears would pick her up easily. She entered the mansion, confident that Network would make sure her entrance back into the party was as undetected by the security cameras as her earlier departure. She followed the saxophone riff from the live band to the ballroom.

"Copy. Channel closed," Network answered.

"Nena, there you are. I've been looking for you for quite a while," her handsome date said, taking her protectively by the elbow. "Are you all right?"

She slipped back into her delicately demure role as quickly as taking a breath, but not before her jaw tightened while she stared intently at her skin, the color of deep walnut with golden undertones, where David held her a bit too possessively for her taste.

She stayed in character. "I got lost," she said breathily, as if relieved her misadventure had ended. She blinked up at the sea-green eyes of her date, the random with whom her sister had made her attend.

"For pretenses," Elin had told her.

More like to torture her. Nena had wanted to attend this event solo.

"I needed a bit of air and decided to walk the grounds—which are huge, by the way. Then I got turned around. I'm glad you found me."

David's chest swelled, the happy hero. "Are you up for a dance? Or do you want to leave?"

She did want to leave. But she also didn't want to hear Elin's mouth about abandoning her familial obligations to cement relationships with potential business and political partners. Building wealth and power for the Tribe wasn't Noble Knight's only vision—building for his family, ensuring they remained powerful inside and outside the Tribe, no matter what happened, was equally important.

She gave in, allowing David to guide her to the middle of the throngs of guests dancing and laughing beneath a domed glass ceiling, from which they could see a black sky blanketed by innumerable twinkling stars.

"Do you mind having the bloke not whisper sweet nothings into your ear? He sounds loud as hell through the earrings," her older sister's voice suddenly cooed with syrupy sweetness through Nena's earpiece. Nena didn't buy the false sincerity for a minute. "You only have to bugger around with him a bit longer."

She should have known Elin wouldn't be gracious enough to leave her be the whole night. Now that the job was done, Elin wanted to crash in on a comms channel to toy with her, especially when she knew Nena couldn't reply or turn her off just yet. She could rip the earrings off and toss them, but then she'd have no backup if something were to go down.

David twirled her slowly. He held her waist, pulling her closer. She could tell by the growing bulge in his pants as he held her close and the way he stared down at her with glazed eyes that he hoped to bed her tonight, but hopes were meant to be dashed. *What would he do if I let the air out of his hard-on with my dagger?*

"You are so beautiful," David whispered, his eyes glassy and lustful.

His reaction was interesting to her. She wondered what he saw as he looked down at her, hovering over her full lips and the oval outline of her face.

"Thank you," she said politely, remembering that her shift as Echo was over and she was Nena Knight right now. But even Nena wouldn't kiss this guy, Tom Cruise looks or not.

Again, she questioned who she was. Nena had worked as her alias, Echo, for so long. Again, she wondered which role was the real her, the rich socialite gliding in the arms of this equally rich Adonis, or the athletic killer who'd ended lives just a few miles away. And what had happened to who she used to be *before*, when she was Aninyeh? What had happened to that fourteen-year-old girl? Oh yeah, she'd died.

"You could act like you're actually into the bloody bastard," Elin taunted, pulling her from her thoughts. "I pulled your vitals up on screen, and they're dropping," she cackled. "The wanker is lit-err-ally boring you to death. Like, as I speak, down they go!"

Nena's mouth tightened, biting back a retort. She hoped Elin had remembered to switch them to a private channel. But she knew her sister, and Elin likely had all of Network listening. She enjoyed launching these small tortures against Nena. Enjoyed it far too much.

Elin snorted gleefully. "Well, we both know you aren't going to fuck him. Maybe I should? Naturally, if it wasn't for Oliver. Do you know who David favors? Tom Cruise. It's why I picked him for you, because you go all doe eyed when *Mission Impossible* comes on."

She didn't. Elin was lying.

"I'd screw him two ways from Sunday, if I could."

She tuned Elin's voice out until it was just white noise in the background. Her mind slipped back to the girl in the Cuban's bedroom. Had she escaped? Was she smart enough to steal the gaudy jewelry to sell and start a new life? Hopefully, the girl wouldn't be recaptured. Nena knew about captivity too.

David murmured, "How did I get this lucky?" as he nuzzled her, no doubt putting a nose-shaped dent in her beautifully coarse, coily hair. Her hair was one of the few things she took pride in, one of the few things she kept cultivated, just as her mama had taught her before she'd passed.

These three parts of Nena, always at war with each other, always at war with one another for survival. She wasn't sure which she wanted to be the victor. Nena or Echo. Echo or Aninyeh. Aninyeh or Nena. When the war finally came to an end, she didn't know who she would be.

Nena willed herself to lay her head against David's chest. She let the rhythm of his beating heart take her back to a place far away, beyond the Cuban's torture chamber, across an ocean to a lifetime ago.

David said he was lucky to be with her. But would he still consider himself lucky if he knew the woman in his arms took lives for a living, and that her story began, back home, with the betrayal and decimation of her simple little world?

# 6

## BEFORE

The rat-a-tat-tat draws me farther from my family's compound like a fish on a reel. Villagers are shouting. Their gut-wrenching cries send riptides of electric fear from my scalp to my toes. These are the cries of my people in pain. The gunfire barely pauses for breath. I force my feet to keep going, one in front of the other, even though all I want to do is run back.

Strange men dressed in camouflage clothing, none of whom I recognize, zoom past in trucks, the odor of diesel trailing behind them. The trucks slow, and some of the men jump out. They run into homes, and screams follow. My hands fly to my ears to blot out the noise. My eyes squeeze shut so I do not see when they begin to drag people from their homes. When I can, I force my legs to move, clinging to the shadows against the walls of homes, hoping I remain unnoticed as these men seek out victims who will better feed their hunger for chaos than I can.

Up ahead, the men are corralling N'nkakuweans in the middle of the village square. They threaten the villagers with an arsenal of weaponry— guns, knives, machetes—which they use to herd our people into a small, indefensible space.

They begin setting fire to homes I thought were empty. Until I see people begin to run out, engulfed in bright-orange flames that no one is allowed to extinguish, screaming in such agony my legs refuse to listen to my brain because my brain can no longer function. I can only stare at the figures in their grotesque dance as they suffer. When the first one drops, my feet move without my even knowing it, the cries of the burning chasing me toward the square. Acrid smells of cooking meat turn my stomach. When my stomach lurches, I vomit everything down the sewer ditch that runs the length of our main roads.

Using the back of my hand and then the hem of my dress, I wipe the mess from my mouth. Where are Wisdom and Josiah? Ofori and Papa? Each passing minute deepens the dread coursing through my veins. And though I try not to, I search the dead for my family. I search the howling mass of my people. One of the aunties' children is wrenched, screaming, from her arms. She tries running after the child but is clubbed down by an intruder while two others pull the children kicking and screaming toward a line of open-bed trucks. Another uncle is cracked over the skull with the butt of a gun as he begs for the life of his wife, a wife who is already gone from this earth. I spied her body on my way here.

"Aninyeh," someone calls from within the dark throngs of people.

Rough hands grab me, forcing me to the ground amid a gaggle of arms, legs, and sweaty bodies that ooze the stink of fear. My immediate response is to strike whoever has touched me, but Wisdom enters my line of vision, and my struggle abates, as does all my resolve. I want nothing more than to fold into him and be told this is all a horrible dream.

"Shhh," he breathes, his eyes imploring me to listen for once.

Next to him Josiah is wild eyed and watching our every move. His eyes most echo mine, full of terror, of confusion, with a question at their very center. *Why?*

"Where is Papa?" I pant through clenched teeth. "Is he—?"

"There." Wisdom motions in front of us. His face shines beneath a film of sweat in the suffocating heat. There lies the problem. The heat. It is not supposed to be this hot. This is not normal. None of this is normal. Therefore this, all of this, must be a terrible dream. Either that or we are in hell.

Josiah's eyes move rapidly, taking in everything around us. He is listening to us but saying nothing, a rarity for him. I finally follow Wisdom's hand, looking beyond the huddled mass.

"Where is the chieftain?" one of the intruders, a soldier I do not recognize, demands. He stands amid the cowering crowd, the sleeves of his uniform rolled in cuffs above his elbows. On his head is a black-and-white checkered scarf wrap. I know this covering. These men might want to appear as if they are military, like the real Ghanaian soldiers, but they are not of them. And if these men are not the government, then who are they? And why are they here doing this to us?

The intruder holds up one of our village elders, bleeding significantly from a wound above his eyebrow. In his other hand, he raises a club high. "Show yourself, or Uncle suffers the consequence of your weakness."

Knee-jerk reaction and rage make me nearly shoot to my feet, but Josiah's hand stills me, warning me to remain as I am. Therefore, Josiah would be the perfect advisor to Wisdom. Impulsivity never overtakes him as it often does me. Most of the time to my detriment.

"I am here," Papa answers, his rich voice carrying across the sea of cowering heads and trembling bodies. He stands. His clothes are heavily stained with sweat, dirt, and blood. It is the first I recall seeing Papa disheveled in front of his people. He has always presented himself in his very best. And yet now, dirtied as if he has rolled in the dust and muck, with his hair in disarray, still he stands erect and assured and fearless.

"Now," Papa commands, his voice without any trepidation, "remove your hands from that man."

The heat from the fires makes the night unbearable, sucking out all the air. The intruders cast demon-like shadows in the fires' light. But Papa's features do not betray anything but a decree of calm for the rest of us to follow. The soldier still holds the club, but his fingers begin to unfurl from the old man's shirt collar, his will bending to Papa's as if entranced.

"Why have you people come here?" Papa demands as the old man sinks to the ground, a bag of weighted rocks dissolving into tears.

A large man, so heavy that when he drops down from one of the open-bed trucks, it springs back happily, unleashed from its burden, walks toward us. He schleps along as if he is about to reason with Papa. Perhaps this is all a mistake.

Instead, the man raises the butt of his rifle and smashes it against Papa's head so viciously that a collective gasp is emitted from the villagers like a stadium wave. Again, I want to rush to Papa's aid, but both Wisdom and Josiah net their arms around me to contain my struggle. That is my papa he has hit. That is my papa staggering from the blow, shaking his head to clear it from the dizzying effects. A hand is over my mouth. Three others hold me tight, and Josiah murmurs as if chanting:

"Be still. Be still."

I heed him, stilling myself, because it is all I can do.

# 7

## AFTER

The Cuban and the party nearly two weeks behind her, Nena left her little cottage home, locking the door. She'd been a recluse, keeping a low profile, watching her movies, and enjoying the backyard oasis that had taken her years to perfect. She was glad only one job remained before she'd have some real time off. She had last-minute preparations to make for her Baxter dispatch, but for now all she could think about was hitting her favorite burger hangout.

When she arrived at Jake's Burger Spot, located in a sketchier part of town, all the stores were closed and the streets relatively empty, but Jake's remained open a little longer for those working late shifts. Nena noticed an emerald-green Cadillac parked along the street not too far from the bus stop. Etched on the top of its trunk were five playing cards: an ace, a king, a queen, a jack, and a ten.

The Royal Flushes, a local gang.

She saw *Holding all the cards* scrawled in a flourish below the winning hand. Nena frowned. She wasn't into Keigel's business, but even she knew the Flushes were on his "turf." And she was pretty sure whatever the reason, it was for no good, and Keigel wouldn't be pleased if he found out.

But Keigel's gang business had nothing to do with her, though she hoped one day he might think of the African Tribal Council as family, like he did his gang. Maybe eventually, he'd work for the African Tribal Council and make the pledge to unite all African countries—and by association all Black people of the diaspora—and work to make them a strong, legitimate force, equal to all the other supreme forces of the world.

That conversation, however, was for another time, because Nena was hungry and Jake's was calling her.

Only two other patrons were in the diner, a Hispanic man and a White one, both finishing up their dinners as she took her usual booth in the back corner of the restaurant. She liked that spot because she could see who came and went. The two men paid the waitress, Cheryl, bestowing some jokes on her that elicited her laughter. It was the kind of laugh a person made when the joke wasn't funny. The men, both wearing County of Miami-Dade sanitation-department jumpsuits, busily discussed their time sheets as they exited through the front doors, the bell chiming their departure while the buxom Cheryl began wiping down the table where they'd eaten.

When she was done, Cheryl approached Nena with a smile that said she recognized her. Nena put down the menu, giving Cheryl her full attention.

"What's up?" Cheryl asked, waiting for Nena's usual.

"Hi," Nena replied. "Could I have a bacon cheeseburger, Coke, and onion rings?"

"And a chocolate milkshake to go?" Cheryl cracked a smile.

Nena nodded. "Please," she added, not meaning to be rude. "And thank you."

"Gotcha." Cheryl smiled down at her, and the tiny diamond stud in her nose seemed to sparkle. She returned to the counter with a sway to her ample rear. *Little at the top, big at the bottom.* Keigel's words popped into Nena's mind as she watched her.

Nena's order was prepared quickly, since she was the only customer, and she devoured it just as quickly. As she was working on the last onion ring, Cheryl brought the milkshake and a refill of Coke. At the same moment, the door chimed. Both women looked up to see a young girl with a head of wonderfully natural hair, giving off #Blackgirlsrock vibes as she walked in, trying to pretend she belonged there.

Nena waited for the rest of the girl's party to waltz right in after her, but there was no one. The girl couldn't have been local. If she was, she would have known Jake's was about to close for the night. Nena took a moment to study her, her slight build, no more than five feet four, the way she looked around the diner with wide-set eyes against a creamy-brown complexion, taking in the red-and-white decor and the checkered floor. If Nena had to guess, she was thirteen, maybe a year older.

The girl considered where to sit, her gaze sweeping over Nena. Their eyes met briefly, and Nena's head cocked to the side, transmitting a silent question: Why was the girl here, and where were her people? The girl blinked, still wide eyed, and chose a stool at the counter.

Nena resumed perusing her iPhone, still wondering what the girl was doing there alone. She had an inkling that maybe she should stay, but all she really wanted was to go home. She remembered the Cadillac parked outside. Surely there would be no problems. The girl had likely passed the car without incident. If there had been something, she and Cheryl would have heard it.

Nena was deep in her thoughts when the girl's dinner arrived just as quickly as hers had. No doubt Cheryl and Jake, who manned the kitchen, wanted to close the grill and get home. Nena checked her text messages. One was from Elin, complaining about Mum being too nosy about her love life. No surprise there. Another was from Mum, asking if Nena could explain why Elin was so hardheaded and to talk some sense into her sister. Probably not a good idea to tell Mum that she and Elin were more alike than they'd care to know. Nena sighed at the irony. The killer of the family was also the one who kept the peace. While their powerful dad ran from the line of fire as much as possible.

She was reading a Twitter rant by a well-known author when the door chimes sounded again. The wind gusted in, as if out of a bad movie. Nena glanced up, expecting that the girl had left, but instead, she saw a young man, a member of the Royal Flushes, sauntering in.

He ambled toward the counter, not looking Nena's way. His demeanor read pompous, and Nena labeled him one of the soldiers of the gang, not a leader. Curious, she took a long sip of her milkshake.

"Let me get a couple cheeseburgers," he demanded, pounding his fist three times on the counter as if Cheryl weren't standing right in front of him.

Cheryl pointed at the red-and-white Coca-Cola clock on the wall. It read 10:05. "We're closed," she said flatly.

"Fuck that, you still got two bitches up in here. You open," he said. "Now get my motherfucking order if you know what's good."

Nena assumed he was counting her as one of the bitches. The slur didn't rattle her. But the fact he'd disparaged the girl shrinking away from him rankled Nena. He was going from zero to a hundred quickly, and it didn't bode well. She slipped her phone into her rucksack.

Cheryl left quickly, likely going to find Jake. While she was gone, the Flush took a long look at the girl, slithering onto the stool next to her. The girl tried to ignore him and focus on the Cherry Coke in front of her, but he was persistent.

His voice rang through the room as if he were sitting right next to Nena. "Do you know who the fuck I am? Who you're fucking with?" he asked the girl. "You know what set I rep?"

The girl was on the edge of the stool, one leg on the floor as if she were preparing to run. Not a bad idea, Nena thought. Jake appeared from the kitchen, catching the tail end of the Flush's big talk.

34

"We're closed, man," Jake said behind a thick, mostly gray mustache. "Catch us tomorrow during hours. We'll get you right. Now leave the girl be and get on."

The Flush wasn't hearing any of that, and the two of them had a go at each other for a few seconds, the young man becoming more incensed with Jake's unflappable calm. What if the Flush drew a gun on him? People had been hurt for lesser offenses, and Nena weighed intervening. If she did, there would be questions. Too many questions and too many witnesses she wasn't sure would keep quiet.

The Flush hopped off the stool, pulling his sagging white jeans over his nonexistent hips. "All right then," he said to the room. He walked to the door; all the while Nena watched for him to make a move for a piece hidden on his body. He didn't, opening the door to the chime of the bell.

"All right then," he repeated as if making a last stand. "That payback, though . . ."

*Is a bitch,* is what he didn't finish. He sucked his teeth, casting one long, menacing glare around the room, before backing through the doorway and slinking off into the night like some tacky villain.

As Jake spoke to the girl, Nena took her leave, leaving a hefty tip on the table for Cheryl and the trouble that had found them all. On her way out, she heard the girl explaining that her dad was on his way to pick her up.

"I was at the library and took the bus here to grab a bite, but I just texted him. He's coming."

Jake eyed her suspiciously. "Library's a ways off."

He was right. The library was twenty minutes out of the way from here.

"And you came here to get a bite?" he clarified.

She shrugged, rolling her eyes with the annoyance only a teenager could muster. "Heard this place had the best burgers around," she said. "And like I said, my dad's on the way."

Nena knew no one was coming for her except those Flushes. Because when a little man-child like that took offense, he'd burn everything down to get retribution. Even his very soul.

# 8

## BEFORE

Through the waves of heat and smoke, recognition flickers within me. The men call him Attah Walrus, a name befitting his enormous girth, but Papa had called him by his name, Desmond. It was not a month ago when he and two others—Paul, who I had taken to be the leader among them, as he had done the most talking, and a younger man they called Kwabena, or Bena for short—had come to our home for an audience with Papa.

"Do you recall my last visit, Michael? Do you recall the unwise choice you made? My offer was most beneficial to you and your people." Paul paces slow circles around my father. He spits on the ground. Seeing spit always makes me queasy, and I force myself not to stare at the splotch it makes in the dirt.

Papa scans the crowd of interlopers, his gaze lingering on Kwabena, then Attah, then finally steadying on Paul. Even from where I stand, I can see how troubled he is at Paul's words. "Do you recall, Paul, what I said your so-called offer sounded like? Sounds like hundreds of years ago. Will you have Ghanaians spirited away on ships from Elmina using my people as conduits in some modern-day Atlantic slave trade?"

"You do not want to pass on this," Paul says assuredly. "You want to be on the profitable end."

"Profitable in what way, eh?" Papa inclines his head, dismay washing his face in the light. "I want no part of this. And I think it best you and your men leave back to Kumasi or Accra, wherever you came from, and stop all of this."

Paul chuckles. "Ask your people." He holds his arms out and raises his voice. "They will want the riches this venture brings. They will want their children given the opportunities living abroad can bring them. It is your responsibility as chief to take it to your council of elders for a vote. Let them choose to get off this mountain and into the real world."

Papa gives Paul his hard look. His tone flattens. "Leave this place, Paul, and never return. The village council is already aware of your offer, and they want no part of you or your dirty dealings."

There is a finality in Papa's tone that causes a niggling inside me to sprout from a little seed to a bud. These men are beyond rebuke. They have killed already. They will not leave just because Papa wills it so. Even I know that.

Paul says, "You would deny me again? Take what's mine from me once more?" The fires crackle and spit in the background. The square is unnaturally quiet.

Confusion breaks on Papa's face. What has Papa taken from this man? Papa, who is the most giving man I know.

Pained, wounded, Papa says, "I never took from you, Paul. You cannot possibly believe . . ."

"If it wasn't for me," Paul cuts in, "you would not have passed the exams or been chosen for uni."

Papa acquiesces. "Yes, you tutored me well, but it wasn't me who prevented you from taking the exam and going to uni with me."

"No, my father had that pleasure," Paul seethes. "And I promise you I have thanked him for his prevention in kind."

*In kind.* The way he says it sends icicles down to my toes. Coupled with the laughter of his surrounding men, it makes me suspect Paul's "thanks" to his father was unpleasant.

"But you, you owe me, Michael. Permit this deal. Let me finally prosper as you have. It is my time, brother."

Papa shakes his head. "Not like this, Paul. Not on the backs of people, of children, I cannot. I will not let you run routes through our roads to ferry people into twenty-first-century slavery. A true brother wouldn't ask it of me."

Paul stares at him for a long time. It's a stare so full of malice it makes me quake where I sit. His voice is so low I strain to hear. "You have made an unwise decision, o."

Papa says, "Then so be it. Leave our village." His voice is heavy with the burden he carries. "Leave our home."

Paul looks at him as if he has suffered an affront. "You do not get to kick me out twice in a lifetime, Michael. I go and stay where I please."

"We would never participate in selling our brothers and sisters!" someone shouts from the crowd.

My father drops his head. "My people have done nothing to you." The traces of despair threaded in his voice unnerve me. If Papa is worried, then I need to be terrified.

Paul breaks into a gregarious smile that is so disconcerting my stomach drops. He gives Papa a mocking half bow, saying, "They do as you wish, Chief. Then your people *have* wronged me."

His smile falls, changing his looks from movie-star handsome to something monstrous. The change is so rapid I involuntarily cry out, wondering how a human can change so quickly, quicker than a chameleon. My sound must be louder than I think, because Paul instantly searches for the root of the noise and finds me. Malevolence emanates from him like a death shroud, and in the second our eyes connect, I know what evil looks like.

Papa believing a man like Paul would take no for an answer was a gross miscalculation—the first mistake I have ever known my father to make. Nothing between them was over.

Not then.

Not now.

# 9

## AFTER

Nena wasn't sure what she was doing or why. She left the diner and got in her car. She kept telling herself none of it was her business. The Flush's temper tantrum wasn't her business. The girl was not her business. She shouldn't have been out in the city going around to places she had no business being at this time of night.

Nena had nearly convinced herself to get the hell on out of there when the Cadillac with the Royal Flush insignia again caught her eye. It was farther down the street now, closer to the bus stop, hidden in the shadows where the streetlight was out. Nena sighed, knowing her decision was made whether she liked it or not. Cloaked in darkness herself, she slid into her Audi, tossing her rucksack inside.

She searched the back. She had nothing but her backup gun, sans silencer, and her push daggers concealed in her belt. She was weighing her options when the diner's chimes alerted her someone was leaving. It was the girl. She looked both ways, as if about to cross the street, but seemed to decide against it. She tugged at her backpack straps and began walking in the direction of the bus stop. Maybe she was a runaway, though she didn't give Nena those kinds of vibes.

The girl was passing a couple of large metal city trash containers when a figure materialized from their shadows. It was the Flush from the diner. He spoke to her, and while he did, one of his colleagues sneaked up behind her. He grabbed her, silencing her scream with his hand. A third man appeared as they dragged the girl into the alley.

Nena waited another moment, thinking of one of those clown cars and wondering how many more Flushes would tumble out. When no more did, she got out of her Audi and followed.

Like idiots who thought they had all the time in the world, the three gang members were standing in the alley debating which was better: robbing the diner as retaliation or just kidnapping the girl and making her one of their bitches. They were so engrossed in their bickering that they didn't notice Nena as she moved stealthily toward them, keeping to the walls.

One of them threatened to rape the girl. Why was the first thing men resorted to exacting dominance over women through violation or defilement? Why did it always have to be rape? Because, Nena thought mirthlessly, that was all these types of males knew.

The girl said, "If you kill me, I'll haunt your dumb asses until the day you die. Which probably won't be very long anyway."

It was a weird thing to say, at the weirdest time, when anyone else's fear would render them silent. The girl was a fighter, and Nena liked that immediately. But her high voice betrayed her true feelings. Though she was a fighter, she was a terrified young girl.

"Well, if you're gonna haunt me, guess I'll call you Casper," the Flush from the diner snarled, slapping her hard while the others stood by.

"'Cept I'm not friendly."

The girl's bravado was impressive, even in the presence of imminent danger.

They laughed at her.

Nena knew the laugh well. It was the laugh of people when they thought you were nothing, less than nothing. It was a laugh a person would never forget. And it was when Nena announced herself.

"Let the girl go and there won't be any problems," she said, stepping to the middle of the alley. "This is Keigel's turf."

They gawked at her, likely trying to figure out who the hell she was and where the hell she'd come from without them seeing. They didn't care about the options she'd given them. They had retribution and lust on their minds. Had they been thinking clearly, they might have chosen better.

"Bitch, fuck you," the diner Flush said, advancing on her. "Just like a bitch to not mind her damn busine—"

He was close enough. She stabbed him in the throat with one of her daggers, leaving her gun holstered in the back of her belt. As if on cue, the girl bit the hand of the big treelike Flush holding her. He yelped, yanking her, then sent her slamming into the wall. She crumpled to the ground, curled and whimpering in pain.

The diner Flush hadn't yet realized he was a dead man when the other two surrounded Nena.

He gurgled out, "Bitch," as he held his hands to his throat, blood seeping through his fingers. She should have saved him for last, since he was to blame for what she was about to do.

Nena was no longer a fourteen-year-old girl, cowering at every movement of the men around her. This time, she was thirty-one, with a whole lot of death notched on her proverbial belt.

These boys wanted to play at being killers, but she was the real thing.

The diner Flush dropped to his knees, his life spilling out of him. The giant one lunged at her, his force throwing her onto her back. He let loose a flurry of blows, as she attempted to dodge the brunt of them. She twisted her hips upward, springing her feet out at his midsection to buck him off. She got to all fours, scrambling behind him before he could gather his bearings. She wrapped one of her arms around the back of his neck, the other beneath his chin, one hand locking over the other wrist in a reverse choke hold that quickly had him upside down and staring at the building rooftops.

Systematically she began squeezing off each breath he tried to take, pulling, contracting her muscles in her arms like a boa constrictor. He flailed at her, as they always did, trying to tug her arms away, but she had the upper hand. She could feel panic rising in him when he couldn't get her off, while his energy, his breath, oozed out of him like his partner's blood.

With all her strength and as fast as she could, she bore down, a move so sudden and unexpected she caught him unaware, and they both heard the sickening crunch of his neck as the delicate vertebrae cracked and dislodged from each other.

She released him, and his body hit the ground. Nena whipped around, prepared to take out the last one, briefly wondering why he hadn't attacked while she was occupied, but he was nowhere in sight. Maybe after witnessing his leader's stabbing and the tree crumbling like the Berlin Wall, he'd run for his life, his rep be damned.

Only Nena and the girl remained. The girl was staring at the dead bodies, her eyes wide and her breathing so loud Nena worried it would call attention to them. Or worse, that the surviving Flush would find some friends and return.

"We need to go," she said.

The girl looked up at her, and Nena assessed her as best she could in the dark. She didn't look physically harmed. Maybe her stomach would be sore the next day. Nena couldn't attest to her emotional state. She'd been through a lot just now, seen even more, but after only a moment's hesitation, she got to her feet and followed Nena to her car.

Once they were buckled in the Audi, and Nena's gun was back in its rucksack and her dagger wiped clean and sheathed once again, she pulled away from the curb. She didn't speak until she got some distance between them and those guys.

When she was more comfortable, Nena asked, "Where do you live?"

The girl rattled off her address—one Nena instantly recognized.

She turned her head to stare at the girl harder, her eyes narrowing. What were the chances? Slim to none, that was what. Nena keyed the information into her GPS while her mind raced. Coming across this girl meant something. It was a sign, had to be, and Nena wasn't one to believe in signs or kismet or any of that.

"Aren't you a ways off from home, yeah?" she asked, recalibrating her tone so the girl didn't notice anything might be wrong—aside from all the wrong that had just happened, that was.

The girl watched the city lights passing by her window. "I like taking rides around the city." She sounded tired, her adrenaline crashing, likely. "Beats staying home alone all the time. My dad works crazy hours."

"You have a dangerous hobby."

The girl shot her a look. "And yours isn't?"

Nena's mouth dropped open, but nothing came out. The cheekiness! She regained her composure, opting to confirm what she had already begun to suspect. "What is your name?"

"Georgia," the girl answered. "Georgia Baxter." She let out a huge yawn, resting the back of her head on the headrest and closing her eyes.

Georgia Baxter. Daughter of Cortland Baxter, the federal attorney who was about to try Dennis Smith. The same federal attorney who the African Tribal Council had marked for dispatch by Nena's hands. If Nena were one for laughter, she'd do it now, because the chances of this meeting were a zillion to none.

Nena guessed she wouldn't bother with a lecture about making wiser decisions about where the girl roamed at night. Georgia Baxter had a parent for that. At least for a little while longer.

# 10

## BEFORE

*An unwise decision* echoes in my mind as Paul makes a motion with his hand and Attah strikes my father again, hitting him with the butt of his rifle. The force is so massive my own teeth rattle. Witnessing Papa struck in front of me is too much to bear, and I pry Wisdom's fingers from around my mouth, twisting away from the mesh of limbs that are his and Josiah's arms.

I am on my feet, rushing to Papa before I have a chance to consider what I am doing. My father tries to wave me back, but I ignore him. He's been hurt. Blood trickles from his lip. I wrap my arms tightly around his waist, something I've always done when in need of his comfort. But this time our roles reverse, and Papa needs my protection.

I hear scuffling, an uprising of some of the villagers, the swelling murmur of the few men not yet silenced. Papa holds out a silencing hand when the villagers' murmurs increase toward indignation.

His pain evident in his voice, Papa says, "Let us be reasonable. What you are doing here . . ." My father's voice falters. He shakes his head as if to clear it of a fugue; likely, he is concussed. "When the government catches wind . . . when the president learns of it, they will put you in a cell."

"You do not get to tell us shit," the Walrus barks.

Paul's answer comes from behind us. Where did he get off to? He reminds me that you should not take your eyes off a predator on the hunt, because the moment you look away, they pounce. Yet somehow I took my eyes off Paul, and he disappeared into the smoke and mass of bodies and reemerged.

"Michael, I had hoped you'd be more welcoming this time," he says.

Papa straightens, covering my shoulder with his broad palm and easing me behind him.

Paul's movie-star looks are back in place but do not match the menace in his voice, which slithers like an anaconda preparing to squeeze and eat. "Fuck the government and their figurehead politics only put in to appease the West against us 'savages.' Despite all your university learning, your doctorate and degrees, your multiple languages, and your association with Westerners and colonizers, do you realize they still regard you as a savage? They think you run around here naked with beads and piercings, yelping into the air with spears, taking ten wives, and bartering goats. I make Ghana thrive, not your politicians."

"Ah, but why do you play with him so?" the Walrus grumbles, cranky, even sweatier than before. "Let's be done with this shit, eh? It's fucking hot."

"It's Ghana, Attah," Paul scoffs. "It's always fucking hot." But he snaps his fingers and calls, "Bena."

Kwabena appears from the back of one of the trucks. He is considerably younger than Paul and the Walrus, maybe twenty at the most. He may be younger, but I soon learn he is just as ruthless.

Bena and another man hold up someone by his shoulders. His head hangs, chin touching his chest. A thin strand of spit drools from his mouth. When Bena yanks him, his head jostles violently, revealing his face to me. It is Papa's youngest brother and closest confidant.

Daniel's left eye is swollen shut. His deformed face looks as if it has been stung by a dozen wasps. His skin glistens, not with sweat, like the men who imprison us, but with his blood.

"Daniel!" Papa's body stiffens, and as if on a string, my head twists toward him, seeing the anger flash in his eyes. Papa's hands fist at his sides. "Release him immediately."

Paul smirks. "So this is the brother who has taken my place?"

"Uncle!" Wisdom and Josiah yell, abandoning their earlier attempts to quell knee-jerk reactions.

At the same time Papa implores, "There is still time to stop this."

My eyes jump from my father to my brothers, then to my trembling, bloodied uncle, frailer than I have ever seen him. Paul is smirking. His eyes are bright and dancing; he's clearly enjoying the scene he has created for the rest of us.

"Maybe you can save your entire village and yourself." Paul holds out his hand. "Attah."

The Walrus ambles over, begrudgingly relinquishing his weapon. Paul walks to us, holding the butt of the rifle out to Papa.

"Perhaps now you will reconsider my offer and do what you must to save your people, your children, your family. Will you sacrifice the one to save the many? Does your loyalty run that deep, *Chief*?"

He does not have to say the words for me to know what Paul means for Papa to do. The choice is sickening, one no one should be forced to make.

My father is beside himself. "Surely you jest? Daniel has done nothing. These villagers are innocent." He looks imploringly at the man he was once schoolmates with. "Take me if you wish. I am not a threat. We can renegotiate. We can talk about opening up the village to your business." Papa's voice cracks. "But please, have mercy, Paul. Please."

My father is begging. Pleading for the life of his brother, his blood, the future of their Fanti village, which he left in order to learn how to be a good leader from Papa. Daniel, who is only six years my senior and is supposed to continue school abroad. Will he be able to still?

Paul's face is impassive for so long as the two of them stare at one another. Suddenly, he breaks into a conciliatory smile, and a glimmer of hope peeks its way through.

"Yes, you're right. Mercy." He shakes his head, flipping the gun muzzle so it points in the air. "What have I done? How could I ever ask you to do such things?"

Papa visibly begins to relax, his body deflating with each measured breath.

Paul's violence is so sudden there is no time to react, to even comprehend what is going on.

My uncle jerks as a succession of bullets explodes from the muzzle, slamming into him with such force he's propelled backward. His jaw locks in a grimace of surprise; his body spasms. Bena and the other intruder yelp like hyenas, jumping away so Paul's bullets do not hit them. Within seconds, Daniel drops to the ground.

The gunfire reverberates even after Paul stops firing. My uncle's eyes stare, unseeing, motionless in a perpetual state of incomprehension. His face in death is forever seared into my memory, not the bright, enigmatic young man who introduced me to horror books and movies and comforted me when my mother died.

Paul approaches, leaning over me so they sandwich me, the slice of meat between Papa, the angel, and Paul, the demon. Through all the commotion around us, Paul's words to my father are clear. For the rest of my days, I will never hear words more chilling, more filled with promises of utter doom.

"Tonight"—his voice slipping over me like a funeral shroud, coiling itself around me, feasting on my insides—"your world will cease to exist. All you love will suffer and die. Your sons will die. You will die. And your princess will sell to the highest bidder. You, Michael Asym, who have had every damn blessing imaginable, have run out of them tonight."

# 11

## AFTER

Georgia Baxter turned out not to be as sleepy or traumatized as Nena had thought. She began talking and didn't stop until they made it to her house. Nena figured it was nerves. During the ride, she told Nena what she already knew, that her dad was a federal prosecutor. Nena's fingers tightened around the wheel, a tell she wasn't proud to be displaying. She shot a quick look at the girl to see if she'd noticed. She hadn't. Nena shrugged away any more thoughts of divine intervention and pressed the petrol to get the girl home a little quicker.

She'd barely pulled the Audi to a stop when the front door to the ranch-style home flew open and Georgia's father burst through the doors, still in his suit, top buttons undone and tie slackened.

Georgia muttered, "Shit," under her breath. She hesitated before opening the door of the idling car. She sneaked a quick look at Nena. "Thanks again for—um—you know. Earlier." She couldn't seem to reconcile what had happened to her. "And for the ride home."

She didn't give Nena a chance to respond before she was out the door and heading her dad off in the middle of the walkway. Nena watched as he gesticulated wildly, his anger and fear apparent. He peered over Georgia's head, no doubt wondering about the strange car and who was in it.

Nena weighed her options. She could just toot the horn and drive away, like she'd seen one of those carpool moms do in a movie when she'd dropped neighbor kids off. If she got out, there would inevitably be questions. But something drew Nena out of the safety of her car, curiosity maybe, because now she wanted to see her mark up close and personal—this man the Council said had to go.

Georgia looked back at Nena, now standing on the other side of the car, before turning to her dad. Nena heard the same story about a library. Only now, Georgia had lost her money too.

Nena smirked. This one was adept at lying. She wasn't sure if that was a good thing or bad. Clearly, Nena wasn't going to be truthful about dispatching the Flushes in front of his fourteen-year-old daughter (she had been quick to correct Nena when she'd wrongly guessed the girl's age). Even if they got Georgia's father to believe it was self-defense, which technically it was, he wouldn't understand why they hadn't called the cops. He was essentially "the cops." Plus, Nena didn't want questions about her ability to put those men down the way she had. While she preferred complete truthfulness, she realized tonight she'd need the opposite.

A voice in the back of her head warned she was pushing her luck as she rounded the front of her car to approach the Baxters, but she dispelled it. In the light of the streetlamp and the walkway lit with little round solar lamps, Nena got her first look at Cortland Baxter, up close and personal. And he got a look at her.

She released a measured breath, letting her exhalation absorb the shock of feelings assaulting her. She kept her face placid, was able to speak naturally, as if she hadn't broken protocol and her heart wasn't fluttering ten thousand beats per second. She could hear those beats drumming in her ears and worried Georgia and her father could hear too.

The force of the—attraction, was that what this was?—made Nena take a reflexive step backward. She again wondered what kind of fate had brought her into the path of this family. This never happened. To have saved the life of the daughter, only to rip her heart out in a couple of days' time. How was Nena to reconcile that?

Her attention shifted to Cortland, who had spoken and was waiting for her response. She hadn't heard.

"Sorry?" she asked, startled.

"Dad wants to know where you come in," Georgia answered pointedly.

"Please, the blame is mine," Nena began. "I happened across Georgia in distress with no money—"

"And my phone was smashed," Georgia interjected.

"That too," Nena agreed. "She looked hungry and said you were working late, so I suggested we grab supper; then I brought her home. I should have thought for her to call you from my phone."

Georgia shook both her head and her hand at Nena. "It wouldn't have mattered anyway, since I don't know Dad's number by heart."

Nena nodded. Made sense. Smart girl. "You probably should have important numbers memorized. At least your dad's."

"Why," she asked, "when it's programmed in my phone?"

Cortland chimed in. "The one you smashed, right, Peach?" He placed his hand on the crown of her head and gave it a little shake.

A ghost of a smile appeared on Nena's face. Peach. She found the nickname endearing. And she liked the way Cortland sounded when he said it. When her eyes met his, he was staring at her. It rattled her, and she immediately worried he might recognize her from somewhere.

Or perhaps—her stomach soured slightly—perhaps his own intuition was alerting him that danger stood right before his eyes. He wasn't looking at her as if she were a threat, though. No, he was looking at her as if he had something more to say. The intensity of his gaze sucked her in, making her feel uncomfortably warm.

Nena found herself liking the way he looked at her. It was the first time she could remember ever welcoming the attention of a man. They stood there looking stupidly at each other, forgetting about the girl between them glancing suspiciously from one to the other. Then Georgia cleared her throat loudly, likely bored at the staring contest these two were having.

The spell broken, Cortland thanked Nena. His eyes, she noticed, were framed with thick dark lashes, like Georgia's. It was too dark to tell their color. From the intel Nena had received, he was six feet two. The photos she'd seen did him no justice up close. She had already taken in his pronounced forehead, athletic build—not overly muscular, not too skinny.

She shook her head to clear it. Two days from now, she had a dispatch to do. She couldn't get sidetracked even if Cortland Baxter was the first man she'd ever noticed, ever considered . . . in that way. He grinned at her, his natural smile nearly making her reciprocate until she remembered she never smiled unless on a job. Wasn't she on a job now? He was her mark. She should smile, then. Her lips twitched instead.

"Right," she said, gathering her wits. "Right. Night, then." She turned before either had a chance to respond and made haste to her car. The two of them remained on the walkway until she was out of sight.

In two days, she'd do her job as planned. She had to, emotions and confusion and hesitation be damned. Once the dispatch was completed, Nena would never have to think about Cortland Baxter, or Georgia, again.

# 12

## BEFORE

Blood saturates the ground, mingling with the fertile soil of my home. All around, people are screaming. The cacophony is so loud my hands clamp over my ears to drown it all out, but to no avail. With Paul's words to Papa, he unleashes his men in full force upon us. Villagers, in last-ditch efforts to save their lives, attempt to flee up the mountain. They are gunned down like dogs. The rat-a-tat-tat permeates the air, followed by muted thuds of bodies falling to the ground. Mere hours ago, these people were laughing, believing themselves safe, believing all was right in the world.

The men are creative with their kills, chasing people down, shooting, hacking with dirty machetes as if my people are sticks of sugarcane. The intruders drag people I have known all my life away by their hair or clothing. They drag these people who have done no harm to death, to rape, to mutilation—whatever these monsters desire, and they desire all of it. I begin to believe my little village has somehow greatly offended God. This must be his wrath, this hell he has unleashed upon us. All because my father refused to be a participant in Paul's illegal business? It all sounds unbelievable to me, transport routes and selling people.

Paul returns to his truck and throughout it all sits in the passenger seat. He observes the chaos while Attah Walrus and Bena bark orders about what to do with whom. They gorge themselves on the wealth and flesh of N'nkakuwe.

They snatch the women and children for their own perversions, taking them while they force husbands and fathers to watch, if they are still alive. Usually, the mountain is alive at night, the animals who inhabit it active and chattering. However, during the spurts when the men reload their weapons, the mountain is a silent witness to our eradication.

Meanwhile, Paul eats from a bowl of palm-nut soup and fufu. He smacks his lips, sucking the soup from his fingers and the marrow from a goat bone. Attah stands beside him, his eyes tallying the death count.

Attah asks, "Ah, but do you think our benefactors will approve? Did they intend for all of this?" His machete-filled hand sweeps before him.

Paul doesn't look up from the bowl. "Do you think I give a damn? There is no benefactor here. There is just me."

Paul does not even notice Attah's embarrassment. He compliments the chef.

"She's dead," Attah says banally.

A small pout plays on Paul's lips. "Perhaps it wasn't a good idea to kill her, no? We could have used her at the Compound. God knows the one we have now is for shit." He runs his fingers along the inside of the bowl. "See if you can find another cook, and tell the men not to kill everybody. There must be some here we can use."

———

After what feels like hours but is not, Paul climbs out of his truck and approaches us again. The screams have been whittled down to whimpers because there are so few of us left. The backs of his trucks fill with N'nkakuwe's youth. Those not selected for the trucks are herded together, off to the side, awaiting their fate as we await ours. My brothers, my father, and I have come together in all of this. We hold on to each other. Papa, his voice gravelly from begging Paul to stop his madness, asks after Auntie. Who has seen her? None of us have, and the guilt I have been feeling for leaving her in the house calling my name gnaws at my bones.

Paul stands reflectively, a hand at his chin. Maybe he has tired of the misery he has inflicted. He casts a long, dissatisfied look at the lot of us.

"Paul." Papa coughs, and a trail of bloody saliva drips from his swollen mouth. I use the hem of my dress to wipe it. He can barely get his words out now, his voice practically gone.

"The spoils here are disappointing, Big Man." The honorific is usually spoken with reverence, to show a man's importance, but from Paul's lips it is a slur. "All I ever hear about in Ghana are the N'nkakuwe's beauties. Have they all gone on holiday?" He chuckles. "Or maybe you make them work too hard in this backwater village, and these shriveled-up husks you call people are the result. And you say I do them a disservice."

He trains his black orbs on me. "But your daughter, Aninyeh, she is a beauty, o. You must have spared her the hard work, eh? Raising a chieftain's daughter."

Papa bristles. "Do with me what you will, but spare my children and whatever is left of this village." He attempts to stand, but Paul kicks him back down with his boot heel. "Have you not done enough, taken enough?"

Paul casts him a baleful look. "It is never enough." His jaw tightens beneath his skin. "Take her."

"No!" Papa yells, grabbing for me as unknown hands attack me.

His yell does not overpower my own as I kick and scream, trying to twist from the rough hands wrenching me away from the safety of my father and brothers.

"Papa!" If I thought I knew terror before, it is incomparable to what I feel now. Will I be shot dead like Daniel? Hacked to pieces like our good neighbor Auntie Pep, who made the best kenkey on this side of Aburi Mountain? Or worse?

"Help me!"

My brothers try in vain to grab for me. Even Ofori, who up until now sat nearly catatonic, stretches his arms, the ones I used to tease endlessly because he had no muscles, toward me to keep me with them. To no avail.

"Make his boys tie her down at that tree," Paul instructs, pointing to a sapling only yards away. "Make sure their *papa* has a front-row view." He gawks at his men. "Do you know what that means, you imbeciles? It means move the fuck out of the way so he can see, God dammit."

My heart thunders in my chest. Josiah and Wisdom stand defiant when the men toss ropes at their feet. They remain defiant even as the men raise guns to their heads, and they continue to refuse.

"Papa." I want someone to save me. I can think of nothing else but self-preservation. "Papa, please, please don't let them take me!"

The men force me to the ground, on my back. The men will put bullets in Wisdom's and Josiah's heads if they refuse much longer. I am a mixture of begging my brothers to listen to their orders and begging to be released. Wisdom and Josiah are statues.

It is Ofori who steps forward, taking charge and grabbing the rope. He approaches me and begins tying my wrists together above my head to the tree. He ties my hands as loosely as possible without making it seem so and gives my arms slack so they do not hurt too much. Pained arms are not what I fear the most.

The ground is alive with bugs fleeing the burning buildings, and every one of them must be running across my back and throughout my clothes. But I would rather have insects traipsing all over my body than what comes next.

The group of men swallows up my twin brothers as they converge on me like bloodthirsty jackals. One of them hits me, forcing my legs open, pushing up my dress, tearing my underwear. They expose me to everyone, my father, my brothers, Paul. It is humiliation unparalleled, the likes of which I have never known.

Until.

Paul demands my brothers take me.

"Are you mad?" Papa blubbers, his voice raised in unadulterated horror. He struggles against the men holding him, fighting them to save his children.

"She is our sister!" Josiah shouts incredulously. His head snaps back and forth between me and Paul. His hands are out as if to placate the horde of men, as if to reason with Paul, who cannot be reasoned with.

"We would never." Wisdom shakes with anger. His hands fist and release. Fist and release. The cords of his neck bulge so much they are near bursting.

"This I want to see," Attah says, bemused and lecherous.

"You, little Michael, will do as I say or suffer the bullet," Paul says blandly, as if offering Wisdom a choice of which vegetable he'd like with his dinner.

"I won't do it." Wisdom's defiance flashes in his eyes. "Fuck you, you depraved asshole. Rot in hell."

Three things occur in succession: a gunshot; my father screaming an unholy sound I have never heard before; and Wisdom, my eldest brother, falling a few feet from where I am bound. His eyes stare through me. I cannot scream; my voice has died in my throat. My body spasms from such pain that only a couple of tears manage to squeeze from my swollen eyelids.

Overcome from witnessing the death of his twin, Josiah is out of his mind when he lunges at Paul. He grabs Paul's shirt, pulling at it so hard he yanks Paul down to his height. Josiah has always been short for his age, even though Wisdom is—was—tall. Before he can lay his other hand on Paul, Josiah is run through with a machete magically produced in Paul's hand.

Josiah freezes on the blade, emitting a sick sound. I can only see the back of him, the blade jutting through. But Paul's face is visible. I strain through my own pain to see some semblance of repentance, some realization from him that he has gone too far. There is none. Josiah might as well be a specimen in a petri dish.

Paul grips Josiah's shoulder, pushing him unceremoniously off the blade, and Josiah lands on the ground near Wisdom. His arm falls on Wisdom's shoulder, finding his twin, even in death.

When all eyes turn to me, seeming to accuse me of these deaths, I pray my own will be as swift as my brothers'.

# 13

## AFTER

Nena had never left a trail of mess like she had tonight, but her encounter with the Baxters had rattled her, really rattled her. And she wasn't sure how she'd work through it. She prided herself on sticking to routine, minding her business, and doing her job without issue. But this had been nothing like routine.

When the shower was hot, nearly scalding, the way she liked it, she stepped in. The tension seeped from her body and down the drain, intermingling with the soap and water. The events in the alleyway of Jake's Burger Joint weighed heavily on her. Now that Nena had time to think, she concluded she might have screwed up twofold, not only by jeopardizing Keigel's delicate gang turf but by going off script with Cortland Baxter as well.

Ever since dropping the girl back with her father, Nena couldn't stop thinking about them. And she couldn't stop questioning the dispatch she'd been assigned to complete, the hesitation she'd felt ever since her father had brought it up to her and Elin. It was those questions that scared her, because Nena never questioned a job. Yet since meeting the Baxters, she had done nothing but.

She turned off the water, stuck an arm out to grab a fluffy dark-blue towel, and wrapped it around her body. She took a smaller towel and tied it in a turban around her head. She ignored the next phase of her cleansing routine, moisturizing herself before her damp skin dried, and found her cell to call Elin. As she did, a glint on the bureau caught her eye. Georgia's school ID badge, which she'd found wedged in between the seat and the armrest in the Audi.

When had Nena ever cared about a mark?

*Tonight.* The words sneaked up on her before she realized. *Tonight is when I cared.*

A sudden weariness weighed heavily on her. Her finger hovered over the phone icon to call her sister. And say what? Ask to be let off the job and risk being retired from Dispatch? Or having a team sent for her? Would they do that? Her father would have to follow the rules he'd created, the rules of the Tribe he lived by.

Nena fingered the smooth plastic of the ID. The Knights had given her life. She couldn't betray them because she was smitten by a cheeky little girl and her dashing dad.

She thought about asking Elin what these swirls of emotions meant, because they were alien to her. They scared her, too, made her feel unlike herself after she had fought so hard to feel a semblance of self again. Elin had always been her biggest support, would give her own life for Nena, defy their father and the Tribe's wishes for her. Nena would never ask her to do that because she would never again allow a sibling to give their life for hers.

She set her phone back down on the bureau and walked away.

# 14

## BEFORE

Ofori rises, trembling violently, while Paul looks on expectantly, waiting for him to choose—will he defy Paul's orders and share the same fate as Wisdom and Josiah?

I take a gulp of air. "Ofori," I croak. He is my blood, my brother. I want him to live more than anything, but not if it means doing this unthinkable thing to me. Ofori takes a halting step toward me.

Paul cocks his head to the side, watching curiously, a smile playing on his lips.

"No, no, no, Ofori, no." Papa is beside himself. "Be strong. Not this."

Death is better than what Paul commands Ofori do. Papa would rather the last of his sons die than commit this unconscionable act.

"See how your father wishes you dead?" Paul bends low so he speaks directly in Ofori's ear like the devil he is. His voice like an oil slick. "He did not say that to your brothers."

Ofori looks to our father, who compels him not to do this thing, then to Paul, who encourages, then to me, who cannot bring myself to say anything.

He takes another, more certain step toward me. The debate rages on his face. He does not want to do this, but he does not want to die. He is a cauldron of emotions I cannot discern.

In the end, self-preservation wins out. My last remaining brother, the one who thinks himself out of place because he is neither a firstborn nor a twin nor the only girl, drops down next to me. He tries to be as gentle as possible as he prepares to do the devil's bidding.

I feel him fumbling with himself. My body tenses, muscles taut, preparing to reject any touch from the brother only nineteen months older than me. "Ofori, no."

This cannot be real. This morning I woke to the sun shining on my face, excited about the trip to Accra we were going to take this weekend. My body is so rigid it begins to cramp from its fortification against this immoral violation.

If Ofori does this thing, we are marked forever. We will be Adam and Eve after they ate of the fruit, no longer able to look upon each other in innocence. We will be forever damned.

"Sorry," he whispers dully. His fingers are clumsy as he fumbles with his pants.

"Ofori Kwaku Asym." Papa's voice rings out, tremulous but angry. "Do this, and you'll be damned, me ba barima." *My son.* "Please—" Papa's voice cracks.

"Shut up!" someone snarls.

A tear slides down Ofori's cheek.

Papa is cut off amid a flurry of grunts as the men assault him again, silencing Papa's protests.

I wish to shut my eyes, but I cannot turn from Ofori. I stare into his frightened eyes, at the tear that trails down his face. His shame is evident, but so is his resolve to save himself.

Ofori frees himself. His eyes shut as if he doesn't want to look. But I do. I must see my brother as he does this thing to me. Even if by force, he had a choice. And Ofori chose wrong.

My brother, the weak. His choice was to survive no matter what, no matter who. He positions himself awkwardly, preparing himself. I suck in air, a feeble attempt to move away from him, even if only a millimeter.

He comes even closer to me, the tip of his tongue flickering out to moisten his chapped lips.

I whisper, "Please. Please, please, Ofori."

His lips are moving, but no sound comes from them. He is limp against me. At least there is that, and he is finding no pleasure from this.

My eyes bore through his closed eyelids. I hold my breath for an eternity, unable to breathe because if I do, it brings me that much nearer to *that* piece of him that should never be so close to *that* piece of me. But my body is fighting to breathe. I am at war with my physical self and my mental, as every facet of physical me begs to take a breath while my mind says, *Do not. Do not make it easy for him, Aninyeh.*

I hold my breath for an eternity. And just when I am about to pass out from lack of oxygen or succumb to my body's need for air, just as I am about to be forever damned by my brother, miraculously, just as he . . . *touches* me . . . the weight of him suddenly lifts off me. All the air inside me releases; then my body convulses from sobs.

"You are a perverted son of a bitch, you know that?" Paul says incredulously. "I don't know whether to be repulsed by you or impressed. I can't believe he was going to do it."

"Well, you are quite convincing," Attah Walrus deadpans. "Who would say no to you?" He looks down at the dead bodies of my brothers. "Or the bullet?"

There is raucous laughter from the men as Ofori hurriedly fixes his clothing, his shoulders bowed in complete shame.

I have never felt so betrayed.

I have never thought I could hate my brother as I do in this moment.

And I have never thought I would feel gratitude to Paul for ending the incestuous horror before it was enacted, even though the command came from him. Because Paul is not my brother; Ofori is. And Ofori will now be exactly as my father declared. Damned, damaged for eternity, because of what he was willing to do to his sister to save himself.

My eyes close, tired of it all, tired of living. I want nothing but to see the darkness.

"You have promise, boy." Paul sighs. It sounds regretful. "But unfortunately, you are useless with your father's blood coursing through your veins. Put him with the others."

Ofori cries, becoming crazed, "No! Uncle, I only did as you asked. Only as you asked!"

His reference to Paul, using a title of a respected elder, is another nail driven through me. His groveling stirs no affection in me. Only contempt that grows like a snowball as they throw him in with the crowd of waiting villagers. My brother. Ofori, the weak.

Moments later, I hear rapid firing, screams, wails. Then silence, and I think, *Good. He is gone, and there is nothing left.*

But Paul is not yet finished with me.

———

Paul, voyeur puppet master, directs Bena and another faceless, vile soldier to have a go at me, and they do. No one stops them this time.

My agony sears through hoarse whimpers because I have no voice left. Papa weeps for a virtue cleaved from me like a hot knife shears through butter. My body tears in two.

Paul ignores him.

The men laugh.

The laughter is worst of all, laughter at my pain, my humiliation, my being made nothing at all. It is laughter that will haunt me for the rest of my life.

They hold Papa's head so he cannot turn away. His eyes implore me for forgiveness. He suffers with me as obsidian dread takes over.

Papa's eyes are the last things I see. The intruders' laughter is the last thing I hear before giving way to the only escape my broken body can provide me. I thrust myself into a realm of unconsciousness, separating mind from body. I cocoon myself so I am not there when they do what they do to me.

# 15

## AFTER

Cortland Baxter was still on Nena's mind the next day when she stood three doors down from her house, at the end of Keigel's walkway, until two of his men moved aside to let her pass. Waiting for entry was common courtesy, and it was better to keep up pretenses that their number one had her respect. Plus, as far as friends went, their boss was the closest thing she had to one.

"When are you gonna sell me that bike of yours?" was his greeting. One she knew was not serious but had become their routine. "Saw you riding it earlier today."

Her metallic thunder-gray Hayabusa sport bike, one of three modes of transportation that she indulged herself with, but by far her favorite. When on her bike, Nena felt nothing could touch her.

"When you learn how to ride it," she answered easily, approaching where he sat on a cheap plastic chair on his porch.

He cracked a smile. "Word on the street," he began, "is that a couple of Royal Flushes got clipped on Fifth and Mercy, by a female."

"A female what? Elephant?" She hated when he—when any man—referred to women as *females*. She'd keep correcting him for as long as he kept speaking ignorantly.

He rolled his eyes, throwing a hand in the air. "A wo-man, okay."

"You know, male, female, those are the sexual distinctions of animals. Shall we discuss sexual classification? There are more than just male and female now—for people, I mean."

He waved her off.

"But the story would be much more interesting if it really was a female elephant," she deadpanned. Nena normally had two facial expressions, serious and very serious. Hers was currently the former.

Keigel released a slow, exasperated breath, ignoring the nearby snickers of the gang members lucky enough to overhear Nena's once-in-a-lifetime joke. They had business to square away. The streets were probably abuzz after her late-night diner save. He snapped his fingers, and within seconds the immediate area around the porch cleared, leaving them alone.

"Real talk, you nearly caused a war, Nena, a war I can't have right now. I'm trying to get this money up, not lose lives."

She took a seat next to him, choosing the chair with its back to the wall. She preferred to minimize her blind spots.

"You already have plenty of money."

He snorted. "Could always use more."

She analyzed him. "You could give up selling the drugs and guns. There are other ways to become wealthy. Better ways."

Keigel scratched his perfectly groomed beard. "Maybe when I grow up." He cracked a wry smile.

The corners of her mouth held a whisper of amusement, and she relaxed just a degree, waiting patiently for what she knew was coming next.

He leaned in, placing his elbows on his knees, matching Nena's look of seriousness. "Real talk, what happened last night?"

She pursed her lips. *Nothing much.* Nena swallowed. *Just met an interesting girl and her father. Turns out I'm supposed to kill him.*

"What are you thinking about, kid?" he asked, narrowing his eyes. "Your face just got all dreamy."

Nena blinked, ignoring him even though she was older than his twenty-five years by six. "The night might have taken some unexpected turns."

She cleared her throat and her mind of all things Baxter.

"Talk to the Flushes. They encroached on your territory, which means two things. First, they disrespected you by starting trouble on your turf. Second, they would have left a body, and a young one at that. That's police attention." She shrugged. "Sounds like whatever woman clipped them—that was the word you used, yes?—did you a favor."

Keigel's look was begrudging. "Well, dude she let live says otherwise."

"Of course." She hadn't let him live. He'd already been running away by the time she'd killed the second one, but that was inconsequential.

What else would the Flush say? That one woman had taken out all three with no backup? Her lips curved into a tiny smirk. Actually, she wished he would say it.

"They want retaliation." Keigel looked at her firmly. "And the one dude who survived describes a woman who looks a lot like you."

It wasn't Nena's concern. It was Keigel's. He had to figure out how to clean this up. If it were left to Nena, she'd order a dispatch of the whole crooked Flush crew for the simple fact they liked to prey on the unprotected, something she and the Tribe vowed to disallow.

She studied him. Keigel needed to start thinking on another level if he wanted to continue in the Tribe's good graces. People joined the Tribe because they wanted to, not because they were forced. And to do so, they needed to be aligned with the Tribe's beliefs. Keigel dealt drugs, and while the Tribe didn't believe in peddling poison to their own people, they didn't stop him from doing it either. They allowed him free rein to do as he pleased in his little Miami world. Because he was under Nena's protection, he was under the Tribe's as well. That was their gift to him.

Maybe one day, Keigel would move beyond wanting to only make fast money and seek more for himself and the people in his territories, find a greater cause to fight for. Nena could only hope. But right now, Keigel served a purpose for her. She needed to be able to move freely about this area of the city. She needed to be like a ghost to do her dispatching and Tribe business unencumbered, and Keigel kept the other, smaller gangs in check so she could do so.

"I'm sure all she did was remind them they were on your turf, especially after they said, 'Fuck Keigel.'"

His jaw tightened, and his eyes went flat. Keigel could be a clown, rough around the edges even, but he knew what respect should look like and demanded it.

"Don't tell me that."

"If I were you, I would make a clear statement. You're chief around here. Send a clear message. Let them know they owe you for causing trouble and bringing it to your turf. You won't have any more problems from them or any of the others if you do that. They owe you." She kept her voice even. "And you owe the woman for taking care of those idiot would-be rapists."

He pulled a face. "How do you figure that?"

"She put you in the perfect position to affirm your authority over your territories. Who knows, maybe they'll be scared now, thinking you have some secret killer to take them all out. Maybe they'll all fall in line now, hmm?"

They had an understanding, Keigel and Nena. No one messed with the quiet woman who lived alone at the corner house in the neighborhood. The woman who came and went as she pleased, looked like a goddess, and was lethal as hell—Keigel's words, not hers. Keigel would clean up the mess with the Flushes. He'd send a message like she recommended. And he'd do it because he had no plans to end up like them,

72

taken down in a dirty-ass alley. There wasn't a need to tell him the girl was the child of a federal attorney.

Nena sighed, begging her mind not to think about Cortland Baxter, how he'd looked at her when she'd brought Georgia home, and how she wanted him to look at her like that again. The feeling was unsettling. Her hands, she realized, were trembling, and so she folded them into her lap, where Keigel wouldn't mistake her emotion.

Nena had thought she would never want a man to look at her with the interest and the want that Cortland had looked at her with the other night. She didn't want it, love, a relationship, did she? Was it even possible for her after all she'd endured?

No, she didn't want it. She couldn't want *him*. Because tomorrow, she'd have to do her job, be Echo again. There was no room for Cortland Baxter in her world, or any world, because the Tribe had decreed his dispatch. And Echo was the one assigned to carry it out.

# 16

## BEFORE

When I come to, my stomach heaves, but nothing but bitter bile comes up. I turn my head, spitting out the slimy mess so I do not choke or vomit even more.

Maybe I should choke and die. Death would be better, so I am not forced to live with what these men have done to me. Nor do I want to live with what I have seen: the death of my brothers, the dissolution of my father, the destruction of my home and everything I know. The destruction of me.

My body is ablaze from the insects scurrying across the ground beneath me. It burns from the inside; the molten lava between my legs liquefies every part of my insides. I do not need a doctor to tell me something in me is ruined. I know my body well enough to know it is broken beyond repair, somewhere inside, somewhere down there. Never again healed, and I, never again whole.

Someone—I do not know who, nor do I care—eventually cuts me loose from the tree. They do not attempt to make me walk, hoisting me up roughly upon their shoulders and tossing me into the bed of a truck already teeming with girls of various ages. Whoever drops me among them does so with no care, and my body is again awash with new pain. But I cannot give up here. I must see to Papa. I must see what has become of N'nkakuwe in my absence. With effort, using the sides of the vehicle to assist me, I pull myself to a sitting position, ignoring the whimpers and squeals of the girls around me.

The sky is the blackest night stretching like a canvas above us, dotted with white blinking stars that are as clear as if we were standing on the cliff. There is no moon, for even it does not want to bear witness to this genocide. There are bodies strewed everywhere in the square, the bulk of their extermination done. Paul's men drag the bodies into homes with no ceremony, as if yanking the carcasses of dead warthogs. The homes are then set ablaze, illuminating the blanket of thick, tall trees that covers us. Paul's end goal takes shape. There will be no autopsies. With the right amount of money and threats, no real investigation will take place.

The girls in the truck wear hollowed expressions I likely mirror. We do not speak, fearing we will call more attention upon ourselves. We have had enough attention to last a lifetime.

"Michael." Paul's voice pulls my attention away from the other girls.

A flutter of hope blooms in me. Papa still lives! I locate Paul, maybe ten meters away, standing amid a circle of his men. Papa sways on his knees in front of Paul. His shoulders are hunched, his hands tied before him. He lists heavily to the left, and each time his body falls too far, Bena tugs him up viciously.

"Kwabena," Paul says. "Easy, o." I will never forget it, or him. Behind Papa is Attah Walrus, who brandishes a large machete, larger than I think I have ever seen, coated with dark, thick, sticky residue I can only imagine to be dust and gore. The blade is so long it drags on the ground when he lets it. My eyes widen.

Paul removes a hunting knife from his belt and uses its curved tip to clean beneath his fingernails. His actions, his tone, belie everything going on around him. It is his preternatural calm that renews fresh fear in me. Paul has no soul. I know this now like I know my name is Aninyeh Ama Asym.

"Michael, our time has ended. Any last words?" He speaks as if asking Papa to quote a final price at market after hours of haggling.

"Brother, Paul, haven't you done enough? Haven't you taken everything from me? My children? Please release the people in the trucks."

When Papa says "brother," Paul flinches as if stricken. I am stricken as well. For the briefest second, I hate my father for his stoicism, his duty to save the rest of the villagers. What about his duty to save me?

And then a deep chasm of shame erupts in me, for my evil thoughts, for my anger at Papa—because he still tries to do what is right despite all he has lost.

Briefly, Paul looks unsure. Maybe Papa's words hit their mark and have reminded Paul of his humanity. Perhaps Papa has removed the veil from Paul's eyes, showing him all the horror he has inflicted like a movie reel. But the next instant, I see I am wrong. Paul's moment of doubt is so fleeting no one catches it except me.

"Brother," Paul repeats incredulously. "I haven't heard you say it in, what, ten years? Never thought I would again." He gathers himself, shaking off all remnants of nostalgia.

"Was I your brother when you left me behind for university after my father beat me so badly I couldn't properly take the entrance exam? You swore you would never leave me behind, and yet you did. Was I your brother when you thrived and prospered abroad while I wasted away here? Did my brother remember to come back for me? Remember when we were boys, planning how you would become chief, and I would be on your council of elders? You returned from uni, took a bride, and became chief here, forsaking your own village and people."

"I didn't," my father replies. He raises his head to look at Daniel's crumpled form. "You have forsaken them. You killed their chief."

Paul follows my father's gaze. "Who, that boy?" He scoffs. "Was I still your brother when I came to you just last month, palms out"—he splays them before him—"asking you allow me these trade routes? This mountain serves as great cover against the government. If I am your brother, is N'nkakuwe not my home as well?"

"You turned criminal, running around cheating and stealing from honest people. Your commodity now is selling people. You are better than that, me nua."

"How do you call me your brother," Paul says, the cords of his neck bulging, "when your sons are dead and your girl sits in my truck, with a fate worse than theirs?"

Paul bends until he is eye level with Papa. He tilts his head, shaking his index finger as if he's now understood the joke. "I know you too well. You use this word to try to break me, and you cannot. You lost sway with me when you left me behind, here, to rot."

Papa's body bows from fatigue, from his losing hope. "I never left you behind."

Paul regains his full height. He looks regal against the backdrop of homes consumed by red-and-orange flames with oppressive plumes of black smoke and heat billowing from them.

"And now one good turn deserves another, right?" Paul says. He cracks a gregarious smile, that preternatural look about him again, then spits out, "Nua."

I thought I knew fear. I thought I had already experienced the worst acts imaginable.

But when Paul says *brother*, dread rolls over me, emanating in waves that roil up into the ink-black sky.

I know Paul's worst is yet to come.

# 17

## AFTER

Nena surveilled the grounds of the federal courthouse. There was law enforcement everywhere. Expected. The setup wasn't ideal, but there wasn't a better option, so she would make it work. She'd gone over the intel repeatedly, driven the streets in different autos to learn the routes in and out. Her eye in the sky, Network, did its thing monitoring cameras and police chatter, but today's mission would happen without Network in her ear and in her head. She needed to be alone with the feelings still warring with her duty. Witt had opposed her cutting comms, but he'd allowed it.

*What if this time I didn't pull the trigger?* Her thought was treasonous.

She'd situated herself in the back of a run-of-the-mill family SUV, a Toyota 4Runner, on the eighth level of the University of Miami medical school's parking garage. It was a bit farther than she would have liked from where her mark would arrive on Twelfth Avenue, but with her high-powered rifle and scope, she'd be able to do what she needed. The advocacy center across the street from the courthouse would have been perfect, but it was much too close and visible. It would be the first place locked down when the bullets flew.

She'd parked the burgundy mom mobile backward in its space, then set up her tripod and rifle. She found the car acceptable, the way its roof jutted out like a visor over the back window, providing more cover. That, along with the tinted windows and the blinds she'd added over the partially open one, ensured she'd go unnoticed. She checked her nav system. The tracker on Cortland Baxter's car indicated he was close. She ignored the flutter of her heart and the way her stomach soured at what she was about to do.

Through her scope, she scanned the front of the courthouse. Smith was scheduled to attend a pretrial hearing, though word was he and the prosecutor's office were going to meet in a last-ditch effort to make a deal that would keep Smith out of prison.

They said he was a bad man, financial crimes and the like. Didn't mean anything to Nena. She'd known bad men half her life. This one was no different, and since the Council decreed him an asset, he was of no consequence to her mission.

She checked the tracker, ignoring the twist in her gut when she saw that Cortland had arrived. She knew he'd park his vintage Chevelle SS in the employee lot and then cross the street, entering the federal building from the front entrance. He'd linger to catch a glimpse of the defense team's arrival. From intel she knew getting a first look at the opposing team was part of his ritual on "game day." How Network secured information like that, she couldn't fathom.

A succession of sleek town cars pulled to a stop in front of the federal building. Figured Smith would come with an entourage. She let out an annoyed breath as she rechecked her rifle's calibrations. The crosshairs needed to be just right. The suppressor was on, so she wasn't worried about sound. She used the scope to search for Cortland, finding him as he made his way toward the building. He was joined by another suited man—could be a coworker—and they shook hands, chatting casually as they waited for the others to exit their cars. Cortland grinned at something the other man said, and Nena, watching through the scope, recalled how that grin made her feel when it was directed at her.

She had to let this go. She'd be taking away Georgia's last parent, but Georgia would survive the loss. She was a survivor, like Nena.

Nena glanced at her watch. Eight o'clock. Her heart thumped. It was time. Now she'd pull the fucking trigger.

But.

She faltered, her finger hovering. Swallowed the forming lump in her throat. Beat back the pounding in her heart. Could she? She couldn't. There had to be another way that the Tribe could pacify the new member. Maybe they could buy Cortland off. Persuade him to drop the case against Smith. Anything but kill him like this. That was not the Tribe's way.

She tried pushing those treasonous thoughts from her mind. Focus. Her job was not to understand the Tribe's decrees or to find solutions to their problems. Hers was only to execute them.

A grim expression replaced the smile Cortland had worn seconds earlier, tightening as he watched the defendant get out of his car. She saw Smith from the back. Who was this man? She hadn't asked for intel on him. She should have. But when she received an assignment, she had tunnel vision, her sole purpose being to learn the ins and outs of her mark. Smith was insignificant since he was supposed to live, for better or for worse—*worse*, she decided.

She swung the scope toward the bustle of local news media jostling for the perfect shot of the defendant. Smith turned and waved as if he were some politician on the campaign trail and not a criminal.

And Nena's world stopped spinning on its axis.

It was as if the last decade and a half hadn't happened and she was fourteen and back in N'nkakuwe.

He was still morbidly obese with watery, yellowed eyes giving away years of nicotine abuse, eyes as deadly as the most venomous snake. He might be older and richer and use a different name now, but he was the same Attah Walrus.

He was supposed to be dead. The Tribe had said Attah, Kwabena, and Paul were dead. Nena had let herself believe. Yet here he stood, still up to no good, grinning from a well-lived life he didn't deserve. The gall of him. He basked in the glow of his celebrity, not embarrassed, not ashamed. He didn't look like there was a day he thought of the countless tortures and rapes and mutilations he'd inflicted on her people.

Of all the places in the world for him to show up, he turned up in the one place she had made a home.

Her memory went to Attah as his arms came down, machete in hand. She heard his phlegmy laughter piercing through her screams.

Her breathing slowed.

She could taste the salty sweat flung from his disgusting body as he plucked her and other N'nkakuwean girls from their parents' clutches. Bile rose in the back of her throat.

She moved her scope to her mark.

*Focus, Echo.*

Her eyes narrowed, honing her vision. She couldn't waver. But she couldn't help the questions crowding her mind. How was he alive? And if he was, what about the others?

She blinked.

Then exhaled, the air released in a steady stream from between her lips.

And squeezed.

By the time the crowd realized what had happened, she had the window rolled up and was disassembling her weapon. She placed it in its case, then the case in her backpack. She pulled the blind off the window, rolled it tightly, and slid it into a cylindrical portfolio case.

No one noticed the woman with sunglasses and box braids driving her 4Runner down two levels and parking it on the other side of the garage, where the Cleaners would pick it up to dispose of it. No one noticed her wiping down the car of any leftover prints. There were no second glances at the young lady in med-school scrubs wearing a rucksack. They didn't see her enter the hospital stairwell and leave through the front doors on the ground level, now clad in navy-blue Converse All Stars, dark-washed denim jeans, and a crisp striped blue-and-white button-down shirt.

She even stopped to help a woman struggling with a flower delivery while entering the hospital. Nena caught the falling vase, placed the rogue bouquet back on the woman's cart, and asked what was with all the sirens.

"You're a lifesaver," the older woman gushed, checking her deliveries. "There was a shooting or something at the federal courthouse over there. Some guy who was supposed to be on trial. It's like a scene out of *Law and Order!*"

Nena widened her eyes as she cooed, "Love that show."

"I know, right?" The woman clucked her tongue. "Anyway, dear, thanks ag—"

But when the florist turned to properly thank her Good Samaritan, no one was there.

# 18

## BEFORE

Papa finds me among all those jackals, and our eyes lock. He stares seemingly through me to the depths of my being. "Aninyeh," he says, "*this* will not break you. Let it make you stronger." How I manage to hear him from where Papa kneels, surrounded by men ready to pounce, I do not know.

All that is good about him, Papa gifts to me in that moment. *There is only your before and your after.* How many times have my brothers and I heard this and not known what Papa had meant? *It is what you do after that matters.*

"What the fuck does he even mean?" Paul snarls, enraged by Papa's stoicism. It must be driving him mad, because he lunges at Papa, grabbing his shoulder and plunging the knife he holds deep into Papa's chest.

Papa's eyes widen like saucers. His mouth drops open, and his intake of air reverberates in my ears. He shudders when Paul unceremoniously yanks the knife out as quickly as he plunged it in. Paul retreats, taking stock like an artist proudly admiring his handiwork.

I imitate Papa's silent scream. I can feel the open wound in my own body. It is as if Paul stabbed my heart. It is my blood seeping into my shirt, a growing dark circle. I rocket to my knees, my hands gripping the metal edge of the truck bed. With no more thought, I swing my leg over the side, preparing to jump down and save Papa, but hands are gripping me, pulling me back inside, even though I fight them with the ferocity of a leopard.

"No, no, you cannot," a chorus murmurs around me. It is the other girls, suddenly brought back to the world of the living by my screams, by me trying to escape.

I struggle, but they hold me tighter.

"Mepa wo kyɛw." *Please.* "Stop, ma, abeg," someone pleads. "Please do not anger them more."

"They will kill us!"

"Sister, please."

What do I care if Paul and his jackals are angry or if they kill me? I do not care about anything else they can do because there is nothing worse than what they have done to me, what they are doing to my papa. I only care to make it to Papa before—

Paul gives the Walrus a pointed look. The Walrus nods in response as he moves into position behind Papa.

He raises his machete.

I tear away from the hands, finding a voice, ragged and coarse, sounding not like me, and I scream Papa's name.

In one fluid motion, Attah Walrus whips his damnable blade through the air, the one already crusted with sticky blood and gore, and—

"Papa. Papa. *PLEASE!*" I am in a frenzy, and the hands—the hands will not let me go. The murmurings of the girls will not cease. They will not let me pass.

—slices the blade through one side of my father's outstretched neck as Papa's eyes still lock onto mine—

"I beg," I say, weeping, unable to comprehend what I am witnessing. "I beg."

—and through the other side, below my father's chin.

As if in slow motion, Papa's head pitches forward and tumbles down the front of his body. His head drops with a thud to ground muddied with sweat, blood, and piss.

He rolls, gathering dirt, coming to rest on his left ear. Papa rocks until finally he stills, his mouth agape, eyes half-closed. He is like a mannequin head.

He cannot be Papa.

And yet he is.

At the same time, his body topples unceremoniously to its side, his hands still bound in front of him.

My mind plummets into unreality. What is real? What is false? Why am I still here?

Papa is gone. My brothers are gone. Auntie, my uncle, my village, all gone. There is only me left alone in this world, the last Asym of N'nkakuwe, the last of my people. Never again to feel safe, loved, protected, or settled. All fight leaves me. The hands manage to pull me back inside the truck.

But they do not prevent me from watching Paul squat down, scrutinizing Papa's head as if he were a scientific specimen. "At least the blade was sharp, eh?" he jokes, looking up at the Walrus with a smile that could light up the sky. "Clean right through, Attah. Well done."

Raucous laughter thunders in my ears, forever changing the course of my life. If there is a life left to have.

Paul pokes and prods Papa's head, defiling him as I look on through eyes blurred by hot tears. His audacity has no bounds.

He lets out a satisfied breath, seeking me out, finding me through his men. He tilts his head to the side, holding me in his viselike stare. He appraises me and says, "You still live, Aninyeh, while your family lays scattered about and dead. They died for you. They died because of you." His face becomes stone. "Do you understand what I am saying, girl? Your family's, your people's, blood is on your hands."

I hang my head in shame. He is right. Papa and my brothers, their deaths are because they tried to protect me.

Blame is a cold, viscous thing that consumes every inch of me. I should have died with my family. I should have fought like them, succumbed for them as they did for me.

I collapse into the truck, all will to live draining from me like the blood from Papa's neck. It is the night my first life, my *before*, ends. And because I cannot imagine life devoid of the people I loved, I reject any *after* with every fiber of my being.

# 19

## AFTER

Nena was already seated on the couch in her sister's elegant two-story flat when Elin arrived. She heard the keys jingling and the heavy steel reinforced door closing behind the clicking of Elin's heels. Nena counted the number of locks engaging. Three. She heard the alarm activated. Good. Her sister did, in fact, heed her warnings and locked up when she was alone. Only this time, she wasn't.

Elin dropped her keys and mail in the crystal dish on the mirror-and-chrome side table. Nena made a mental note to remind her sister to keep her keys nearby.

"What the hell for?" Elin had asked once, scoffing at her overly careful sister. It was easy for her to be flippant about security when she wasn't the one directly engaging in the risky behavior.

Nena had replied, "For quick escapes."

Elin let out a yelp when she noticed Nena sitting on her couch. It took her a second to regain her businesslike demeanor. She narrowed her liquid brown eyes, the color of chocolate. Her expression switched to mild irritation with the crook of a freshly arched eyebrow. Her regal frame and mahogany complexion thrummed with electricity.

*She really does look just like Mum,* Nena observed, waiting for her sister's first words. Or wrath. One could never be too sure, but from Elin's rigid stance, Nena thought the latter.

"Nena, what the hell? Say something simple and easy, like, *Elin, don't be scared; I'm sitting like a freak on your couch.* Something like that."

Elin took the one step leading down into the sunken living room, her heeled sandals clicking on the white flooring, then silencing when she reached the plush rug. She sank into the oversize mauve chaise.

"Wasn't my intent," Nena said flatly.

Elin waved her off, her rings catching the rays of sunlight in the brightly lit room. She gave Nena a stare down of gargantuan proportions while her finger subconsciously tapped against one of her front teeth.

"What," she said, launching into the meat of what they had to discuss. "The. Actual. Fuck, Nena?"

News traveled fast. "Was a change of plans."

"An unsanctioned change of plans. And Dad's pissed, you know. And you know what that means, right?"

Nena inclined her head.

"Yeah, he and Mum will pop up in town. And you know how much I hate their pop-ups."

Nena inclined her head again. Both knew full well that a visit from across the pond meant Elin's carefree lifestyle would come to a grinding, albeit temporary, halt.

Nena squared her shoulders. "It was a good kill, Elin. This man was evil."

Elin shot her a baleful look. "Aren't they all? That's your job now? To decide who dies and who not? Smith was not the mark."

"The lawyer is insignificant. He's a one-off, remember? You even said so. However, the other man—Smith—he would have sold out the Tribe, no question."

"And you know this how?" Elin countered. Her face reflecting her disbelief.

Nena didn't respond, and Elin flounced back in her seat in a huff. She didn't stay there for long. She was too riled up, and when she was in this state, she had to move around . . . or smoke.

Before Nena could decide how to elaborate, Elin's computer, the secure one, chirped with an incoming video call. They looked at each other, Elin wearing a smug expression and Nena a resigned one.

"Oh, it's Dad, all right," Elin said, answering Nena's unasked question. "He's big mad. Probably had Network track you here to call." She gestured with her fingers that Nena should answer.

Noble's face filled the screen, and immediately Nena saw the disapproval on his face. She managed a tiny hello before their father started in.

"What the hell happened, Nena?"

Nena flinched almost imperceptibly, waiting anxiously for him to unleash his fury at her and demand she return home to London so the Council could properly reprimand her. The sensible part of her knew Noble Knight had never raised voice or hand to her. He spoke gently, with love, even when correcting her misbehavior. And he wouldn't change now. But a small part of her, the *before* part of her that had never died, feared that one day he'd turn out like all the other men she'd encountered after she was taken. She often woke up thinking, *Today might be the day.*

She didn't think Elin had noticed her concern, but Elin had. The sisters made eye contact. Nena could read that Elin wanted to reach out and comfort her, but she wouldn't. Elin knew doing that would make Nena feel weak. Nena tore her eyes from Elin and focused on the screen, her body hunching over in embarrassment. She was supposed to be the enforcer, the one who took care of business, not the one who needed taking care of.

In a softer tone, Dad was saying, "This will take some discussion with the Council members."

Elin said, "But you have the final word as High Council."

"The Tribe and the Council are not an autocracy."

"No, Dad, but the buck stops with you."

His distinguished face contorted, thick dark eyebrows with flecks of gray like the rest of his beard and hair crinkling in annoyance. They could see the familiar background of his London home office with the picture of the African continent spread across the wall behind him like a mural. "I've let you stay in America far too long. You're beginning to sound like one of them."

"Blimey, Dad, you're going to have to get over it. We lost that war, okay? Been a few years at that. About two hundred thirty-seven, I'd say." Elin loved reminding him of that little bit of English history.

He steepled his large hands in front of him, leaning into the video, his voice deepening. "What have I always told you girls?"

"Even High Council must adhere to rules," Nena answered promptly. "We have these rules because if we don't have rules, then we have anarchy."

"Life-and-death rules."

"Yes, Dad."

Elin groaned. Nena was always in tune with their father's thoughts. She understood him in ways Elin didn't.

Nena continued, "High Council must lead by example." She squared her shoulders. "Dad, I am sorry for any trouble it may cause the Tribe. I accept any consequences for my insubordination."

"Elin oversees the business side; Network guides; you dispatch," Dad said, too far into his fussing to stop at her apology. "That's the job. You do not deviate from the plan."

"I understand."

"The Council's concern, my concern, is that this lawyer may get too close. What if this killing only compels him to look further into Smith's dealings? What if it all leads back to the new member we're about to vote in and subsequently the Tribe? We cannot have undue attention.

We are so close to cinching our place and being seen as more than a third world continent. Do you understand?"

"He won't, Dad."

"Ah, but how? How can you be so sure, my girl?"

She thought about the plastic school ID on her bureau. "I can figure out a way to see what he knows," she offered.

He scoffed, looking at his elder daughter, who pursed her lips and flipped her wrist as if she wanted nothing to do with the conversation. "Do you hear your sister? She's a spy now instead of a dispatcher." He let out a string of Yoruba that said something about *nerves* and *these children.*

He pointed at the screen. "Elin, you make sure she keeps a low profile. No further jobs until I smooth things over with the Council."

"What? Dad, no! I'm not her bloody babysitter," Elin protested. She threw a withering look at Nena, to which Nena mouthed an apology.

Having had enough of the both of them, Noble disconnected the call.

Nena turned from the screen and gave Elin her undivided attention. If she could make Elin understand the machinations of her mind when she'd seen the man through the lenses of her scope without having to explain her feelings, it would be much easier. It would be too difficult to explain how easily she'd been snatched back to the darkest time of her life, how easily she'd been taken back to her burning village, how quickly she'd felt small again, like nothing, made to fear, introduced to terror, married to grief and loss, just at the mere sight of that man. No, Nena wished not to explain any of it to anyone.

"What's going on with you? It's not like you to not follow directives. Smith was the *wrong* man. He was *not* the mark."

*But he was not the wrong man,* Nena thought, though she remained quiet for the moment. Smith was the right one, the absolute right mark. She'd thought he'd died long ago.

And if he was around, then Paul and Kwabena were not far behind him.

93

# 20

## BEFORE

The journey from what used to be N'nkakuwe takes the rest of the night. As we travel down the mountain in a caravan of trucks, each jostle over unpaved roads awakens new blooms of pain. They make me drift in and out of consciousness. Unconsciousness is better than having to think about what and who we left behind.

The sun is at the highest point in the sky when we arrive at an encampment, what I soon learn is the Compound. It is to be our prison, a large, sprawling facility comprising numerous cement buildings of different sizes enclosed by walls of cement and iron gates.

Our long line of autos enters through the massive front gates, which open electronically. Atop all the gates and walls are thick razor-covered wires so that even if we were able to climb, we would tear ourselves on the sharp needles. The gates grind to a close and lock behind us, sealing us in, confirming to us there is no escape. Dotting the outer perimeter of the walls are small towers—guard towers where the men currently on patrol duty look down at us with indifference, their automatic rifles pointing in our direction as they watch our arrival and whisper to their mates, sometimes gesturing at us. They are already picking out who they might like to visit once Paul has broken us in.

We drive into a circular clearing, where the men disembark from the trucks, open the back doors, and demand we get out. They corral us in the middle of the circle and tell us to sit. We do, huddled together, and wait.

Paul appears from a building dressed in an army-green shirt and camo pants with black combat boots. It is the basic uniform of the men here. He looks fresh, rested, and clean from the bath he undoubtedly took, while the rest of us wallow in filth. Attah Walrus and Kwabena flank him.

He begins, "I believe in being transparent about what comes next for you." He paces in front of us, while Kwabena stands at attention and the Walrus looks bored, swatting flies and spitting on the ground.

"You are scared, of course. Understandable. But life for you can be relatively easy." He grins. "*If* you follow the rules. No trying to flee, no fighting us, no wishing you'll be saved." His minions laugh around him. "There is no saving. This, my dears, is your new reality. Embrace it."

The girls with me are the same ones from school. Lived in homes next to mine. Socialized with me just yesterday. We were playing a guessing game about which boys we would marry—boys probably burned to crisps now. It seems eons ago. Childish and superficial.

"N'nkakuwe is gone. It was unfortunate, true. However, there is no use dwelling over—what do Americans say—spilled milk?" The chuckling around him increases.

Raping, pillaging, beheading, hacking people to pieces is *not* spilled milk.

Paul continues his sales pitch. "When you leave here, you will be sold—"

*Sold!* My heart thumps violently in my chest, and my fingers go numb. My mind reels. *Like slaves!* A murmur rises from the abducted, the blasphemous word awakening us like the paddle of a defibrillator.

"—to the highest bidder. Take care of yourselves."

The grounds of the Compound resemble a bull's-eye, the clearing at its center. Surrounding it is medical, the mess hall, the latrines, and Paul's quarters. He stays close to the main and perimeter gates, which are the only real ways in or out. The next ring consists of our quarters, small, cramped one-level buildings. Tin roofs that jut out and connect to the buildings on either side cover them. We are lucky to have small windows in our quarters, so at least there is that.

Behind our quarters is a lower chain-link fence that serves more to slow any attempted escapes than to stop them. Behind that fence are the guard quarters, and behind those are the perimeter gates and the walls with those strategically placed guard towers. Beyond them are the carports housing the trucks used to transport us. Every inch reaffirms there is no getting out and no going back.

Paul continues to pace, slowing in front of me, hands on his hips. "Behave. Keep clean and be presentable."

I zoom in on the dark stain on his boot toe, wondering if it is blood from when he poked Papa's head.

"Because if you break any of those rules, we will kill you."

---

We are nothing but entertainment for the men, who are cruel, gluttonous children. The Compound is their candy store, with a bounty of young, nubile confection ready for selection every night.

Our quarters consist of maybe ten to twelve girls. We speak infrequently and only in whispers. We abhor attention because it brings nothing good. Every night, we are listening for approaching boot steps, knowing when the door bangs open, an intruder, maybe two, will be there to peruse the candy aisles.

While he does, we hold our breaths, guiltily hoping his eyes fall on someone else, not us. We try to avert our eyes without looking obvious, because the men tend to pick the girls who look like they want to be chosen the least. When the selection is made, they drag one or more of us kicking and screaming from the room. They pull us past the chain-link fence, into one of their quarters. They return us before daybreak and threaten death if we do not clean ourselves well enough so Paul does not know they have sampled the merchandise.

The day of my selection, the guard remembers who I was before and takes extra pleasure in having a chieftain's daughter. He finishes, spent and lying next to me as if we are lovers, and that is when he makes a grievous error.

"Your father's head sounded like a bowling ball when it dropped. *Bamp!* Like that. Off with his head, o." He cackles at his pun, his breath foul like refuse. He is still laughing when my arm shoots across my chest, fingers curled.

I claw at his cheek, my nails digging deeply into his flesh, intending to tunnel into his mouth so I can rip out his tongue. I roll onto him, biting his ear, all thought blotted from my mind. I grind my teeth until they connect, determined to take his ear off. He screams bloody murder, bucking beneath me.

I do not consider his screaming. I should have grabbed his gun. Killed him, silenced him, then ended myself before the others came.

But they come, pouncing on me. They punch and kick me until they force me off the guard with half his salty, flabby ear in my mouth. I spit it out on the ground. My curses rain down as I kick at him. His blood trickles into my mouth. I spit saliva and blood at the group of them. He writhes on the ground, clutching his ruined cheek and ear.

I am a force for them, a feral animal locked on its prey. It takes four to restrain me. I am alight with lunacy. I want blood, all of theirs. I want death, my own.

Maybe they will make an example of me, drag me into the middle of the courtyard and put a bullet in my brain, take me from this never-ending hell and from my guilty mind.

But they do not.

Instead, it is the Hot Box for me. It is hotter than hell in that little box, only half the size of a coffin. Memories of my family, of Papa's cologne, and of Mama's moisturizer torture me. I remember the soccer squabbles my brothers will no longer have. I recall Papa's language lessons, him telling me I need to speak as many languages as possible so no one can ever lie to me.

In the box, I sing in French. I count in English. I recite prayers in both Ewe and Twi. I meditate in Ga. I mutter the little bit of Spanish I managed to learn before my world dissolved into fire and brimstone. Now, I may never have the chance to learn any more if the Hot Box melts me. If these demons kill me.

Or if I lose my mind.

# 21

## AFTER

Fresh from their father's reprimand, Elin stood from her chair abruptly. "Maybe we should have tea? Yeah?"

Nena's words were soft, barely audible. "That man, Dennis Smith, was Attah Walrus."

The name hung between them like a guillotine. Elin stiffened, having not heard it in years. "Maybe a shot then." She hurried to the bar at the corner of the living room and selected the first open bottle she could find—whiskey. She was allowed two shots before Nena continued.

"Do you remember who he is to me?"

Elin stepped down into the sunken living room and resumed her place across from Nena. She folded her long legs beneath her, holding the tiny glass containing her third shot. "How could I not? The way you described the lot of them—him, Bena, Paul—they were like the horsemen of the Apocalypse." Elin shivered. "But Nena, remember, Dad sent a massive number of soldiers scouring Ghana looking for them. They found the Compound in ruins. The locals said Paul's own men turned on him and killed him. Said he refused to pay them. I'm pretty sure Dad had scouts looking throughout all of Africa in case Paul happened to turn up. Dad knows how to find people."

"Dad doesn't know Paul like I do." Nena's face was stony. "Paul is . . . resourceful. He knows how to survive." *Like me.*

Elin rolled her eyes. "It's a bit overdramatic, you think?"

"Still the truth."

Elin was tapping her front tooth with her nail again. She cursed, reaching into her bag for her pack of cigarettes. She was supposed to quit, but Nena knew that wasn't happening anytime soon. Nena scooped up the gold-plated lighter with sparkling crystals—only the best bling for Elin—from the mirrored centerpiece lying atop the ottoman and tossed it. Elin caught it deftly.

"God, you're insufferable. They're all dead. Trust Dad on this, yeah? You mixed this Smith bloke up with the other guy."

Nena focused on her hands, folded in her lap. She nodded. The man was Attah. She'd know him anywhere.

"These back-to-back jobs we assigned you scrambled your mind." Elin pointed at her. "And if anyone asks, tell them the wind was fucked up this morning and threw your bullet off or some gun shit like that, okay? But don't tell them this crazy shit about sex traffickers coming back from the dead."

Elin was right; no one would believe her without more proof.

Nena's lips pursed. "I won't say anything to anyone. Not even Dad. Not until I figure things out a bit more."

"Let's just tell him, and he'll fix this bloody thing."

"Tell him and crush what he's spent his life building? The African Tribal Council—his baby? Because that's what we'd be doing, crushing Dad's dreams. You want to crush his dreams? You heard him say how close this new member gets them to achieving their goals." She looked pointedly at Elin. "Truly?"

Elin groaned. "I really hate when you make sense."

Nena looked at her soberly. "You're the one who said we needed proof so no one would think me mad. Very sensible of you."

"I hate you; you know that?" Elin's pretty face, a perfect blend of their mother and father, contorted into a pout. "All I wanted to do today was gossip with you about Oliver. Like, we're getting serious now—"

"After a month?"

Elin shot her a dirty look. "There's no time limit on love. You'd know if you gave it a chance," she returned. "And no knowing where you find it, because who would have thought I'd find a guy I actually wanted to keep around? There's something different about him—"

Nena's eyebrow quirked. "More different than John before him? Or Nathan before John? Or when it was both Giles and Felipe at the same time? That was *very* different." A half smile played at Nena's lips.

"I already *love*," Elin stressed, ignoring her sister's dry humor and placing a hand over her chest dramatically, "every bit of intense, strait-laced, by-the-book Oliver. I want you to meet him."

Nena's lip twitched. Elin's theater study from their school days was reemerging, as it often did when Elin wanted someone to pity her.

Elin said, "Apparently, Oliver will have to wait."

She rolled the lighter around in her hand, intently watching the sunlight catching the crystals. Nena imagined all possible contingency plans playing through Elin's calculating mind like a movie reel on fast-forward. Elin got that masterful mind from their mother.

"You sure about this guy and about not telling Dad?" Elin finally asked, her cigarette remaining unlit. "Truly? Smith was Attah Walrus?"

Nena gave her a single nod, adding, "Yeah."

Elin balked. "What if Attah Walrus was lucky? The other two could be dead, and he was the only one to survive. Dad's teams couldn't have missed all three. Those assholes aren't that good even on their best day."

"Also a possibility, but doubtful."

Elin continued to fidget with the lighter, giving her cigarette long looks that told Nena how badly she wanted to go to the balcony and smoke. She didn't know why Elin didn't just go. She was fine, for now, maybe. She'd managed to drive away the memories threatening to strangle her ever since she saw his yellowed eyes and face that looked like a melting Hershey bar. The years really had not been kind to him.

"The Council may call for consequences."

She was resolved to take whatever punishment should come from her actions. "There should be consequences for me."

Elin pinched the space between her eyes and said thinly, "Maybe docked pay."

"I wouldn't have accepted payment anyway." Nena recalibrated. "I would have given my life savings to kill that man."

"Nena, you can't go saying that to the Council. You'll need to show a mea culpa for what you did. Just go with the bullet-and-the-wind story I mentioned earlier. Or say you're overworked. Maybe that will keep the Council off your back and—"

"Those are excuses." Nena paused. "However, I am sorry that Attah's death was too swift. He deserved to suffer for a long time."

Elin groaned, long and defeated. "Nena, that's not how remorse works."

Nena's anger simmered so close to the surface she feared she'd explode. She was always calm and collected. Her restraint was the only thing she took pride in. That and dispatching.

"He took everything from me, Elin." The rage she suddenly felt, something long hidden, surprised her. And from Elin's wide eyes and frozen expression, she'd surprised Elin as well.

Elin stood, walking toward her balcony, which overlooked Biscayne. The view was what had sold her on the flat. "Okay. I'll see what I can find about Smith and the other two, but chances are this Attah Walrus guy was an oversight."

Nena remained quiet because what she was really thinking about the term *oversight* would only incite more of Elin's wrath. Elin wouldn't understand the danger Paul and Kwabena posed. No one knew, except Nena.

"Meanwhile, don't do anything without telling me first."

Nena extricated herself from the couch expertly and without using her hands for balance. She couldn't make that promise.

Elin cast a long look at her. "While you're waiting for word from the Council or me, go out and have some fun. Do something wild. You're wound too tight."

"Copy," Nena said, watching as Elin glanced at her gold Rolex for the third time since she'd stood up. "You have somewhere to be?"

"Mm-hmm. Date," Elin responded dreamily, lighting her cigarette.

The corners of Nena's mouth curved slightly. "With this *different* Oliver. Can't wait to meet him."

As Nena neared the front door, she threw over her shoulder, "I do hope this guy is as different as you say, because it would be unpleasant if I had to dispatch him."

"Fuck you, bitch," Elin answered merrily as she took the first drag. Her eyes closed in pleasure before she called out, "Oh, and I'm planning a dinner so you, Dad, and Mum can officially meet him. I'll let you know soon as they tell us when they're coming to town."

"Okay," Nena answered, relieved to have Elin's benefit of the doubt. She needed her sister by her side. If Elin doubted her . . . Nena couldn't think about any of that.

The next time she'd play it safe. The next time she wouldn't run off half-cocked and be so reactionary, without a plan. She'd ask for Witt's help, too, if he'd give it—he wouldn't refuse her, would he? And she'd just make doubly sure there were no more ghosts left to haunt her.

# 22

## BEFORE

Mixed in with the guard quarters are the Hot Boxes, tiny metal boxes conducting heat that reach nearly oven-high temperatures. They are specially reserved for the greatest offenders, those of us who dare fight or flee. As far as I know, no girl who spends time in the Hot Box ever goes back. She either learns her lesson or succumbs to the sweltering temperatures before the men have a chance to get her out.

I am not sure how long I have been at the Compound. I have lost track. Weeks must have passed, because until the guard took me for his, my wounds had begun healing. The pain inside and out had lessened to a throb. And my body, which no longer felt like it belonged to me, moved robotically, doing what it needed to survive—eat, drink, wash, defecate, rinse, repeat, all without my mind willing any of it, at least not that I knew of.

But when the guard ridiculed Papa's death, I was reanimated. I was Frankenstein's monster sparked by his insolence. A spark propelling me to act, to lash out, to rip his dirty, stubble-filled face off with my bare hands.

The action brought me here, to the Hot Box, where I have been for God knows how long, because in here, time stands still. And in here is where I am in the process of dying.

I am nearly there, I think, when ironically enough, Paul saves me. He flings open the door, bathing me in blinding light. My arm rises to shield my eyes, but I relish the wisps of cooler, dry air that flood in and drive the blanket of heat out.

"I told you not to fuck with this one," Paul growls. "I leave for two days, and this is what you do?"

Only two? No, it has been two hundred years.

He continues, "Fuck his ear. Kill the bastard for disobeying my orders."

An unrecognizable voice asks, "What should we do with her?"

"What do you think? Get her to medical and have her looked at! I told you imbeciles to leave the girls alone. We have a big sale next week. You need to fuck around, then do it with the whores in town. These here are merchandise. You understand? And no one wants to buy fucked-up merchandise."

If my mind had not turned to jelly and my limbs hadn't become petrified wood, I might react properly to being called merchandise and the knowledge I am to be sold the following week. But all I can think of is water. And sleep. And maybe death, because the thought of it seems sweetest of all.

Two of his men lift my body, frozen into a question mark from the cramped box. The pain drives my screams into the air. They drop me back on the floor.

Paul is livid. "You see? She's all fucked up. If I can't sell her to the Frenchman, you take on the debt."

My eyes crack open, blinking rapidly, trying to adjust and focus on his face. He grimaces at mine, undoubtedly bruised and swollen. His nose wrinkles at the smell of my blood, excrement, and vomit. I hope he gets a good whiff. I hope the Frenchman tells him to go to hell and refuses my used merchandise. And then I hope he kills me.

My thoughts become nonsensical because when the men lift me again despite my howls, white-hot currents rip through my body, and I fall into darkness.

I awaken on a cot with a rough spun blanket covering me. Cold compresses battle the swell of my face. The pain has now receded to a dull ache, and I am surprisingly hungry. Gingerly, I sit up on my elbows, surveying the room. The other cots are empty, but I am not alone. There is a young woman, maybe eighteen, watching me. She has a healthy glow about her, is without the vacant, catatonic look most of the girls walk around the Compound with.

"Welcome back to the world of the living," she says through a wry smile. Her eyes are the color of chestnuts. A simple patterned duku is wrapped around her hair. She is tall, pleasant looking, her husky voice reminding me of a warm desert breeze.

She brings me a bowl of light soup, urging me to eat. "The spice will revitalize you."

It is the hottest meal I have had in—again, I try to recall how long we have been here. I yearn to ask, but I refuse to speak just yet. If she is here tending to me so freely and without guards, then she must work for Paul. She looks too well to be one of us—the captives. My first instinct is to trust those kind eyes because to trust is all I ever learned before the attack, but I am learning hard lessons about trust and good and evil. The only girls who flourish here are the ones who have become amenable to the guards' wiles, thinking it will keep them alive and off the sales rack.

"You've been here for two days."

Abayisɛm. *Witchcraft.* She must be using her juju powers to read my thoughts.

I do the calculations in my mind. Two days here, plus two in the box. Before that, how long in this wretched place? A fortnight? Three weeks? A month? Eternity? There is no sense of time in this place, and it destabilizes me. The soup slides down my throat. I relish the burn all the way to the bottom of my stomach and immediately feel better. An angry rumble erupts in protest. My hand flies to my belly. I hope I do not get sick.

"My name is Essence," she says. "I was here when you arrived."

I chew my bottom lip, considering whether to converse or continue my stony silence. There is nothing I have to say, but my mind is a cacophony of questions. There are things I need to know.

She leans in, her voice conspiring. "They tell me I'll go to America. Maybe that is not so bad. America is full of rich people, o? Land of the free."

Of which she will not be. Does she jest or truly believe what she says?

She waits for my response, and when it does not come, she continues. "You need to get well or get dead or find something to contribute that they can use."

"I think—he said there is a Frenchman for me."

Essence's eyes widen as she claps softly. "That's good, o! France is the country of lovers. I'll have a rich man, and you will have a loving one. You won't be so bad off, eh? Anything is better than here."

"We are being sold," I hiss, my anger untethered. "Like animals." That she would try to find a positive aspect in this black hellhole of ours is confounding. "Or maybe you have already sold yourself out."

Her eyes flatten as she peers at me. She leans back, unimpressed with my accusations. "I do what I have to do to survive. You would do well to follow the same plan." She turns in a huff, leaving me to eat the rest of my soup and contemplate my future.

I am content to spend the rest of my recovery in solitude and silence, but Essence is not built for silence. She inches near, sending me furtive looks.

"Is it true?" she hedges.

"Is what?" I gaze forlornly at the empty bowl, wishing I could grab it and lick it clean.

"About the guard. Is it true that you bit his ear off? For true *bit* his ear off? Like this?" She mimics what she thinks I did, gnashing her teeth against an imaginary ear. I nearly laugh at the look of her. She has her answer.

She whistles, dropping back into the chair. She is impressed with me now, but I still see the warning in her eyes. "You should be careful."

"Why?" Being careful in this place is an oxymoron.

"That guard—Paul had him killed as punishment for you ending up in here. Because of you, one of theirs is dead."

Her words tumble around in my mind. Because of me, one of theirs is dead. There is no guilt at this discovery like there is for my family.

"They will seek retribution."

I am okay with being the reason their numbers are minus one. I would subtract the whole lot of them if I could.

The thought becomes my fantasy, making me giddy. Visions of killing each one of these bastards, especially Paul, bring me immense joy, though I know I will not be given the chance. I will either die here or die at the hands of whatever trash Paul sells me to. Essence leaves the medical building, but I am too far into my fairy-tale world to notice.

I would save Paul for last. I would make him watch as I dismantled his life and everything he holds most dear—money, power, respect. He is nothing but a covetous man who takes from others to make himself feel big. He will try and try and never achieve what he wants more than his own humanity.

These thoughts help me mend. These are the fantasies that wile away the endless time at the Compound. These are the wishes that help me bide my time as I await the inevitable.

The arrival of market day.

# 23

## AFTER

Two days after Nena took Attah Walrus out and practically gave her family a heart attack, she was pulling onto the private school's grounds, trailing behind another car that led her to where the students congregated to meet their rides home. She surveilled the property as she pulled to a stop in the curved driveway, wondering for the hundredth time why she'd come. She stepped out of her luminescent white Audi, shutting the door behind her. Her eyes jumped from point to point, mapping the location with the precision of a cartographer.

There wasn't security past the gate she'd entered. Teachers dotted the grounds, but they were more involved in their own conversations than in what the students were doing. The adults in the car line were too busy using their phones or speaking with each other. Students milled around, some playing sports, some talking. The place reminded her of the preparatory school she and Elin had attended. The school didn't seem like Cortland's or Georgia's cup of tea, but what did she know?

She spied Georgia sitting on a bench on the plush lawn, glancing at her watch. The girl looked up and noticed Nena. Georgia's first reaction was shock, not fear, Nena noticed, pleased. Georgia jumped off the bench and nearly ran to where she stood.

As she neared, a student passing by asked, "Who's the Audi?"

Nena's brows crinkled as she looked at her car. It wasn't any different than the expensive imports lining the pickup line.

"Don't worry about it," Georgia said, reading Nena's expression. She stopped short of her, breathless and flushed. "That's how kids here at Prep refer to the cars they're riding in. I guess you're an upgrade from my dad's Chevelle, so they noticed."

Nena nodded. These kids had life easy if car types were all they noticed.

"How'd you know where to—" Georgia stopped when she recognized the school lanyard Nena dropped in front of her. The ID twisted in the breeze, sunlight glinting off the plastic.

She groaned, accepting the ID. "Where were you when I needed this?"

"Indisposed."

Georgia's eyebrows furrowed as teen angst emanated from her. "I had to serve hours for two days."

Nena's blank stare prompted her to add, "After-school detention." She slipped the lanyard over her head, patting the ID three times.

"For good luck," she explained. "Thanks for bringing it."

"You're welcome, Georgia Baxter." Nena slipped her hands into the back pockets of her dark denim jeans as she tried to think of what came next. Awkward. She wasn't sure what to say to a kid. She didn't usually deal with them in her line of work. What did people this young like to talk about?

Georgia toed the earth with her sneakers, eyeing Nena warily as the wind blew at the thick coils around her head. She brushed them back impatiently, her eyes moving all over: from Nena's face to her car, to the ground, to Georgia's Vans and Nena's All Stars. All the while, Nena watched patiently and waited for the girl to say her piece.

"Are you like a cop or special agent or something? A spy, maybe? *Mission Impossible* or *G.I. Jane*, which is one of my favorite movies, by the way?"

Nena was amused. "Noted."

Georgia grinned back. "Yeah." She looked away bashfully, as if deciding whether she should continue.

"What's on your mind?" Nena prompted, leaning back against her car. She wasn't ready to leave just yet. And she wanted to figure out why.

Georgia took a step forward, her eyes trained intently on Nena's. "The other night was like a scene right out of *Black Panther*."

The tiniest smile played at Nena's lips. She'd heard this before. She and Elin had gotten a kick out of the movie when it had come out, musing about how it captured the essence of the Tribe and Africa. Their dad had groused, "It's nothing like Africa." But his daughters knew he liked the idea of it as well.

She leaned in closer to Nena. "How—how did you . . ." She swallowed and cleared her throat. "The thing with the big guy's neck. I didn't think it was possible to break a neck with your bare hands."

Nena cocked her head at an angle. "Separating the vertebrae is not typical or easy. It was the first time it actually worked." Nena had thought Georgia's eyes couldn't get any larger. She was wrong.

"You must have a considerable amount of upper-body strength," Nena added. "You can't just twist it like you see in movies. More of a one-two-three combination and a lot of luck."

Georgia's gulp was audible, and five whole seconds passed before she could speak again.

Nena scanned their surroundings. What was keeping Georgia's father? Most of the students had dispersed. The car riders' line had thinned, and a group of four girls was headed Georgia's way. Nena made ready to leave; she'd kept Georgia from her friends long enough.

Georgia squinted against the sunlight. "Anyone ever told you, you kind of look like Yetide Badaki from *American Gods*? Maybe Lashana

Lynch? She's the new 007, you know. Was in *Captain Marvel* too. Love her."

Nena frowned. The girls were nearly upon them. "You watch a lot of TV."

"What else is there to do?" Georgia countered. "You sort of sound like her too."

Nena's lips pursed. "Because all British people sound alike?" She rather enjoyed watching Georgia squirm.

"No." Georgia's hand shot out, grasping Nena's wrist, to both of their surprise. Nena looked down at the light-pink polished fingernails. The last person who'd touched her without invite was no longer of this world. Gently, she twisted her hand from Georgia's grip.

"I-I just mean you sounded like there was something else too."

Nena nodded slowly. "The 'something else' is my Ghanaian accent. I also come from around London." Why was she telling Georgia this? It was like Nena was trying to impress her.

"I get that. My mom was Haitian Cuban, and Dad's African and Haitian, although I'm not sure where in Africa. It's down the line."

Nena didn't respond. She wasn't looking at Georgia, her attention hijacked by the arrival of the quartet. She straightened, palming her key fob so she could really leave this time. One chattering teen was enough for one day. Five was a nightmare.

Georgia turned to where Nena gazed and let out a groan. "Great. Sasha."

The first girl, Nena assumed, the blonde-haired, blue-eyed, all-American girl who led the pack with the other three in tow. And from the way dread covered Georgia's face like a death shroud, Nena could tell this Sasha was unwelcomed. The vibe emanating from her rubbed Nena the wrong way as well.

"Georgie, my driver's here," Sasha started, stopping nearly between them, forcing her way into the center of attention.

Right, kids here could afford fancy drivers, not Lyft or Uber, to drive them wherever they wanted to go.

Sasha asked, "Want a ride?"

Georgia pursed her lips. "My dad will be here soon."

"Speaking of, what's it like for your dad to have brains splattered all over his face?" Sasha asked, widening her sparkling blue eyes in faux concern. "Freaky, right? He's okay?"

Nena didn't like the way unease gnawed around her edges at the mention of the shooting.

Georgia's tone grew uncomfortable and her face shuttered. "He's good."

"What happened with Georgia's dad?" A second girl, Asian, looked alarmed. Her concern for Georgia, Nena noted, was genuine. Georgia should go home with this one, not the fake Barbie.

Sasha turned to her friends. "Apparently, her dad was, like, right next to the guy who got his head blown off, Kit."

Georgia mumbled, looking down, "Wasn't quite like that."

Except it kind of was. Only Nena wasn't going to share that with the group.

The one called Kit asked, "Is he okay?" She reached out to touch Georgia's shoulder. Nena watched Georgia seem to melt at Kit's touch, the authenticity cutting through her defensiveness.

Georgia nodded. "Yeah."

The anguish on Georgia's face made Nena uncomfortable. Knowing she was the cause of the trauma both Georgia and her father were going through brought on spasms of guilt. Another new feeling Nena had never had before and didn't care for at all. She never thought twice about a mark or a kill.

Nena took a step to leave when the one called Sasha spoke. "'Kay, we're out then. Catch you later, Curious George."

There was a slight breeze in the air, and yet it was as if they'd been sucked into a vacuum. Nena, having experience with all sorts, expected insecure people like this girl to make other people feel as bad as they did. She let their insecurities roll off her back like beads of water, but she caught how Georgia dipped her head, shame covering her face like a mask. Rage bubbled up within Nena, a protective type she wanted to blanket over Georgia so she'd never have to feel like she was less than again. Nena knew that feeling, that loss of self-worth, the inability to call someone out for speaking untowardly. She knew how it felt to be at the mercy of others. And there was no way she'd let it happen here when she could put an end to it, unlike she'd been able to do before.

# 24

## BEFORE

We are on the way to some unknown location, trussed up like life-size dolls. Just as my nerves are at the point where I believe I am going to jump from the moving truck bed and fall to my death, the truck squeals to a stop. Trace scents of burning torches fueled with kerosene and a sprinkle of laughter are on the wind. The girl beside me is breathing heavily, although the breath could very well be my own.

The younger girls relax, allowing themselves to be lulled into a false sense of security. Laughter and music have always meant something good in N'nkakuwe, so it must mean good here too.

"Maybe they have changed their minds? Will return us home?" Yaa asks, sounding much younger than her twelve years.

"Our home is gone, stupid," Constance says bitterly. Before all of this, she was going to be a runway model in America because of her height. No one will likely find her model quality again. Not with the scar that crosses her face from scalp to chin, gifted to her the night the intruders came.

Yaa blinks several times, forced to remember there is no more N'nkakuwe. "Something must still be there," she whispers, refusing to give up entirely. "Our families have relocated to nearby towns, and the authorities are looking for us this very moment."

Constance asks, "Then why have they not located us?"

Yaa shrugs. "Ghana is big."

"Not that big," Ester says.

No one argues. Ester is likely a year older than Yaa, with big round eyes and full lips that used to always curve into a smile back home. Not anymore.

In total, we are six. Ester, Mary, Yaa, Constance, and Mamie. The injuries I suffered at the hands of the guards and from the Hot Box are not entirely healed, but over the last week Essence has cared for me as best as she could. I willed myself to be well enough to be present at this ridiculous sale because I want out of the Compound, and by whatever means necessary. Thus, I grit my teeth, bear the pain, and pretend my ribs are not sore to the point of immobility, that when I urinate it does not sting and is not tinged pink. My kidneys, Essence guessed when I told her. They will heal. Perhaps they will. If Paul and his hounds permit it.

The flap to the back of the truck opens, and guards tell us to get out. A warm breeze greets us as we disembark one by one. The guards touch us enough to help us down in the uncomfortable shoes they make us wear. Paul has us dressed piously and pure, as if we are young brides. Truthfully, we are nothing but fancy whores for purchase in an even fancier brothel. No manner of white and frills can mask that.

I take in my surroundings. We are at some estate nestled in a cove of tall trees that obscures it from the travel-heavy roads. The house is brightly lit with wide windows that show everything. Through them, I see mostly men, some women, a melting pot of nationalities.

Each of us has an assigned guard to accompany her throughout the night until she becomes sponsored. *Sponsored.* It's the word Paul says the buyers prefer to use. It makes them feel less like slavers and more like people "sponsoring" a new life for youth in need.

Parked amid a row of luxury cars I have only seen on the television is Paul's forest-green BMW, an older model. He exits it, dressed in a fancy suit that likely is worth more cedis than I can imagine.

We stand at attention while Paul walks down the line, inspecting, ensuring we are presentable enough to be sold like the slaves we have become.

Paul says, "Do not speak unless you are told. Be demure. You're not sluts, for God's sake."

Is he daft? His men have made us so ten times over.

"Smile and look like you want to be here, because if I do not fetch a price for you, if you are not sponsored—"

*Sponsored.*

"—you will not return to the Compound."

Paul is strictly business, smoothing his suit beneath the orange glow of the lit torches lining the premises. His words feel directed toward me, since I am the one who got a man of his killed.

He might still believe I am a valuable prize for my lineage, but I am no more than any of these girls. They are, in fact, better than me, because they hold out hope all will turn out well. However, all hopes died weeks ago back in our village. And dead is what these girls and I will be if we do not fetch a price for Paul. With the thought looming in my mind, I follow the others along the stone path toward the brightly lit house filled with our future masters.

It is hard to maneuver across the stones in the heels, but I manage. No one speaks, not even Paul, as we follow him up the steps and into the auction house. The air-conditioning is refreshing. I am immediately cold as the sheen of sweat on my skin freezes.

The guards guide us to various locations within the house, our elbows firmly within their grasps. There are curious glances all around, as buyers appraise the stock. I avert my eyes, not wanting to make contact. My life is no longer my own. The eyes roving my body make me feel like the algae slime that floats in stagnant water.

Thoughts of algae cause me to stumble, and my guard grabs me sharply, annoyed that he has stumbled too. His mouth sets in a firm line. He wants to hit me. I can tell from the way he fists his free hand, but he cannot touch the merchandise. So instead, he glowers at me. It is a threat from him to me.

*Don't. Fuck. Up. Again.*

# 25

## AFTER

Sasha's words sent lightning bolts through Nena, and her response came before any of them could adequately register the insult, much less think of a comeback.

"What did you just call her?"

The blonde shifted nervously from one foot to the other. She gave Nena a guarded look. "What are you talking about?"

Nena's eyes narrowed. She spoke slowly enough to make the rest of them fidget uncomfortably, even Georgia, whose lips twisted in concern. "Do you know what Curious George is?"

Georgia, Kit, and the other two girls looked on, watching this game of tennis with trepidation. Georgia had seen Nena in action, and Nena couldn't imagine what was running through her mind. She probably thought Nena was going to snap the girl's neck like she had the big thug's.

"A cartoon?" Sasha drawled questioningly. She gave Nena the teenage *are you stupid?* look, not noticing how her friends backed away a few steps, abandoning her to her fate.

Nena cocked her head, looking even more menacing than she had before. Sasha took a reflexive step back, and her wide baby blues were what reminded Nena with whom she was dealing. No, she wasn't going to kill the girl for being stupid or a racist. She was going to school her.

"You call her that, or anything else improper, again, you'll deal with me. You understand?"

Sasha's face flushed a deep crimson, which only made her very blonde hair look blonder. "What did I say?"

"Let your mates explain it to you. They seem to understand the negative association a Black girl with the type of animal your cartoon, and your racist remark, refers to."

Sasha's mouth opened and closed like a fish. She gawked, swallowed hard, voice now at a higher octave. "Racist! I'm not . . . I'm not . . . my best friend is Chinese!"

"Korean," Kit and Georgia corrected in unison. Georgia's hand flew to her mouth, covering it.

Kit gritted her teeth. How many times did the girl have to remind Sasha where she was from? Nena wondered.

"I didn't . . . ," Sasha sputtered, blinking rapidly. "I meant—"

"Yes, we know what you meant. You won't mean it again, now will you?" Nena swept her gaze casually over the other girls. None of them moved, and Sasha continued blinking, her mouth opening and closing with nothing coming out, much to Nena's satisfaction.

"Well, off with you, ladies," she urged when no one seemed to be taking their leave. "Driver's waiting and all."

Kit and the other two mumbled goodbyes and were full of *ma'am*s as they tugged a still-stunned Sasha away toward her ride. However, a few yards away, Sasha regained her ability to speak.

"Did you hear how that weirdo lady talked to me?" she asked in a shrill voice. "That bitch!"

Kit snatched her elbow, ushering Sasha away before she stepped in any more shit than she already had.

Georgia watched Nena watching the girls' retreating figures. Georgia gave a resigned sigh. "I'm sorry about that. Sasha's—"

"A privileged, rude, racist Barbie doll?" Nena said helpfully.

"I was going to say 'different,'" Georgia finished.

"Which would be wholly inaccurate. Don't make excuses for the girl." Nena gave her full attention to Georgia's troubled expression. "Why does your schoolmate dislike you so much?"

Georgia blinked, her eyes taking on a shine Nena didn't care for. She worried the girl would cry, and she wasn't equipped to handle chattering teens, much less crying ones.

Georgia asked, "Is there ever a reason?"

"Sometimes."

Georgia lifted her shoulders. "The other students think I'm a snitch because my dad's an assistant US attorney. Even though Sasha's is a judge, and most of their parents are, like, uptight businesspeople. But I'm not," Georgia said emphatically. "I would never betray a trust."

"Georgia," Nena began, her tone softening, "your name is the first thing your parents give you, besides life. Don't ever let anyone take that away from you. So when someone calls you a name you don't like, like Curious George, for example, stand up for yourself. Don't accept it just because you don't want to make a fuss."

Georgia's body deflated, and she looked away, unable to withstand Nena's scrutiny. "It's that obvious, huh? That I'm hard up for friends." She laughed dryly. "I'm a joke."

She refused to make eye contact, and Nena knew it was because she was crying.

Nena thought back to her school days in England and a boy who had tormented her. "When I was younger, the kids at my school used to call me 'gorilla,' 'bush girl,' and 'African booty scratcher,'" Nena said softly. "I was new there, and the school was like this, not very diverse and also extremely minted."

"Minted?"

"Rich. Sorry. Anyway, I was not rich before attending the school. The kids were cruel. One boy, Silas, was like your Sasha."

Georgia quickly thumbed away the tears before they fell. She swallowed. "What did you do?"

"My big sis stood up for me. Made them stop. And then she told me the same thing I told you. Later, my mum made me an awful dinner. She's a horrific cook."

Georgia couldn't smile. "I don't have a big sister. And my mom is . . . well, there was a car accident." Her voice hitched.

"I understand." It was time to go, because Nena wasn't prepared for this deep a conversation in a school's parking lot. She'd made contact and returned the ID. What next? She was a dispatcher, not James Bond. She needed to know what Georgia's father knew (if anything) about the Tribe. But how exactly?

Nena opened the passenger-side door of her car and rifled through the armrest until she found what she needed, an old receipt and a pen. She scribbled something and handed it to Georgia, who blinked back the tears that refused to go away so she could focus on the ten numbers scratched on the scrap.

"Man," she mumbled, squinting. "Your handwriting is pretty shitty."

Nena closed the passenger door. "You're a cheeky one, aren't you? Perhaps you and the blonde *should* be friends after all. Two rude little girls."

"You could have just asked for my phone and typed your number in. It's what people do now."

Nena stared at the insolent child, growling, "I like . . . to write."

Georgia laughed. "Ooookay. Anyway, thanks again for bringing my ID and for totally freaking Sasha out."

Nena rounded the front of her car for the driver's side. She gave a slight wave at Cortland's approaching 1970 electric-blue Chevelle, not yet ready to face him after the shooting.

Georgia looked as if she wanted to say more. Nena stalled, waiting.

"Maybe you can come for dinner or something sometime?" Georgia asked hopefully.

"Perhaps," Nena answered, slipping into her car. "Put my number in your phone, yeah?"

As she pulled away, glancing at Cortland standing with Georgia and Georgia excitedly showing him her ID, she hoped Georgia would ask to see her again . . . for reconnaissance, sure. But also, because Nena liked the little lift she felt when she thought about being around the Baxters again.

# 26

## BEFORE

After my guard parades me around the party of potential owners of actual humans, I am reunited with the other girls. The younger girls are giggling and drinking from small plastic cups. How can they be so happy? Do they not realize this "party" is no more than an auction block masked in fanciness and revelry?

"They gave us punch," Mary announces, her teeth stained pink from the red liquid. "It's the most delicious thing I have tasted. So sweet. How many sugarcanes do you think they used for this?"

"Bush girl," Constance scoffs, glowering at Mary. "Don't be simple, as if we live in trees and do not know about granulated sugar."

"Be still," Mamie says. "Let her enjoy."

Constance sucks her teeth and sips her own cup of sugary sweetness.

My guard hands me a cup, then stalks off to join his comrades huddled a few feet away. I sniff the drink, checking for anything odd. Only a sweet and fruity smell makes it up my nose, and I take a tentative sip, concurring with Mary. It is the most delicious thing I have ever tasted, better than Coca-Cola or orange Fanta, which are now my second and third favorites.

"I wonder if they will allow us to eat," Constance says, looking forlornly at the overflowing trays of roasted meats and seafood, fruits, vegetables, and bread. The food looks like TV food, no creamy peanut butter soup or banku, which has no taste, so it must be accompanied with fried fish, a spiced spinach or palm-nut stew, or shito pepper sauce. Where is the rice?

"If they serve food like this wherever we go, then it cannot be that bad, eh?" Mamie whispers to Constance and me. Instead of answering, I down the rest of my punch, then plot how to get more.

As time passes, one by one, the guards return and escort their assigned girls away. They do this when a customer approaches them. Each girl shoots a look back at the rest of us as she is led away. I cannot help wondering if this is goodbye. Or if we will see each other again.

Sometime later, my guard approaches. Mamie and I are the only two left.

"Come," he tells me. Mamie stares ahead forlornly. Paul's words come back to me. *You will not return to the Compound.* For her sake, I hope she does fetch a price. Words I never thought would cross my mind.

The back patio has a secluded gazebo. In it, a stocky obroni, a White man, waits in a wicker chair. There is a lit firepit in front of him, flames lapping at the air. My guard directs me to the opposite chair. I sit stiffly at the edge of the seat. Being away from the house and other girls is unnerving. The way this man observes me is unnerving. It is difficult to tell in the lighting, but his closely cropped hair is ginger or maybe blond. His eyes are small, hard. Thin lips and a prominent nose with a bulbous tip.

The guard remains near but far enough to allow a little privacy. Why all these formalities? If they mean to sell us, then do it quickly! But I rein in the bloom of anger and watch the White man watch me.

"Bonjour. Al-lo."

I understood his French the first time, but my gut tells me not to let on. Better they do not know the depths of my knowledge.

"Wo din de sɛn?" he asks in butchered Twi. *What is your name?*

"Aninyeh." The only reason I answer is that I cannot pretend I do not understand.

In English, and louder, he asks, "Can she speak? English?"

My guard shrugs. He does not care for this man any more than I do. It is the only commonality he and I share.

"A little," I say hesitantly, pinching my thumb and index finger together to show him how little, although I am fluent in English too.

He is pleased. He points to himself. "I am Monsieur Robach. I live in France. You know France?"

I pinch my fingers together again. My father has been—had been—there to study abroad. I pored over all the history books I could find about it as I learned the language.

"I like you very much, Aninyeh," Monsieur Robach says. His eyes intensify, no longer looking at me politely but more like I am one of those trays of roasted meats or a specimen. "You are a beautiful girl. Very pretty. Paul says you're special, of good lineage."

I say nothing to this.

"I would like to take you to my home in France. It is lovely there, and I think we shall get along very well. Don't you?"

I say nothing to this either.

"I think you will like my home. It will be your new one."

His home will never be mine, and I do not believe for one moment he thinks it will be.

When he has had his fill of me, he coughs once. The intensity in his eyes evaporates, much to my relief. He looks away from me, at my guard, nodding at him. "Tell Paul I approve of her and the quoted price. I will wire the money immediately."

The guard does a quick bow. "Very good, sir."

I do not need prompting to stand because I am already on my feet, ready to leave. I walk away briskly, not wanting to be around the man one moment longer, knowing they now consider me his property.

What does this mean for me? What manner of servitude, degradation, or worse will he subject me to? All at once I begin to second-guess my desire to leave the Compound. I am marching into an unknown world, moving away from a devil I know to one of which I have no idea.

The guard leads me to a back bedroom where three other girls wait. The guards stand vigil at the closed door. Another is outside the window. I can see his shadow pacing back and forth. This room has a lavish bed, and the movie *Spider-Man* plays on a large TV. Though the movie is a couple of years old, it still holds the girls' rapt attention.

The girls tell me Yaa and Ester have already left with their sponsors as soon as all the funding went through. There were no goodbyes.

"Do you know where they're going?" I ask, sitting with a plate piled high with the glorious food we saw in the other room. The other girls work through their own mountains of food.

"Spain and Luxembourg. I'm going to Germany," Mary answers.

I turn to Constance with my eyebrows raised.

"America," she answers in a husky voice.

My eyes go to Mamie questioningly. Constance slowly shakes her head. Mamie quietly chews her food as she stares intently at Spider-Man and Mary Jane kissing while he hangs upside down.

"I have not seen this one before," Mamie says softly. "Must be nice."

She looks at me with the slightest flicker of hope dancing in her eyes. "To be kissed like that?"

I cannot hold her gaze. Her look is one that will haunt me.

We watch the movie with a heaviness upon us. We are thinking the same thought but cannot bring ourselves to say it aloud.

If Mamie does not fetch a price, *Spider-Man* will be the very last movie she watches.

# 27

## AFTER

Miami was in the midst of one of its pop-up tropical rain showers. Nena nestled in a swinging chaise longue beneath the security of her gazebo so she could enjoy the shower without getting wet.

She was soothed by the mundane neighborhood sounds—kids playing ball at the park, cheers from a Little League football game, the occasional bump and rattle of some car's bass. She could pick out the banter between Keigel's soldiers as they walked their rounds, making sure all was well in their little piece of the world. People would complain the neighborhood was never quiet, but Nena loved that it reminded her of the bustle of N'nkakuwe. Twi and Ewe were replaced with English, but the motions were still the same. Children playing, adults adulting, life moving on as it should.

The high fence walls surrounding the stucco cottage provided ample privacy and seclusion in her backyard oasis. Exotic trees, elephant-ear plants, and vibrant flowers fit for botanical gardens grew lush under her care when she was home and were well tended by the sprinkler system when she was on a job. Her serenity fountain with its gentle gurgles as water wound between white and brown rocks, dappled light, and bright-orange koi offered a peace Nena could never find beyond those walls. Here was where she could be most at ease.

Successive beeps alerted her to an incoming call on the secured laptop, and she slipped in the earpiece.

"Good evening," she said. Her body automatically straightened at the video image of her longtime mentor and trainer.

"Evening." The many years training and working Dispatch had kept Witt lean and fit. Only the increasing gray of his speckled goatee indicated he was older. Nena was never quite sure just how old—younger than Dad, maybe by ten years? Or less? They didn't ask those types of questions.

She waited for him to begin, had been waiting for his initial contact since her botched job, but he'd bided his time, likely waiting to see what the Council would decree he should do with her.

When she couldn't stand his speculative observation any longer, she blurted, "Say it." Witt was the only one who could beat Nena at the waiting game. With him, she was always the sixteen-year-old trainee.

"This is the second time you detoured from the plan. Now I'm tasked with ensuring you're still an asset to the team."

"Sir, I absolutely am. The 'detour' you refer to—"

Anger flashed in his eyes. "Was not sanctioned. There were no directives to dispatch Smith."

She watched her team lead rub his eyes. She hated disappointing him. Her respect for him was second only to her respect for Noble.

"Do you trust me?" Witt asked. "Are you still a member of Dispatch?"

"Without question." None of what she'd done was about Witt or the team or the Tribe.

"Then tell me what is going on. The thing with the Cuban and the girl in his room . . . I get it, okay? The Council gave it a pass. But Dennis Smith was not the mark, yet he's the one dead."

She'd already heard this all before, from Dad, from Elin. She didn't need to hear it again. What she needed was Witt's help.

"Your parents are due to visit you and your sister in the next few days. There is a video conference scheduled for the Council members where they will be discussing you. Your father will need to assuage their discontent with your work, justify your actions."

His thick eyebrows furrowed as he leaned in close, his bald head shining just a bit against his dark background. Was he home? She'd never been there. Maybe in an office at Network's headquarters in London. She'd never been there either. Only Dispatch's team lead got to go there.

"I can speak for myself."

"You don't run anything in the Tribe yet. You don't get to speak to them. You just get to listen to them berate you."

*Lucky me.*

"People get retired from Dispatch for detours."

His words served as a reminder of one of her former teammates who'd botched a job and been excommunicated from the Tribe, or "retired"—she guessed the Council members thought it was a nicer word. And Witt was warning her that she wasn't immune to the same punishment, even if she was the daughter of the High Council.

"I understand all about retirements." Her little stab of insolence surprised them both. Quickly, she clamped her mouth shut.

They regarded each other before Nena again broke the standoff. "Witt . . ."

His face broke into a wry smile she rarely got to see. "Now I'm Witt."

It was now or never. "Yes. I need some intel from you. I'd rather it be you than Elin because I don't want her involved too deeply in something that may blow up in my face."

"So I'm expendable, then." Witt let out a laugh. "I taught you well."

She took a cleansing breath and pushed on. "Smith was Paul Frempong's number two, back then in N'nkakuwe. Do you remember who—"

"I remember." His tone was sharp, his eyes like razors cutting into her. "Explain."

"I'm concerned there are bad actors within the Tribe," she said. "Someone lied and said Attah was dead when he was not. And maybe they've kept him alive all this time, been his benefactor."

"For what purpose?"

Nena spread her hands. "Money, power, control of Africa's commodities by using ruthless people to get it. Lucien Douglas could be the benefactor. Perhaps that's why he wanted Attah alive and the attorney dead."

This was what she treasured about Witt the most. He never interrupted her, not like Elin, allowing her to fully present her argument before he rendered his judgment.

"Or perhaps Lucien Douglas is also a pawn being used by someone else within the Tribe, someone who wants to ascend the ranks by any means necessary."

Witt narrowed his eyes. "What you say is treasonous, Nena; be careful." It wasn't a warning. It was a plea, because Nena read the concern in Witt's stormy dark eyes.

"Or what if"—she took another deep breath, because saying this scared her the most—"what if Paul is alive as well? And Kwabena? What if they all lived and were lying in wait all this time?"

"To come after you?"

"No." She shook her head. "They haven't thought about me since they sold me. But what if they went underground and have been biding their time to infiltrate us and take over, with the help of members who seek to betray the Tribe?"

"Nena, I went to Ghana myself. The Compound was in ruins. The soldiers Paul used had turned on him, killed him for nonpayment, and then we dispatched all of them. We cleaned house."

"What if they lied?"

Witt pursed his lips.

"Paul is like a—a—" She searched her mind for the proper word. "A crocodile. He can wait right beneath the smooth, tranquil surface for the right time to jump out and snatch you into the waters. You're dead before you realize it."

"And your father? How can we keep this from him when he is High Council? He has to know what you suspect about members of the Tribe."

"To tell Dad now without concrete evidence would destroy him and put my family at risk. Dad's put his soul into establishing the Tribe. He is the Tribe, and I'm not ready to blow up his world just yet.

"Please." She hoped he could see logic in her reasoning, that he could find the seed of doubt to make him help her. "Could you gather intel on Dennis Smith? See when he suddenly appeared? Because if Attah Walrus lived, it means Paul lives, too, and is waiting just beneath the water. And Paul couldn't have hidden all this time without help. I need the proof first, and then I'll tell Dad."

He was still dubious. "And the attorney? What of him?"

She held his critical stare. "I'm working on it."

The sky was darkening by the end of their call, with Witt finally agreeing to make inquiries. Nena knew what the things she was saying could mean for the Tribe. They meant dissension in the ranks. They meant a housecleaning of those who were not truly for the cause. But if she was right, so be it.

And if she was right, she'd make sure for herself that Kwabena and Paul were gone for good . . . by her hand. And most importantly she'd protect her family at all costs from any threats, outside or in. Even if it meant going against the Tribe's wishes.

Even if it meant her death.

# 28

## BEFORE

In the bedroom at the party, watching the movie with the other girls is a welcome respite, a vacation into normalcy, which is very needed in our new reality. There is no more pretending away what we are now, or what will become of me or Mamie.

"Maybe I should kill myself," Mamie whispers, her head bowed toward me.

I cannot look at her, to see the wild and worried expression I know to be there, because if I do, I will break, and I cannot, not right now. I say nothing at first, considering her words. Dying by her own hand is infinitely better than dying at their hands.

"Maybe he doesn't mean what he says. You are worth more alive than not."

Mamie takes in a breath, which relieves me. I pray I have provided her a bit of reprieve, a little hope, if only for a short while. What goes unsaid is that Paul is a man of his word. Mamie will not return to the Compound alive if she does not fetch a price. Gently, I pat her hand. It rests on her lap, trembling slightly. I sneak a quick look at her, catching the small tears pooling at the corners of her eyes. My own are stinging; seeing Mamie suffer is more than I think I can endure.

The door opens, and my guard enters. Mamie and I tense. His eyes sweep the room, landing on Mamie, on Spider-Man swinging in to save the trolley car full of children, and finally on me.

"Come," he says gruffly. "Time to go."

I hesitate. Mamie and I share a look.

"I said it's time to go. Now!"

I ignore him. Instead, leaning close to Mamie, I whisper, "Do what you must to survive." My words come out so low I cannot hear them above the noise of the TV and the barking guard. But I hope she can.

Angered by my disobedience, the guard snatches my arm and twists it, forgetting I am someone's goods and he is not supposed to touch me. He raises a hand to strike, but I spin on him, ignoring the pain in my arm.

I snarl, reveling in renewed rage, and threaten to scream that he is manhandling me, an offense Paul or my new White benefactor would not take lightly. I stare into the guard's eyes, daring him to touch what Paul considers merchandise. The hatred I have for him, for all of them, ignites a vigor I thought had abandoned me for good.

My words must snap him to his senses, because he releases me. "We must go," he says, his voice coiling with anger that parallels mine. We stand like boxing opponents.

The adrenaline seeps out as quickly as it came upon me. I look once more at Mamie as the guard leads me out. She offers a slight wave, a forlorn smile. Then she turns back to the movie and watches it as the door closes on the last vestiges of my old life.

A dark car idles in front of the house, waiting for me. Paul is nowhere. In the back seat, a raven-haired woman awaits me. She smiles when the door opens, motioning that I should join her.

I hesitate. Who is she? Monsieur Robach's wife? Daughter? I have not seen her all evening, and with no choice, plus the guard's not-so-polite prompting, I climb inside the car.

Before the door closes, I give him a withering look that I hope shrivels up his balls into raisins. I wish him an eternity in hell. He extends his middle finger at me in farewell.

The woman has on a silvery dress with rows of bracelets on her tiny wrists that jingle together. She keeps smiling, showing all her teeth. I will not give them satisfaction by asking questions, looking afraid, or showing apprehension. I work to wash all the emotions from my face.

"What is your name?" she asks as the car begins to move. I concentrate on the dark windows, which make the outside world look like a black hole. She is also French, another obroni, with a voice that is older, gravelly. Not what I expected.

"I'm Bridget." She sighs when I don't answer and leans back in her seat. It is unsettling, driving into an abyss of nothingness. "It's okay if you don't speak much. Monsieur Robach likes them quiet."

The acrid smell of smoke indicates she's lit a cigarette. She rolls the window down for the smoke to escape. "I'm sure you have questions. So this is how it will go. I will be your escort to France and drop you at his home. He is already on the way to the airport and will leave ahead of us. You and I will stay in Accra for a night. Tonight Ghana, tomorrow France."

I can't help myself. I turn to look at her.

"I travel with you because fewer questions are asked when a little African girl travels with me, fewer questions than if you traveled with a White man. Don't you agree?" Bridget answers my silent question.

"Is this what you do? Escort children?"

Bridget laughs. It is not unpleasant. "Whatever you want to call it, chérie. I prefer 'babysitting,' or to call myself a recruiter."

Her conversation and laughter do not fool me. Nor does the fact she is pretty and has nice clothes and a smile I am sure makes people bend to her will. But she is no better than them.

What Bridget does is worse than any of the men I have encountered. What she does is deceive and deliver. She is the siren. She is the gingerbread house used to attract and ensnare. She is Charon, the mythological Greek ferryman.

And I am the sailor to be dashed upon the craggy rocks hidden just below the surf. Hansel and Gretel to serve as a meal for the evil witch. The dead soul carried off to the underworld.

Bridget says, her voice saccharine, "Consider this as an adventure toward a brand-new life, Aninyeh. You can have whatever you'd like."

"My freedom?" I blurt before catching myself.

"Except that." She studies me through the darkness with a smile full of false sympathy. "Profites-en maintenant, chérie." *Live it up now, sweetheart.* "With Robach, you will need these memories."

# 29

## AFTER

Just as Witt had said, Noble and Delphine Knight made it to the States for their American business interests and to see about their daughters. Nena and Elin were on their way downtown to meet their parents, who had arrived the previous day, planning (much to Elin's chagrin) to stay indefinitely, or until Miami became too hot for them. They'd become accustomed to London weather and hated the muggy, stifling nature of Miami weather that the upcoming summer months would bring.

"I wonder why they didn't wait until the Council meeting ended to come here. Dad prefers to have face-to-face meetings in London," Elin said. "When Mum and Dad are too close, it makes me edgy." She shot a quick glance over the rim of her oversize sunglasses at her sister sitting in the passenger side.

"Probably to decide what to do with me."

"No, not you." Elin checked her appearance in the sun visor, touching up her lipstick. "It's for Lucien Douglas. They're voting him in officially."

Nena's jaw tightened, but she wasn't sure if it was from her concerns about the man or from Elin's reckless driving. Both, she decided, digging her nails into the armrest.

"And we have the dinner with your boyfriend," Nena reminded her. Which was why Elin was a nervous wreck and nearly about to cause one on the expressway. "But they've met Oliver before. What's the big deal?"

"Yeah, but this dinner is the *official* official meeting. They've only seen him in passing, really, because they've been too caught up in his dad and squaring that away." She side-eyed Nena as they pulled into the lavish grounds of the condo where their parents owned a flat. She stopped to allow the guard to open the gate. "You're not trying to flake on me, are you?"

"I'm not." Nena was enjoying Elin's panic. It was rare that her older sister was ever rattled about anything.

They took the elevator to the top floor of the building, Elin complaining every step of the way.

"Do you think they'll stay on beyond my dinner?" she asked, following Nena down the hall to where one of the family's personal guards stood sentry at the door. Nena shrugged at Elin and nodded at the guard as he opened the door for them. She could hear her father speaking loudly from his office.

"You know how I feel claustrophobic with them in the same city," Elin whispered in Nena's ear. "I don't know why they bought a flat here. Can't they do like normal parents and stay at a hotel for a bit and then leave?"

Nena shushed her.

Delphine Knight greeted them in the foyer with a finger to her lips. She gestured for them to follow her into Noble's office, where they could see him behind his dark mahogany desk. Several large-screen monitors lined the wall, each filled with the image of a Council member, eleven in total. The twelfth screen was blank, the one that would be for Lucien Douglas when they voted him in as representative of Gabon.

Delphine took her position standing at Noble's side while Elin took a seat at a small desk and opened her laptop, preparing to read financials to the leaders representing Ghana, Nigeria, the Republic of the

Congo, Liberia, Kenya, South Africa, Tanzania, Senegal, Mali, Eritrea, and Sierra Leone.

"The Council expands as more countries join," Noble was saying to the members. "Remember our cause, brothers and sisters. One Africa. If one eats, we all eat."

"But how will we get anything accomplished if we have members from each African nation?" one representative asked. "Could you imagine all the strife we would have? Too many opposing views. We'll never agree."

"I hear you, brother," another said. "But just like America has senators and congressmen, we can vote, majority rules."

A third countered, "And America has a president. Eh? The president?"

"Let's not go there. You remember what he called us, o."

They grumbled for a full minute about "shithole countries." It was a line they would never forgive or forget. Nena wouldn't either.

"My point is America has senators for each state that vote on American matters."

Another: "America is one country. We are many countries. And we are not a government, eh. We're not politicians; we are businessmen."

"And women."

"The point is we don't need representatives from every damn country we get on board. We can make the rules the rest of the Tribe will follow. Simple as that."

Like big business or government lobbyists who influenced politicians to do their bidding and push their interests, Nena came to learn, that was how these wealthy Africans wielded the amount of power they had to do whatever they wanted.

Noble cut in, terminating the debate. "We are *one* Africa. This is our vision, eh? All of Africa united into a large multinational business entity—thriving, prospering, and cultivating our own lands and resources and gaining riches and selling as we choose. Imagine Africa as the sole benefactor of all our unmined resources and minerals. Leaders instead of workhorses."

Nena had heard this speech a time or two, and she believed wholeheartedly in her family and the Tribe's vision. But her job was to enforce those ideals, not chat about them.

"I still think we should allow more time before voting," someone said. "Think this through. Make sure this new member is worth all the trouble to secure his seat at the Council table."

Nena kept her head up, staring at the screen without moving, when what she really wanted to do was slink away. She wouldn't let the rest of the Council see her squirm. Her parents would want her to remain stoic despite the fact she did feel some shame at not following orders, and at the little glimpses of disappointment she caught from her dad whenever he looked her way.

Another representative, one who hadn't yet spoken, said, "If Lucien's business merger with territories in Gabon is successful, then it's worth his spot. We're going to bring all coastal countries into the fold of the African Tribal Council for imports and exports. Then we will shore up the central countries and align them to our goal of a unified Africa. Soon the Tribe will be like the United Nations, but even better because it's for Africa, by Africans."

"I like that better," the rep who'd brought up the president's insult chimed in. "I'd rather be like the United Nations than the United States."

Nena liked him. He was a jokester. The room exploded in laughter, and Nena relaxed now that the conversation had veered away from land mines. She felt a buzz in her back pocket, and as the voting commenced, she checked her phone.

GEORGIA: Dinner at our house? 6 ok?

It was nearly three thirty. She'd need a bit more time to finish up the meeting, chat with the parents, and freshen up.

NENA: Can do 7.

GEORGIA: You like lasagna? Dad says we can have something else if you like.

Lasagna wasn't her favorite. She didn't like the texture of ricotta.

NENA: Lasagna's fine.

GEORGIA: Great!

Nena's mouth twitched. She still couldn't figure out why she found the girl so endearing when she'd never had a place for children in her life before. Never gave them a second thought and had lost any notion of being a mother. Yet here she was, her heart swelling weirdly with pleasure at the lines of silly smiley face, plate, fork, and knife emojis Georgia assailed her screen with.

Then a slither of unease followed when Nena remembered her promise to her father, her sister, and Witt—find out what Cortland Baxter knew of the Tribe. Now, she had the way in.

# 30

## BEFORE

Which is worse? The physical or psychological cruelties Robach inflicts on me? I do not know. What I do know is once I arrive at Robach's home in Paris, it does not take long for his sadistic nature to show itself. He enjoys small tortures, needling me with instruments or repetitive irritants, like flicking the tops of my ears until they sting so badly I shrink whenever he raises a hand, like a dog trained to stay away from an electrified fence.

I have easily memorized the parameters of my prison. The cellar is belowground. No windows, just a large square box. Across from the staircase is a hidden door, the entranceway to the tiny dungeon where I reside. The entrance to this room is behind a shelf of Monsieur's gadgetry. When he is gone, my door is closed, and the shelf is secured in front of it. No one knows it's there. Therefore no one knows I am there either. When I am allowed out, there is a tiny bathroom consisting of a shower, sink, and toilet where I can clean myself.

One day, Robach opens the door to my dungeon and announces I may leave. I can walk out. The first day he does this, I eye him. My mind whispers, *He lies,* but hope for freedom overcomes the voice. He moves away, freeing the pathway to the steps that lead up to the kitchen and beyond it, to the world and freedom. Freedom I have not known in who knows how long. Time, for me, is one endless stream.

I take a few tentative steps. His expression is apologetic, and he holds his hands out as if promising not to touch me. I take another halting step. My hackles rise, but my need to flee overcomes my fear. I move faster so as not to tempt fate with slowness. My footsteps on the first stair. My fingers grasping the edge of the railing.

Behind me, he is blubbering, "Due," *sorry*, in broken Twi, butchering my language. "Fa me bɔne kyɛ me." *Forgive me.*

A bit more courage pushes me to climb. The taste of freedom is sweet on my tongue, permeating every fiber. Each step brings me closer to liberation and farther from him. My arm extends toward the cellar door, which is open a tiny sliver of a crack. The bright, natural light I almost forgot existed beams through radiantly, energizing me.

I am barely aware the blubbering apologies have stopped behind me. The tips of my fingers graze the inside of the door. It feels odd, padded like stiff Styrofoam. Later, I learn it is material to mask the screams that come from his cellar, cries sometimes from others, sometimes from me.

Another step. My fingers push the door ever so slightly, widening the crack. There is a window and, beyond it, a bright, shining, sunny day. A kitchen where wonderful aromas of baked bread waft in the air. My stomach growls its response, and my eagerness to leave this wretched place blots out all caution.

Initially, I am not aware when rough hands as thick as sausage and strong as steel grab me by the back of my neck, so focused am I on the door and the world beyond it. They yank me off my feet. The apologetic butchered Twi switches to angry, vitriolic French, a barrage of horrible names and a multitude of curses. With his free hand, Robach grabs the door handle and slams the door shut. The sound reverberates in the stairwell, ricochets like a bullet in my ears. The cutting off of freedom, literally, figuratively. The impending of my doom.

My mouth opens, but no sound comes out because terror has paralyzed me completely. With the door now secured, Robach turns his full attention on me. He lifts me off the stair by my neck. His strength is nearly inhuman, the way he can hold me up as if I am a limp doll. Perhaps it is not that much of a feat. I have not eaten well since I arrived here. The bottom of the staircase pitches precariously under the harsh recessed lights. My feet sway lightly, my toes dangling in the air, trying to gain purchase on a bit of step, somehow.

Then he throws me.

I am airborne, still reeling at how quickly he came upon me, how quickly freedom was just within my grasp and snatched away. I still have not entirely come to terms with the fact I have not freed myself until I crash near the bottom step, my right shoulder taking the brunt of the force. It is when my body tumbles head over heels onto the cold cement that I realize what he has done to me. The side of my head whacks the floor. Silvery-white firecrackers explode. The pain is beyond excruciating. My teeth sink deeply into my tongue, filling my mouth with a geyser of blood.

"Stupid cunt," he says in a mixture of giddiness and disgust that I fell for his ruse. I lie crumpled, helpless, with waves of pain paralyzing me. The wooden stairs vibrate from his heavy footfalls as he bounds down them. He grabs my ankle and tugs. My body twists horribly when he spins me around. My screams flow freely now. But as he pulls me, kicking and screaming, toward my dungeon, they are of no concern to him. He is laughing. Each scream makes him laugh harder.

This is my first significant encounter with Monsieur's true nature. It is not the last. We play this game a few times more because my need to flee overcomes my want to remain healthy every time.

Monsieur is the chat, *cat*.

I am Souris, his pitiful trained mouse.

And so he renames me Souris, one name among many. One of the kinder ones he uses. And eventually, Monsieur and I fall into our dangerous game of jouer au chat et à la souris. *Cat and mouse.*

---

The things I learn with Monsieur:

He prefers to watch.

He likes prostitutes, lots of them; the gender is of no consequence. He brags to me about being an equal-opportunity employer. And by *employer*, I mean *monster* and *murderer*.

He tells me I am lucky he does not like "Blacks" in that way, for which I am grateful to him. I have never been happier to encounter bigotry than when it is the factor that keeps Monsieur from raping me.

Whenever he complains about "my kind," I want to ask, Why, then, did he buy me? But I bite my tongue, choosing my battles. Does it matter why he has me—to be his pet on which he can unleash his most unconstrained anger? He has his sexual proclivities, and it is a gift I am not one of them.

He likes to inflict pain on everyone he brings to visit. His house is a cockroach trap; some check in and never check out. I have yet to witness this visually, but I have heard plenty.

He likes to hunt—no surprise—big game, exotic animals, rabbits in the forests, people.

But most of all, his enjoyment comes from tormenting me, from promising me a slow and painful death when he tires of me.

"I jest, Souris," he says in the next breath. "I shall keep you as my souris for eternity. You would like that, oui?"

A true answer would incur his wrath, so I refrain.

Monsieur has several CCTV screens lining an entire wall, monitoring various areas of the house, the grounds, and the street. He watches them always. He does not record the screens, except sometimes when there is a visitor he wants to visit a couple more times after the visitor is gone from the world.

My job, when Monsieur is at work on his workbench, where rows of instruments, tools, and knives gleam in the lighting, is to clean. I scrub the floors from his hunts. I throw hot water on the concrete, brushing the gore-filled mess into the drain in the middle of the floor. I clean his many tools under his watchful eyes. While I do, he smirks, daring me to use the tools on him.

Sometimes he speaks on the phone, always in French, because he still thinks the language is unknown to me.

Whatever he does for business is bad, evil. He discusses his distance from the airport, from the train station, from Paris. I commit all this information to memory because maybe one day I can use what I secretly learn from him.

He's sometimes gone for days at a time. And when this happens, he locks me in. It means endless time in my dungeon, but it also means I have peace from him, though not from my mind. I had never been alone for so long until Monsieur brought me here. At least in the Compound, there were other girls. Before then, I had a village. The time alone forces me to contemplate all that has happened. I am ashamed of my failings. And I agonize over the deaths of my family due to my cowardice. I should have fought harder. I should have died with them. But maybe this place is my penance, my hell I am eternally doomed to.

It becomes so long since I have heard my given name that I start believing my name is Souris because I lost the right to be called by any other.

He leaves rations when he is on one of his excursions so I do not starve, and because my room is hidden when closed, no one can hear or see me—the way he wants it. No one knows I am here. But no one comes down here, except Monsieur.

That is, until the woman appears.

# 31

## AFTER

Later that night, Nena was seated at the Baxter table, the turtle and key lime pies she'd brought waiting patiently on the kitchen counter for their turn on the plate. Nena had been pleased to learn that both were favorites of father and child.

"I hope you like it," Cortland said shyly, placing a warmed plate piled high with lasagna in front of his guest. He watched anxiously as she scrutinized the pasta bake before picking up her fork to take a small bite. Nena could sense his nervousness. Georgia looked back and forth, finding immense pleasure in his awkwardness. It was like a National Geographic episode, the mating rituals of a single father.

"If you don't like it," he added, "we could order Chinese."

"You always tell me if I don't like it, I can starve," Georgia pointed out.

He shot her a silencing look, the dad look. Nena and Elin had received the very same kind of look from their own father.

"No," Nena said, raising a hand. "This is good. Delicious. And I kind of hate Chinese."

Cortland and Georgia shared a look. He said, "That's a . . . rather strong word."

Georgia's nose wrinkled. "Never heard of anyone hating Chinese." She dug into her food. "It's good, Dad, cheesy, the way I like it. Pass the parmesan, please?"

Nena passed the container of grated cheese. "I had a very bad experience with Chinese food." She glanced up at him, again transfixed with a spatula in hand. "Cortland, sit and eat?"

"Call him Cort."

He sent Georgia a warning stare and said, "Or Cortland. Whichever is fine." He ignored Georgia's look of incredulity.

Georgia reached for the remote control and turned the TV on. She flipped through the Guide channel until something caught her eye. "Look, Dad, *Jaws*. Just in time."

"Peach, maybe *Jaws* isn't Nena's type of movie."

"I love *Jaws*," Nena said between mouthfuls. "It's one of my favorites. Love *Pet Sematary* too."

"She's a keeper," Georgia deadpanned.

"Peach," Cort admonished, with a mixture of embarrassment and horror at her inappropriateness.

Nena's mouth quirked, taking a delicate bite. They ate in silence as the movie's ominous theme music played in the background.

"What do you do?" Cort asked, sitting back from his nearly empty plate. Nena waved away his offer of wine. No Chinese, no alcohol.

"I'm an assassin," Nena replied simply, with a bland expression to match.

Georgia erupted in a coughing fit, choking on her food. Her fork clattered to her plate. Her eyes bugged, watering as she tried to take in air. Her dad jumped up, nearly knocking over his chair to reach her. She waved him away.

"I'm okay," she wheezed, reaching for her sweet tea and taking deep gulps.

He hovered above his seat, ready to aid his daughter should she need it.

"Are you well?" Nena asked, an amused glint in her eyes as she watched Georgia choke.

She nodded, giving both a thumbs-up and a pointed look of her own at Nena. Her dad finally took his seat.

"That's a good one, Nena," Georgia said, one last cough forcing its way out. "Assassin. Ha ha." She looked anything but amused.

"Definitely not something one hears every day. Hope you're good at it," Cort said, playing along with the joke.

Nena returned her attention to him, studying him with a hint of a smile. There was a time when smiling had come so easy to her, until there had no longer been reason to.

"I am the best," she answered. When she caught Georgia's wild-terror-filled expression, Nena pivoted. "We're a family business. My parents deal with trade and commercial real estate. My sister and I oversee our American operations."

"You're from the UK? If I'm placing your accent correctly? And a little something else."

A quick nod. "Born in Ghana and grew up in the UK. Have you ever visited either?"

He shook his head.

"Dad and my mom backpacked through Europe in college," Georgia informed her.

He nodded, sipping from his glass. "It was a great experience. I hope to return one day."

"Maybe one day, you might." Nena looked at him, her head angled.

"Maybe," he said modestly.

Not for the first time, she found herself enjoying the way Cortland—Cort—looked at her, like she was desirable, more than a commodity or someone's pet or a killer.

She'd never seen herself with a man in any romantic capacity. Usually shied away from their attention. But with Cort, she didn't mind so much. Curious.

She asked for the restroom.

"Down the hall, to the left," Cort replied. "Want me to show you?"

She didn't. She demurred and excused herself, walking down the hall as if she were on tour in a museum. She studied the photos of Cort and Georgia, always happy, laughing, in various places and at various ages in Georgia's life. She saw the photo of Georgia's mom sitting on a white bench in a park, floppy hat and book in hand—a beautiful honey-toned woman with a smile like Georgia's staring straight into Nena's soul as if to say, *Protect them. They're yours now.*

Nena had nearly blown up this family's world, leaving Georgia with nothing. A pang not dissimilar to guilt nicked at her, and she pried herself away from the photo. The door to Cort's room was open. It was immaculate, not a paper or dirty sock in sight. The bed was made. Impressive.

Nena quickly moved down the hall, passing Georgia's door—slightly ajar—and then another room. Looked to be both a guest room and office? She checked the hall in case either had come looking for her, but Georgia and Cort were in a highly energetic conversation. She went in, going for the desk by the bay window. She gave it a cursory look. Not much and hard to see in the dark with only the light from the hall to guide her. She couldn't risk turning on any lights here. But she spied something on the floor next to the desk chair. Cort's attaché, maybe? She went to it, finding it open with a manila folder peeking out. She looked at the door again while synchronously pulling the file out. She took out her cell, turned the flashlight on, directing it to the pages. Quickly she rifled through. Nothing she knew and nothing that jumped out at her. The last page was stamped *EVIDENCE*. It was a photocopy of a business card reading *The Lotus Flower*.

Didn't stand out to her. Good. It was also time to get back.

When everything was put back where she'd found it, Nena went to the bathroom as she'd asked, returned to dinner, and enjoyed the conversation between a daughter and her father, hoping she could do as Georgia's mother seemed to ask from the photo. Protect them.

# 32

## BEFORE

The sharp clicks of the unlocking door alert me Monsieur has returned. I am tense, not knowing how I shall receive him. Thoughts of what kind of torture or psychological terror he will dole out nearly loosen my bowels. I hate the way I cower, the way I am so weak at the sight of him.

My dungeon opens, revealing him in a bathrobe and house shoes. His hair stands on end, a funny picture I am too scared to find amusing. He holds a pitcher of liquid in one hand and a crate beneath his other arm of what I hope is hot food. He looks satiated. Either his business was successful or he has had a visitor. Whatever it is, he will soon tell me, as he always does.

He sniffs. "Jesus, Souris, you smell horrible."

My head drops. I try my best to keep as clean as possible. During his stretches of absence, I must choose between cleanliness and survival. Therefore, the container of water he leaves is for consumption. There is also a bucket for my waste that cannot be emptied until he lets me out of my little room. So yes, there is a smell. I am now accustomed to the debasement Monsieur subjects me to. Me, the daughter of a chieftain, a princess. It is almost laughable.

He places the crate of supplies on the floor, uses his foot to push it into the room, and beckons me to come out. He holds a bar of soap and a rough towel. I take them quickly in case he changes his mind, but again he is in decent spirits, so he lets me be. I quickly pass him to enter the small bathroom, noticing the door atop the stairs is ajar. I eye it longingly.

"Eh, Souris, you forget something, oui?"

The bucket. I cannot forget. Anything can ignite his wrath.

"Apologies," I murmur, rushing to get my bucket of shit and piss I will empty into the toilet. He goes to his workbench, where the surveillance monitors are up and running.

I rinse the bucket and use my bar of soap and water to make suds, then let it soak while I bathe. The bathroom has no door. And while he says he would never lower himself by being with me, I do catch him watching me on occasion. If that is as low as he will go, I can live with it.

Neither of us hears the creak on the steps until it is too late. I am readying the shower, wanting the water to be as hot as it can. Fortunately, it is very hot.

The gasp behind me makes my heart skip a beat. It is not from me and surely not him. I spin around at the same time Monsieur looks up from his worktable. His face is a blank canvas.

She is halfway down the steps, has long, tousled dark hair, and is wearing a glittering dress that reminds me of Bridget's. A sizable green leather purse loops over her shoulder. Her eyes are as round as saucers as she takes in me, wrapped in my too-short towel, and Monsieur in his half-opened robe.

We stare at her, and she stares back. She is pretty, a bit overly done with the makeup. She is older, more voluptuous, and the lights do not complement her sallow skin.

Silently and with a foreboding that deepens within my gut, I twist the faucet knob until the water drips to a stop. And I wait for what comes next.

# 33

## AFTER

Georgia ditched the adults to finish homework. Nena and Cort sat together on the living room couch in awkward silence while she nervously played with the hem of her shirt. Her behavior, her shyness, was different than it'd been the night they'd met, and she worried he was disappointed. She should have told Elin where she was going. Maybe Elin would have given her some pointers—*after* Elin laughed so hard she peed herself and called their mother.

Nena blurted, "Why Georgia? I mean, it's a lovely name; don't get me wrong. But why Georgia and not Dakota or Arizona or Virginia?"

He settled into the couch. "I was born in Haiti, my wife, Donna, as well. We grew up together in a little town that was . . ." He trailed off. "We had a difficult life."

She nodded for him to continue, folding her legs beneath her.

"Donna and I said we'd come to the States to go to school and have the all-American life. We worked hard, really hard, saved everything we had, and bought our way here when we turned eighteen. We worked our asses off while we got our degrees—hers in nursing and mine in law. Atlanta was the first real vacation we ever took. We were always going without to make ends meet. Finally, one day, I was like, 'Let's go somewhere.'"

He shrugged. "We chose Atlanta and fell in love with the city. I mean, we came back broke as hell. Had to play catch-up for months, but it was worth being able to have fun for a few days. Not long after, Donna told me she was pregnant, and when we found out it was going to be a girl, Georgia was the only name that made sense."

"The nickname makes sense to me now too."

His laugh was a deep, boisterous, belly-rumbling laugh that reminded her of Papa. "Yeah, she's my peach."

Nena pursed her lips.

He laughed again. He beamed talking about his daughter, reminding Nena of how Noble doted on her and Elin. She realized she really liked Cort's laughter. It was like being at home, settled and secure. Even more, she liked being the cause of his laughter.

"Why become a federal prosecutor?" she asked, hoping to tamp down the sudden assault of emotions. She was worried about what she was starting to feel and whether she could control it.

Cort chuckled as if to say, *Where do I even start?* "I was a cop for a few years. Loved it and worked with my best friend, Mack. Then I got my law degree and had been working in the Economics and Environmental Crimes Section at the US Attorney's Office for about seven years by the time Peach's mom died."

"I'm sorry."

He shrugged. "Don't be."

"Economics and Environmental Crimes?" she asked. "A mouthful."

He laughed. "I work General Frauds, which handles investments, securities, Ponzi schemes, to name a few." He thought some more. "Suddenly I was a single parent to a little girl, trying to make a name for myself, which was—is—tough, especially for a Black man, you know? They're so busy thinking you don't know as much, or you won't work as hard, or you got where you were because of affirmative action or to check a diversity box. Or they stereotype you. I had to know more, work harder, and be more of a hard-ass than my White counterparts. The work is how I got to where I am now, handling cases like the one prosecuting Dennis Smith. And I enjoy it because I like serving up a piece of the justice pie. Which screwed with me when the guy was shot right in front of me. That easily could have been me."

If Nena made it through the night without exposing herself to Cort, she deserved a damn Emmy.

"You like taking down the bad guys."

He shrugged. "There are laws, rules, in place that people have to adhere to."

"But what about when people do things outside your rule of law for a good cause?" Was she really having this conversation with him, a federal prosecutor, about what was just and what wasn't? She was playing with fire.

"What do you mean?"

She tried finding the right words. "I mean justice by your own rules, but for the betterment of people."

"Justice is not just black or white, you know. There are shades of gray. I get that. Still. We have a justice system in place for a reason. People should leave judgments to them."

"Or there is chaos."

He squinted an eye. "Yeah," he said, nodding. "I guess." He held up his hands in surrender. "There is no perfect system. Mistakes happen."

An understatement.

"Not everything is perfect, not even in my office. I guess we all just have to do what we can."

Her mind was traveling places she hadn't wanted to revisit. "Yeah, all of us do what we can. And sometimes, it's all that we can do."

He agreed, pausing as if he were having an internal debate. "Don't know if you heard about the big cartel leader killed last month."

She kept her face placid. The image of the girl on the bed, the way her fingers had fumbled with the key to unlock her way to freedom. Then, as quickly as the image had come, she washed it away.

"The way he was killed was personal. Not like anyone else on the property, who were all shot."

What was Cort getting at? What should she say? If she said the wrong thing, revealed information that hadn't been made public, she'd raise suspicion. So all she said was, "How do you mean?"

"I really shouldn't be discussing this"—he shifted on the couch—"but it's been a minute since I was able to talk work out with someone who has nothing to do with any of it."

Her lip twitched before she had a chance to stop it. She needed to remain in control. She needed to be clearheaded around this man who made her want to lose herself in him. She also needed to find out what he didn't know so she could clear him with the Tribe and they wouldn't give him a second thought.

"I was talking to my buddy Mack, who worked the scene, but he doesn't buy it. He thinks it was just a hit. But this guy's death was a message. Personal."

"Bit of a stretch?" In her mind, she thought, *Spot on.*

Her practiced confused face prompted him to explain. "Because it was up close. Not a shot like all the others. The killer cut his neck. Takes a lot of balls to cut a man's neck."

If she didn't know any better, Nena would think Cort was impressed. And that pleased her entirely.

Took a lot of something to rape and sell young girls too. But Nena didn't share that part.

"Not to mention the guy who was killed in front of me." Cort grimaced, his conviction slipping as the memory hit him. He blew out a breath. "It's still hard to think how close I came to death. Like, what if it was me in the crosshairs, not the other guy?"

Nena frowned sympathetically.

164

"Georgia would have been an orphan."

Cort's words plucked at the chord of guilt thrumming in her chest. She didn't need reminding of what could have been.

"But the guy I was going to prosecute and the cartel guy, they were linked."

"How?" This question was real because she herself wasn't entirely sure. Would Cort realize both Smith and Juarez had an affinity for human trafficking?

"Money. There's a money trail that links one of Smith's schemes to some of Juarez's investments."

Her thoughts went to N'nkakuwe and the Compound. The way the Walrus had laughed when her father's head had rolled. Money schemes and investments. Cort had no idea what Smith had really been into.

"Is it a stretch then to say justice was served?" she asked. "You say both men were bad men. If what you're saying is true—"

It was.

"—and their deaths are connected, or personal, or whichever . . ." She frowned. "Is it wrong that they're gone? Justice served?"

He looked at her, resolute. "No."

"Which is it?"

"Justice wasn't served."

"Even though they were bad men?"

He shook his head.

"Why?"

"Because we have a system for this. A legal way to exact justice."

"Would the man you were going to prosecute have been sent to prison?"

"I would have tried my damnedest."

"But what if he got off? What if he was exonerated? Where is the justice then?"

She could see Cort's torrent of emotion as if his face were a movie screen, the war raging between systematic justice and moral justice. She quelled the urge to reach out and touch him. The intensity of the feeling both terrified and thrilled her. Nena wanted him to see that justice was more than a system of unbendable laws. She wanted to tell him all systems were fractured, and laws were colored shades of gray. Cort would work himself to death trying to live by rules no one else played by.

"It's my job, no matter which way it falls."

There were some jobs not meant to be done. She thought of the bullet marked for Cort that had gone into Attah Walrus instead.

"That's very commendable." She pitied the day when his idealism would be crushed.

Cort beamed at Nena before reaching for the TV remote. Nena gladly took it as a signal they'd gone deep enough for one night. He flipped through the apps.

"Have time for one more movie?"

"I do. Yes," Nena answered without hesitation. She watched as he relaxed into his seat and followed his lead, settling into a more comfortable position on the couch, feeling her guard lower with each passing moment. She asked, "Any new releases?"

"I can help with that!" a singsong voice called from two rooms over.

They looked at each other, at first wide eyed at Georgia's eavesdropping on their conversation. Then amused when she suddenly materialized in the doorway. Without prompting, she invited herself back in and nestled on the couch between them, sitting closer to Nena than to her dad, as if Nena had always belonged there, with them.

# 34

## BEFORE

"What the hell is this, Robeeee?" the woman drawls, reminding me of John Wayne movies.

An American? Here? *And who is Robe-eeee?*

"Who's the kid? And what the hell is going on here?" She gets her second wind. "I like kinky, but I don't do kids, okay?"

She is so busy gawking at me she does not notice Monsieur's slow rise from the bench or the stealthy steps he is taking toward her. He is a predator, she the prey. He closes the gap between them. My anxiety is growing because he will undoubtedly blame me for his forgetting to properly lock the basement door.

"I thought you left," Robach says, standing at the foot of the steps. His voice takes on a honeyed tone, as American as apple pie.

What is his game here? Why has his accent changed?

"She is my housemaid."

"Then why wasn't she upstairs cleaning or something?" She narrows her eyes at me as if I am competition, about to take her prize. She takes two steps down. "She's also naked under that towel, and you're here. It's weird, Robeee."

Monsieur's smile is disarming. He does not fool me one bit. "Really, dear? How is it weird? She lives down here. Can't have the help living upstairs with me, can I? Plus, who can want a waif like her when I have a woman like you?" He holds a hand out for her to take.

I am wound tighter than the skin on a drum. Why can she not see the trap Robach lays for her? I have been on the receiving end more times than I care to count.

She considers him. Looks at me with hooded eyes. Her heels clomp down the stairs, and she clears the last couple of steps. How she does not fall on those stilts, I have no idea. She takes his hand, allowing him to pull her into him.

They kiss for a long while. He fondles her rear. I look around, wondering if I should resume my showering, retreat to my dwelling, or stay as I am.

He pulls away from their kiss, looking down at her, stroking her mane of wild hair. His hand trails gently along the edge of her jawline. He gazes at her. She swoons, exhaling. Her eyes go all gooey and romantic like in one of those black-and-white movies my auntie liked to watch. I scratch an itch on the back of my neck, my every sense electrified.

"My dear," he says in a disappointed sigh, wiping his hand over his face as if weary, "why couldn't you mind your fucking business and leave?"

Her head jerks back as if slapped. "What? What do y—what do you mean?" she stammers, confusion filling her rapidly blinking eyes.

She tries to step away, to make some room between the two of them, but he grips her firmly by the waist with his left hand. His other hand snakes up to her neck. My mouth goes dry and my mind numb.

When he speaks, he no longer sounds regretful that she has happened upon us. And his French has returned. "You should have left when you had the chance."

His voice is cold, colder than I have ever heard, and it nearly stops my heart.

His huge paw of a hand curls around her pale throat. His thumb presses into her larynx; then the other hand sidles up to join it. Together they mash into her throat, closing her airway, damaging the delicate bones, tendons, and nerves that help her breathe. He means to make her suffer. It is as if he blames her for his having to kill her.

Her eyes bulge. The purse drops, sounding loud and heavy. It tips over, and its contents, tons of makeup, spill all over, going this way and that.

Her hands slap and claw at his. She tries going for his face, beats at him. Her fight is in vain. When he is like this, he is not human. His face does not register emotion.

The struggle she puts up is no match for this hunter, this apex predator, the enslaver of girls, the oppressor of souls. My feet shuffle until I am at the bathroom's doorway. I should run. Turn away. My heart is in my throat, but I cannot tear myself from what I am seeing.

He yanks her forward, then wrestles her to the floor. Terrible sounds erupt from her, tight, gurgling, gagging sounds.

I am not watching to relish her death. I am learning his moves. If I ever get a chance, a big if, I can never allow him to get me beneath him. He cannot wrap his fingers around me like he is doing her. I would never get him off, as she cannot. I will need to maintain the upper hand.

He grasps the sides of her head in his bear paws, lifting it. Our eyes connect. There is utter fear in hers as they beg for help. And before I formulate a thought, Monsieur smashes the back of her head on the floor so hard I become disoriented. Her grip loosens, and an arm flops to the floor. The other wavers in the air.

Her breathing is a wet wheeze. He lifts her head again, gathers himself on his knees so his weight is entirely in it, and smashes her head back. And again. The dull sound her skull makes on concrete is sickening. Her other hand drops, and she no longer moves. He continues straddling her, watching as the last bits of life ebb from her. Then he smiles, takes his finger to her chin, and turns her head toward me.

Her blank eyes stare in my direction, without fear this time because there is nothing. The silence after so much noise is deafening. He looks at me with bottomless black orbs, grinning like a Cheshire cat.

"A shame." He pouts as if he dropped an ice cream cone. "I rather liked her." He licks her cheek with the tip of his tongue where a single tear has fallen and takes a deep inhale of her hair, sticky with the blood oozing from her shattered skull. Her dead eyes ask me if her death is on my hands too.

There is no answer from me. Instead, I retreat into the bathroom and turn the shower back on, waiting for the hot water to wash away the stink of death.

When I finish showering, towel dry, and slip on the loose blue jogging suit Monsieur has left for me to wear, he is no longer sitting by the dead woman's side. He is at his workbench sorting out an array of shiny metal instruments a coroner or butcher might use.

His hands glide lightly across the instruments, finally settling on a large cleaver, a mallet, and a slender boning knife. "We have a series of unfortunate events, Souris."

Does he mean it to be a pun, alluding to the children's book?

"I cannot call the authorities for obvious reasons." He points to me and at her. "And we cannot leave it here."

She is "it" now, no longer a woman he spent time with, no longer human. She probably never was to him. This is the first time he has killed in front of me. Usually, I am locked in my dungeon, and anything he does in the cellar, I only hear. My imagination runs wild as I try to visualize what he is doing beyond my prison doors, but to see Monsieur end a life with his own hands resonates deep within me.

He walks to the metal shelf filled with storage items, selects a couple of huge dark duffel bags, and tosses them to me. He goes to a large roll of thick, frosted white plastic, attached to a wall and hung like a roll of paper towels, and pulls a long length from it. The vinyl comes away at the perforated edge with a rip. He juggles the cleaver, boning knife, mallet, and plastic sheet before setting them all on the floor next to the woman.

He spreads the vinyl out, then rolls her body onto it. She left quite a bit of blood from her head wound. Robach sprays the puddle with liquid that smells of ammonia and begins preparing his knives, reverently laying them out in a neat row near the massive capped drain in the floor.

"Come." He beckons with his fingers.

I acquiesce.

There is no time to unpack my feelings, a whirlwind of emotions: Perplexed at how he treats her like she is a slab of beef, curious about what he will do—although I am beginning to get an idea—and repulsed because whatever he does, he will make me watch. And I am afraid, always.

"Kneel."

I do a few feet away, not wanting to be too close. He places the boning knife between us. We make eye contact. One look reminds me he expects me to take a chance.

No—if I try, it will be by surprise, when he least expects it and his guard is at its lowest. I wait for directions.

"I have a place, an incinerator, where I can dispose of this body, but I cannot walk out of here with a full-size body, you understand?" He pauses, waiting. "Because I did not plan for this. I did no intel. Anyone could be out right now."

All I do is nod, unsure why he bothers telling me any of this, as if we are confidants.

"We need to make it travel size." He chuckles.

Who will miss her now that she's gone? Does anyone know where she went and with whom? When she woke this morning, she did not imagine her lover would smash her head in with his bare hands.

"You will assist me with cutting it up, so time will move faster. I would like to retire to bed soon." He considers me. "You are not my first pet, Souris, but you are by far the most intriguing. You don't cry or beg. You don't simper like others have. You're quiet, and I like that in girls, you know? If you continue to behave, perhaps your welcome won't be worn out as quickly."

His charity knows no bounds.

He talks me through the process as he begins to hack at her with the cleaver. It is ghastly work, and he soon deserts the instrument. He shows me how to use the boning knife to get between her joints. "So that I miss bone, like deboning a chicken. You see?" He ponders a minute. "I'll need my saw for the big parts. What was I thinking, eh?"

He returns, saw in hand. "When I cut a part away, you quickly place it in a bag. Two bags should be enough. Good thing they are waterproof, yes?"

The least of my concern.

"Try not to get any more blood on my floor. It is hell to get out, as you can see already. And it'll be less cleaning for you." He chuckles. "You see how I look out for you, Souris?"

"Yes, Monsieur."

He falls into a rhythmic silence as he sets to work. With the saw, he works deftly at detaching her limbs with the precision of a butcher. When the first part falls off, thumping onto the plastic, I jump. I stare at the leg, cut right above the knee. My mouth is slick with spit, and I desperately want to vomit.

The blow to the side of my head is so sudden and intense it knocks the wind from me, leaving a ringing loud enough to prevent my hearing anything else. I lose my equilibrium and tip over to the side. My hand braces on the floor to steady myself. Tears spring from the explosion of pain, but I bite back a yell, clenching my teeth, breathing through it all.

He leans toward me. Too close. I feel the heat of his breath on my neck as he growls, "What did I tell you, girl? Put the shit in the bag. Without delay."

"Yes, Monsieur."

He does not have to remind me again. I stuff the half leg into the bag. And when the next part of the dead woman detaches, I scoop it before it has a chance to hit the floor.

# 35

## AFTER

Nena was running late for her sister's dinner party, where Elin was to officially introduce her latest boyfriend to the family. She didn't hold out much hope for this one, no matter how serious Elin said they were. Elin was as promiscuous as she was shrewd. She fell in and out of love so swiftly that the rest of the Knights could claim whiplash. It had been this way ever since she and Nena were teenagers.

Their mum hoped to have grandchildren one day. There was no way Nena was popping out any kids, which left Elin to be the baby factory, and if it meant going along with this boyfriend or that to get a husband, then Delphine welcomed them. Elin swore that if she wasn't married and pregnant by thirty-eight, she would thaw out some of those eggs she'd frozen without her parents knowing and bake a baby for them. She had six more years to go.

On the night of the great family meeting of Oliver, Elin desperately needed her sister to get there so their mother wouldn't scare him away with talk of heirs and whatever else. She'd given Nena this same spiel three times already and was working on her fourth.

"Nena, say you're on your way? Because Mum and Dad just arrived," Elin said frantically over the Audi's speakerphone. "I can't find anything right to wear tonight. I'm on outfit number five."

"I am," Nena answered. "But are you sure you want to officially introduce—"

"Oliver."

"Like, once you tell Mum and Dad this is the guy, they will be looking up venues for your wedding. Mum will prepare the aunties. Is this thing with Oliver a business deal, a love match, or just a fling?" Nena had to be the voice of reason here. "Is he old or young?"

Elin's silence alerted Nena that she was irritated. "Are you trying to throw cold water over my parade? He's my age or a tad older. Who cares?"

"I don't think that's the proper saying."

"I don't give a damn if it's the proper saying," Elin hissed. "Yeah, okay, right, I've dated a lot. But it was only because I was searching for a certain kind of mate."

"You should want a relationship like Mum and Dad's," Nena said. "Someone who is the other half of your mind. Someone to run all of this with."

Elin, incredulous, said, "That position's already taken, little sis, by you. I don't need a man for what Mum and Dad have, because you are my other half. I want a man who will let me do my work with no questions asked. He can have his own businesses, but he leaves ours alone."

"How can you be sure he will adhere to that? His dad is a Council member now. He'll want to run the business with you."

"He won't. Dad won't let him, and neither will I. Plus, he's too vanilla for what we do. He's scared of clowns, for God's sake!"

Nena paused. "Well . . . no one actually likes clowns."

Elin sighed. "I really, really like this one, Nena. I think I can settle down with him. For real this time."

Nena couldn't help herself. She tried to remain serious. "I should forget about all of the other 'the ones,' then?"

"Oliver makes me feel like I'm wrapped in a security blanket," Elin cooed, ignoring her.

"You know, Amazon sells massive amounts of those. Weighted ones at that. I like the one I bought."

"Fucking comedian," Elin grumbled. "I'm deadly serious, Nena."

Nena was making jokes, but the way Elin sounded, hopeful and excited about this guy, made Nena think about the dinner she'd had with Cort. The whole situation with him was so complicated. At least Oliver knew about the African Tribal Council. At least Elin didn't have to hide part of herself from him.

Before she knew what she was doing, Nena recounted her evening with Cort and Georgia. The words came so effortlessly, and she realized something new about herself. She liked talking to her sister about this kind of stuff.

"You really care for this bloke, yeah?"

Elin had asked the question so softly, so thoughtfully, that Nena was taken aback. Startled, really. *Care* was such a big word. She wouldn't say *care*. Would she?

"I mean, they're pleasant to be around," she backtracked. "And remember, I was there to determine what he does or doesn't know. It was work, really."

"Mm-hmm," Elin said teasingly. "I'm checking if the world's gone topsy turvy."

"Come again?" Any warm-and-fuzzies Nena felt about confiding in Elin were quickly gone.

"Because that's the only way my little sister is going to get a boyfriend."

"Elin! He's not my boyfriend," Nena practically screeched, entirely unbecomingly.

"Oooh, listen to you," Elin said. "Now I know it to be true. And it's about damn time, sis. And well deserved."

But was it? Nena had gotten herself involved with an American (which would irritate her dad, for one), and a prosecutor at that. How could she ever share the Echo side of her—not that she'd want to—in a relationship built on lies? Even lies by omission. If she allowed it, Cort would lay himself bare to her while she'd keep a massive part of her hidden, all the while enlisting his own daughter to deceive him. Didn't seem very fair of her.

"I am sorry I teased you about Oliver," Nena said. The realization her sister might be serious about a man had a sobering effect. "I see now it's a bit different with him, so I look forward to meeting him tonight."

"And what about Mum?"

Nena snorted. "You do realize no one *handles* Mum, right? However, I will try," she promised. "Relax and enjoy your evening. I'm almost there."

# 36

## BEFORE

I have come this far. I did not die in my village. I did not die in the Compound or in the Hot Box. I have not died here yet with this monster. Still, I cannot help but question again what kind of hell this is. What god permits this? What did I do to deserve this? Oh, that's right . . . I survived.

All is complete when I zip up the second bagful of the dead woman. I am now a coconspirator in her death and disposal. I am damned and want only to curl up on my cot with my thin sheets and die, but Monsieur is in a celebratory mood. He opens a bottle of his favorite whiskey and orders Chinese, which I find unbelievable since two duffel bags of dead American sit on the basement floor.

When the Chinese food arrives, we sit next to the filled and sealed bags. Monsieur pours himself a generous portion of whiskey, then downs the entire tumbler in a large gulp. He belches and pours another. With a grunt, he pushes the thick glass toward me. I dare not decline. My ear still rings from his earlier strike, a reminder of what any delay in following his commands brings me.

I take a tentative sip from the dark liquid that smells like paint thinner. The liquid leaves a blazing trail to my stomach, and I erupt in a violent coughing fit, thinking Monsieur has poisoned me. I retch, sputtering, to his enjoyment, evoking deep belly laughs. He always laughs at my expense.

"Jesus Christ, Souris, you can't hold your liquor." He looks at me as if he just had an epiphany. "Connais-tu Jésus?" *Do you know of Jesus?* "Or do you savages pray to the sun or wooden totem poles? Or water sprites?" He slides a white carton of food and two wooden chopsticks toward me.

He has traveled to my country enough times to know we Ghanaians are as Christian as he is supposed to be, but I temper myself. He might be in a playfully insulting mood, pretending we have suddenly bonded through the dismemberment of a human, but I still tread carefully. He can strike as quickly as a rattlesnake and is just as trusting. He takes another drink, straight from the bottle this time, because the cup from which I sipped has undoubtedly been tainted to him.

"Menim Yesu." *I know Jesus,* I answer in my language.

The alcohol blooms a slow burn in my belly, and I do not care for how queasy it is making me feel. Monsieur's movements are dulling. His speech comes out in a slow drawl. I do not trust him. He is testing me, like with the staircase. The food on the ground is a test. He wants to see if I will slip and lower my guard. Then he will do to me what he did to her and stuff my cut-up parts into another of those waterproof bags.

The psychological warfare he plays with me over the overflowing box of Chinese food is damning. My stomach cramps violently at the aroma wafting from the hot meal. The thin vegetable soup he gave me for lunch earlier is long gone.

He shovels long, thick noodles into his mouth, giving me and the carton he left for me sidelong glances. "Eh? Don't you want this?" he says in French. "What is your problem?" he tries in Twi.

I wish he would stop speaking in my father's tongue. Monsieur's is not the last Twi I want to hear before I die. But luckily, he switches back to French, which I used to think was the language of love, but now . . .

"J'ai entendu dire que ton père était un porc. C'est vrai, Souris?"

My gut twists when he calls Papa *swine*.

He is becoming annoyed at my refusal to respond, but he is unable to see how my fists ball and unfurl with each passing second. Or how my muscles are tightening as I wish he'd shut up before I lose myself, death be damned.

The alcohol makes him meaner. "You understand me, stupid little cunt? I heard il a pleuré comme une chiffe molle quand il a été renversé."

I look down at my hands. No, Papa did not scream like a little bitch when Paul had him run through.

"Your brothers also squealed like dirty pigs when Attah and his men fucked them. Est-ce vrai?"

Lies. Attah and his men murdered them. Took my father's head.

He sneers. "La tête de ton père aurait été belle sur mon mur de trophées, non? Même si ce n'est pas moi qui l'ai tué." *Your father's head would have looked nice on my wall of trophies, yes? Even if it wasn't my kill.*

Then Monsieur begins to laugh at me.

So far, nothing he's said has moved me to act, not even when he grips my thigh so roughly a bruise immediately begins to form. A bruise on top of a bruise on top of a bruise. My molten rage at the lies about my family is white hot, otherworldly. It is a feeling I have never experienced, a feeling that is awakening me from the deepest of slumbers.

My family died honorably. They gave their lives for me, for me to live this damnable life as someone's mewling pet. No, this cannot be what their deaths end up meaning. I, in this place, cannot be the legacy of the Asyms of N'nkakuwe.

My fingers grope the floor around my feet.

His laughter sends me back to the village, to the laughter of the men when they violated me. The sound of him drowns out all logical thought. He is all I hear when I snap.

I round on him, bringing up the wooden chopstick in a swirling rush.

"Ne parlez jamais de mon père ou de mes frères. Fils de pute." *Never speak of my father or my brothers. You son of a bitch.*

His eyes are so huge they are nearly all white at my speaking in his language.

My arm arcs and, with all my might, drives the chopstick into the closest thing. Robach's right cheek. The cheap wood pierces his flesh, snapping when it hits teeth. He is too surprised to react swiftly, and it is all I need.

Before Monsieur has a chance to recover, before he becomes the predator and I the prey again, I pounce on him. I am a primal, animalistic creature grabbing one of the knives from the bloody plastic sheet. I stab him, pushing the blade to its hilt. He reels, lashing out at me, catching me on the cheek with the back of his hand. It destabilizes me, but only slightly. I am back on him quicker than he can recover.

He rolls, bellowing and knocking the knife from where I impaled him. I leap on his back, wrapping my arm around his neck, trying to choke the life out of him. I cannot. He is too broad, his throat too thick, for my malnourished body. But the rage his laughter incited breathed new life into me. I do not release him.

The knife is on the floor, unreachable. He grunts, whirling in dizzying attempts to get me off. I cling to him, safer on his back than at his front. I claw at his face, my grunts matching his. We crash backward into his worktable.

I ignore the pain, daring to let one hand scoop up the closest instrument within my reach. I plunge scissors—long, shiny, silvery, extremely pointy ones—into his exposed pink neck, into the artery pulsating against his skin.

I pull the scissors out. And drive them back in.

Again.

Again.

I do not stop. I jab their sharp edge into every soft part of him. I force myself to continue even while my strength is draining. It is not easy, killing a person. It is exhausting work. But I must finish him because to let him live is not an option.

He staggers, dropping heavily to his knees, pitching me forward. His blood spews and drips all over us. He topples forward, clutching himself, writhing, grunting curses.

I scamper on all fours toward him, climb onto him, and straddle his upper chest, slicing, stabbing. His curses turn to groans for mercy. How dare he ask me—Souris—for mercy, after what he has done to me. After what he did to the woman. After what he made *me* do to her.

I carve deep trenches into his skin. He grapples for purchase, but his strength is nearly depleted, and his fight against me is feeble. We are bathing in his blood. There is so much of it. I do not stop until his arms fall to his sides with a wet splat. I lean forward to watch his eyes darken as the last vestiges of his evil soul leave his body.

Blood bubbles up as his lips try to form words.

"Souris?" he asks, eyes filled with wonder.

"Aninyeh," I correct, so close our noses nearly touch.

I have seen plenty of horror movies where the villain leaps up at the last moment. I wait until I see him pass into death, and when he is gone, to hell, I curse him to an eternal life where he is sold like a slave and chopped up into a million little pieces, over and over again. Forever.

I finally tear my eyes from him, noticing his carton of noodles is splattered with blood. I pull over the carton that was meant for me. I suppose this was his payment to me, his gift for helping him rid himself of the inconvenient woman. I open the carton, inspecting its contents. I sniff the food, finding it unremarkable.

I remain on top of him, using him like a piece of furniture, while I eat. The congealed noodles are cold, not dissimilar to gooey worms. It is the worst thing I have ever put in my mouth—maybe not the worst; there was the ear of the guard at the Compound. I toss the mess between the newly dead Monsieur Robach and the bags of dead American.

In the bathroom, I wash his blood from my face and hands. I rinse the taste of those noodles and Monsieur's blood from my mouth. I search the basement for any articles of clothing I can change into, and in a box, underneath a workbench, behind some plastic containers, I find the clothes I arrived from Kumasi in: a pair of white Keds sneakers, a pair of jeans that are slightly too big, and a sweatshirt with a My Little Pony character on it.

With the scissors in hand, I walk up those elusive stairs. I push open the door into the dark kitchen. Monsieur's keys hang on a wooden key rack, and I pluck them off. His black leather wallet is on the counter, and I take it too. The air that greets me when I walk through the front door and close it behind me is cold, pure, and crisp. It is a wonderful smell. It smells like freedom.

It is in the driver's seat of his car that I nearly break down, the events of the night rushing at me like poltergeists. I am bone tired but cannot believe I am alive and Monsieur is not. I cannot believe I have escaped. I cannot comprehend that I am alone for the first time since this horrible nightmare began. There are no guards. No weeping girls or screaming ones. No murderous psychopathic killer making me his pet dog. There is just me.

However, now is not the time to loiter, because I cannot tempt fate and allow one of his neighbors to see me. I will not be recaptured, and I must leave from this place. Monsieur's car is a manual shift, and while I do not know much about driving, Uncle Daniel taught me the basics in one. So I manage as best I can and flee in Monsieur's car.

I drive until the car runs out of gas, managing to follow the signs heading toward the city. The car makes it nearly to Paris before it rolls to a stop. I leave it stranded by the side of the road and walk the rest of the way. There is a coat of Monsieur's in the car, more money in the pockets, and in his glove box a hunting knife. I rifle through his wallet for anything I can use. Credit cards are out. They will only bring questions I cannot answer. There are bills stuffed in the wallet, thankfully. Not much, but enough.

I take it all, even the coat, which I abhor wearing, but I am no idiot. It is freezing out there. The walk in this cold, strange land lasts forever before I finally see city lights. Every time cars pass, I run from the road, hoping no one sees me. What if Monsieur's people have found him and are looking for me? What if the authorities? Or Paul? Those questions drive me into the shadows to hide.

In Paris, I spend several nights in the streets, sleeping in alleys cloaked in darkness. I shy away from populated areas. No one sees the dirty, crazy-looking girl roaming the streets. She is but a ghost with her hunting knife at the ready, the scissors too. They are my trophies.

Newspapers tell me I have spent six months with Robach. The time with him and at the Compound has conditioned me for these cold, often wet nights wrapped in whatever I can find next to steam vents to keep warm. I do not go hungry, knowing about the currency from my studies with Papa.

I live off hot black coffee and sandwiches with delicious meats piled high in them. Soon, my money will run out, and I will need to figure out how to get more. But that is a thought for another day. Because while life on these unfamiliar streets is hard, it is infinitely better than where I have been.

# 37

## AFTER

"Nena!" Elin was breathless.

Before she greeted her sister, Nena double-checked that the attendant hired for Elin's evening dinner closed and locked the door behind her. Even here Nena stayed on high alert, always making sure the security measures remained in place.

"Finally! You're here. I thought I'd have to deal with Mum and Dad all by myself." Elin twisted her perfectly done top bun, patted down her elegant wrap dress as if it were disheveled, which it wasn't.

"I said I was five minutes out."

"Mum's in rare form tonight. She's on Oliver like he cuffed the queen's jewels."

Nena's lips quirked. "Maybe he did," she answered, following Elin into the living room, where her parents stood with a tall man wearing a finely tailored suit. They turned when Nena entered.

She approached the trio. Oliver had an immaculate low haircut that twinkled in the room's light. He was pleasant looking, and Nena could appreciate why Elin had taken to him. Intelligence wafted from him like pheromones. When he saw her, he broke out into a wide smile. Nena inclined her head in response, trying to appear equally pleasant.

"Hello, Mum, Dad." She allowed her mother to pull her into a quick embrace and her father to dot her cheek with a light kiss. They knew she couldn't tolerate extended displays of affection.

"All is well?" Dad asked.

"It is," she replied, stepping closer to the man of the hour. Elin took her spot next to him, wrapping her hand around his bicep.

"Nena, this is Oliver. Oliver, my sister, Nena."

Oliver's grin widened, yet he seemed not at ease with his environment. Perhaps he was nervous about meeting their parents. His father didn't seem to be there yet.

"Good to finally meet you, Nena," Oliver said, his voice a deep baritone that held a hint of an accent. She didn't know why she'd assumed he was born in England like Elin, who was the only natural-born Brit in their family. Nena and their parents still held traces of their homelands' original accents fused within their British one.

"Hi," Nena said, assessing Oliver.

He said, "I've heard a lot about you. Almost feel as if I know you."

Nena's eyes slid to Elin, accusatory. Sometimes Elin talked too much.

"Really?" she asked, unamused. Oliver returned her assessment with a cool, curious look, as if he were mining for something hidden deep within her. His scrutiny was annoying, but she shook it off, thinking he was just trying to get in good with her.

Whether his mysteriousness was good or bad, the jury was still out, although Oliver Douglas didn't register as a foe. He had a nerdy quality to him that Nena was surprised Elin liked.

Elin cleared her throat, trying to mask her guilt as she announced, "Dinner's ready. Shall we proceed to the dining room? The chef made beef Wellington." Under her breath, Nena heard her mutter, "The sooner we start, the sooner this blasted shit can be over."

It was a thought on which they both agreed.

Elin grabbed Nena's wrist, slowing the two of them as the rest of the group headed toward the dining room. "Don't even think about shagging off and leaving me by myself either," she said, properly reading the sister she knew all too well.

Nena offered a slight shrug, twisting from Elin's grasp to join the rest of the family. She supposed she could wait a little longer to see what fate had in store for her.

———

"Is your father typically averse to being on time?" Delphine Knight asked, disdain permeating her tone and the air around the dinner table. She couldn't stand when people were late and said it showed their disregard for others' time. Thus, the reason they started dinner without Lucien Douglas.

Noble cleared his throat as a gentle warning. *Not in front of the guest.* Nena ate a forkful of perfectly cooked beef Wellington while Elin shot a hostile look at their mother.

Oliver remained occupied with his dinner, reluctantly pulling his eyes up to meet the hard gaze of Mrs. Knight. "Yes, ma'am, he sends his apologies and is on his way as we speak. He promises the business that held him will please you and the Council."

"Understandable," Noble said, sipping his drink. "That is our kind of business, right, dear?" He sent a pointed look at his wife.

"Hmm," Delphine answered through tightly closed lips, spearing a sautéed green bean.

The doorbell rang, followed by security chimes, indicating one of the servers had answered it.

Nena, who'd said very little until now, added, "It's a nice idea to come bearing good news when you've kept everyone waiting." She rather liked when Delphine's ire was directed at high-level members.

Elin glared, her fork clattering onto her plate. "Oh, now you speak."

"When there is something worth saying."

Before Elin could retort, one of the attendants entered, followed by their newest guest.

"Ah, there he is," Oliver announced, pushing his chair back to greet his father.

Noble got out of his seat, as did Elin. Delphine plastered on a frosty smile, as frosty as the white-chocolate-and-raspberry-truffle ice cream that would be their dessert.

Nena took her eyes off the son and landed them on Lucien Douglas as he shook Noble's hand warmly, clapped her father's back, then ended their handshake greeting with a loud snap of their intertwined fingers. The greeting of the Tribe.

Her vision tunneled. Background noises and sights fell away. The blood rushing in her eardrums was deafening as the room suddenly became unbearably small. Lucien's eyes connected with hers before his gaze left her, moving on to her mother.

*At least the blade was sharp, eh? Clean right through, Attah. Well done.*

Paul. Lucien Douglas was Paul?

The sight of him made her gut constrict with a fear she hadn't known for years. Her stomach roiled, and her mouth slickened, her body rejecting the food she had consumed. She stood up too quickly, causing the tableware to clatter, startling the others. She murmured apologies as she rushed from the room, the back of her hand to her mouth to keep from becoming sick.

She barely made it to the restroom, where she vomited into the toilet in violent heaves. Her body was burning and freezing simultaneously until there was nothing left at all. Her head pounded. The tortured screams of her people, mixed with his men's laughter at her, visions of Paul poking and prodding at her father's decapitated head, all a cacophony of hell. All brought on by Paul, who had made her into nothing.

And what was worse was that he hadn't recognized her. That was clear enough by the way his eyes had moved past her. He hadn't remembered who she was. After all he'd taken from her, the least he could do was to know her when she fucking saw her!

Her hand moved to her push daggers, their sheaths hidden as part of the design of her belt. She itched to use them on his throat. She thought about the Glock she had stashed in the kitchen that Elin didn't know she kept for "just in case."

*Kill him now,* her mind shrieked. Sweat dotted her brow in the increasingly hot room. She wobbled to her feet, feeling weak. She grasped the sides of the sink, waving a hand under the faucet to activate the sensor's release of water.

*End him,* the voice continued to command. *Now, while he's here.* And she would. She turned to go, then stopped, the rational side of her pushing past. A summit of intergalactic proportions raged in her mind, her fists clenching and unclenching.

*I can't kill him.*

*Why not? He won't see it coming, like we didn't back then.*

*He is a Council member. He's untouchable. I cannot kill him now.*

*All these years, and he lives and thrives. He is supposed to be dead.*

*I cannot kill him with his son watching.*

*Had he the same consideration when he forced Papa to watch his sons murdered or you raped? Had he any concern for you when he commanded that your father lose his head?*

*Fine. Then I cannot kill him with my family here.*

The voice pushing her to kill Paul stopped. Because her rational side was right. She couldn't kill Paul with her family there. She would not put them in harm's way, executing a Council member as he dined at the home of the High Council's daughter. That Elin and Oliver were seeing each other inextricably linked Paul to Noble, and if she killed him now, everyone would think Noble had decreed it as a power grab for Gabon and whatever other power Paul had.

She was no monster, unlike him. She wouldn't kill him in front of his child as he had slaughtered her father before her eyes, leaving her with a lifetime of memories and nightmares.

She wouldn't do any of that. At least, not here.

# 38

## BEFORE

The screams in my dreams drive me awake with visions of Monsieur's bloody body coming for me. The night is wet, with thick drops of water that douse you all the way through. Earlier, I made a nest for myself, burrowed within shrubs at the base of a tree in a small park. Sleeping among the trees reminds me of the openness of home, where we did not have all these tall buildings to blot out the sun.

There is a street near the park, and across from it is an upscale hotel called Le Monantique Hotel. It is busy at all hours of the day and night. The people who bustle in and out look wealthy, hopping into cars that look more like small spaceships.

Based on my calculations, I have been on my own for a week and am growing used to the city's smells, sounds, and people—both good and bad. No one sees me, which I like. I can walk among people without them giving me a second glance. This makes me witness to many things—both good and bad.

At the corner across from the hotel is a small all-night store. They have good hot chocolate, and tonight, I convince myself to get warm and buy a cup. Besides, I notice two men hanging around. I have not seen them around before, and they shift their gazes everywhere, as if they're nervous about something. They huddle together, casting furtive glances toward the hotel's rich patrons. I cannot place the warning emanating from them, but I do not like their look. They could be here for me; who knows? They could be police, which puts me on high alert. But a burst of frigid wind distracts me, and my thoughts switch back to the store's heater and hot chocolate to warm me.

The bell tinkles when I enter the store. I shake the water off, surveying the room. The overhead light gives off a bluish-white hue, and the store is practically empty, save the clerk behind the counter. He doesn't care much for me.

He barely looks up from his tabloid, saying in clipped French, "Make it quick."

I walk the aisles. My stomach growls, reminding me I have not eaten in hours, wanting the rows of tightly wrapped food. But money is low. Papa said stealing was dishonorable, but I have done many dishonorable things in the name of survival. I think he would understand.

Up and down the rows, I walk, passing a woman dressed in fur and heels. My fingers graze all the incredible merchandise. I slow in the health-and-beauty aisle when a familiar bottle on the shelf catches my eye—*Olay* written in black script.

I know it immediately. I grab the bottle labeled *Tester* and open the cap, bringing the bottle to my nose. I inhale deeply, suddenly transported to a time when I knew nothing but happiness.

Memories flood me with my mother's scent, filling me with the sensation Mama is around the corner, sautéing chili spices and onions in grease for the shito pepper sauce she cooks to accompany the kenkey. The generous portions of fresh fish are dusted with flour and salt, ready to be fried. My tears are so thick they blur my vision.

I must have it. It is Mama.

I cap the bottle and slip it into my rucksack. There is not enough money for it, but I do not care.

An idea dawns. If I found Mama's scent, then perhaps this store has Papa's too. Seconds later, I am staring at it in the fragrances section. I grab the heavy glass bottle, spray it into the air, and step beneath the mist. Tiny droplets shower my skin as if enveloping me in Papa's deep embrace. He is all around me. Overcome, I let out a small cry, then clamp my hand over my mouth to stifle it.

It has been so long since I was near him, since I felt his warmth. His smell made me feel protected. Mama's scent made me feel loved, the feeling you get when all is right. I put Hugo in my sack too.

"He's seen you, darling," a melodious voice says from behind. I turn, facing the fur-clad woman from earlier. I must look like a caged animal. Still in my bag, my fingers release the cologne and reach for the scissors. I will kill again before giving up these items.

She points to the ceiling. I follow her gloved hand, noticing the sizable cylindrical mirror in the corner. In it, I see the clerk, rigid as a board, glaring at me from behind the counter. I weigh my options. I doubt this woman can take me, and if I am fast enough, I can run past him and never be seen again.

That is, unless he locked the door.

"It's locked."

I draw back. How could she possibly know my thoughts?

We are at what my brother Josiah would have called a stalemate. The woman is regal like an African queen. She smiles, seeming kind enough; however, I will not be fooled.

"Where are your parents, child?"

I look between the mirror and her.

"Okay," she says, also checking for the clerk, who has now moved from the counter. "Ces articles, la lotion et l'eau de Cologne. Tu en as besoin? Ils signifient quelque chose de spécial pour toi, non?"

*Yes, I need them, the lotion and cologne. They are very special to me. They are my mother and my father. I need them more than I need to breathe.* But I refuse to say any of it aloud.

Her French is like musical bells. Mine sounds more like garbled marbles.

"I'm calling the police for this vagrant." The clerk slows to a stop beside the woman. "I've seen her before coming in and out of my store, always scheming things to steal!"

They face me. Two sentinels against one. My hand remains on my scissors. I do not want any trouble. I wish to harm no one. But I am leaving with these items in my rucksack, and no one will stop me. My understanding of the stalemate is clear. Only one of us will be victorious, and I mean that one to be me.

# 39

## AFTER

Elin's flat was two thousand plus square feet, but for Nena, it felt no bigger than the Hot Box. By sheer will, she kept herself from leaping over the dinner table to attack Lucien Douglas with the salad fork. She focused on pushing her food from one end of the plate to the other, unable to tolerate the act of chewing and swallowing. All his presence did was make her want to vomit.

Finally, she was able to get some space, venturing out onto the spacious balcony. They were in there laughing, talking, him most of all. Her father thoughtfully answered Paul's incessant questions and batted away his multitude of platitudes. *He's so slick,* she seethed. *Playing it up for Dad so he can be a big man, the Council.* Her back against the railing, she scowled at him through the sliding glass doors. He had them all fooled. Had them all believing he was a friend when he was really the epitome of a foe.

The salty, warm Miami air did nothing to quell her urge to kill him. Her body shook from her fight to control herself. She was afraid she wouldn't be able to hold off much longer. Thoughts of what Paul had done to her, to her family, fed her rage. She tried to clear her head, remain present and focused.

How had he survived all these years? How had he made it into the folds of the Tribe? She squeezed herself against the corner of the glass railing. So deep was she in her murderous machinations that she nearly missed him standing from the group, pulling a cigar case from his blazer pocket, and approaching the balcony.

Her finger found a blade. He passed through the sliding glass doors held open by one of the servers. She watched him close the gap between them, wearing the same brilliant smile from so many years ago.

Her stomach constricted. All these years believing him gone, believing she had survived him, only for it all to come crashing around her ears in the space of an hour. He was a beautiful monster, aged like fine wine. He looked better than she remembered. Her family was dead, and there was Paul, living better than he had before.

"Beautiful out here, yes? I find the sea air and the lights of the city refreshing, don't you? Spectacular. You don't see sights quite like this in Lagos." He stopped a foot away, his back to the party inside. He pulled out a lighter that was more a torch, pushed the tip of his cigar into the flame, and puffed until it caught.

Every molecule of her was electrified, yearning to toss out all her years of training and run him through with her blades.

When she wouldn't answer, he squinted. Took in her features. Considered her for a long while. "I'm not sure what it is." He held his index finger up, shaking it as if he were trying to shake out a memory. His vile cigar in his other hand. "But damned if you don't seem familiar. Have we met in passing? Maybe you attended an event with Oliver and Elin? Accompanied your father on Tribe business?"

This was the moment. This was when she'd declare who she was and kill him when he attacked her. She could claim self-defense, and the Tribe would forgive it. She straightened her shoulders, pulling herself to her full height.

"Could be we met sixteen years ago, in a little town where you beheaded my father and then sold me to a homicidal psychopath." Her words came out low, measured. She could fling the devil incarnate from the balcony railing and watch his body break and bleed on the grounds below.

She zeroed in on him, watching as his curiosity moved from surprise to a split second of fear; then finally he shuttered himself from her, regaining his composure. His relaxed, controlled smile slid across his face.

"For true? Aninyeh?" he asked, his amazement evident. "This is you? Still alive?"

"As are you." She bared her teeth.

He barked a laugh, slapping his palms together as if he were with a long-lost family member. "I had heard the bastard Robach was dead years ago." He paused, drawing back to look her over like some proud uncle. "I knew you had it in you, girl. A survivor. I knew it!"

Her eyes narrowed. As if he'd done her a favor.

"And beautiful." He put his hand to his chin, cheerfully. He looked at her with appreciation. He clapped once. "You would fetch quite a price on the market now, Nena. Much more than before." Another casual smile, sickening her.

He must have seen something in her eyes, because he waved his hand. "It's a joke, Aninyeh, a joke. That time was eons ago, yes? Haven't we grown, you and I? Matured? Look at you now. One of the Knights. A daughter. I gave you this life." He bowed low, magnanimously. "You are welcome!"

Her blades nearly came out at his audacity. She couldn't let her emotions cloud her judgment.

Witt's training during hand-to-hand combat replayed in her mind. *Never take things personally.*

No. This was personal, very personal.

Paul's laughter died, realization dawning on him. He looked at her deeper, reading her anger. "That explains Attah," he mused softly.

She didn't respond.

"He was valuable to me, you know. I even paid good money to get him off on those charges. I had members of the jury in my pocket to ensure no conviction."

"Then why have the Council dispatch the prosecutor?"

"I like to hedge my bets. And I wanted to see just how much the Council wanted me. Always have a plan B, dear girl."

Silence had always been her best quality. She needed it more than anything now. She kept reminding herself not to react. *Don't be foolhardy, Nena.* She struggled to believe that Paul being here was not a mirage or a nightmare, that he was really here in flesh and blood, because up until this point—even after Attah Walrus—she'd never truly believed Paul could still be alive.

Her silence was unnerving, and Paul cast cautious looks at the caged tiger in front of him. He looked back at all the unknowing people inside. He stepped to the glass railing, looking down. She could push him, she thought. Right now. She gripped her hands behind her back.

"Your new family—these Knights—are good, generous, powerful people. You've received a second chance, a better chance. You're not wallowing in the dirt, wed to some poor goat-herding chieftain. You sit atop the throne of modern-day African royalty."

He waited a long beat. When he spoke next, he dropped all traces of earlier joviality. "You would do well to let bygones be bygones. You have made your point with Attah. Don't you agree?"

This was the Paul she knew and loathed. Her mouth twitched. So many things she wanted to say. Attah's death was not enough. Not by a long shot.

"Aninyeh, let this pass. Your sister loves my son and vice versa. My strongholds in Gabon and links with its government and other factions will further solidify the Tribe's power. But if you tell anyone who I am and alter the scenario . . ." He sighed, looking at her solemnly. "It will all go to shit for the Tribe . . . for your family." He gave her a long, pointed look that speared her all the way through. "You know what I can do, Aninyeh."

When she refused to answer, he nodded, taking his leave.

Only she knew how dangerous Paul was. Only she knew the gravity of his presence. To drive home his implicit threat, he went to Elin, bending to kiss her cheek. He moved to Delphine, taking her hand and feathering it with a light peck. Delphine smiled, warming up to him. He clapped Noble on his shoulder as he grabbed his outstretched hand to pull him upright and grasp him in a warm embrace. They shook hands again and snapped their intertwined fingers. Then, while holding her father, he turned to her, still alone on the balcony. He smiled at her, a smile as treacherous as she remembered.

Beside Paul, her dad turned, spotting Nena on the balcony and breaking into his familiar, dashing smile. Noble gave her a boisterous wave, beckoning for her to join them. She shook her head, begging off. He waved at her in a joking *forget you then* gesture, mistaking her actions as one of her usual solitary moods.

She tore her gaze from her dad, hating how close he was standing next to the man who'd killed her papa. Paul, alive and more well than he ever deserved to be, was watching her with a calculating smirk playing on his lips. Paul's message was plain and simple, a reminder of how easily he could touch the most important people in her life again.

But now Paul also had something important to him. Didn't he? Her eyes shifted to the young man with his arms wrapped around her sister. He had his son.

# 40

BEFORE

The woman in the fur coat is the first to break our three-way stare down.
Maybe she reads the determination on my face, a look that says I will
not give these items up without a fight. I know I can do it, fight . . .
until the death. Once you have killed your first, another may not be
as difficult.

"Monsieur, it's fine. She's picking up items I asked for."

"Madame? How so? You two did not come in together."

She turns to me with a hint of a smile. "But darling, you need to
get the new ones. Not the testers." She steps to the shelf, picking up a
box of Hugo, and holds it out to me.

"Madame, no. She is nothing but a misérable, a vagabonde. The
police can handle her accordingly."

*Wretch* and *vagrant*. Two more names to add to my growing list.

The regal queen rears on the clerk. I would never want to be the
recipient of the look she gives him. "You will take my payment." She
pauses while the weight of her words settles on him. "Wait for us at
the counter. Elle est à ma charge et nous achèterons tout ce que nous
prendrons. C'est compris?" *She is with me, and we will buy everything
we collect. Understand?*

Shrinking beneath Madame's glower, the clerk opens and closes his mouth several times before stumbling back to the front of the store and waiting as told. Through the mirror, he glares at me. At her. She holds the box out to me again. She gives me an encouraging nod. Hesitantly, I take it.

"Don't put it in your bag yet. We need to pay first, and I don't want to give him any reason to call the authorities." She waits for a response. When none comes, she says, "Tell you what, put the test lotion back, too, and pick up a sealed box." She points to little baskets stacked at the end of each aisle. "Get whatever you want, but do not steal anything. I will pay for all of it. Deal?"

Her kindness does not make any sense to me. She doesn't know me. I am a nobody to her, a vagrant, as the clerk said. Why give me a second thought? And what will she want in return? Because one thing I have learned is there is always a price. My eyes shift to the shelf, to the mirror, then back to her.

Finally, I nod quickly. She rewards me with a smile that surprisingly makes me shy. She leaves me, heading toward the counter. While she gives the clerk commands, ignoring his protests and insisting that he take her money for anything I want, I pull the tester bottle from my sack and put it back in its rightful place.

"Madame, vous m'avez donné trop d'argent."

"Then give the child the change."

She moves away from the counter, about to leave with whatever item she came in to purchase. As the clerk scurries to unlock the trap he set for me, she looks at me one last time. It's as if she wants to say more, then thinks better of it. She pushes open the door, the bell chiming her departure.

My rucksack is laden with my bounty. I have Olay, Hugo Boss, plenty of tightly wrapped packages of food, hot chocolate, and €284 in change. The door does not fully close behind me before I tear into the sack, grabbing a package of Oreo cookies. The onslaught of cookies and hot chocolate sends a jolt of sugary energy coursing through my veins.

I catch a whiff of my father's scent, feeling gutted when for the briefest of moments, I believe he is behind me and only empty air greets me instead. But now, anytime I want, I have Papa's protection and Mama's love. Anytime I want, I can spray a cloud or squeeze a drop, and they will be right there with me.

Thoughts of my parents consume me to the point I take little notice of my surroundings. I pass the dark and narrow breezeway next to the market. There is scuffling coming from within, which I figure is rats. They can be big, nearly the size of kittens. But when I hear a sound that sounds more human than rat, like a woman's voice, it gives me pause.

"Don't," the woman says.

"Keep ahold of her. Ne la laisse pas s'échapper." *Don't let her get away.* The second voice is male, menacing.

I know the woman's voice. Quickly, I take cover, peeking around the corner of the building. I strain to make out the dark shadows, trying to sort out the moving shapes—two, maybe three. I sweep my eyes up and down the street, looking for help as I bite the insides of my mouth. The safety of the park feels miles away instead of right across the street. The street was bustling not too long ago, yet now there is no one in sight. There is only me. I look longingly in the direction of the park. This woman's trouble is not my concern. I should mind my business.

*As she minded hers back in the store, Aninyeh?*

It is not me who asks the question. It is like a blend of my mama and papa. I shake my head to clear my muddled thoughts. Their scents are clouding my judgment.

*Or did she help you?*

My feet refuse to move. The woman was kind to me when she had no reason to be. She protected me, helped me. The heaviness of my rucksack is proof of it. I owe her, and Papa said to pay your debts, the good and bad.

203

Nothing comes without a price, and it seems my time to pay is upon me.

I consider my options. I have the scissors, which served me well. But I choose the knife. First, I stow my rucksack in a corner, where I hope it remains until my return, if I return. Then carefully, I follow the voices.

"She's loaded. Look at her jewels. Maybe we should take her instead, hold her for ransom. Her people will pay."

The first man's back is to me; he is kneeling in front of a prone figure. His partner hovers over his shoulder, watching. He is the one I take down first, thrusting the knife into his neck until its tip comes out the other side. He lets out a gurgle as his hands grab the point of the blade. The blood spurts like an unclogged spigot, steaming in the cold.

I yank the blade out when he begins to fall. I need to close the gap between me and the second man before I lose the element of surprise. The second man is too fixated on the woman to notice his partner is gone.

"Shut her racket before someone hears," he says.

The woman moans as he attempts to take her jewelry. He hits her.

"Maybe you're right, Jacques. Maybe we'll take her shit and kill her." He grunts as he struggles with her, unaware his friend Jacques is a corpse.

The woman struggles desperately. He slaps her again, harder. I can tell because I hear her head smack the ground. It reminds me of the woman in Monsieur's basement. I move to grab the man's neck—I seem to like necks—but he catches my movement in his peripheral vision. He twists, yelping a curse, and knocks me back. I fall, tripping over his dead friend.

"Jacques!" He sees his friend beneath me and lunges. With a dead man at my back and his partner's weight on top of me, I am pinned. The man's grasp on me is weak, slick with water and grime. He punches me on the side of my head.

*Mon dieu!* Stars flash in my vision.

I have come too far to die at the hands of this thief, to be a victim of yet another man. Again, my will to survive ignites me, taking me to the primal place, as it did a week ago.

We grapple, and I lose the knife. He launches curses and squeezes, trying to get a firm hold around my neck. I try to hold him off with one hand, my knees digging into his belly. My other hand roots around the oily ground for the dropped knife. The only things saving me are my legs, but I do not have enough leverage to push him off. I can only keep him at bay. Until my fingers touch something hard beneath me. I yank on it, desperate for something to save me. My hand closes around the handle, and I realize it is a gun. I have never held one. I do not know if it will work. There is no time to think. So as the man pushes his weight on me, I lift the gun, trying to get a better angle and my finger on the trigger. I point away from me. I pull.

A flash in the dark. An explosion in my ear that briefly robs me of my hearing.

The man topples over on top of me, dead.

I lie there, sandwiched between him and his equally dead friend, sucking in mouthfuls of burning air.

"Est ce que ça va?" the woman croaks. I can hear her moving. "Merci de m'avoir sauvé. Es-tu blessée?"

She repeats in English, "Are you okay? Thank you for saving me. Are you hurt?"

Instinct tells me to run, and I need to do so because if I remain here any longer, the woman will call the authorities, because now there are two dead men, and she must. My nest is no longer safe for me. The police will have too many questions I do not want to answer.

I will never be taken by them—or anyone again. I shift beneath the weight of the man, wiggling free from within the cocoon of the dead.

# 41

## AFTER

Through Nena's earbuds, Witt said, "Hold for the intel you requested."

Seconds later she watched a file download itself to her computer, then unzip and open. She tapped the mousepad, watching as the contents began popping up on her screen, images of the men as they had been long ago. Images of who Attah Walrus and Kwabena were now, both older, though Kwabena was still younger and much better looking.

"This info was buried so deep it was damn near impossible to find. That's why it took me a bit of time," Witt said apologetically.

If a week was a long time to gather intel, then Nena guessed he'd taken forever, but in the span of one night, she'd forgotten all about Bena. All she could think about was how Paul had slithered back into her life and threatened everyone and everything important to her.

She couldn't leave Elin's fast enough, pretending to feel unwell. Her mum had insisted on checking her temperature as if she were a child, all under the hawkish gaze of Lucien—Paul. She'd spent the rest of the night alternating between vomiting in her toilet and curling up in a ball on the floor of her bathroom. She'd awoken to the sound of an incoming call on her computer.

Witt hadn't let her appearance faze him. He regarded her with troubled eyes but continued with their business. The information flashing across Nena's screen woke her up, gave her something else to think about for the moment, something other than the stark terror she felt whenever she thought about Paul. She'd thought she was strong. She was a stone-cold killer. And yet, knowing he had been inches from her not twelve hours ago regressed her to fourteen all over again.

Kwabena now went by Kamil. He was in town, convenient. Had to come in because of Dennis Smith's death to handle their business dealings. And one of their businesses was a place called the Lotus Flower. She immediately recalled the photocopied business card from Cort's office. Okay. But where'd she seen it before that?

"It's a day spa," Witt was saying when she refocused on him. "Seems innocent enough."

Nena knew its true purpose because just like mental connections seemed to do, something clicked, and she remembered. "It's not," she said. "It's a front for human trafficking, and the people who 'work' there are being trafficked, most likely. If you check for business partners, you'll find the Cuban was a client of the spa."

Witt sat with the information for a moment. "Well, that's your proof right there, yeah?"

But was it enough? "The Council was willing to go off script, kill a man just doing his legitimate job, to gain more power and territory. Do you think they'll care that these guys were selling people?"

"Noble will care, and he'll set things to rights. This justifies your dispatch of Smith and will get your dad to look further into who backed them, like Lucien Douglas, for example."

Hearing the name of Paul's alter ego gave her a visceral reaction she wasn't sure she had masked fast enough.

"What is it?" Witt missed nothing.

She told him.

He might have been a master at showing no emotions, but this was too much. He gawked at her incredulously. "Are you sure?"

Nena managed to keep back a biting retort. She was tired of everyone asking if she was sure about these men. Their faces were forever seared into her mind.

"My God, how can this be?"

She wanted to say, *You tell me. After all, you're the one who was supposed to make sure he was gone.* But she didn't. She kept her mouth shut and her face impassive. She didn't need to say it, though, because Witt could read it in her face. He knew they hadn't been thorough enough. Nena placed her hand against her hot forehead, leaning back against the chair in her office and releasing the frustration and accusations she felt toward Witt and the Tribe at the moment. They were not the real villains here. They did not know, as she did, what chaos Paul was capable of, how he was always waiting just beneath the tranquil surface for the right moment.

"Someone within the Tribe is Paul's benefactor," Witt surmised. "Just like you guessed."

"Yup."

"Who?"

She shook her head. She couldn't even think of that now, and she told Witt as much. "I need to compartmentalize, to focus."

Witt warned, "If you dispatch Paul's third man, you'll poke the bear."

"Then he'll know I'm no longer the scared little village girl from before."

# 42

## BEFORE

The woman and I consider each other as we stand in the wreckage of the ordeal we have shared. She has a cut just above her eye, but despite the blood, disheveled clothes, and ripped pantyhose, she does not look too bad off. She does not even seem too shaken, which is perplexing. Surely a woman as high class as her should be quaking in her shoes, of which she is only wearing one.

"I should have been more careful. I saw those men hanging around before going into the store." She searches the ground, locating her purse and her phone within it. She places a call.

"I have something for the Cleaners, double order. Yes. In an alley across from my hotel. I'm leaving now," she says tersely, tenderly touching the cut. She ends the call, then turns back to me. I am concerned about my rucksack and wondering where I am going to sleep tonight, because the area will be too infested with police to stay in the park. "Noble is going to be angry with me."

I just look at her. Not sure who Noble is and why he would be angry with her for being attacked. He sounds quite the opposite of his name if that is the case. Not my business. I want only to return to my own life. However, the woman has other plans.

"Can you speak?" she asks in French.

I nod.

"Will you speak?" she asks in English.

I hunch my shoulders.

Her eyes narrow as my mistake dawns on the both of us: I understand English too.

"Where is your family?"

There is no way I will answer in either language.

She nibbles on her lip. She does not know what to make of me, nor I of her. I am still trying to figure out how I was tricked into disclosing anything about myself.

I wilt beneath her scrutiny. For the first time, I am ashamed of my appearance. Here I am, bundled in my clothes from Robach and the coat from his car, all caked with dirt and grime.

She inches closer but halts when I tense. "We need to leave here now. You cannot stay, or the Cleaners will take care of you too. Do you understand me?"

I do not see any issue with cleaners. I could use them. I remember watching, on the CCTV, cleaners pick up Monsieur's dirty clothes. But the way she's made them sound, maybe that is not what these cleaners do.

"For your trouble, will you return with me to my room? You can sleep in a nice bed and get real, hot food, not processed food from the store. And tomorrow, we can decide what the next step will be."

*Tomorrow? We?* She must be concussed. She speaks of us as a pair when there is only me, and *I* will be long gone.

She checks the area once more, gingerly stepping over the men. She pulls her lost shoe from a corner where it landed during the assault. Satisfied there is nothing of her left, she walks briskly to the street, toward the hotel, pausing to watch me root around for my knife under the foul man's body. I push him a little to pull it from under him, let his body fall back in place, and extract what dangled in his hand. Then I kick his corpse for good measure, feeling nothing as I look at the men. No remorse. No joy. Nothing at all.

I tug my rucksack out from where I stowed it. I sling it over my back and turn toward the park.

"Please," she says, "won't you come with me?"

I look toward the park. Look at her. Look at the hotel. What if she is like Paul or Bridget or Monsieur? What if she is worse? I cannot take the chance. I shake my head. She visibly deflates, sadness and disappointment washing over her face. It surprises me, is confounding. But she says nothing else and resumes her walk to the hotel.

I catch a whiff of my father's scent. What if she isn't like them? What if she's better, and this is Papa telling me to go with her?

I jog to her side and touch her elbow lightly. She stops, and I hold my closed fist out toward her. She looks at me, puzzled, then looks down. She opens her hand, and in it, I drop what I took from the dead man.

Her smile is the sun, warming me all the way through. My lips twitch in response, having long ago lost a reason to smile.

"Noble gave this bracelet to me for our fifteenth anniversary last month," she says.

I nod at her since it seems the appropriate thing to do.

"I'm Delphine," she says. "What's your name?"

My name. What do I tell her? The adults I have dealt with lately have not been kind to me, have betrayed me in every way possible. Am I making the right decision? But this lady has something about her that rings honest and safe.

I need safe.

We begin walking, crossing the street to the entrance of Le Monantique Hotel.

Who am I? I cannot be Aninyeh. I lost the privilege of her when she died with my family and my village. Whore and bitch, from Paul's men? Souris, from Monsieur? Wretch and vagrant, as the man in the store referred to me?

Who am I?

Like a ghost from the past, I pull a name no one has ever called me except Papa—his own special name for me. Then I look at the woman and answer, "My name is Nena."

# 43

## AFTER

"I didn't peg you for a cheeseburger-and-fries type of lady," Cort said. He opened the door of Jake's, looking up when the chimes announced their arrival.

Nena surveyed Jake's Burger Joint, the scene of her recent crime, noting the diner was bustling with the midday lunch crowd, very different from the night she and Georgia had been there. She was feeling a flood of emotions: anticipation for what she was preparing to do with Kwabena; a twinge of concern about when Witt had said she was "poking the bear"; a rush of worry about what the ease and quickness with which Paul was able to ingratiate himself in the Council meant for the Tribe and, even more so, for her family; and lastly, hope that none of what she had to do meant there would be a bigger target on Cort's back. She didn't want to think of any of that at the moment. Right now, Nena just wanted to enjoy a guilt-free afternoon with Cort and a burger and a milkshake.

Nena shrugged. "I'm a bacon-cheeseburger-and-fries type of lady," she replied.

She knew it meant she was a total glutton for punishment, or playing with fire, or both, that she'd suggested she and Cort meet here, of all places, when he'd proposed they grab lunch.

Cheryl wasn't on duty today. It was another pleasant-faced server wearing red and white. Nena chose her usual booth, selecting the side against the wall where she could see who came in and out.

Cort took another look out of the large-paned window at the busy street. He read the street signs. "You know," he said, his eyebrows furrowed in thought, "I know this place."

Nena knew what she wanted. It was the same order every time. "Yeah? Been here before, then?"

He shook his head. "Nah. There was a killing that happened here not too long ago. Two men affiliated with a local gang were killed."

"Are you investigating that too?" she asked innocently.

He refocused on his menu. "Nope. Doesn't fall under my jurisdiction." She forced herself to chuckle with him, all the while wondering again why she'd brought him there.

*Playing with fire, that's why,* is what her mum would say.

Perhaps Nena was.

Or perhaps she just wanted to be a normal woman for once. Go on a lunch date in the middle of Cort's workday with him in his business suit and talk about nothing and everything, all at the same time. She wanted to know him, and he her. First, she needed to know who she was—beyond being a killer. And she couldn't help wondering if the woman currently on her first lunch date was the woman she might have been.

"Earth to Nena."

She blinked away her surprise, forcing herself to return to the present, where Cort was smiling at her, and the server—Janice—was waiting with a knowing smile. Pen and paper at the ready.

"I'd be daydreaming, too, if I was sitting across from a man like that," Janice said conspiratorially.

Her boldness flushed Nena's cheeks with heat and made Cort look away sheepishly, as if women ogling him was new to him.

"And he's in a suit too. Ummph," Janice continued, swinging her long dark ponytail. Nena wondered how she could see through those extralong eyelashes. She wanted to touch them. Janice laughed at her patrons' unease. "What are ya having?"

When Janice finally left with her inappropriate comments and their order, Nena allowed herself to relax. She was too aware of Cort's eyes on her. They sat quietly because she didn't know what to say. This wasn't a job, and she was out of her element when it came to this stuff.

He said, "You're a mystery, you know that?"

"My mum says the same thing quite a bit," she replied, amused.

He squinted. "But I'm betting there's a story behind it. A reason for your distance and caution when you're around me." He sat back in his seat, throwing an arm across the top of the bench.

"Story?"

"Yeah," he said encouragingly. "Who are you?"

She opened her hands as if she didn't know what to say. "Nena Knight. I explained about my family and where I'm from. There's not much more story than that."

They paused when Janice returned with a tray heaped with their orders. Nena's usual of bacon cheeseburger, onion rings, and Coke—milkshake to go. Cort had decided on a grilled chicken club with fries and a Sprite. Nena judged his choice of a sandwich over a juicy burger.

"But there is a whole history I want to learn about."

Now she knew where Georgia got her chattering from. She swallowed her bite. "Like what?"

His eyes widened as if he might have offended her. "No. I don't mean to pry. It's the lawyer in me, I guess. Always questioning. I'm sorry. I just . . ." He shrugged, shaking his head. "I like you is all. I just want to get to know you."

She needed to ease up. Cort was being truthful. His questions weren't coming from a place of suspicion. He was truly interested in knowing who she was.

"You're very intuitive," she said, looking at him from beneath her eyelashes. "At reading people."

"You forgot what I do for a living?" He laughed, making her feel good inside.

She pursed her lips again. "Have you returned to Haiti?"

He shook his head. "Not since Peach was a baby. I send money every month as every good Haitian does, but I haven't made it back like I should."

"My parents do the same."

"Where to?" he asked slyly.

She raised an eyebrow at him. He was slick, trying to get her to talk. He gave her a sheepish grin.

She said, "I'm adopted, but my mum is also from Ghana, and my dad is from Senegal."

He gesticulated with his hands. *Go on.*

She let out a sigh, resigned to the fact Cort wouldn't let up until she opened up, and even more, that she wanted him to know about her.

"My mum found me living on the street, and they took me in. Been with them ever since." Nena looked intently at her plate of food. "They saved my life."

"They sound like great people."

"They are lovely. And that is all you're getting for now."

"Well, all right then," Cort said, laughing again as he dipped a fry in ketchup and popped it in his mouth. "You're the boss."

He grinned at her.

"Naturally," she replied, and before she realized what she was doing, Nena was grinning right back.

# 44

## BEFORE

The last time I had a night of uninterrupted sleep eludes me. So does the last time I slept without fear of harm, of being ripped out of whatever passed for sleep at someone's whim. Without the fear of death or recapture. Up until tonight, the idea of peaceful sleep has been unfathomable.

But when I fall asleep in Delphine's hotel room, on her lavish bed, which makes me feel I am sleeping on clouds, I sleep like the dead. I sleep so deeply I dream of my family, hoping they are at peace. In my dreams, Papa tells me to sleep, rest, let my traumatized mind and battered body recuperate.

When I wake, Delphine is fully dressed and on the phone, giving instructions in that take-charge tone I heard the night before. She notices I am awake, smiles at me, then turns back to her phone call. There is an important message in her actions. She is showing me there is trust. But I am not so trusting and again consider fleeing. I wonder if someone has found my nest and has taken it as their own in the short while I have been gone. Then I wonder about the men I killed the night before. Were they found? Did the Cleaners take them? Will the authorities come for me next? Is the woman on the phone with the police now, planning my capture?

I sit up in the bed. My own comfort confuses me because I cannot understand what compelled me to agree to staying here for the night, or how I could sleep the sleep of the dead when I haven't known a good night's sleep since leaving N'nkakuwe.

But I realize I am tired. Really tired. I am tired of living in the streets and of fighting every day with hunger and cold and fear and the threat of incarceration. I cannot yet put my finger on why, but she feels safe. So with my decision made, I remain. For now.

I swing my feet to the side of the bed and hop to the floor. My rucksack is still on the chair next to the bed, where I left it. I keep her in my periphery so I can track her. I peer into my sack, ensuring the Hugo and Olay were not disturbed. Monsieur's knife and scissors are there, too, along with the rest of my possessions. Everything is untouched.

I leave the rucksack, walking the length of the room to the large window. The world is bright and beautiful beyond the white curtains. The street bustles with people on their way to work or wherever they are going. There are no authorities. No police tape blocking the alley across the way. No one coming to question me about the murder of two would-be—what? Rapists? Robbers? Murderers? There is nothing, only me and her.

"Nena," she says, startling me.

I forgot I gave her my name the night before. My behavior is confounding. How is it I let my guard down with this stranger? Without knowing her true intent?

She holds her phone, wearing gorgeous red high heels, so high I wonder how she maintains balance in those things. Her black sweaterdress hugs her athletic but womanly frame. She reminds me of a Hollywood movie star from the times movies were black and white.

"Won't you have a shower?" she asks in English. "I took liberties and got some clothes for you. Breakfast is here when you're ready. Tea too."

"Thank you," I say, my voice coming out scratchy and unsure of its volume. I have not used it in so long it is alien to me.

I do as told, entering the luxurious bathroom, where I spend what feels like eternity cleaning every part of me. My hair is wild and rough without the lotions and oils Mama, then Auntie, helped me use back home. It is in knots, damaged, brittle, and broken. The state of my hair devastates me. It has always been my greatest joy.

To my delight, the shower water never turns cold. The room fills with so much steam I can barely see in front of me. I shower off all the grime, dirt, and blood. Monsieur's, the prostitute's, the men's, and mine—all cascade off me in rivulets. I wash until the water runs clean, and then I wash again. I do the same to my hair with the little tubes of shampoo and conditioner I find on the counter. I use the handheld showerhead in an attempt to wash inside of me until I can no longer tolerate the heat or pressure from the nozzle. I wish to be clean of all violations from the inside out.

When I am wrapped in fluffy white towels, beneath a turban of another towel, I wipe the mirror of condensation. I brush my teeth with the toothbrush given to me. I brush four times, then use Listerine. The golden liquid burns my mouth in such a way I gasp. It reminds me of the alcohol Monsieur made me drink before I killed him, so I do not think I will use it again.

I take more time to comb and brush through my softened hair. There is almond oil, a wide-tooth comb, and a brush. I oil my scalp and ends until they are soft enough to detangle the knots. The parts that are too fused together, I cut away with my scissors until my misshapen hair has some form again, a much, much smaller one. With hair this short I am a perfect likeness of my brothers, and it is like a stake in my heart as I grieve the loss of my family and my hair . . . my beautiful hair.

The woman has provided jeans, a pale-pink shirt, and an olive-green army-surplus jacket with plush lining that feels like heaven. After I lace up the russet combat boots that are my size, I assess myself in the mirror. I look like me again. I look like I belong somewhere and to someone. It makes me sad and elated. Guilt nibbles at me for my selfishness at being pleased by my appearance when appearance no longer means anything to my dead family.

She is on her phone again when I leave the bathroom and force myself not to rush to the breakfast table. I make myself choose wisely, knowing that overindulgence will mean getting sick later. I choose fruit, some scrambled egg, and bacon that is perfectly cooked, neither too crispy nor too limp. I have a large cup of hot chocolate with whipped cream.

She is still on her call when she joins me at the small table. She pours herself tea and sips from it as she continues to make travel plans, from the sounds of it. Hopefully she will allow me to fill my rucksack with any leftover food, of which there will be a lot, because who knows when my next meal will be. I think of a good argument for why she might let me leave with the food, suspecting she will not. And why should she? When she finally dismisses me, that will be the end of it all. She will have repaid my saving her with a good night's rest, a hot shower, and food, and I do not fault her for it.

I tense when she puts her phone down on the table. She picks up her cup, studying me. She's thinking of how to tell me to leave and when. She doesn't have to; I can do it for her.

I push my empty plate away. "Thank you, Madame," I say. "Is it okay if I take some food with me when I go?"

She continues to eye me critically. Her expression is unreadable. "No," she says plainly.

I expected as much. And yet a wave of embarrassment cascades over me. I misread her kindness. I wore out my welcome. Used up my sympathy card. I should have just stolen what I needed and left before she awoke. Then she would not have had to tell me to go, and I would not have to suffer the humility of being tossed back like bad fish.

But I know I am lying to myself. I would not have stolen a thing from her. I am no thief by choice, and especially when someone has shown me kindness, even if they did it because they pitied me.

"Okay," I whisper, ducking my head so she can't see my inflamed face. Out of everything, this is the worst feeling, the feeling I have just reminded her that I am a wretch and not a hero.

"It's unnecessary for you to take this food," she begins, "because there will be plenty where we are going."

"Madame?" I look up at her, bewildered. Fear cuts through me as I did the man last night. She is taking me to the authorities. Back to Paul.

She smiles at me with warmth I feel is genuine. "Where we are going," she says, "is to London, where I live with my husband, Noble, and my daughter, Elin. She is maybe a year or two older than you, sixteen. Would you like that, Nena?"

There is warmth in her voice and a want that nearly brings me to tears. "Would you come home with me and be a part of my family, as my daughter?" she asks.

Her words have rendered me speechless. Quite senseless, to be exact. I wait for clues alerting me that she is being dishonest. I wait for my instincts to urge me to run for my life because she means me harm. But they tell me she is being sincere. I already know I am safe with her and that she needs my acceptance, as she has accepted me. With that new knowledge, I answer, more assuredly than I have ever before. "Yes, Madame. I think I would like to. Very much so."

# 45

## AFTER

Spotlights lit up the nightclub, and lines entering the double doors wrapped around the building. Hopeful patrons had decked themselves out in their Saturday best. Nena was dressed for the occasion in a short leather skirt and black fitted bodice that showed more skin than she was accustomed to. She wore one of her favorite wigs, the black bob with burgundy-tipped ends. According to Witt's intel, the club was where Kwabena would be most vulnerable, where she could most easily separate him from his people.

She joined a raucous group of women already toasted from a night of bachelorette partying as they entered the club so she wouldn't have to wait in the seemingly endless line. The place was packed with writhing bodies that took up the expanse of the wide room, its bright electric colors and fog machine adding to the promise of a fun-filled night. She reminded herself she was supposed to be in character. So she let the rhythmic bass drown out all the noise in her mind, and before she knew it, her shoulders began to jiggle, and she allowed herself to get lost in the thumping and bumping of the song.

"Dance?" asked some random guy with a complexion as creamy as the suit he wore, no shirt. He held out a hand, wiggling his fingers for her to take. She cast him a sidelong glance, swaying her hips as she moved away. She smirked when he clutched his chest as if she'd broken his heart. She moved through the crowds in sync to "Daddy Yo" by Wizkid.

The VIP section was in the middle of the club for the most prominent view. It was a raised white circular platform, like a crown in the center of the dance floor. All the non-VIPs danced around it, hoping they'd be chosen to join the elite. She waltzed right through them all.

She spied him, Kwabena-now-Kamil, and her directive returned as she danced in front of the platform, refusing any other person who tried to dance with her. She was performing for a party of one, hoping she'd catch his attention. She would, because what drew a man to a woman the most was when she seemed untouchable.

—

"May I?" a voice from behind asked above the din of the music. She accepted, moving in time with the music and with him. She didn't let him get too close. She thwarted and teased his attempts to hold her waist. She kept just out of reach, wanted to make him yearn for her, be enthralled by her.

When she tried to drift away, he grabbed her hand. "What's your name?"

The grab was electrifying, driving her to that moment with dirt and rocks digging in her back while Kwabena hovered above her, causing her to feel more pain than she'd ever imagined. The taste of his foul breath in the back of her throat while her mind was going, going, gone.

She could take him down right here. Her push daggers were in her belt. There was enough crowd to conceal her act. But that would mean too quick a death, like Attah Walrus. She reflexively snatched her hand away and saw him shrink back at her sudden hostility. But wasn't this why she was here? To draw him out?

*You need to cool it.* She forced herself to play at being coy, to reel him back in, make him follow her.

"Hey!" he called out. She ignored him, moving farther away.

He called after her again.

She paused for a group of club goers to pass. As she did, he caught up, jogging over to her, slightly out of breath.

She said, with faux surprise, "You're following me?"

His smile was not unpleasant, but she'd love to scratch it off him. "How could I not? You took my breath away in there," he panted.

Easily, she maneuvered toward the door. "A good thing."

"I don't normally chase women."

She smirked. "And yet . . ." *Easy. Not too much.*

Her Dispatch training included ways to engage people romantically, but her best teacher was Elin, and Nena tried to channel her now.

She bit her bottom lip, showing a bit of teeth. She looked at him, taller by a foot or so, through her eyelashes. He was nothing but arms, legs, and a rounded little potbelly. They were at the doors now. "What do you want from me?" she asked.

He held up a finger. "One night. One night with you, and I'll make your life brand new."

He'd already done that, now, hadn't he?

She let out a throaty laugh. "You think highly of yourself . . ."

He gave her his name.

"Kamil." She let the name roll off her tongue, as if becoming accustomed to it.

She cocked her head to the side, looking coquettishly at him with a hint of hesitation. "One night?"

He held up his finger again. "Just one."

"Where do we go for this 'one night'?"

"I know the perfect place."

She knew where he'd want to go. To a place not so public. And it was indeed perfect.

She looked beyond him, at the couple of guards weaving toward them through the crowd. "And your friends?"

He looked over his shoulder at his approaching men, then back to her. He really thought his boyish looks were disarming, and maybe to any other woman they would be. "I'll take care of them."

———

Nena let Kwabena drive her several blocks away in his latest-model Bentley. Ostentatious, but what more could she expect from a man like him? He pulled into the dimly lit back lot of a strip mall.

Pointing to a door with a blue flower painted on it, he said, "We can go in there. It's very nice. I own it."

She made a point of looking at the door, then him, in awe. "Perfect." Her voice was husky with anticipation. She unbuckled her seat belt and left the car, beckoning him to join her.

The Lotus Flower was deserted at this time of night. All the girls who were forced to work the spa were likely at a shared house, recuperating from another day of being forced to give massages and prostitute themselves to earn their keep. One of the numerous ways traffickers used their merchandise: in their businesses, in their homes, moving the girls from one location to another . . . always moving. And when the merchandise was all used up, it was disposed of.

He unlocked the door and stepped aside to allow her in first. She swallowed her unease at the door shutting and locking behind them as they stood in the dark hall. The place smelled of flower fragrances and sea salts and opulence that contrasted with the burgeoning anxiety of being in a small, unknown space.

She didn't lie to herself that this job was like the others. This job wasn't for the Tribe. It was only for her. She took his hand and pulled him down the hall.

———

They entered a room Kwabena said was one of his favorites. She'd cased the spa a few days earlier, both as a wife looking to purchase a package for her husband, and after hours to get the layout of the back rooms. From the outside, the business appeared high end, but it was much more sinister when the patrons knew what to ask for.

He rambled about how this was unlike him, to bring a beautiful woman here alone.

"Then I'm honored."

He chanced a quick glance at her. "There's something beguiling about you, making me ditch my security detail and bring you here to my spa."

She threw a sly smile over her shoulder as she walked the length of the room, ensuring there was nothing new since the last time she'd roamed the premises. He turned on the moon light, and the room was bathed in warm recessed lighting.

"Make yourself comfortable? I'll get us some champagne."

When he returned with an ice bucket holding a bottle of his finest, she was waiting for him. She gestured for him to join her. He set the bucket down and did as told, snuggling into her neck, inhaling the scent of her. He ran his arms over her body, exploring her curves and the heat of her skin. He went in to kiss her supple lips, and she tilted her head up so he trailed the tip of his tongue along the length of her jawline instead. She couldn't bring herself to have his lips on hers.

"Me on top," she breathed into his ear.

He gladly traded positions. She ran her hand up and down his leg. She traced it up and down his thigh, near his manhood, then teased it away.

She kicked her long leg over his lap, straddling him and easing her body onto him. He unzipped his pants. She quelled the urge to jump off him, the feeling of his penis flopping like a fish out of water beneath her making her think horribly of her brother Ofori. She breathed through the urge to vomit.

"Let me taste you," he growled, gripping the hem of her skirt and hiking it up. His animalistic urges were overpowering his gentlemanliness. He was tired of seduction—and she was tired of seducing.

She said, "Tell me again what you want."

He answered as if it were the most natural thing in the world. "To fuck you."

"To fuck me?" Her hands slid down his arms, which were wrapped around her rear. "To know me?"

"Yes." He strained against her. "Yes, baby, yes, to know you."

She pulled back. "But Kwabena," she breathed, "we already know each other."

At the sound of his name, Paul's third-in-command snapped his eyes open in muddled confusion. Beneath her, his body stiffened. He searched her eyes for understanding.

"What—what did you call me?"

Her hands were moving beyond his vision. "You know me. Intimately."

She produced her push daggers from the belt of her skirt. In one swift move, she plunged the blades into his chest. She leaned her weight into the daggers as he thrashed beneath her. She dug them deep under the breastbone, the blades tearing through his left and right ventricles.

"Perhaps you remember me from N'nkakuwe."

She watched his eyes grow round and his mouth open. Close. Open. Close again. He wheezed. She studied him, wanting to see every last second of his life. He coughed, blood spurting from his lips, running down his throat, and then dripping fast onto the floor.

His hands dropped from her, swinging like heavy pendulums until they finally stilled. When he was done, she got to work on the rest of her plan.

She walked the halls, entered all the rooms, the outer ones for legal massages and the inner chambers for illegal acts. She checked the explosive charges she'd placed in each one. When she set them off, this place would be leveled and Kwabena with it. But first . . .

She returned to the room with a small red condiment bottle of accelerant and matches. First she wanted to watch Kwabena burn.

When it was done, when he'd gone up in a quiet and satisfying whoosh, she walked away from the building, pressing a button on her burner cell phone to remotely detonate the charges.

Two down.

One to go.

# 46

## BEFORE

If anyone had said I would be riding in another fancy black sedan before being whisked away to England in a private plane, I would never have believed them. Of all the things I envisioned for the future, this was not it. I believed I would die in Paris, frozen on the street, and that no one would realize it until I thawed in the summer and the smell of rot became too pungent to ignore.

I consider pinching myself to make sure the house looming into my vision as we ride down a long, curved, tree-lined driveway is real.

The mansion is a sprawling L-shaped home of stone and wood that looks as one might imagine an English house does, turret and all. It sits on 2.5 acres of lush lawn and greenery in Hammersmith, made of light-colored stone with a dark rooftop and large bay windows. It is an eight-bedroom, twelve-bathroom mammoth to me, but—

"It's a simple home," Madame says. No, where I came from was simple. This is otherworldly.

Our car rolls to a stop in front of the brightly lit home, and the driver exits to open Madame's door. My door pops open. Another man dressed similarly to the driver has materialized from thin air and waits for me to leave the car. I take a moment for my heart rate to slow.

She waits patiently for me as I take in my surroundings. I swallow down the bud of nervousness threatening to sprout. What hides behind those doors? I am unsure. I wait for a twinge or stirring, alerting me danger is afoot. There is nothing.

"Ready?" Madame asks.

I hesitate, worried she is going to offer her hand to me as we enter. I do not want anyone to touch me. But she doesn't, as if she is aware of my thoughts. Instead, she motions toward the front doors. "Shall we meet Noble and Elin?"

And by "we," she really means me.

I start biting my bottom lip, my hands rubbing up and down my pant legs, as I follow her up the stairs. The swath of red beneath her heels catches my eye. I have seen shoes like this on TV, on models. This family must be richer than their royals to be able to afford what people on TV do. The driver and the other man pull her bags out of the car. I shift my rucksack on my shoulders—my only possession.

As if by magic, the front door opens, and an older, stout Black woman with graying hair tied in a bun greets us. Her smile to me is immediate and welcoming as she ushers us in out of the cold.

"Welcome home, Ms. Delphine," she says. *Ms. Delphine*, not what I have been calling her. I like this better. The older woman's voice is pleasant, welcoming. Her voice is rich and full of soul. I bet she has endless stories within her, like the elders of my village. She turns to me. "Welcome *home*, Nena."

My body goes stiff and my throat tightens. Again, having such kindness shown to me and hearing myself referred to by an actual name is alien to me. I feel unworthy of the attention they bestow on me. Terror overtakes me. I am going to disappoint them, and they will realize their error in selecting me. The thought nearly makes me run out of the door.

"Margot, hello." The two women hug and kiss each other's cheeks. "Where are they?"

"In the kitchen finishing lunch. Ishmael has a spread for you both, not knowing what Nena likes to eat." Ms. Margot looks at me, and I shrug. I cannot afford a food preference. "Well, I'm sure we'll figure it out soon enough."

We walk down the front hall into a kitchen of gray quartz countertops, white cabinets, and dark-stained wood flooring. It is pristine with a cook busy at the counter, chopping away. Beyond in a large alcove is a round cherry table topped with even more food than was at the hotel room. My stomach growls, but thankfully the noise is drowned out by the sizzling pots and the chatter from Ms. Margo and Ms. Delphine.

A man rises from the table, dark and slender. He is taller than his wife or me but not too tall. His hair is dark and cut very low. He is clean shaven except for his perfect mustache. He removes his reading glasses and opens his arms as he approaches. Behind him, a lanky girl with his same coloring trails behind. She is beautiful. Absolutely beautiful. Graceful. And she must be Elin.

*She will hate me.*

"My love," the man says. He pulls his wife into a hug and kisses her as if she's been gone eons. I take several steps back, not wanting to intrude on their reunion, trying to blend into the walls so no one sees me.

But Mr. Noble spies me pressed against the wall, nearly out the doorway we entered. "This is Nena?"

Ms. Delphine throws an arm out to me. "Nena, come. Why are you all the way over there? Come meet my Noble and Elin."

I sneak a look at Elin as I shuffle toward her mother's outstretched arm, stopping short of her wriggling fingers. Their daughter is studying me with a curious expression. It is not hostile, and I am relieved, but only a little. She does not say anything, watching with that same expression.

I stand before Mr. Noble, a ball of nervous energy. He, too, studies me, and I realize he is judging me. This is when they are deciding to

235

keep me or not, like some stray dog off the street. I nearly laugh because is that not what I am?

Up close, I see how handsome he is. The air around him exudes power and authority, which instantly reminds me of Papa. It is a long time before he speaks.

"Delphine tells me we have you to thank for her coming home to us relatively unharmed."

Only herculean effort makes me speak because I cannot *not* answer him. I can tell just by the look of him.

"Was luck," I whisper.

"Oh, that's not luck," he says, looking down at me with dark, dark eyes that I will learn can express everything from gentleness and love to cold calculation when he condemns men to their deaths. But today, he looks upon me with appreciation.

And then.

Then he opens his arms to me. I am frozen. What am I to do? Every man's touch since I have been in this nightmare has resulted in immeasurable pain and humiliation. I peer into his eyes again. The acceptance, the love, and the warmth I see in them envelop me, driving back the horrors I endured for so long.

Gingerly, I walk into his arms, warring because while the thought of touch makes me cringe, the need for a father's embrace is too great. However, I can only stand it for a moment. I alert him to this by tentatively patting his back thrice, then pulling away. Ms. Delphine and Elin share an amused look. He is just pleased.

"Dad is a hugger. You'll need to get used to it," Elin quips.

I look to her, stricken. Is it a deal breaker if I cannot?

"Only with my girls," he clarifies.

I pause. Am I now considered one of his girls? I search for the proper feeling. The four little words bring me joy but also trepidation.

"Well, come on then," Elin says brightly. "Let's find your room."

*My room?*

My expectation is that I'll be relegated to the basement, tucked away like some unwanted guest, shut away in a cupboard under the stairs. But we go up instead of down, through a maze of halls and rooms. She shows me one, two, three, four, five bedrooms before we reach her own.

"This is my room," Elin says, motioning to a massive room decorated in lavenders, light greens, and creams. She looks at me. "Are there any rooms we passed that you like? Do you like this one? Because you can have it."

My mouth drops open at her words. Surely, she must be playing me false to offer her own room.

"You saved my mum," she explains simply. "I owe you everything because she *is* my everything. Her and Dad."

I still cannot answer. She continues.

"You'll get used to Dad; he's a big softy with us. And by us, I mean you too. You're a Knight now, Nena."

Another four words that bring me such incredible joy I nearly buckle at their weight.

"But why?" I blurt, truly confounded by this family and their total acceptance of me.

Elin frowns, as confused as I. "Why not? Mum is a perfect judge of character." She flips her ponytail. "If Mum gave you her seal of approval, you are in. Relax. Besides, I've always wanted a little sister." She glances around the room, unsure. "Anyway, back to the rooms. You don't really want this one, do you? I know I said you could have it, but hell, I didn't mean it."

Her honesty is amusing. "No, it's yours. I'll be okay wherever you put me."

"Well, Mum and Dad's room is on the first level because Dad doesn't want to bother with stairs, so you want to be up here with me. You'll have more freedom without them breathing down your neck. They're cool and all, but they're still parents, you know?"

I nod because I can think of no better response.

Elin chooses another massive room a couple of doors down from hers. She says it is so we have privacy but can still be close. But maybe it is so she can keep an eye on me in case I turn out to be a thief. Thievery is one thing Elin, or anyone, will never be able to attribute to me.

Because I only take when my hand is forced, and that includes when I must take lives.

# 47

## AFTER

Waiting for the fallout from Kwabena's death already had Nena on high alert, so when she received a frantic call from Cort, she arrived prepared for a gunfight. However, they were in the midst of a full-blown panic for a different reason. Georgia was in tears and threatening to never leave her room again.

"I don't know what to do," Cort said, answering the door before Nena could knock. "She asked for you."

The desperation in his eyes hit Nena like an arrow, and all she could think was that whoever had hurt Georgia would pay. She ran down a list of possibilities: something with Cort's case; Paul having somehow found out about them and threatened Georgia; something about Kwabena's death? No, if any of those were the cause of this mayhem, Cort would not be asking for her assistance.

"Is she okay?"

He stepped back, running his hands over his face the way he did when he was stressed, and she entered the foyer. Nena could hear music blaring. "What happened?"

"I'll let Peach tell you."

He looked terrified, as if he didn't want to go near the room with the howling girl. This big man, as he'd be considered back home, was practically pushing her toward Georgia's door so she could deal with whatever was behind it.

"I'm handling it with the school."

She stopped to look at him. The school? Nena wasn't one for group hysteria, but the way they were acting out of character was alarming her. She didn't like changes, and this behavior was a change.

He stopped abruptly, as if remembering himself. He reached out, holding her arm and making her feel all sorts of jolts radiating from the touch.

"Thank you for coming so quickly."

"We'll get it all sorted," Nena said as stoically as she could.

They split up, Cort to the kitchen with his phone in hand and a look of relief on his face. The irony was not lost on her. He was sending a killer to sort out his daughter.

She arrived at the door and knocked on it. "Georgia?"

The music cut off immediately. Her sign to enter.

Nena opened the door wide enough to see Georgia sitting in front of her dresser, comb in hand, attempting to work her way through her massive bushel of hair. She was in sweats and a T-shirt, damp from having come out of the shower. She was trying to tug a brush through the tangles, but through the mirror Nena saw the frustration and anguish etched on her face.

Georgia turned in her seat, her eyes red and puffy. "They put gum in my hair," she said, hiccuping. "And Dad had to cut out the chunks. My hair is ruined!"

Nena let out a breath, understanding perfectly. She remembered the horror, the shame, when she had gazed at her own coarse, dry, knotted mess of hair in her mum's hotel room. There was unbelievable pride in Black women's hair. Their hair was their crown, their superpower, something women taught each other to care for, as Nena's first mother had taught her.

"I can kill them for you," Nena said. "No one will know."

Georgia's eyes saucered, her mouth dropping open with brush still in hand. Then she burst out in laughter at Nena's obvious joke.

"Can I help you?" she asked, happy the girl was consolable.

Georgia turned back to the mirror, her hands dropping to her side, leaving the white-and-black-handled brush nestled in her hair, which Nena carefully extracted. Nena made a concoction with the products they had. It took a considerable amount of time, but she finally got Georgia's hair to the point where it felt buttery soft. With a wide-tooth comb, she separated her hair into quarters and worked through each section with precision and gentleness, as if handling a Fabergé egg, all while Georgia recounted her argument with Sasha over an answer Georgia had corrected her about in front of the class, and then the gum in the bathroom.

"And she didn't just throw it in, you know," Georgia said. "She put a massive wad in and then mashed it until there was no way it was coming out without cutting. Bitch."

Nena agreed with her. Putting gum in another girl's hair was an attack.

"I miss this," Georgia said, surprising Nena because the girl had fallen silent, eyes drooped, and Nena had thought she'd fallen asleep sitting up.

"Miss what?" Nena asked.

"Someone doing my hair. Like, my dad's done real well with my hair until I got old enough. Don't get me wrong." Georgia's voice cracked.

She looked at Nena through the mirror, her eyes welling with huge droplets of tears that made Nena swallow in discomfort.

"But I miss my mom doing my hair." Her voice held immense sadness, and she sounded all of five. "Do you ever miss yours? Your birth one?"

Nena frowned at the tuft of hair in her hands, not trusting the cavern of emotions this girl brought about in her, this girl who was so very much like her and yet so very different. This girl who was much more than her.

"I miss her every day," Nena whispered.

"And when you met your mom and got adopted, did it change anything for you? Change how you felt? Did you ever worry you'd forget who she was or what she looked like?"

Nena continued working on Georgia's hair, understanding Georgia's true meaning. Georgia wanted assurances she'd never forget her mom no matter who came into her life. Nena wasn't ready for this. She wanted to run, wanted to do a dispatch, anything but talk about dead mothers and their memories.

But wasn't this what she was essentially signing up for by being here? To be that person for Georgia like Mum had been for her?

Finally she said, "No one will ever take the place of your mum, Georgia. Some little details of her face may fade, but the most important parts always stay." She paused. "Can I show you something?"

Georgia nodded, tilting her head this way and that as she looked at herself.

Nena jogged to the living room, where her rucksack sat on the couch—not where she'd left it. Cort must have moved it. There was a gun in a secret panel within the bag, but seeing as how Cort hadn't come running, he hadn't found it. She lifted its straps and hustled back to Georgia's room, where Georgia still admired Nena's handiwork.

Georgia joined Nena on her bed. Nena opened her bag, and Georgia looked on curiously as she pulled out a white container and a bottle of cologne.

Georgia shot her a quizzical look. "Olay and Hugo Boss? Are they for my hair too?"

Nena almost laughed, but her response was to open the plastic bottle and give it a quick sniff before holding it out. Georgia leaned in, taking a deep inhale. Nena sprayed a fine mist of the cologne in the air, and Georgia leaned into that too. She regarded Nena, who gazed at the two bottles, one plastic, one glass, with all the love of the world, and waited.

"These are my first parents, the scents of them, and what I remember the most about them," Nena said. "I've kept these with me for half my life. They comfort me. Ground me. Settle me. They remind me of who I used to be and who I used to have." She checked their tops were on tightly before slipping them back in her bag.

"When I'm in my darkest moments, missing my mama or papa, I pull them out and put some of Mama on or spray my papa. Feels like a kiss and a hug. They're always with me."

Nena wiped at the tears now sliding down Georgia's face. "Find the thing that helps you remember your mum the most and keep her with you, because you don't have to let her go, ever. But you also make room in your heart for others to get the privilege of loving you as well."

"I already have."

Oh, Nena wasn't ready for that. Or for when Georgia threw herself into Nena's arms, wrapping her arms tightly around her waist in a breath-sucking embrace. Nena hesitated, and then slowly, she put her arms around Georgia's shoulders. She inhaled the coconut shea of Georgia's hair, a new scent she'd cherish. She'd rushed to Georgia's aid because Cort had called her and Georgia needed her. But Nena knew it was really her who was the one in need of them.

# 48

## BEFORE

Assimilating into the Knights' lavish lifestyle the past few months has been difficult. Most of the time, anxiety plagues me. All this sudden good fortune could be snatched from me at any moment. I cannot relax well enough to enjoy any of it. I live each moment in this opulence like it is my last, because I have conditioned myself. Nothing good stays good, for me.

They are a good family, treat me very well. They give me space. They never ask me about my past, and I am thankful for that, since I am not ready to share my story. It embarrasses me, believing once they know of my cowardice in my village, that my people gave their lives to protect me and I did not try to do more, the Knights will be ashamed and no longer feel I am worthy of them, as I already believe.

Each day is a discovery of new freedoms. I walk the grounds, pushing to see how far they will allow me to go, memorizing and mesmerized by my surroundings. They never stop me. I speak little, only answering when spoken to. But I like to listen, enjoying how comfortable and loving they are with one another. They remind me of my family.

I learn about everyone's idiosyncrasies. Ishmael, the chef, hates when anyone peers over his shoulder while he cooks. Raul loves to discuss plants and flowers and allows me to prune and pluck with him in the greenhouse. He tells me to name the plants so they will return my love and grow for me. I find horticulture very soothing. The head of security, Montreal, is funny and a ladies' man. He is seeing two of the maids at the same time, but they do not know. He winks at me to keep his secrets.

I do wonder about the number of guards looking after the family. They go everywhere we go, especially when Mr. Noble and Ms. Delphine travel, which is often. It all has to do with Mr. Noble's business dealings, of which I am unclear. I have heard "Tribe" and "Council." I cannot make sense of any of it.

"Why do you call Mum and Dad Ms. Delphine and Mr. Noble? You sound like all the people who work for them, and you don't work for them, Nena. You're family," Elin says one morning as we prepare for school. The Knights have enrolled me in the same private school Elin attends, one vastly different and more formal than what I am accustomed to.

We dress in matching blue plaid skirts, light-blue button-down shirts, and navy jackets with a blue-and-white tree etched on each jacket pocket.

I stop packing my schoolbag. "What else should I call them?"

"Mum and Dad, of course. They would love it." She sweeps her hair up into a ponytail, her favorite style. "I would love it. Then we'd be real sisters."

Her answer rolls around in my mind. I would like that, too, but calling them Mum and Dad, calling Elin sister, feels like I am shutting the door on Mama, Papa, and my brothers.

Elin has been my biggest source of comfort, much to my surprise. I really thought she would hate having to share her parents and life with me, but all she has shown is kindness. She takes care of me. Nightmares plague me often, waking me up in cold sweats, sheets twisted at my feet, my face slick with tears.

Each time, Elin is there in my room, having heard my screams. She gathers me to her and assures me I am safe and okay, that it is all over.

I want to believe her; really, I do.

But the nightmares are driving me insane. They are worse now than when I lived them, because in these dreams, Monsieur and the men from the Compound turn into ravenous monsters that devour me alive. And Paul. Paul is the devil incarnate. After Monsieur and the men consume me, I am sent to Paul in hell, where he torments me forever. He holds my family—Papa, the twins, and Ofori—in cramped cages above a firepit of boiling black oil.

The worst nightmares are when I fall into hell and see not only my birth family, doomed to his torment, but the Knights and Margot there as well. My worst fear is that I am now cursed and will visit upon them what my first family suffered. That I have no way to save them, failing as I did the first time.

Elin cradles me, begging, "Please, Nena. Please, what has happened to you? Tell me how I can help."

I can never say.

After Elin falls asleep in my bed, I rummage under my pillow for the two items that give me a semblance of serenity, Hugo and Olay. I inhale the scent of them, biting down on my tongue to keep from crying out from the agony of missing my parents. Eventually, I, too, fall back asleep.

The obsession over my fears makes me withdrawn at school, where I am not popular or accepted by the students at first. There are other Black kids, like Elin, but they are all English born. I guess I look too "African" for them because my hair is natural and braided, twisted, or sometimes out in its full afro glory. My accent is different from theirs. I do not know the nuances of their rich worlds or the slang of their language. Most of them are from old English money, with ancestors of royal lineage or parents in Parliament or the government.

They ridicule me, trying to antagonize me, and call me names.

"Look at the little gorilla," a boy named Silas taunts as I sit beneath a tree in the courtyard attempting to eat my lunch of tomato soup and grilled brie sandwich. The courtyard is one of the few places I find refuge from these loud children who hate me for no reason.

Silas has been exceptionally horrible to me. He is the one who calls me names, the one who reminds me of a little Robach. I add his insults to my tally: whore, bitch, Souris, and—

"Gorilla," Silas finishes amid a chorus of laughter from his compatriots, lemmings who pretend his asinine jokes are funny.

I squint up against the sunlight.

"That's what you do, innit? Live in bushes like wild people, naked, and shag animals?" he asks, his voice getting louder. Students crowd around, sensing a good show is about to commence.

"Bloody hell, check out the likes of you. You're so black. The only time we can see you is at this very time."

My fingers tighten around my spoon; images of using it to scoop out his blue eyes flash to mind.

"Silas Balderdash the Third." Elin's voice rings out. The crowd of onlookers makes way. There she is with her two besties flanking her. She marches through them right up to where Silas looms above me. Elin and I make eye contact, and for a moment, she sees murderous intent in mine. She holds a hand flat, a signal to say, *Be calm.* "You should leave her alone."

"Fuck off. What's it to you?"

"There are two things you should know, you mongrel," she says, getting up close and personal to the boy. "You will stop teasing my sister and calling her racist names. You understand that?"

Silas laughs. "And what's the second thing?"

She rocks back, cutting his laugh short when her foot shoots up and smashes into his groin. The crowd's gasp is collective, and Silas is bowled over, dropping to the ground. His body curls into a tight ball, the pain so paralyzing he cannot scream or breathe.

Elin bends over him. "Second thing is I will fuck you up worse than this if you"—she looks up at the rest of the spectators—"or any of you fuck with her again."

They never again call me names at school.

Later that night, when Elin finds me clutching my throat in the throes of another nightmare reenactment where Monsieur's giant paws are around my neck, she hugs me, opening a tiny fissure that I finally walk through.

I grip her, not wanting to let go, the need to relieve my burden so great it is like I am suffocating from beneath it until I finally say, "I need to tell you my story."

# 49

## AFTER

Nena and Georgia were putting away all the hair-care materials when Cort stuck his head in the room.

"Hey," he said, then stopped when he saw his daughter's perfect braids coiled upward into a high bun atop Georgia's head. It didn't look dissimilar to the low version Nena sported. "Wow, look at you, Peach. You look amazing."

Georgia gave a tentative pat of her hair. "Thanks. I wanted Nena to do one like hers."

He nodded, shooting Nena an appreciative smile, then gazing again at his daughter, free of the tears and turmoil from earlier. "God, I almost forgot. Nena, you have a guest."

Nena stilled. "Me?" she said, sharper than she intended. No one knew she was here, except . . .

"Your sister?" Cort said, a little unsure if he'd delivered good news or bad. "She's waiting out front." But Nena had already pushed past him without another word.

Elin wouldn't. Nena marched toward the front door, half expecting Elin to be waiting for her there, nose in the air as she gave the lived-in home a once-over with her highly expensive, highly critical eye. Elin wasn't in the foyer or the living room. She wasn't in the house but rather was leaning against the driver's-side door of her white-as-snow Tesla. She looked as annoyed as Nena felt.

"What the fuck?" Elin said as her little sister neared her. "You don't answer messages or my calls now?"

"What do you mean?" Nena frowned, feeling her pockets for her phone, which wasn't there. Rucksack, she thought. "You rang me?"

"No, I just popped up to make bloody small talk." Elin rolled her eyes, pushing off her car and sauntering toward Nena, tall and regal as usual. And annoyed. Couldn't forget that.

Nena scanned the street. Where was Elin's security? She asked, but Elin waved her off. "Is it Mum or Dad?"

"They're fine. And I don't need security when Oliver's with me."

Nena did a double take. Not only had Elin appeared, but she'd brought Oliver, when she knew how much Nena wanted to keep the Baxters separate from their lives for now.

"You brought Oliver?" Nena strained to see around her insufferable sister. "What's so damn important that you had to hunt me down? And with him?" Nena gestured toward the car. She couldn't see him through the tinted glass.

Elin flipped her hand. "We're on our way to Vegas. And because my sister refuses my calls."

Nena had never wanted to wring her sister's neck as much as she wanted to at this very moment. "What. Is. It?"

"A warning. That little spa day you had not too long ago? It's been noticed."

Nena made no response. She'd expected as much. Maybe not this soon, but still. "All right."

"Intel came in through Network about it. I don't think it'll make big waves because no one knows or cares about the bastard. But if it's coming through Network, it means your big bad has likely heard through his own channels. You need to watch your back until we find Paul, wherever he is."

Too late, Nena thought grimly. Paul was already found.

While Nena had told Elin about the intel Witt had provided, she hadn't told her sister who Oliver's father was. She couldn't do that to Elin just yet, burst her idealistic dream by telling her that her boyfriend's dad was a sadistic monster. Plus, Paul's threat against her family weighed heavily on Nena's mind—heavier now that he likely knew Kwabena was dead.

"Has anyone else said anything? Oliver?"

Elin scoffed. "Are you mad? Oliver is an altar boy. Give the man a financial sheet, and that's the most excitement you'll get from him. I can't even get him to go anal on me, he's so fucking squeaky clean."

"Please," Nena begged, the vision of her sister and Oliver assaulting her. She was used to Elin's garishness but wasn't ready for this.

Elin was grinning down at her squeamish sister, proud of knocking her down a peg. "I just came to say be careful."

Nena nodded. Her eyes were on Elin's car, whose inside light had suddenly come on. The passenger-side door opened.

Elin continued, "Stay the course, right?"

Right. Nena already knew. No more detours until she knew what play Paul would make. She thought of her conversation with Witt, of how she might have poked the bear.

"Your man's joining us," Nena warned in hushed tones, her pulse quickening. She didn't like this. Didn't want Oliver here, much less these two sides of her life colliding.

A sly smile slid across Elin's face as she gazed past Nena's shoulder in the dimming light. "So is yours. And the kid." She sounded much too gleeful.

Sure enough, there they were, Cort following a now-glowing Georgia down the walk. Nena faced a smirking Elin, warily watching Oliver make his own approach.

"Look what you've done," she growled.

Elin was loving it. "Aww, sis, are you ashamed of your family? Don't you think it's time I met this illustrious man who"—she lowered her voice, leaning in as both sides were nearly upon them—"made you disobey orders for the first fucking time? I rather enjoy seeing you flustered. Another first."

Elin straightened, brandishing a huge smile as the Baxters stopped before her and Oliver came from the rear. "So you're Georgia." She held out her hand, which Georgia took and pumped energetically, surprising Elin.

"You're Nena's fancy sister."

Elin's eyebrows rose. "Is that what Nena called me?"

Georgia shrugged. "Kinda hard to miss," she answered, indicating Elin's attire and her car.

Oliver laughed as he moved beside Elin, his eyes sweeping Georgia, then lingering on Cort, then Nena, then back to Cort. "It's true," he said. "She's very fancy. You're pretty astute, er . . ."

"Georgia," she answered. "And I know."

"Peach," Cort warned, shaking hands with Oliver and introducing himself.

Elin looked down at Georgia, her nose flaring in distaste. "So you're the reason my little sister had to run off and wasn't answering my calls."

Georgia pursed her lips and, without missing a beat, replied gravely, "You've had her all to yourself for a long time. Time to share Nena with the world."

Elin's mouth dropped open in a most unbeautiful manner as she was struck speechless, despite Oliver laughing as if he were at a comedy show and Cort placing a firm hand on his daughter's shoulder while trying to mask his amusement.

"She's a regular spitfire, yeah?" Elin said, bemused. Elin wasn't used to someone having faster quips than she did. She quickly regained her ultracool. "You may borrow her for a little, but you must return her every so often, because I rather like her."

Georgia nodded. "Deal," she said.

"Okay, enough of that," Nena said, feeling warm inside and anxious to get Oliver, who was chatting it up with Cort, out of here. "You two should be off now. I'm also about to head out. Have to sort some things out."

Elin raised her eyebrows as the men said their goodbyes. "Stay the course, little sister."

"I appreciate your concern, Elin." Nena tried to be as cool as she could manage.

She watched Elin and Oliver return to the car, and then Elin sped off far too fast for the neighborhood. She begged off an offer of dinner from Cort and asked for a rain check. She got in her Audi, waved at the Baxters, and drove away wondering what the hell had just happened.

Later that night, when she was back home alone eating takeaway lemon-pepper wings and blue cheese, which Keigel had graciously brought her, and watching *Pet Sematary*, her phone chimed.

CORT: Ty 4 what U did 4 Georgia. She's going thru her mom's stuff looking for a keepsake.

NENA (after wiping her fingers): Good.

CORT: UR something else, NK.

If only he knew. Heat rushed Nena's cheeks. She didn't know how to respond to that. All she could do was reply with: TY. Not so bad yourself, CB.

He ended with good night, but as Nena continued to watch the movie, she wondered why the husband buried his wife in a cursed cemetery knowing what it would do to her. Maybe the message was that it was better to have those you loved in any capacity—even if they came back murderously evil—than to not have them at all.

She shifted in her seat. If she were honest with him, could Cort decide to be with her, in any capacity? Like that husband? Nena couldn't answer that, but how would she ever know what they could be, if she didn't at least try?

# 50

## BEFORE

Two weeks after I take Elin into my confidence, the mornings are brighter, and I feel as if some of my burden has been lifted.

Elin and I are different in every conceivable way. We are opposite bookends. She is stylish and highly sociable, assured and unabashedly unafraid. She speaks her mind and can be as tactful as a royal or as brash as a sailor.

I refrain from commenting. I question every decision I make. I prefer clothes that cover my developing body. I wear what allows me to blend into my surroundings so I may go unnoticed.

Mr. Noble, Ms. Delphine, and Elin are already at the breakfast table when I come down to eat. Ishmael excuses himself to gather ingredients for lunch from the pantry. Margot sets a steaming cup of hot chocolate in front of me, velvety and topped with whipped cream. She knows how partial I am to sweets. She hovers over me a second too long, and when my eye catches hers, I know she knows everything and that Elin has told them all.

Despite all my caution, I have grown to love this family and become comfortable in these new settings. But now they know of my disloyalty, of how I betrayed my first family by surviving. And now, instead of being dead with them, I am living lavishly in a lifestyle fit for royalty.

Elin offers an apologetic smile. I am not upset with her for breaking my confidence. To be honest, I feel nothing but relief that the job was done for me.

"Darling," Ms. Delphine says solemnly, "will you sit?"

"Yes, Ms. Delphine."

She hates when I refer to her like that, but what other options have I?

"Nena." Mr. Noble folds his newspaper, then lays it on the table beside his partially eaten scones and scrambled eggs. "We won't dally around. Elin told us what you told her."

I am nodding and swallowing, forcing my eyes to remain on the melting white cream. I try to save them the trouble.

"Yes, sir." I swallow down the painful blockage in my throat. I rocket to my feet, prepared to leave immediately. My story, who I am, is more than these people have bargained for.

A long stretch of silence passes, and I cannot tell what any of them are thinking. I finally chance a look at Ms. Delphine and find not the disgust or pity I expected but sadness. She has tears in her eyes, and her lips are trembling. Mr. Noble appears just as stricken.

Mr. Noble begins, "Nena—"

"Darling, we would never ask you to leave," Ms. Delphine cuts in. "Never."

Mr. Noble silences his wife with a steady hand. "We had no idea what you have endured. We cannot fathom what has been done to you and your village, your father and brothers." His voice cracks.

In wonder, I watch him overcome with unexpected emotion; his eyes are so unbelievably sad I have a fleeting urge to comfort him.

"I have already made calls to locate Paul and his men. We'll find them and deal with them accordingly."

*Why?* The question does not transmit from my mind to my lips. I clear my throat and repeat it aloud.

Mr. Noble looks baffled. "Why what, Nena?"

Ms. Delphine holds Elin's hand. Elin looks at me, wide eyed and worried.

"Why did you take me in? Why are you doing this?" This has been on my mind for months. I drill an imaginary hole into the tabletop, awaiting their response.

"Nena, I owe you my wife's life. You risked your life for hers. There are people I pay to do that, but you did it without a second thought, without an expectation of payment. You did it with no thought to your own safety."

His voice gains strength. "The moment Delphine brought you into this house, I knew you were meant to be a part of our family, another daughter for me. I know you are loyal, and you are brave."

I shake my head. "I'm not. I am neither brave nor loyal. If I was, I would not have sat idle as my family was slaughtered."

Elin reaches out, nearly touching my hand. I slide it back before she has a chance. "There was nothing you could have done."

"I could have died with them."

Ms. Delphine sucks in air at my truth. "Don't ever say that, darling. You have done nothing but survive. That is the best thing you could have done for your family."

"I was selfish."

"You survived," Mr. Noble corrects.

I fall silent. There is no moving me—or him.

"What is it that you want more than anything right now?" Ms. Delphine asks. "Anything in the world?"

The answer comes out as quickly as breath. "To not be afraid anymore."

Elin looks at each of us worriedly, her face unable to hide her feelings.

Ms. Delphine says, "But you're safe with us. No one will ever harm you again, darling."

How can she ever understand what I mean? There is no amount of safety to keep you from harm. There is only the safety you can give yourself, and that type of safety is what I need for me.

"No, ma'am." My palms are sweaty. Their requirement for me to articulate my wants has me in a near panic. "I want to be able to make myself safe. I want to learn how to protect myself, to know how to this time, to keep others safe. I want to walk around without fear."

How do I explain my burning need to make sure no one ever touches me uninvited? To once again revisit how it felt when I plunged the chopsticks and then the scissors into Monsieur's face and body, and the knife into those men in the alleyway, in defense of myself? How do I explain the assurance of being able to stop someone else from hurting me?

Mr. Noble nods, absorbing my words. "You want your power back."

I look him squarely in his eyes, my heart lifting because he understands what I want, what I need to begin to heal.

He shares a knowing look with Ms. Delphine. "We can give that to you."

# 51

## AFTER

"Whose grill is this?" Cort growled at his longtime friend and lead detective for the Miami-Dade PD, John "Mack" McElroy. Curiously, Nena observed the two men bickering back and forth as they stood before the rectangular god Cort called a grill, which was currently emitting noxious plumes of smoke that Nena was pretty sure was the wrong kind of smoke.

It was her first time meeting Mack. Both Cort and Georgia were always talking about the sandy-haired, ruddy-faced man with warm brown eyes. He now gesticulated emphatically at the pieces of meat that ranged between charbroiled and barely singed. She immediately decided she liked him.

Nena wasn't used to consorting with so much "goodness," and knowing that brought about twinges of unease . . . about herself. Like, what was she doing here? What would her lifestyle bring down upon this family? But she pushed those thoughts away because the men's continued bickering was much more entertaining.

"The temp's uneven, man!" Mack griped as Cort stiff-armed him with one hand from coming any closer, while holding a bottle of lighter fluid in the other. Nena frowned, utterly perplexed at this display of male behavior.

Georgia pulled out her cell with a sly smile. "What do you like on your pizza?"

In the patio seat next to her, Nena gave her a quizzical look. "What about your dad grilling dinner?"

"Unfortunately, he still continues to try." Georgia looked at the grill wistfully.

There was a flare-up, and Cort quickly shut the grill top to smother it, gray ropes of smoke streaming out of the edges.

Georgia said, "Cheese or the works?"

"The works."

She tapped away at her phone. "That's what I thought."

There was a high-pitched yelp from the grill, Mack jumping backward as Cort yelled out, "God dammit!"

Mack doubled over in laughter. "We're all right," he called, waving a hand at Georgia and Nena. "Everything is under control. Except maybe Bax's dignity."

Defeated, Cort said, "Order me a meat lover's."

"Don't forget the mozzarella sticks," Mack wheezed. "And garlic knots."

Thirty minutes later, the four of them were seated around the Baxters' backyard wrought iron table, splitting two pizzas, the sides, and a pitcher of Country Time lemonade (a Georgia specialty) while the grill cooled in the background.

"I should take the grill back to the store. Something's gotta be wrong with it," Cort muttered, grabbing a third slice.

In Georgia's cough Nena could swear she heard her mumble, *Or with your grilling*. Cort didn't even notice because he was too busy glaring at Mack, who, at the same time, said very loudly, "Bullshit."

Silence descended on them as they each replenished their paper plates with food. Nena couldn't remember feeling as content with anyone other than her family as she did right now. She looked forward to Cort's occasional texts asking how she was doing. Or Georgia's flood of meme- and GIF-filled messages wanting to know when Nena was going to show her some of her fight moves.

"Shop talk?" Mack asked, breaking the silence. "Just for a second."

Cort's eyes flicked to Georgia, then back to Mack, before he gave in and pushed his plate away.

"Chill, Dad. I've seen *The Wire*." Georgia propped her feet on the chair and pulled her phone and earbuds out. "Nothing scares me anymore."

Cort's nose flared at his daughter before he gave Mack his attention. "What is it?" He wiped his hands with a paper towel, then balled it up. Nena stilled, her ears perking while she appeared to remain semiclueless and only mildly interested.

Mack said, "You know about the day-spa homicide?"

Nena regulated her breathing. If Mack was bringing up Kwabena in this conversation, it wasn't good.

"What about it?" Cort asked.

"The spa's name is Lotus." Mack gave Cort a meaningful look Nena couldn't quite decipher. She looked back and forth between them. Georgia had her earbuds in and paid them no mind.

At first Cort was confused. He squinted at Mack, who kept looking at him, widening his eyes as if Cort should be picking up what he was clearly laying down.

"Lo-tus," Mack enunciated.

It took another second for Cort to fully realize Mack's meaning. Nena was mesmerized at how it dawned on him, the dots he had to be connecting in his mind to come up with, "The business card from the Cuban?"

Mack thudded a satisfied, beefy fist on the table. "Damn straight."

"What is a lotus?" Nena asked, because if she didn't speak, it would look weird.

Cort said, "Remember when I told you a little about the dead Cuban cartel member when you came for dinner a while back?"

She nodded. She knew a bit more than that.

"There was a business card in his room for a massage spa called the Lotus Flower."

She nodded again.

"And," Cort added meaningfully, "Dennis Smith was connected to the Cuban. Laundered money for him."

She gave him a look as if to say, *So what?*

Mack chimed in. "There was a murder last week at this very spa. Someone killed the man who owned it and burned the place to the ground. The business card—"

*Connects the three killings,* Nena thought, her mouth drying. Why hadn't it occurred to her that Cort might connect the pieces? Damn.

"Connects the three killings," Cort said.

Mack said, "These three men, if we can prove it, had business ties with each other. We know the Cuban dealt with human trafficking. Smith was facing charges for racketeering. We now suspect the Lotus Flower was like a way station for funneling both money and maybe some of the people they trafficked, so whoever killed these three men did it as either a business play, a show of strength, or . . ."

"Or to settle a personal score," Cort finished.

That would be why they were a federal prosecutor and lead detective. They were good at their jobs. And so was she. She absorbed their theories, easing back into a sense of calm. Still no mention of Paul or the Tribe.

She scanned the backyard, noting it was enclosed by a chain-link fence instead of the high privacy ones she had installed at her home. She felt too exposed out here. What if the Tribe was surveilling them, listening to Cort and Mack get too damn close to a member of Dispatch? If they decided that he was a clear threat to their cause, there was nothing

Nena could do to stop them from sending a team to dispatch him, and her with him if she tried to stop it.

"But this is all just conjecture between two guys with overactive imaginations. We need proof, and we don't have it."

She nearly snorted. These "two guys" were spot on. It was all happening faster than she could think of new game plans. Her job wasn't to plan these things, it was to carry them out, which was probably why she was making such a mess of everything. She wasn't even sure when Paul would strike back for Kwabena, if he would.

"What's for dessert, Bax?" Mack asked, switching topics. "That's the most important meal of the day."

But Nena had tuned them out. Her phone was ringing, with *Maybe Mercy Hospital* displayed on her screen. Could be one of those calls asking for a donation for some fundraiser. She considered ignoring it but knew she'd better not.

Her chair scraped the stone of the patio flooring as she moved to get up. She held her phone in the air. "Will you excuse me? I have to take this call." She was away from the table and entering the home before either had a chance to respond.

A voice on the other end asked, "Ms. Knight? Nena Knight?"

"What's happened?" Nena was out the front door now and needed the porch pillar to hold her up. She could hear loudspeaker announcements in the background and, over them, the words, ". . . charge nurse at Mercy Hospital . . . admitted your father earlier today . . . rushed to the ER by ambulance."

Fear wrapped its icy fingers around her throat and squeezed, but she forced her voice to remain steady. "Is he—" She couldn't bring herself to finish.

"He's undergoing tests to determine, but your mother is with him. She asked us to notify you and ask you to come."

"I'm on my way," Nena said and disconnected the line.

While the only thing running through her mind was that something was wrong with her dad, she couldn't just leave without saying anything at all. She went back outside, where they were debating whether to have ice cream or key lime pie. They all looked up when she appeared, their faces falling when they saw her expression.

"What is it?" Cort asked at the same time Georgia asked, "What's wrong?"

Nena looked from one to the other. "My dad's in the hospital."

Cort was out of his seat. "What happened? In London?"

"No, they are here on holiday."

"Can I take you?" he asked, his eyes full of concern.

"Yeah, I can watch Georgia. Go ahead," Mack offered, worry lining his face.

Georgia was nothing but worry. "Nena?"

She shook her head. She just had to see about her father. Alone. "No. Thank you, but I'll call, okay?" She spun on her heel and retreated the way she'd come, barely registering the rush of feet to follow her.

"Nena, wait." Cort was right behind her. However, she was faster, moving at a near sprint to make it to her car without having to engage in any more conversation. She didn't want to answer questions or receive any more pitying looks. She only wanted to get to her father's side and find out what had happened.

———

Nena rushed into her father's hospital room. Her mother was fussing with the blankets on his bed. She looked up at Nena and seemed years older, with red-rimmed eyes, hair slightly askew, and worry etched all over her face. Nena allowed Delphine to wrap her in an embrace. It was typical Delphine, always taking care of her family before herself, as most good mothers tended to do.

"What's wrong with Dad? How is he?" Nena asked, straining to see him around her mom. She extracted herself so she could properly assess him.

The Noble in the bed was not the dad she knew. His pallor was ashen, and he no longer seemed bigger than life. He no longer looked domineering and debonair, like he had all the answers. In that moment he looked vulnerable. Like he could be snatched away from her in an instant. Nearly had been.

"What happened?"

Delphine collapsed into the nearby chair, allowing herself a moment. Her shoulders heaved once as her head dropped in her hands. Panicked, Nena rushed to her and put her hands on her mum's arms to comfort her.

"Mum," she said, "what do you need me to do?"

Delphine put a hand up, shaking her head as she got herself together. "I'm fine." She swallowed her pain. "I don't know what happened, actually. Your father was at a luncheon, and when he came home, he seemed fine one moment. The next he was vomiting, complaining of dizziness and stomach pains. Then he was foaming at the mouth and passed out. It was horrendous."

Her mother shuddered, as if trying to shed the images. "One of the men called the paramedics, and here we are awaiting test results."

"Was Dad feeling ill prior to that?"

"Not really. Maybe a headache or stomachache here and there for the past week." Her mother stood up, making her way back to the bed, where she held Noble's limp hand. "I just thought it was fatigue from the meetings he's had with the Council and Lucien."

Nena's stomach plummeted. Her dad had been with Paul.

"He'll be fine, darling," her mum assured her when she noticed Nena's angst. Their mum was always the one with the stiff upper lip. "And while your dad's recovering, I'll run the Council. Elin? Is she on her way?"

"Yes, Mum, she and Oliver should be chartering a flight to get back here."

Delphine nodded. "Good. Because we need to keep a united front. We're not cracking up in front of that lot, no matter what happens with your dad," she said.

"Which will be nothing," Nena added quickly, slipping her hand into the curve of her father's and feeling its warmth. A warm hand was a good thing, a living thing.

"Nothing at all," Delphine agreed, offering a thankful smile. "I love you, Nena."

Nena ducked her head. Those words never ceased to make her a little anxious, although she had no reason to be. She constantly worked to make herself deserving of them, hoping beyond all else it wouldn't be the last time she heard them from either of her parents.

# 52

## BEFORE

Not even a week after the Knights asked me what I wanted, Ms. Delphine announces once breakfast has ended that she and I are going to an appointment. Imagine my shock when she takes me to see a doctor who handles woman issues. When Ms. Delphine explains to me what a gynecologist does and where in my body the gynecologist will look, I consider running.

No one has seen any private part of me since Monsieur forced me to change in front of him. I am in a state of near hyperventilation until, in the waiting room, Ms. Delphine places a warm hand on mine.

"Please, darling," she whispers. "We have to do this. We have to make sure you are well."

"I *am* well," I say through gritted teeth.

"Well in *there*," she enunciates.

What if I'm not? Will they throw me back into the water like a fish too small to keep?

I sit so rigidly my lower back hurts from the strain. The whole time, Ms. Delphine keeps her hand on my arm to either soothe me or prevent me from leaving. I'm not sure which. I do not need a doctor to tell me my insides are ruined. I knew it the moment Paul's men raped me.

The nurse calls me. Ms. Delphine stands, making me do the same. I loathe doing this. I do not want to again feel vulnerable, but I trust Ms. Delphine's decisions. The room the nurse leads us into has a small bed that goes up and down, sits up and back. There are metal attachments at the end, which I learn are stirrups. They are nothing like the ones used with horses. The nurse is pleasant enough and asks me questions I cannot answer because I can't remember.

"When was your last menses?"

I do not know.

"When did you first have your menses?"

I cannot remember. Since the village and the Compound and Robach, things have been different, down there—inside.

"Are you sexually active?"

If my look could kill, there would be one less nurse.

"Were you sexually active before . . ." She trails off. There is no soft way to ask if I was a virgin before I was raped.

At any rate, I was a virgin.

"She would have only been fourteen."

The nurse clears her throat, sounding nearly as uncomfortable as I feel. "I'm sorry for the questions. It's just we have to ask about your sexual history, even at that age."

Ms. Delphine is offended on my behalf, and I sneak a look to see she is glaring at the nurse. "Let's move on, shall we? These questions are irrelevant. What is important is now."

"Yes, ma'am." The nurse asks me to remove my clothing and don the paper robe.

She leaves us alone. Ms. Delphine tries to avert her eyes when I turn my back on her so I can undress. I worry about what the doctor will say about me, because I will not be able to bear her pity. When we return home and she tells Mr. Noble and Elin what she has heard, they will pity me too.

The doctor is not only a woman but the same color as me. She is older, maybe sixty, with big round glasses and a comforting smile. I relax a bit. Her hands are warm and soft, and she does not talk down to me or make assumptions.

"May I?" she asks before touching me.

She will never know how grateful I am that she asked first. I nod, sneaking a look at Ms. Delphine, who earlier refused to leave when the nurse suggested that she wait outside during the examination.

"She is my daughter," Ms. Delphine told her. "You're mad if you think I'm leaving her."

My entire chest expanded so much I was afraid it would explode.

The doctor tells me what she is doing every step of the way. She shows me the speculum before she puts it in. Despite my effort to keep quiet, I cry out from the pain, from memories of my defilement by those men. Down there, the doctor makes sounds I cannot discern to be good or bad.

"Nurse, let's have an ultrasound."

Once the technician completes the ultrasound exam, the doctor says regretfully, "Just as I feared." The monitor is swirls of gray, black, and white. I do not know what I look at, but she begins to explain. "This"—she points at the screen, tracing a web of what looks like white bands in a sea of black and gray—"is what I was worried about. It's scar tissue, a result of extensive traumatic injury. Untreated scar tissue hardens, which it's done now. Scarring can come from tears in the vagina from forceful entry or could be from untreated sexually transmitted diseases."

"Does she—?" Ms. Delphine chokes out.

The doctor looks at me with compassion. "We've tested for all of it, and the results will come soon. I've put a rush on them. To me, this scarring looks like a result of forced entry."

Ms. Delphine says, "I did explain to you that Nena has been sexually assaulted." She glances at me. "Repeatedly," she whispers as if I have not lived it. She uses her right hand to twirl the large diamond rings on her wedding finger.

The stitching of the doctor's name on the breast of her coat reads *Eddington*. "Yes, and the massive scarring . . ." She trails off. "Reveals a substantial history of abuse."

She didn't need these scars to tell her that. I could have told her that without all this fuss.

"Which is why she's now with us," Ms. Delphine explains rigidly.

I drown them out. The doctor says nothing I do not already know. My scars are not new to me. They are only a part of my story.

She pauses, her duty making her deliver the rest. "I also fear Nena will be unable to carry children without extreme difficulty. Maybe not at all."

My head swivels toward Ms. Delphine, and to my shock, she is crying. I hate these moments. Consoling people is not my thing, but I pat the hand resting on my arm.

*Pat, pat, pat.*

"No children?" Ms. Delphine interprets.

"It looks unlikely. There is too much damage, rendering her body unable to sustain a pregnancy. And if her assailant passed on an STD that went untreated, her ovaries and eggs were likely compromised."

*Pat, pat, pat.*

Our roles reverse because while I am okay with this news, Ms. Delphine is beyond solace.

"My child cannot have her own children?"

There is a lightness in my chest at hearing her say "my child," as if I have been there all along.

*Pat, pat, pat.*

This time, I will not fail them.

"No more tears, Mum," I say. *Pat, pat, pat.* "I will be okay."

Mum looks at me and dissolves into more tears. Have I misspoken? Her shoulders are shaking, and she is a blubbering mess. I cannot tell if it's calling her Mum that has reduced her to pieces or the news I am barren.

And there you have it. I will not bear children. And I am not surprised by it. It is my fate, the final nail in my coffin, so to speak, for betraying my family.

Fitting, no?

Consider it. Death and violence are my legacies.

But watching Mum strengthens my resolve to become the best at whatever I do from this moment forward. I resolve to make amends to my first family, to no longer know fear.

I swear to protect the people of my new family.

Who have opened their arms to me, have invested in me.

Offered me a seat at *their* table.

And have given me their name.

# 53

## AFTER

Hours after arriving at Mercy Hospital, Nena was in the middle of getting tea for her mum when an incoming call made her step away from the vending machine—Mum would have hated vending machine tea anyway—to answer it.

"Aninyeh," Paul began when the call connected. "I hope you are well. I know you've been busy."

"How do you have this number?" She wouldn't exchange pleasantries with her mortal enemy.

"I have my ways," he said coyly. "You would do well to remember that."

"And that means what?" she snapped.

"How's Noble?" he asked. "He was just with me earlier. Seemed very healthy. It's a shame, really, what's happened to him."

Perhaps if she played it cool, didn't give anything away, then he wouldn't get whatever he was fishing for. "All is well."

"Cut the bullshit, Aninyeh; I've been in contact with Delphine. I know your father's fallen ill quite unexpectedly."

Nena's stomach clenched. *Let him talk,* she told herself.

"Your mum is rather unnerved, I'm sure. I offered to assist in any way I can. I'll step in if I have to, even though I'm the new kid on the block, so to speak." He chuckled. "Of course, Delphine wants to keep it quiet from the Council. Doesn't want them thinking your father weak enough to let his guard down and be usurped. I agree with her decision. For now."

His banter dropped, leaving his voice cold and unforgiving. "I told you to leave this alone, girl. I told you to let bygones be bygones after Attah."

She forced herself to be quiet. *Let him talk so you don't say something to make things worse.* But she'd already made matters worse, hadn't she? And her father was the victim.

"But you don't listen. I told you not to fuck up my opportunity with the Council."

"I haven't told anyone anything, Paul."

"I am Lucien Douglas now."

"Funny, you sound and act very much like Paul Frempong."

"Careful, girl."

"They don't know anything about you."

"Yet Kwabena is dead."

She closed her eyes. She'd expected him to find out. She hadn't expected him to go for her dad. Not when Paul was so new to the Council. It was a big play.

"Who's next, Aninyeh, hmm? My child, Oliver? Me? Am I next on your revenge list? Because I know you cannot kill a Council member. You would risk harm to your family?"

She hated it when he used her name from before. He had no right. He'd ripped it from her as he had stripped away her humanity. Hearing him speak it made her knees weaken every time and notched another chink in her resolve. Maybe she should just give up and let him have whatever he wanted again. Maybe then he'd leave Dad and everyone she loved alone.

"Would you?" she countered, hoping her voice sounded strong and assured, a stark contrast to the unadulterated fear and doubt raging. "Because all I have to do is tell the Council and my parents who you really are, and the dispatch would be sanctioned before I finish speaking."

He snorted. "You could," he said. "But then your mother and your sister would suffer a similar fate as your dad. However, they might not be so lucky," he told her. "Your father may well be on his way if you try me any further. This little illness of his is but a warning."

"You hurt them, and I'll kill Oliver."

He laughed at her, a crass sound that chopped her down to nothing. That damn laughter. She hated how it sliced her with fear whenever she heard it. "You don't kill innocents, love. That's my job."

She felt bile rise in the back of her throat.

She remained silent, a stinging behind her eyes. This couldn't be happening again. She would die if she had to suffer another loss of that magnitude again. She would not survive it; of this she was sure.

"Or better yet, perhaps I rid myself of only your father, take Delphine as my wife. She's still beautiful, you know. Aged like fine wine. And I assume complete control of not only the Council but your family as well." He laughed as if he'd made an uproariously funny joke. "I'd be your father, Nena. What do you think of that? Irony at its fucking finest."

Over her dead body would Paul ever be her father. Or assume High Council.

"You've played with me too much, girl, and it's time I remind you of who you are dealing with. There will be no more of your temper tantrums."

As if with the snap of fingers, Nena was fourteen again, taken back to her burning village: to the moment Papa lost his head, to the sweltering Hot Box, to the murderous Robach.

277

She swallowed hard. Willing herself to remain calm, to not let him know how deeply he'd wounded her. Tiny hairline cracks snaked through her usually placid demeanor. Paul was the only person who could make her feel all the fear and insecurity she'd felt as a young girl. He was the only person she truly feared because she knew the depths he would go to take from her again.

His point made, Paul disconnected the call.

# 54

## BEFORE

"Noble, you're mad," Mum argues in a hushed whisper. "We should be teaching her the business like we're doing with Elin. What you're suggesting, it's too much. Hasn't she had enough violence in her life?"

It is late, and I should be asleep, but I woke up thirsty and came downstairs to get a drink. Mum and Dad's bedroom door is open, and they speak freely, thinking they are alone. Candidly, about me. Part of me feels guilty about eavesdropping. The other part of me wants to know their true thoughts of me.

"Del, trust me on this. She won't want to run books and make decisions on the corporate or moral levels about Council territories. She won't want attention on her. You know this."

"Yes, but—"

"But you heard her the other day. She wants her power back. She wants to feel safe and like she has a choice in what happens to her. She needs something physical to do, something concrete."

"And assuming control with Elin when we step down isn't concrete enough? She will help run this entire organization that you have built."

"She won't want to sit behind a desk and make deals and lead the business ventures. Those are for Elin to handle." The volume of Dad's voice never increases. He always remains calm. He always chooses his words carefully. "My fear is if we do not channel her rage, and believe me, she has it, it will manifest in self-destructive ways. She needs to release the demons she harbors inside."

"Are you calling our child evil?" Mum blusters.

My lips tremble, a sob teasing at them. Is that how Dad sees me? As evil?

"Of course not. I'm saying Nena needs to channel her anger. She won't speak of her past anymore. She needs to do something physical— just trust me, Del."

"Well, surely we aren't going to win parents of the year, allowing one of our daughters to do this," Mum grumbles, the steam let out of her fight.

Relieved their disagreement is merely a difference of opinion and not an argument, I relax, about to go back the way I came, until their next words make me stop.

"No, but when the girls are adults and inherit their roles as heads of the Tribe, along with the other members and their children, our family continues its top position. It's only our family I fully trust to ensure the Tribe continues as it was meant to be."

*Tribe. Council.* The words roll in my mind, sounding both ominous and exhilarating. I knew there was more to Dad and Mum's business. Everything sounds very secretive, and they watch their words around me. But now, it seems this Tribe and Council will become my business as well. My water forgotten, I make my way back to my room and shut the door behind me. For the first time since I can remember, I feel excitement bubbling up. Whatever Dad has planned, I hope he will tell me sooner rather than later.

Because I can stand no further delays in reclaiming who I am.

———

There are only a couple of weeks remaining of school before the summer holiday. I look forward to it, hoping the summer temperatures will be more tolerable for my heat-accustomed body. After a particularly uneventful day, Margot directs me to the garden, where Dad awaits.

He sits on the wicker bench and slides over to make room. The garden is vast, with a maze of bushes and trees I like to get lost in. Dad finds the garden as soothing as I do. He is often in it while I toil away at my bonsai and other exotic plants I am determined to make live in this harsh weather. Some do; some do not.

He asks after my day, which has gone fine. Then he crosses his legs, a habit of his I'll eventually learn happens before he "gets down to business," as Elin likes to say. He also tends to tilt his chin up a centimeter and look to the air as if seeking guidance. My eyes travel up as well, expecting to see a face or force looming above. There's nothing there.

"You may or may not already know, but I originate from Senegal, having immigrated here when I was young. My parents sent me first to live with an uncle in Nigeria, where I involved myself with a rough bunch, enjoying my sudden freedom from my parents. I was a pretty bad child.

"When my uncle sent me to England to live with an old girlfriend of his, I continued along my path. I liked what I was doing back home, but I didn't want to be the soldier anymore, the bag boy holding the food or guns. I wanted to be supplying the food, the brains of the whole organization. I wanted to run the money because, to me, money was the most important thing. Because I had gone so long without it, I never wanted to be without it again. I would kill for it. And I did."

I was not prepared for his admission. Murder is something he and I share. He is telling me of our shared experience, but to what end?

"I met Del when I was twenty. She was seventeen and attending an all-girls uni. Her family had immigrated here from Ghana when she was a baby. They owned several markets and a dress shop that specialized in African fabrics and were doing well for themselves. They certainly didn't want me around their daughter, but your mum and I were inseparable from the moment she sold me a cola in one of their stores.

"Eventually, her parents began to accept me. Her brother, Abraham, became my best friend. We grew into this world together—Abraham, Del, and I."

I cannot explain my feelings as I listen to him speak. It pleases me that he is sharing his past with me, that he can relate to something of the life I lived on the streets. However, I am curious where this conversation is heading.

"Have you heard of my father before?" I ask. "Michael Asym? Or of N'nkakuwe and of how it is? Chigali, maybe?"

Dad's eyes dim as he weighs his words carefully. "I did not know your father, not personally."

"My village?" I ask, hoping he says there is something left. A deeper part of me knows the truth.

He shakes his head. "No, Nena, N'nkakuwe is gone. It is as you said, burned to the ground with not a soul left. We scoured Aburi Mountain for any signs, any survivors."

I catch my bottom lip between my teeth to prevent it from trembling. I turn away, my vision blurring and hot. I knew this already, but I couldn't help harboring this one last bit of hope that I was wrong.

"Soon," my father says, "Del, Abraham, and I developed a routine. I hustled, and she had the business sense and knew when a deal was good or not. I trust her above anyone else, and with our partnership, I rose higher and higher in the ranks of one of the local organizations we got in with. There are many organizations from various countries who trade and work together to import and export goods, drugs, arms, money, things like that. Eventually I had enough sway to unite a few of the African organizations working out of London. These became the African Tribal Council."

*The Tribe.* I recall the conversation I overheard between Dad and Mum.

"The Tribe, as we call it, is a conglomerate of countries from all over Africa. Our investors are wealthy people who come from those countries. We dedicate ourselves to the advancement of all African nations and Black people everywhere. You see, we hate that the world thinks of Africa as third world, though there are factions within and abroad who prefer Africa remain split and at war all the time. That we remain unaware of the riches we walk on every day. Those entities seek to plunder us, to take advantage of our trusting and loving nature."

His words have me enraptured, but as I continue listening, a thought begins to develop. What if N'nkakuwe had had the Tribe's protection? The people would all still be alive, and I would have never been taken and sold. The troubling thoughts crash about in my head until I can no longer hold them in.

"Where was the Tribe when N'nkakuwe needed them?" It comes out as an accusation, an unfair one, but I cannot help what I feel—let down, as if the world turned its back on us.

My words wound him. His face crumples, and he sucks in a deep breath, searching for the best answer. I should take back my question. Dad has been nothing but kind to me. But then I think about my dead papa, my brothers and auntie, my entire village, and I wait for his response.

"There's nothing I can say that will be suitable enough, Nena."

That is all he offers, and I don't know what I am supposed to do with it. But I suppose, what can he say? Dad is not God, but how can he claim to be a protector of African people if these things happen beneath his nose?

Dad continues, "Even though the Tribe is focused on advancing the African cause as a united entity, sometimes we must employ extreme measures."

"You mean killing others."

Dad hesitates. "It's not as simple as just killing people. Everything we do is for the advancement of our cause. We do not condone anything that denigrates African people. Our focus is on controlling imports and exports out of Africa. We do smuggle contraband as necessary to make money, to obtain power."

"Do you smuggle slaves?"

His eyes cloud. "We are businessmen and women working in unison for the advancement of Africa and the people in it and of it," he says again. "Do you understand, Nena? We work to make Africa as powerful as the Western world."

My eyes never waver from his. "And the imprisonment of humans, of children? And the rape and torture of them? Does the Tribe trade in that?"

"No," he says firmly. His gaze holds mine. "The Tribe would never knowingly participate in human trafficking."

Dad says they would never *knowingly*, but he cannot say unequivocally, because this Tribe of his is not perfect.

He cannot deny the Tribe dabbles in selling people to others for their entertainment.

"Nena, we have transferred people in and out of Africa, yes, but not to be sold as slaves. Never that. At least, that is not something we condone or would allow if we knew. I cannot dictate what the individuals decide to do on their own or what those under their watch do, but when the Council learns of such actions, we take care of it. We quell it."

Does he realize how naive he sounds? My expression must tell him so, because he frowns back at me.

"What happened to your village should not have happened. Paul performed those atrocities, not the Tribe. Sometimes, we do move people in and out of countries for various reasons—the main reason being that the people want a new life and can't get out properly. However, our transportation of them is not against anyone's will." He looks at me as if checking if I am still with him. Begrudgingly, I nod. "Sometimes, we have enemies transferred elsewhere to repay a debt or as punishment for something they've done. But sometimes—"

"Sometimes, the murder of innocent people, the selling of their women and children to be slaves for disgusting pedophiles, falls between the cracks," I finish between clenched teeth, hands balled by my sides. This moment is the first and only time I ever want to strike my dad, to rain punches upon his head for each and every life lost in N'nkakuwe.

It's as if all his energy has drained from him. "That is what we work against. It's why we work to create legitimate businesses, so our people never have to subjugate themselves to anyone."

I suck my teeth. My anger ignites my boldness. I barely know myself. "And Paul? What of him?"

"Also gone. When your home was razed and your father, chief of N'nkakuwe, murdered, it was an act of treason in our eyes. But because we don't have dealings with Paul, we don't know him. There are many people we deal with in Ghana. Paul is not one of them."

"And the other two? Where are they?"

"Likely dead. We've conducted extensive searches. We sent out our dispatch teams."

I squint at him against the sunlight, still not quite trusting it could all be over. "The Compound?"

"We cleared it. It's demolished now. I believe he has been eliminated, Nena," Dad says comfortingly. "He could not have hidden from my resources."

"Truly?" I look at him, hoping beyond hope.

He grunts and gives a slight nod, and I settle back on the bench, letting what he has said resonate. Dad cannot relate to what happened to my village or at the hands of Monsieur. He does not know how it feels to be sold like cattle.

"Without boring you . . . ," he continues, attempting to get us back on track and away from my accusations.

I continually remind myself I am not angry with him.

"I am at the head of the Council table. I am the High Council. All major deals run through me. Del says whoever holds the purse holds the key. I guess that's why she is the boss of the house, eh?" He laughs, while my mouth twitches at the truth. She does.

He drops his arm on the top bar of the bench behind my shoulders, careful not to touch me, aware of my triggers.

"Delphine and I work well together. She has an affinity for reading people. For knowing their soul, so to speak. It's why she brought you home to us. She could read that you were the missing puzzle piece in our family."

I cannot remember the last time I was this kind of emotional. It feels good, proper, to be tearful because I am happy.

"What we have is a family business. This business is what Elin will eventually run—and, we hope, with you by her side."

My mouth prepares to protest running any business, but he holds up a hand.

"I know you don't want to run a business. But you need to know it so that you can be the other half. Elin will be its face, run the deals and the money. You'll work in operations; you have a knack for getting things done when they need it. And you two will do it all for the advancement of our family and the Tribe."

My mouth closes as I consider his offer. That sounds acceptable.

"Africa cannot have another massacre like N'nkakuwe. Rogues like Paul cannot go unchecked. The channels and ports the Tribe runs need to be free of outside influences, free of inner turmoil and chaos."

He grips my shoulder now, squeezing it firmly. I do not flinch, so enraptured by his words am I. "You heard me mention the dispatch teams earlier. To keep the order, we created a special team of representatives who ensure obedience within the Tribe and its territories by any means necessary. Without order, there is anarchy. Do you understand, Nena?"

I nod.

"I mean for you to become one of these representatives and handle any issues that arise that threaten the stability and success of the Tribe.

The African Tribal Council only recognizes our administration of justice. We take care of our own, the good and the bad."

I nod.

"But most of all, I want our family protected. I want you and Elin to look out for each other and our Knight name above all else."

I nod.

"How does that sound?" Dad asks, looking down at me.

"Sounds good."

"Good." He nods, relieved all has gone well.

"Dad?"

"Yes, Nena?"

"Thank you."

"For?" He raises an eyebrow, waiting patiently for me to continue.

"For trusting me." My hands clasp and unclasp in my lap, and I sneak little peeks at him from under my eyelashes. "And for giving me back my power."

# 55

## AFTER

CORT: How's your dad?

NENA: The same, but stable. Not awake yet.

CORT: Your mom, sister?

NENA: They're well. Thanks.

CORT: What about you??

Nena glanced up from the screen of her cell and looked out the window of the hospital's waiting room. She hadn't left in the twenty-four hours since she'd arrived, seeing to her parents and waiting for Elin to arrive from Vegas, where she'd been with Oliver. Figured. She imagined her sister arriving in a whirlwind of *fuck*s and *heads are going to roll*s.

Though the previous day's call with Paul had rattled Nena so much she thought she might take up smoking herself, she found time to reply to Cort's numerous messages, reject his multitude of offers to come and bring food, and update him on her dad. It was nice to talk to a regular person amid all this . . . well, shit. Shit she'd caused, she supposed. By playing at revenge. By underestimating Paul. By not warning her family that he was back.

How had she returned to this dark place, after fighting for her literal life, conquering death, just so she never had to experience the loss of family again? Yet here she was. Powerless, threatened, and terrified by the same man. Again.

Her cell vibrated.

CORT: Nena?

She had forgotten to reply.

NENA: Sorry. I'm fine, distracted. Can I call you later? Maybe ice cream with G at Azucar?

CORT: Do you one better, a real date? I know it's bad timing, but . . .

Her stomach fluttered as she read the words. Was this really happening? And now? A real date. Could she even do this when her dad was in the hospital and Paul was just looming over her bloody head like a guillotine? Wrong choice of words. She had to get herself together. Maybe she could concentrate better if she just allowed herself this one reprieve. Was she wrong for considering it?

CORT: Your lack of response is killing me. Is that a no?

She mused on how Cort could cut through her dark cloud with a beam of light. Then she wiped her eyes. Suddenly furious at herself.

*I am inept at protecting the people I love.*

The fact that she couldn't protect her family was the worst admission she could make. She couldn't protect her family back then, and she was coming to the realization she still wasn't able to now. Paul was just too good.

CORT: ???

NENA: Yes. OK. A date.

She thought for a second as she closed that message chain and opened the running one she had with Elin, then typed a quick message. She watched the three pulsating dots, awaiting Elin's response.

ELIN: We track teens now? 🤨

Georgia was without protection. Who knew if Paul knew about her connection to the Baxters? She aimed to keep it that way, but Nena would feel better knowing Georgia's whereabouts.

NENA: Yes.

ELIN: Any particular reason?

NENA: A favor.

ELIN: 😑 Figures. See you when you get back to the hospital?

NENA: Yes. Thanks. Be safe.

She felt better now that her bases were covered and the important people were protected until she could determine her next moves. She could have put a trace on Cort, but she didn't want to chance him finding out about it or anything else going on. Besides, Nena already knew how to locate him. After all, he had been her mark, once upon a time.

# 56

## BEFORE

A couple of days later, Dad picks me up after school, and we drive to an industrial section of the city near the port. It is composed of several warehouse facilities for imports and exports. It is not a place I am familiar with, and I stare out the window to memorize the route. It is force of habit that I must know where I am and how to get back home, even if I am only going to the market with Margot and Chef Ishmael.

We pull up in front of a formidable-looking warehouse. Dad doesn't wait for the driver to open the door for him, but he stops me with a glance when I reach for my door. I retract my hand and wait for the driver.

"You are a lady at all times, Nena," he says when we are both outside and I am staring at the grayish-white building. "Even when you are doing your job." It seems my training has already begun.

Inside, there is a lanky Black man with a strikingly lush beard, matching bushy eyebrows, and stern-looking eyes waiting for us at a table in the middle of the room. The inside of the warehouse looks bigger than the outside. It holds a boxing ring, a large area with floor mats covering it, and various accoutrements for physical training lining the wall.

"Witt," Dad says, grasping the man's arm in a half handshake, half elbow-grip hug. They pull away, snapping their intertwined fingers.

"Sir," Witt says. He steps away from Dad, returning my appraisal.

Dad looks down at me. "I'll leave you now, Nena; is that okay?"

I'm not sure it is okay. I do not know this man, but my gut doesn't indicate danger, and Dad would not put me in danger. I nod.

"I will send the car back for you when Witt gives word you're done for the day."

Witt grins. "Shouldn't be too long. It's the first day."

"Not too long" by Witt's standards is six hours of grueling calisthenics and an assessment of what I can and cannot do. I cannot do much.

"You're a bit skinny, do you know that?" he asks me as I attempt push-ups. "Do you eat?"

"Yes, sir."

"You'll need to eat more. Build muscle mass, but not too much. You must retain your natural figure. And you'll need to join sports at school. That way, I know you're exercising when you're not with me."

"Yes, sir," I pant, about to drop. My arms tremble from the strain.

"Don't call me *sir*," he says. "That's for the military, and I'm no military man. Anymore."

My body collapses on the cement. I can sense Witt's eyes on me.

"Why do you want to do this?"

I do not want to explain my reasoning for choosing to be the harbinger of death. This is how I now see myself after the long talk Dad and I had, and I like the sound of it. I give Witt the same answer I gave my new family.

"To be safe and get your power back?" he scoffs. "You don't have to endure this training to be safe. You are a Knight now. That's as safe as you can get. You're safer than the goddamn royals! And being told when and where to dispatch people is not very powerful, if you ask me."

I sneak a look at him. "I need to make myself safe, and I want to dispatch." That's all I say. Luckily Witt accepts the answer, and we move on.

"I am your trainer and will be your team lead when you become part of Dispatch," Witt explains, giving me a tour of the facilities. "Network is the eye in the sky who watches your back when you're out there. I'm in Network, and that means I have your back. We must learn to trust each other more than anything else. You, me, and the rest of the team." He frowns. "It'll take them some time to get used to you, as you will be the youngest team member—if you make the team, that is. I'll teach you everything I know. And shit I don't."

His voice is heavy with accent, but it won't be until months later that I learn Witt is from Rwanda and experienced the genocide of the Hutu, and he wasn't one of the good guys. I will not hold Witt's past against him, because in this present, he is good to me, and he is my teacher. Plus, I learn he has atoned tenfold for what he did in Rwanda, and that speaks volumes.

———

For the remainder of my years in school and university, I do as I am told, joining the soccer team, where I learn stamina and increase my leg strength and endurance. I do not enjoy being on a team, but I do enjoy the thrill of winning games. And I learn how to be on a different kind of team.

"You are on the soccer team to develop passable social skills, Nena," Witt tells me. "You can't only talk to your dad, mum, sister, and me all the time."

"But I don't like anyone else," I answer, doing my last round of burpees. "I barely like you as it is."

"Now, that is a goddamn lie." Witt smirks, handing me rope for me to jump. "Dear girl, you'll pay for that comment."

# 57

## AFTER

It was hard to believe the woman staring back at Nena was her and that she was going out like a normal thirtysomething woman. It wasn't like when she had to dress up for work. Those were uniforms, part of a mirage. Tonight was for her. And yes, Cort too.

A sudden surge of embarrassment hit her that she was giddy with her first boyfriend—if she could call Cort that at her age. And she felt some guilt, too, that she was excited about going out when she should be with her mum, ensuring her dad stayed on his slow but steady path to recovery after he'd regained consciousness. The doctors were still puzzled about what had made him ill, and the only person who knew was Paul, not that she'd ever ask.

She shouldn't be feeling like a schoolgirl, worried if Cort would see her as woman enough. Did she want him to? Did she have what it took to be someone's lover? Would she even like it? Up until this point, the only feelings Nena associated with sex were pain and shame. She looked down at her hands, at her perfectly polished nails. These hands had done things no other woman Cort knew would do. These hands had killed. Could these hands love?

She'd spent her adult life accepting the idea she would never love a man, not in that way. Never again have sex because she wanted it. The thought of intimacy had always repulsed her. But since Cort, the revulsion had grown less and less. The thought had become not so unimaginable.

She was curious about what that life was like, the one where she could give herself to someone and them to her. A life that was beyond the strict and regimented one in which she cocooned herself. The thought was both scary and exciting. Nena was still trying to decide which was stronger when Elin appeared behind her in the doorway of her guest room, which no one used because Elin was not into overnight guests.

"Absolutely not," Nena growled.

"Just a quick chat. It's the perfect pick-me-up for Mum with Dad out of commission and all."

"No." Nena's eyes slid back to the mirror.

Elin produced her phone, pointing the camera at her sister despite her protests. Both knew if Nena had been serious, it wouldn't be happening.

"How'd you get her in that?" Delphine asked in awe. They could see their mum in the hospital room beside their father as he slept.

"An act of God, Mum, truly."

Nena turned her body this way and that, appreciating the way the dress, white with black splotches resembling a Rorschach test, fit her form and fell in soft folds at her calves. The plunging neckline emphasized her cleavage. Her silver gladiator sandals finished the look and matched the silver ropes woven into the front tiara braid of her head. The rest of her hair flowed magnificently past her shoulders.

"I know Nena wasn't difficult," Delphine said knowingly.

"Thank you, Mum," Nena said, shooting her sister a death glare, which was returned with a sweet smile.

"I wish your dad was awake to see you, but they just gave him medication to sleep, and it will be too hard to wake him. I've taken a screenshot, though."

"Shit," Elin breathed. "Mum knows how to do screenshots."

"Okay," Nena called out, turning around. "I should go." She snatched the oversize straw clutch her sister handed her. One with a secret compartment perfect for the small gun she'd carry. She headed toward the stairs.

"Nena!" Elin called behind her. "Do not take the bike."

Nena gritted her teeth. She wasn't entirely inept when it came to men.

"And remember to let him lead," their mother's disembodied voice added, propelling Nena out the door faster.

She arrived early to meet Cort at a Cuban restaurant owned by a well-known Cuban singer. Cort was already waiting for her at the valet, which she really liked.

"You're gorgeous," he said when she was close enough to hear him.

She looked down, trying not to show how pleased she was at his compliment. "You are too." Then her hand touched her lips. How stupid of her. That wasn't how women complimented men.

He smiled. "Thank you."

She felt heat flush her cheeks.

He perked up. "I didn't know you were into cigars."

"Come again?"

"Cigars." Cort fished a plastic baggie out of his inner jacket pocket and handed it to her.

Confused, she held it up with her fingers to take a better look.

"Found it under the coffee table in the den. Please tell me it's yours, because that's who Peach said must have dropped it. If it's not, it means either Mack's taken up smoking or Peach lied to me and I need to rethink my parenting." He cracked a wry smile with only the slightest dash of trepidation.

It only took a second for Nena to understand what was going on. "Yes, I must have dropped it. I was trying to find the type of cigars my dad likes, so I had one. Sorry if I caused trouble for you or Georgia."

When she opened the bag, she recognized the scent immediately, and a rush of anger jolted through her. She hadn't left a cigar. But she knew who smoked ones that smelled exactly like this one. Clearly the cigar was another message, just like her dad's sudden illness was a message. But when had Paul dropped this message off?

*Recalibrate.* She was on a date and needed to focus on it, if only just for the night.

Cort's eyes widened apprehensively. "No problem at all. Just had to make sure, you know?" He reached out as if he wanted to touch her but thought better of it and returned his hand to his side. "Ready to go in?"

She nodded.

The restaurant was busy but beautiful and the perfect place for them to talk and dine. Gradually, she cleared her mind of other worries, and the conversation flowed easily. Nena answered all his questions about England and her travels.

"Your favorite place to vacation?"

"Bay of Naples," she said immediately. "And Bukhansan National Park. It's a forty-five-minute tube ride from Seoul."

"Korea?"

"Yes."

"Tube?"

"Subways."

They shared their entrées, dining on crispy whole fish, palomilla, and chino cubano. They sipped on mojitos while watching the other patrons dance on the floor.

"And your dad's doing better?"

She nodded, taking a bite of the fish. "He is. Thank you. The seizures have stopped, and they're monitoring his heart. Good prognosis."

Cort stood, extending a hand to Nena. She eyed him suspiciously, trying to figure out his plan. Eventually, she gave in, gingerly placing her hand in his and allowing him to pull her to her feet.

He led her through the restaurant to where the music was loudest, where the dance floor writhed with couples dancing to Davido's "Fall." He slipped his arms around her waist, drawing her close. She tensed up, then relaxed, allowing him to lead. He began softly singing the lines to the song in her ear.

She pulled back. Cort was full of surprises. And she liked it. He grinned, dropping his head sheepishly. She touched her finger to his chin, pulling him back to face her.

"Don't stop."

He moved side to side. She quickly fell in sync with his moves, pleasantly surprised his dancing differed vastly from his grilling techniques. Her body fell in line with his, and soon the music, the heat, the lights, the aromas, fused into a headiness that made Nena feel light headed. Was this what dating was like? Because when she saw the way Cort looked at her, it made her stomach somersault and the area she'd thought long dead come alive.

He lifted her arm above her head, twirling her slowly, and when she had revolved entirely and was facing him again, her eyes connected with his.

The music pounded in her ears. The way he looked at her—she swallowed. Why was he looking at her like that?

She fought rising panic. Her first impulse was to make space between them to stop him from touching her like that. But she found she wanted his touch.

And . . . she wanted him to kiss her. She wanted him to . . . maybe even more than that.

No, no, she couldn't. She'd never wanted that, not since they'd snatched her virginity from her, desecrating her. But her feelings were becoming undeniable to her now. She had fallen hard for him, even though it was impossible. He put away people like her. She dispatched people like him.

Her body tensed when he slipped his arm around her waist to slowly pull her in. He stopped when she hesitated, then pulled her the rest of the way when she allowed it. She stepped all the way in. Into his arms.

The dance music switched to Lianne La Havas's "Don't Wake Me Up."

"Love this song," Nena said softly. She swayed to its beat, surprised she was feeling this comfortable. She let the soulful song, let being with Cort, take her to a place of peace she'd never known could exist for a person like her.

And then she thought, *Why not me?*

# 58

## BEFORE

I keep going during the rigorous conditioning portion of my initial training, even when my body screams it cannot move another inch. But after a few weeks I must be conditioned enough, because while I'm at the table, lacing up my combat boots, Witt slides a picture of Monsieur into my line of vision. I look at it without saying a word; then my gaze flicks up to his.

"Show me how you did it," he says.

I drop my head back down to finish lacing. How can I reenact something that is not the same? I am without the primal drive to survive I had then. Why does Witt want me to relive that horror? Why is he not teaching me something new? He taps the picture sharply, and my head snaps up to him.

"Show me," he says. "Count off."

What is his end goal? Is he trying to break me, or can he not believe a scrawny thing like me can take down a being like Robach? But he wants to see, and I acquiesce.

We stand, facing each other. Robach and I weren't standing when I attacked him, and I must bring Witt down to where I can do what I did. I cannot tell him to have a seat so I can stab him, can I? Instinct takes over, and my right foot swipes Witt's from beneath him. He falls with a surprised grunt to the floor, and I lock away the sliver of worry that I might hurt him. I grab a pen that has rolled from atop the table. I feign a stab to his cheek.

"One," I say.

I jump on top of Witt, who bucks me off and rolls. When my body hits the floor, I roll fluidly, scamper to my hands and knees, and spring up, jumping on his back as I did with Monsieur.

"Two."

I cling to Witt's back as he tries to shake me off. He rears backward, smashing us against a wall. Pen in hand, I tap it against his neck.

"Three."

And his throat. "Four."

And his chest. "Five."

Witt tumbles to the floor, and I continue tapping him in the same places I stabbed Monsieur, counting while I do it. When I reach 150, I stop. My hand drops to my side, and I lift myself off my instructor. I stand back, panting, waiting for him to tell me what is next.

He is panting as well. He does not speak to me. Instead, he stands and walks to where Monsieur's picture has fallen on the floor and drops it back on the table. He shuffles through a file I neglected to notice was there. From there, he extracts two more black and whites, photos of the muggers from the Parisian breezeway. I stare at the pictures, amazed. What don't Witt and the Tribe know about what I have done?

He does not need to tell me to show him. I just do.

———

"Your method of attack is intrinsic," Witt says. We are standing outside the warehouse, waiting for my car to collect me. How he is capable of speech after our grueling training, I have no idea. I want to lie on the ground. My body throbs, and I am tired beyond comprehension. I wait for him to continue his assessment, since that is what this is.

"What I mean is it is instinctual. It's also sloppy and has many points in which your combatant can turn things around on you. You leave too much evidence, and you do not think. Your kills to date are from emotion, and from that rage, people can manipulate your weaknesses, your blind spots. You can't let emotion cloud your judgment, Nena. You can't take things personally." He lets that rest, having read me like a book.

"Correction," he reverses. "Robach was rage. The muggers were not. Those kills were more strategic. Those kills were cleaner. Why did you kill them?"

"They were attacking my mum."

"She wasn't your mum at the time you encountered them. Why did you step in?" He looks down at me curiously.

"Because she had shown me kindness, and I owed her."

He nods, approving of my answer. "When emotion is at the helm, mistakes happen. You'll learn to leave all your feelings behind. You must be methodical, Nena, when dealing in the business of dispatch and order as we do. You must think many steps ahead and of the repercussions. What happens after this job's done? Who will this affect? Can I get in and out cleanly?" He speaks as if reading from a laundry list of assassin what-not-to-dos. "You get the job done, though."

He looks at me, amused. "And it looks like you prefer to stab."

The corners of my mouth twitch in response.

———

From his assessment, Witt tailors my training to focus on my strengths. When I get in close, I am the most effective. He brings in several sparring partners of varying abilities, heights, weights, and strengths. He watches us duel until one of us taps out. These men and women don't get caught unaware like Monsieur and the Parisian men. These people are lithe killers and hold nothing back from little teen me. In fact, I think they mean to kill me.

"Use your proximity, Nena; forget the element of surprise here. It's gone," Witt commands as he observes me losing the fights repeatedly. All he needs is a bowl of popcorn to top it off. "Surprise is a luxury you can't always afford, so always assume they know you're coming. Like when you were in the basement, use anything you can find. Any object is a weapon in the right hands, in your hands. Use your surroundings to your benefit."

My eyes flutter open, unfocused. I nearly pass out from the arm pressing into my throat, squeezing both the air and consciousness out of me. Witt's words echo in the distance, as if down a long, empty hall. I grasp for anything of use. I use myself, letting my body suddenly go limp in feigned unconsciousness.

My partner loosens his grip a little, confident he has put me down. When his defenses drop just enough, my fingers grapple for anything, a boot kicked off during the struggle, now by my knee. I grasp the tip of it, then launch the heavy bottom sole with all my might, which isn't much. It strikes my partner in his temple.

After nearly a year of continual training—some phases concurrent—my sparring partner finally taps out, and I am ready to move on. Because of my age, my education in Dispatch takes longer than other prospects'. But during the next phase, Escape and Evasion, I have a little experience from my time with Robach and on France's streets. It only takes me half the time to make an A.

# 59

## AFTER

When Cort kissed her, it began with a peck. And then another, deeper, longer. And in the middle of the crowd, Cort kissed her deeply, passionately, like she'd seen in movies and had always fast-forwarded through when she could get away with it or suffered through when Elin complained she wanted to watch. Nena's arms circled around his neck, guiding him closer.

And it all felt right. *They* felt right. The way this newfound feeling permeated every bit of her being, like nothing she had ever experienced before. She followed his lead, using a little tongue when he did. Biting lightly, slightly, when he tugged. Sighing when he peppered her forehead with feather kisses. She found that more sensual than when he kissed her lips. She no longer knew herself. She felt forever changed by this moment, even if she never had it again.

"Renmen mwen," he said in a language she did not know.

It sounded like French, but not what she'd learned. "Your French is different than what I know."

"That's because it's Creole, like Haitian French."

"Oh." She'd learn it.

"Mon amour." That she did know. *My love.*

Pleasure sizzled through her. She had a new name, and that name was *love*.

———

Later, they walked hand in hand along the Miami Beach shoreline with waves cresting and washing up to meet and wash away their tracks.

She took a deep breath, knowing if she was going to take the leap and open herself to another person, it would have to be now, despite the promise to herself to never discuss it again. "Remember when we had lunch at Jake's? You asked about my past?"

He nodded.

"Well, I lived in a small village called N'nkakuwe. It was a great home, full of love, life, and prosperity. We had a good man, a chieftain, who was kind and fair, giving. Always giving."

"Sounds like a cool guy."

"He was," Nena agreed. "He was also my father, Michael Asym."

Cort slowed, his head twisting slowly toward her. "Wait. Hold up? You mean you're a princess? Like a daughter-of-a-chief kind of princess?"

She shrugged. "Titles don't matter much to me. We were simple villagers."

He cast her a dubious expression that read, *Yeah, okay.* Then he said, "Yeah, okay."

She couldn't explain the urge she had to tell Cort about what had happened in N'nkakuwe. It was like if she didn't speak it now, show him the most vulnerable part of herself, then she never would. And she couldn't continue to not give most of herself with Cort. She couldn't move past the hurt if she didn't let him know the hell from which she came.

She told him what Paul and his men had done to her village and people, what they'd done to her.

His steps halted. "What?" he asked, staring at her incredulously. His eyes searched hers, pleading for her to say it wasn't real. She wished she could. But one look into her eyes let him know every word she spoke was horribly real. His grip on her hand tightened.

"I know shit like this goes on, but to know it's happened to you . . ." He couldn't continue, overcome with anger. "I could really fuck somebody up right now, Nena."

"That's sweet of you," she replied in a tone she hoped was not patronizing. She appreciated his concern, but she needed no one's protection. She'd learned to protect herself years ago.

She went on to describe life at the Compound and the abuse she and the others had suffered there. She spoke of the Hot Box, remembering the heat of it. Her recounting of her time with Robach came out haltingly, ending with the opportunity to run six months later. She left out the American woman. And the state in which she'd left Monsieur.

"I was living on the streets of Paris. Only for a week or so—the days got a bit hazy." She'd relived this story over and over in her mind, had told it only a couple of times out loud, so to hear it from her lips now was unnerving.

"Must have been horrible."

She looked at him, full of determination. She didn't want him pitying her. She wanted him to see her as the survivor she was. "Anything was better than where I had been."

He nodded his head, kept bobbing it up and down. Placing his hands on his hips when they stopped briefly. He looked out into the dark waves lapping at the shore. His jaw moved. He had so many questions, so much to say. She knew this. But she only wanted him to listen. And he knew that.

"I found Mum, or rather she found me. The Knights took me in, adopted me. And here I am. A Knight." She threw out her hands and jiggled them like jazz hands.

But that was only half her story, wasn't it? Nena might be lovestruck, but she wasn't struck dumb. The training, the dispatching, the Tribe, she couldn't tell Cort about.

Nena looked up. Cort's head had dropped as if in prayer. She first thought he was displeased. She was used goods, wasn't she? Soiled. Ruined. He was shaking his head slowly. Maybe she shouldn't have told him all of this, but she had to. There was already too much he didn't know.

She prepared herself to lock away all those amazing first-time feelings, because she understood more than anyone that her baggage was tremendous, more than anyone else should have to deal with. She couldn't ask Cort to be patient with her as she got used to intimacy beyond the kiss they'd shared. The kiss had been terrific, but sex? There was no way she was ready yet. No matter how much her body had come alive tonight.

Nena peeked at his face. What she saw astonished her. Her fingers touched his face and came away with wetness on the tips. She looked down at them, confounded. Cort wept for her.

He passed his hand over his face. He looked at her sheepishly, unsure of what to do next.

"Ocean spray?" she asked with a knowing smile.

He laughed in spite of himself, a deep, rich laugh that elicited a genuine smile, small and rare as it was, from her.

He made a move to hug her and paused, asking permission. She stepped into his arms.

"Oui, mon amour. Damn ocean spray got the hell out of me."

Nena luxuriated in Cort's arms, knowing he was the first man, aside from either of her fathers, with whom she'd ever felt safe. It was a feeling that Nena knew once she had, she never wanted to be without again.

# 60

## BEFORE

Elin knocks on the frame of my open door and finds me reading in bed, my second-favorite pastime after watching movies. What is quickly becoming my third-favorite thing to do is training, especially as the thrill of working with tools during training increases. I look up from the latest Stephen King novel.

"Mum wants us in the kitchen," she says, looking annoyed at having to stop whatever she was up to, to do Mum's bidding.

We enter the kitchen and are immediately assaulted by a chaotic scene. Mum is behind the stove, something we never see. Ishmael helicopters, a complete wreck at having to yield his beloved kitchen to the mistress of the house. He wrings his hands and tries to guide Mum while remaining at a respectful distance.

He pleads, "Madame, please, it's best to use a wooden spoon on the pots so as not to scratch them. Perhaps I should take—" She shoots him a deadly look, making the words fall away from his lips. There is steam everywhere and a barrage of scents, making me wonder if I should be excited or fearful.

"Mum, what are you doing?" Elin eyes the explosion of sizzling stainless steel and bubbling cauldrons warily.

Mum shoots a quick glance over her shoulder. "I'm cooking supper."

Elin pantomimes sticking a finger in her mouth to gag and elicits a small guilty smile out of me. It is something Elin discovered only she seems to be able to do.

"You never laugh, Nena," my sister observed one day as we were looking through her favorite style magazines. "Not even a smile."

I shrugged. I find things amusing. I laugh within.

Elin blurted, "I think Ishmael and Margot are fucking."

I choked at the absurdity of her words. Margot is as old as a grandmother—no offense—and Ishmael is gay, although he has not made it publicly known.

"Fucking with you," she said, turning the page of her magazine. "But wouldn't it be a sight?"

I covered my mouth to hide the giggle that escaped. I find my older sister entirely inappropriate and wildly entertaining. "Aha," Elin said without looking my way. "So you will laugh for me."

"Ishmael, out!" Mum commands, fed up with his hovering. He falters in his hesitation to leave his blessed domain, but one more lethal stare cast in his direction reminds him whom he's dealing with.

Elin and I move closer to Mum's frenzy. There is cubed meat sizzling in a pot. Onions and tomatoes cut in various sizes, almost to a mashed pulp, litter the cutting board. On the countertops are open containers of peanut butter, palm nut, and other ingredients that I recognize. Mum wears a food-splattered apron, and her usually coiffed hair is in disarray. It doesn't look like that even when she is fresh from the bed.

"What are you making?" Elin asks, huge eyes roving over all the mess. She may not want to know.

Mum turns to us, beaming. "I'm making peanut butter soup and fufu and fried kelewele. Nena's favorites." I look over the hurricane that used to be our kitchen. The kitchen back home never looked like this.

"Really, Mum? You couldn't ask Ishmael to do it or have it brought in?"

Mum looks at me. "I wanted to bring a bit of home to Hammersmith for Nena." She offers me a hopeful look, wanting my acceptance. She has stepped out of her comfort zone, done something she never does. For me.

My heart nearly bursts from her display. Elin slides her gaze to me, waiting.

The corners of my mouth eventually pull into a small smile. I nod. "Thank you, Mum. It will be delicious."

Elin lets out a resigned sigh, and Mum hiccups as if she's sucking in a cry. She spins around quickly, returning to her sautéing and boiling.

Behind Mum's back, Elin leans toward me, whispering, "I'll ready the Pepto Bismol. You'll need it, love."

Mum's is the worst peanut butter soup (*pudding* is a better description), fufu (white, gritty, and as hard as stone), and kelewele (a mushy, salty mess made from plantains not ripe enough) I have ever had the pleasure of eating.

I eat every bit of what she puts in front of me. Then I ask for seconds, ignoring the looks of utter repulsion from Elin and Dad.

# 61

## AFTER

Although Nena was still high after her magical date with Cort the other night, the threat of Paul's next move loomed over her head. His cigar was a message that he could reach out and touch anyone. But she'd already known that, hadn't she? That was why she and Georgia were currently pulling up in front of a nondescript building in a warehouse section near the port where they'd fed the gulls earlier.

She and Georgia toured the facility. The gym was small and looked more like a boxing training facility. Didn't have the purple of Planet Fitness or orange of Orangetheory. There weren't a lot of people there, just a thick punching bag suspended from the ceiling and, in a back room, an expansive blue mat taking up much of the floor space. Georgia wondered aloud if they were about to practice gymnastics.

"You asked how I learned to fight," Nena began, settling her eyes on the younger girl. "It wasn't for pleasure, okay? It was for a purpose."

"Okay," Georgia prompted.

"The type of fighting you witnessed that night is called Krav Maga. It's not easy, and it takes years to learn."

"What is it? Like kung fu or something?"

Nena pulled a face. "No. There is no liberal philosophy with Krav. It's about doing whatever you have to and using whatever is around you to be the one that lives. Do you understand?"

"Think so."

"Krav is about acting by your instincts and using techniques that are simple and effective to get you away. It essentially makes you a human weapon."

Georgia cracked a grin. "That sounds pretty fucking cool."

Nena gave her a sharp look.

"Sorry," Georgia mumbled sheepishly. She bent down to untie her shoelaces. "Should I take my shoes off and get on the mat?"

"Do you plan to have your shoes off when you're attacked?" Nena asked curiously.

Georgia hesitated as if trying to determine if she was serious or not.

She was.

"No," Georgia drawled when Nena didn't answer. "I guess not?" It came out as a question. She seemed to wilt beneath Nena's intense scrutiny.

Nena said, "When the girl from your school put the gum in your hair, what did you do?"

Georgia offered a limp shrug. "Do? Where?"

"When you fought."

"I never said I fought."

"You didn't just stand there either. Show me," Nena prompted.

"But what does that have to do with learning combatives?"

Nena didn't answer, instead channeling her inner Witt.

Georgia gave in, positioning Nena as Sasha's stand-in. She pantomimed hitting Sasha in the mouth by tapping Nena on hers. Nena blinked away her surprise at the unexpected force of the blow.

Georgia grinned, pleased she'd gotten one in.

She grasped Nena's arm, recalling how she'd twisted Sasha's until the girl had cried out in pain and embarrassment. When Georgia dropped Nena's arm, she stepped back.

"And that's when Coach came in and broke it up."

"That's all?" Nena asked.

Georgia's head bobbed in several short nods.

"Was quick," Nena observed, lightly touching her smarting lip. Little bugger. "Not bad."

Georgia sighed with relief.

"Most fights are quick. Not long and drawn out like you see in the movies. And you tire fast because it takes a lot of energy to be that physical. Adrenaline is what pulls you through combat. You must use the little opportunity you have to get your opponent in a position for you to either get away or kill them."

Georgia blinked multiple times. "Who said anything about killing?"

"Had you ever fought before? Before the racist girl?"

Georgia made a face that questioned Nena's sanity. "No."

"Self-defense, then. That's what propels you."

Georgia thought about it. "Yeah, especially because of the hair. And she made a slick comment about my mom," she said between gritted teeth, fresh anger flooding her voice.

Nena nodded. She knew all too well about triggers. Nena's own hair was a mass of brilliant, luscious coils now twisted in a thick rope of two braids and swirled into a bun at the base of her head. And there was that one time when Robach had made derogatory comments about her father and brothers. They were the last comments he'd made before she'd killed him.

"So your mother is your trigger."

Georgia shrugged, toeing the edge of the mat. "I guess? And Dad too. No one can talk about my parents but especially my mom, since she's gone."

Who else but Nena would understand? "Let's start with if you're grabbed from behind."

"Why from behind?"

"That is typically the case. Element of surprise." She stopped, pursing her lips. "And I'd like to also work on if someone has a weapon on you."

"A what? You think that's going to happen to me?" Georgia choked out.

Nena frowned. "Hasn't it already happened? Those gang guys?"

"Again. You cut me off before I could say 'again.'"

Nena let out a cross between a cough and a snort. Georgia stared at her, wide eyed.

"I just made you laugh. Sort of. Was it a laugh? You need practice," Georgia said, practically vibrating.

As quickly as Nena's outburst had come upon them, her face blanked. "All sorts of things you never expect to happen can happen to you, and more than once. Remember that. Expect that."

"Okay."

"Let's begin," Nena said, pushing Georgia onto the mat facing the wall. From behind, she continued. "Couple things to remember. Fight with whatever is around you and in reach. Make anything a weapon."

"Anything?"

"I once killed a man with chopsticks." Nena said it as if she'd picked up milk at the grocery.

Georgia snapped around, forgetting they were supposed to be training, her eyes as round as saucers. "Get the fuck out!"

"Language," Nena said blandly. "Now turn back around and repeat the move from your nonfight. I'll react, and let's see what you can come up with to defend yourself."

This time, Georgia did as she was told.

# 62

## BEFORE

Dad and Mum teach me and Elin the ins and outs of Council, although she enjoys it much more than I do. Elin is shrewd, like Mum, knows when a deal is good or bad, plans and thinks things through. And I, like Dad, am better suited to action. We are becoming a well-oiled machine, each with our own roles and purposes. And I begin to feel real comfort at being a part of the family.

My sophomore year at university is when I begin tagging along on light team missions. It took Witt a while to get the okay from Dad, but Witt convinced him that the best way to learn was with on-the-job training. Reconnaissance and concealment go hand in hand. When I tag along with the team or with a member on a job, I usually stay back in what we call an urban assault vehicle. It is filled with cameras and microphones strong enough to pick up a mouse breaking wind, if they did that sort of thing.

I learn the key to recon is to be the observer, not the observed. And to never let a mark see me until it's too late.

———

I practice languages, one of my favorite subjects because of my affinity for them, thanks to Papa. Eventually, Languages and Linguistics becomes my major at uni, while Elin, of course, chooses Business and Accounting. A good decision.

I perfect my driving skills when Dad treats me to a weeklong event at the Circuit de Monaco, where I experience the Monaco Grand Prix. I train with one of the racers for Defensive Driving and High Speed. My first trip to America is to the Daytona 500 in Florida. It is a memorable experience that makes me fall in love with Florida, more specifically Miami, when we shoot down there afterward for Dad to conduct some business.

At the 500, I also learn to ride motorcycles, something to use in tight spaces and for quick getaways.

I undergo all these intense trainings over and over until I not only get a passing grade but excel. My education consists of the University College London and the University of Witt. I hungrily consume both, the illegal and the not, especially anything hands on. And I accept the consequences of my choices, the good and the bad.

———

After one particularly grueling day with the team, I am on my bed. Every inch of my body is racked with pain. When I try sitting upright, a sharp stab ricochets through my sides like a ball in a Ping-Pong machine. I bear down, breathing through the pain. My mind does a body check—I took a course from a field medic at the University of Witt—and I diagnose my pain by comparing it to injuries I have received before. I have bruised my ribs.

The scalding-hot shower I took to help ease the pain provided only temporary comfort, and I stare at the jar of ointment sitting all the way over on the dresser. My body begs for me not to move. But I try to ease off the bed, hissing through the pain.

"Need help?" Elin asks from the doorway.

I close my eyes, knowing what she will say when she sees my bruises. She invites herself in without my answering her, grabbing the ointment. She twists it open as she approaches me. She gets on the bed as carefully as possible, which, of course, makes me hurt worse.

"Sorry."

She gently removes the robe from my shoulders and emits an audible gasp at the dark-purplish bruising over half my body, the side Dana pummeled earlier that day.

"Bloody hell, Nena, how much more of this will you take?" Elin asks as she begins applying a thick slathering of ointment. The room fills with the smell of camphor. "You don't have to do this. It's been years, and you still get fucked up. Haven't you had enough?"

"I like it." I wince. "And I am nearly finished with my training."

"You're always hurt, bruised, cut, broken, or exhausted," she fumes. "I hate this for you." With nimble fingers, she kneads away knots of pain. I grit my teeth, my hands fisting into tight balls and digging into the duvet cover, to keep from crying aloud.

I hiss, "I'll be okay."

"Why can't you stick to the business side with me? Run it with me?" She asks me this every time she nurses me. It has become our routine. "We would be unstoppable."

"I don't want to run anything."

She pulls my robe over my shoulder and watches me inch into the bed, between the covers she has thankfully pulled down. When she tucks me in tightly enough I cannot escape, Elin lies beside me, her head touching mine. "What about a double date? Tomorrow."

Her voice brightens when she says it, and I twist my head to gawk at her, then return to my more pressing matter of finding a comfortable position to sleep in beneath this cocoon she has wrapped me in.

"Ben has a friend who says you're hot." Ben is her flavor-of-the-month boyfriend. Her words, not mine.

"I am hot," I mutter. "Would you mind turning down the heat when you leave?"

She wrinkles her nose. "Not that kind of hot, Literal Lucy. He finds you attractive. You need to shag, sis."

"Never."

"Never?" Her eyes are round as the saucers we use for tea. "You'll never have sex?"

We have had this conversation as well. My sister believes I have had enough recovery time and should enter the world of the sexually active. "I have unwillingly had enough sex to last a lifetime. And I find it quite distasteful."

"What about when you find love? I mean romantic love, not family kind of love."

I sigh again. Elin will never understand how dead I feel inside when it comes to sex, my repulsion when men touch me in that way or any way. I cannot imagine ever wanting someone to touch me like that again. She won't know the ruin I feel, the lack of desire. I have never known romance. Sex was used as a weapon against me. I want no more part of it. Even though she will never understand, I tell her how I feel. Then I open my eyes and look at her.

It is undeniable, the despair I see in Elin's eyes as she gazes at me. I wish she would not. There is nothing to despair. It is what it is. Exhausted, all I want to do is sleep, but Elin has more talk in her.

"Nena," she breathes, "when you came to us, you were this scrawny little thing. And in this short amount of time, you have become the most amazingly strong and bravest person I've ever met."

I can no longer meet her gaze. If I do, I will break right in front of her. With great effort, I say, "Kindly thank Ben and decline the date with his friend for me."

Elin huffs, annoyed with me, but only for a little while. I am not worried it will last. "Also, if you're going to be on Dispatch, you've got to sound more human, more your age," she says.

"Do I not sound human?" Her words are nonsensical. If I am human, how do I not sound so?

Elin touches her forehead as if dealing with a difficult child. "You sound robotic, Nena. You speak very properly, and I know you know multiple languages, and that's wicked, but you sound stilted. You're too tight, need to loosen up." She begins convulsing, jiggling her body in an alarming manner. "See, like this. Loosen up. And you need to use slang and contractions and idioms. Shit like that, or you'll stick out like a sore thumb, and your mark will make you."

"My thumb is actually the one part of my body that's not sore."

"And maybe throw in some cursing too. Say *bloody hell,* or call someone a tool-ass wanker or fucking cesspot."

I frown. "Is *cesspot* a word?" I am pretty sure she is saying it wrong.

Elin throws her hands up as she shrugs. "Who knows? But it sounds good when you're in the moment."

I nod, giving up on any comfortable position in my mummy wrap. "Okay." Elin makes a good point, and if I am going to be an invaluable member of Dispatch, like I plan to be, I had better get to work on becoming less . . . robotic.

# 63

## AFTER

It took Nena a couple of days of soul-searching to decide to tell Elin who Oliver's father was and that he might not be as innocent a bystander as Elin believed him to be. There was no more dancing around the fact that Paul had to go. His attempt on her father and his threats against the rest of the family were bad enough. It was the cigar that solidified her decision—Paul's cigar, its scent easily recalled from their encounter the evening of the supper party. Nena could no longer remain silent.

She'd asked Elin to meet at one of their favorite Mediterranean restaurants. Sitting across from her in her sharp business suit, Elin still looked fresh faced and beautiful despite having just arrived from closing on a new business venture in New York, a meeting she'd had to chair on their father's behalf.

"You're lucky Oliver had to cancel our plans for tonight . . . and that I love sister time and all," Elin said, gesturing to the server for another glass of white wine.

Nena watched her sister finish the first glass, wondering if there was any way she could be wrong. No, she decided. She wasn't.

"Yeah." Nena hesitated. "About Oliver."

Elin set her glass on the table, accepting a second glass and thanking the server with a quick smile. She took a sip and furrowed her eyebrows at the expression on Nena's face. "Jesus, Nena, why so grim? You and the kid's dad have a row?"

"No." Nena stalled, knowing this would be the moment that could divide her and Elin for the first time. "Cort gave me a cigar that was left at his house."

Elin snickered. "That shifty little bird. Is she smoking them or using the wrap for weed?"

"It's not Georgia's," Nena said. "It's Paul's cigar."

Elin snorted. "You must be totally knackered, sis. Where the hell did Paul come from? Last I checked, intel only had Dennis Smith and Kamil Sanders coming up, not big bad Paul."

Nena forged ahead. "Because I remember its smell from when he smoked it the night of the dinner party."

Elin's initial reaction was to lean away, as if whatever amount of crazy Nena had was contagious. "Come again?"

Nena lowered her voice. "Lucien Douglas is Paul Frempong."

She said it as if he were the boogeyman, and indeed he was. She watched as Elin, initially shocked, narrowed her eyes, which were filling with doubt that had never been there before.

"You've gone mad," Elin told her. "Perhaps Dispatch has taken its toll on you. You can't go throwing accusations like that around. Lucien is a *Council* member."

Nena nodded. "And he is Paul."

Elin wasn't buying it, the way she glowered at Nena. She held up a calming hand. "Nena, let's think this through. I know Attah Walrus brought up a lot of past feelings. And then learning of Kwabena, but there was nothing on Paul. Attah and Kwabena had intel. Lucien's intel has only been on the up-and-up. He went through the vetting process. We would have recognized him."

"How, when he had no photos? No one knows what he looks like except his old soldiers, who were dispatched when the Tribe raided the Compound, and any survivors who were there. Me. His face is something I could never forget."

Nena watched as Elin, their mum's spitting image, vacillated between doubt and the belief she'd always had in Nena. Nena had never lied or overreacted, and yet today she was asking Elin for more than she was willing—ready—to give.

"Okay." Elin looked up at the ceiling, no doubt thinking of a million contingencies. "You killed Kwabena, and when Paul, whoever he is, found out, he'd retaliate."

Nena took a sip of her water. "He did. He had Dad poisoned, Elin."

Elin was incredulous. "This is too much, Nena."

"Honest to God. Paul called me when I was at the hospital. He admitted it."

Elin thumped the table. "I thought we were a team, Nena. It's been over a week since Dad. And what about Mum? And if Lucien is who you say he is, he's been sniffing round her 'for moral support,' he says." Elin cast a doubtful look. "Are you sure, Nena? No bullshit."

"None."

"Let's say you're right," Elin proposed.

Nena nodded with great difficulty. Meeting Elin's withering gaze was unbearable, and even more so was the disappointment radiating from her.

"But attacking Dad now, when Lucien's barely at the table two minutes? You should have said something. That night. That very night you saw him, you should have said something to us. Instead, you go off half-cocked on a revenge tirade and make a bigger problem."

Nena shook her head emphatically. "You don't know him like I do. This is what he does. Infiltrate, ambush, bulldoze, take what he wants with no regard for anyone else. If I had told you that night—"

"Then Dad wouldn't be recovering today."

Nena dropped her head. Elin was right. But Nena was right too. "No, Dad wouldn't be recovering today. Because he'd be dead, Elin, you understand me?"

"Nena—"

Nena cut in. "There is no winning against him until I give him what he wants, make him comfortable. Then get him when I am positive you, Mum, and Dad are safe. And the Baxters."

Dumbfounded, Elin asked, "What is it Paul wants?"

Nena sighed. The hard part still wasn't over yet. "He wants Dad's seat. He can't stand for any man to have better than him. That's why he hated my papa. A seat at the Council table isn't enough for Paul, so the head of the table is what he wants. High Council, Dad's seat."

Elin flounced back in her seat. "Bloody hell that would ever happen. There's no way the Council would ever allow him to ascend to Dad's seat."

"And yet here he is, after hiding for over fifteen years, within reach of the High Council seat."

Elin assessed her coolly, her lips pursed. Nena knew it was a low blow. None of this was Elin's fault, and Nena couldn't let her resentment at the Tribe's failures rest on her sister's shoulders.

Elin scoffed. "I mean, the man is a major douchebag opportunist, yeah, but he's not some indestructible supervillain, Nena." She took a long swallow of her wine, then held up a hand. "Still assuming you're correct about Lucien-slash-Paul here, what are you getting at with the cigar your federal friend found at his home? You're saying Lucien—Paul—put it there?"

"He likely had an emissary do it. He always uses others to do his bidding." Who knew Paul better than she?

It was now or never. Nena tried to control her breathing, knowing this would be the straw that broke the camel's back. "That emissary learned of the Baxters and told him about them. And that someone planted Paul's cigar knowing I'd get the message."

"What are you playing at, Nena?"

"Oliver is working with Paul and planted the cigar."

Elin inhaled. "And when the fuck"—she said it so sharply Nena flinched—"would Oliver have done that?"

Nena shrugged. "I don't know. But Oliver knows where they live. He saw me there and knows the Baxters are important to me."

"Bullshit. He never went inside." Elin's dismay was so palpable Nena felt she could reach out and touch it. She looked at Nena with such hurt and betrayal it nearly broke Nena, and she almost took back everything she'd said. Nena forced herself to continue, despite Elin's eyes begging her to stop.

"This is complete bullshit, Nena. You're complete bullshit for even thinking Oliver has anything to do with whatever Paul's got going on." She downed the rest of her wine, watching Nena from across the table. Nena couldn't read her, couldn't tell if Elin even believed Lucien was Paul.

"You don't know what you're doing, Nena, you really don't . . ." Elin trailed off, unable to look at her. She covered her mouth with her hand, shaking her head as Nena waited for her to say more.

All Nena could do was sit back and watch as her sister motioned for a refill, downed it, and then asked for the bottle. Nena was at a loss, knowing she might have destroyed the most important person in her life, her best friend, who'd stood beside her since the moment they'd met, because she had waited too long. If Elin doubted her, if Elin no longer trusted her, Nena wasn't sure if she could survive it.

# 64

## BEFORE

At eighteen, I spend a month of my summer in Sniper Training. My rifle of choice will eventually become a Nemesis Valkyrie because of its lightweight handling. I learn to use it both left and right handed. My second rifle, a little heavier, is a Vanquish 762 because I saw it in a movie once and took a liking to it. I add on gear like nightscopes, suppressors, and detachable magazines, to name a few.

I go through Weapons Training, learning how to handle guns of various sizes and weights, finally opting for a sleek black 9 mm Glock 17 with a suppressor as my personal sidearm. I love the way it feels in my hands. I am already well versed with sharp objects, but now I learn the art of knife fighting: how to hold them, making them extensions of my hands and fingers.

Eventually, I will possess many knives in my private arsenal in my little blue home in Freedom City, Miami, my favorite being a military-grade tactical blade I house in either a side sling or blade holsters. Or, if I'm on a big job or in a remote location, a tactical backpack or go bag. My two little secret push knives are hidden within fashionable-brand belts (thanks to Elin). These are short, tiny T-shaped blades that sit at either hip bone, can go unnoticed by metal detectors, and come in extremely convenient during hand-to-hand combat. These are proximity weapons I never leave home without. I like to call them my utensils.

———

In Interrogation Training, both giving and receiving, I learn all I need to know, and it is still not enough.

"Interrogation goes hand in hand with Escape and Evasion," Rand, his long-roped dreads twisted into one long, swaying, beautiful braid, begins. He is from Jamaica, and maybe one day I'll visit. "The key here is to use your E-and-E training before you are ever in a position to be interrogated.

"There are three main goals you must have when pumping anyone for information," Rand continues. From his usual perch, Witt watches. "What is their weakness? Once you figure that out, how do you exploit it? And what is the best way to extract that information from them? Sometimes, the method of extraction might have to be forceful."

"Torture," I volunteer.

Rand nods.

I look at him. "And what if I'm the one being interrogated?"

He sits backward in his chair, propping his arms over the back. "You better stay free or die trying."

His words are supposed to be a joke, but his meaning is horrifyingly clear. It is in my best interest to never get caught.

# 65

## AFTER

Elin finally set her sights back on Nena. She firmed her shoulders, fighting to keep her voice level but failing miserably. "What you're suggesting . . ."

With Nena, there was no hiding.

"What you're suggesting is that Oliver, *my* Oliver, is a willing participant in Paul's master plan?" She glowered at Nena while waving off a refill of her drink from the server.

Nena swallowed. Her hands were damp from the nervousness coiling through her body, twisting her intestines like a snake. The last thing she wanted to do was hurt her sister, undermine her authority, or go against Elin in any way. Their father had told them to always stand together no matter what. But there was no way Oliver did not know. That wasn't how Paul worked with his inner circle.

"It is my belief, yes."

Elin snapped at her, "A belief, but not a fact." She lowered her voice. "I can't accept this. You have no proof."

"You're right. I don't."

"We don't deal in maybes and beliefs, Nena," Elin hissed. "You know this. We deal with absolutes because we can have no reversals."

"It's a guess," Nena concurred. "But it is probable."

"It's a fucking guess," Elin scoffed, sitting back in her chair. Her eyes flashed anger, but there was something else, too, a sliver of fear that maybe Nena was right, a plea that Nena was wrong.

Nena rarely asked for anything. Never questioned Elin's judgment or her ability to cut through bullshit and do what she needed to do. But now, when Elin had finally found someone she loved and saw a future with, Nena was asking for too much.

"It's how Paul works. His inner circle will always know his motives and plans."

"Oliver is his son. Did you ever consider maybe Paul would shield him from that?" Elin reasoned. "Look, you got a pass on the Attah thing. You took out Kwabena. But now? Now, you're going too far, Nena. Dad is in the hospital. Mum is sick with worry. We don't need any more shit right now."

"I know."

"Then take Paul out, but leave Oliver alone."

Nena couldn't stand the way Elin was staring at her intently, pleading again. She felt herself giving in. Maybe she was wrong.

"Oliver had nothing to do with what happened to you," Elin reaffirmed. "He couldn't."

It was as if Nena's own heart was breaking. "I know."

Elin's eyes pleaded with Nena. Her voice was thick with emotion. "If what you're suggesting is true, then it means I have compromised the Tribe—that Dad and the Council have compromised the Tribe. It means I allowed my feelings to take over common sense, that I'm unfit to lead."

Nena was slowly shaking her head. "It would not mean any of that," she said sincerely. "Paul is just too good, so good he's managed to evade capture, reinvent himself under the Tribe's nose, and then come out to join them. Only he has the audacity to do so. There is nothing you could have done, Elin." Why hadn't Nena believed those very words about herself all these years?

Nena reached out for Elin's hand, grasped it in hers, and held tight. "There is nothing either one of us could have done." Her voice betrayed her, cracking and showing how devastated she was at delivering this news.

Elin took a deep breath. "I love him, Nena." Her eyes were glassy with tears and her voice soft and mournful.

"I know." How she hated herself for what she was doing to her sister. How she hated Paul even more for making her do it.

"And we . . ." Elin gulped, forcing herself to continue. "We eloped three days ago." Her phone began chirping.

Nena's stomach plummeted. Her hand retracted as she sat back in her chair. "Elin," she breathed, not wanting to believe it. Because if she *was* right about Oliver . . .

"When we were in Vegas. We just . . ." She trailed off. "It was sudden. A whim."

"His idea?" Nena asked, trying to keep the accusation out of her voice.

Elin looked at her sharply. "It was both our ideas," she said through clenched teeth. The phone kept ringing. Elin glanced at the number. "Network," she informed Nena, clearing her throat. "Yes?"

Nena watched as her expression changed from business to horror.

"You're sure?" She waited, her eyes connecting with Nena's. "We are on our way."

Nena was already out of her chair and dropping a hundred on the table.

"Where?" Nena asked, back to business. A second look at Elin's stricken face gave her pause. "Who is it? Dad? Mum?"

Elin swallowed. "There's been activity at the Baxters'."

It was all Nena could do to not buckle in the restaurant. The Baxters. Georgia and Cort. Nena never showed fear, never had a chink in her armor, but it was there now, the chink widening each second she didn't know what had happened to the Baxters.

She allowed herself that moment of emotion. But then her face returned to its impenetrable mask, because there was work to do.

Work only she could do.

# 66

## BEFORE

Not long after I receive my field name and become Echo, on a particularly cold and miserable evening, I am on recon. Goon and Max are with me. Goon has become the closest thing to a friend I have in Dispatch. Tonight's mission is to wait for a man—some radical threatening to disrupt the delicate power in a small country government under Tribe protection.

Simply put, he is planning a coup.

Allowing him to unseat the current government and obtain control for himself would drive up trade costs and undo all order the Tribe has created. And Dad's motto is *If there is no order, chaos ensues.* Thus, Goon and Max are here to restore that order. I tag along to observe and learn, although I'm ready to get my feet wet beyond watching and driving.

Max is irritable. Goon prefers face-to-face confrontation. He is the proverbial bull in a china shop. Like Rambo, he wants to go in and fuck shit up—his words, not mine. But a dispatch can start either like a bull or like a lamb. Tonight is the latter. The lengthy surveilling we do in our very ordinary Subaru grates at both men.

"I'm hungry. What the fuck's taking so long?" Goon whines. From the back seat, I look at him through the rearview mirror. The car isn't big. He must be very uncomfortable, further amplifying his irritability. He knows we are supposed to remain undercover and in position, always watching for our mark and the first chance to take him out.

"Fuck it," he says, opening the driver's-side door. "I'll be back. I gotta stretch my legs and make a food run to the cart across the way."

"You shouldn't," I say, the sudden change making my stomach flip. There are too many unknowns when the plan changes. *That* I learned in training.

But Max waves me off. "Grab me something while you're at it. The bugger's probably getting in an extra screw with his whore anyway. Gonna be a while." He pulls out his gun and lays it on the armrest between their seats. "Gonna take me a piss before the show starts." He doesn't wait for me to comment before he leaves.

I am left alone on a mission for the first time. I watch as Max walks around the corner of the apartment building, where the mark is indeed enjoying time with a young woman. At the same time, his wife sits in prison a world away because of crimes he committed, according to the intel reports I study before every mission.

I can barely see Max due to his dark clothing. He blends with the shrubbery. Goon has merged himself into a line that has suddenly materialized at the food cart. It's funny how one second, there is no line, and the next, everyone becomes hungry all at once. I look at my watch, thinking our mark is due at any moment. My fingers tingle with anticipatory energy at what's to come. Correction: my whole body is a mass of tingles.

I scrunch down lower when a Navigator pulls up in front of the building and sits idling, no doubt waiting for the mark. Goon's view of the building's front is now obstructed. He cannot return with the car there, or he'll risk blowing cover and the mission. Max is nowhere to be seen. When the Navigator's front door opens and two serious-looking men file out, sweeping the street for anything out of the ordinary, I know they are the mark's detail. In moments he will emerge, slip into the waiting car, and be gone, as will our opportunity. All our time and resources wasted because Goon got hungry and Max had to piss.

And there is the mark stepping through the doorway, looking satiated in his three-piece suit, as if he hasn't a care in the world.

An executive decision made, I grasp my door handle and open it. A cold wind hits me as I step out and make haste to the building. I have my cell to my ear, pretending to make plans to meet an imaginary friend. The mark's eyes are upon me as he slowly makes his way down the six steps from the door. His men are to his right, one on the same step as him, one on a step above him.

As my boot reaches the curb in front of them, Max reappears, wiping his hands on the back of his pants. Unless he found a spigot, the wetness on his hands is not from water. But there's no time to harp on his poor hygiene. The guards spot him and tense at the same time; their hands automatically reach into their jackets and extract their sidearms.

Max's gun is in the Subaru on the armrest, a rookie mistake when he is not one. He should have another on him, but he notices the men a moment too late. The guards pay me no mind. I am a young girl who has tripped exquisitely over the heels of her shoes. I cry out in false pain and surprise.

The mark reaches the bottom of the stairs, but I stumble in his path, blocking his way to the Navigator. He smiles broadly. From the intel, I know he has a penchant for young women, which is why I caught his attention. Before he has a chance to decide whether he wants to assist me or not—the fact that he has to decide is rude—shots ring out.

His head snaps toward the commotion, as does mine, in time to see Max falling and one of the mark's men, arm extended, pointing his gun at the space Max once inhabited. He shot without provocation. For all he knew, Max was some random man on the street, but he gunned him down. Just because.

People begin screaming, scattering this way and that. More shots ring out as Goon breaks from the line at the food cart and approaches.

He has forgotten his hunger and no longer cares about his cover. He pulls his gun from his hidden side holster. The guards shoot above where I crouch on the sidewalk. The man in the waiting car is shooting.

People screaming, running, falling, everywhere. I can hear Network calling commands to retreat in my ear. I know Goon can hear them too. It is three to one, and Goon takes a bullet in the side, maybe the hip. I am unsure, but the bullets keep coming. It pushes me to action.

*Don't let them see you coming . . .*

The mark's hand hovers in the air above mine. Seconds that feel like eons have passed, and no more must, or Goon will be as dead as Max must be.

*. . . until it's too late.*

My hand frees my piece from the belt at my back, its silencer already in place. Slowly I rise up to position myself closer to the crouched mark. He is preoccupied, looking at his guards, who shout commands among them. I need to get to him before one of them breaks off to help him into the Navigator. My free hand, the one he considered grabbing, snakes out and latches onto him. I yank hard.

He yelps, surprised, and staggers as I unbalance him, bringing him down to me. I press my virgin gun into the softness of his submandibular space, below his chin, above his Adam's apple. I squeeze the trigger. His blood splatters my face, and he goes down. I catch him but do not anticipate his dead weight, so we both fall hard to the ground, me flat on my rear.

There is no time. Quickly I push him off me and get up. His men lay a suppressing fire to keep Goon at bay as he takes cover behind a parked auto. I shift my target. The men are unaware their charge is dead, so focused are they on Goon. They do not see me coming.

I take aim and squeeze. One down.

The shot draws the attention of the other. His head snaps in my direction. His eyes widen at the dead men on the ground, but I allow him no time to gather his thoughts. I squeeze the trigger. He crumples, tumbling down the steps. Two down.

Goon has recovered ground and lets out another rapid-fire burst now that the other shooters are no longer a threat. He riddles the car and its driver with bullets, killing him. There is silence, except the echoing reports of gunfire against the walls.

Goon limps toward our auto while I look down at the mark. He is very dead, but I have seen enough movies. I squeeze one last shot into the back of his head.

"Come on!" Goon commands from the car, its engine roaring. I step over the mark as if he were merely a crack in the ground and hustle to the car. I gaze over at Max's body, checking for signs of life, before slipping into the passenger seat he once occupied.

"Maybe he's still alive?"

"He's not," Goon growls through his pain, focused on getting us out of this hot zone. "Get the charge from the bag."

I reach to the rear seats of the car, grabbing the go bag from the floor. Sirens wail in the background, coming closer. The street is relatively deserted, everyone either having run away or keeping cover. I rifle through the bag until I find the small black box no heavier than a D-size battery, no bigger than an old pager. I check with Goon, who nods pointedly.

I press the button on it, priming it. I roll my window down as I do. When Goon wheels past Max's body, I toss the charge at it. The charge smacks the body, exploding on impact. The explosion amounts to a small firework you can buy for New Year's, but it does its job, eradicating any trace of our dispatch team and the Tribe.

The mission has gone awry. Max is dead, and Cleaners will take care of his remains somehow. However, the objective has been met and the mark killed, even though I was only supposed to tag along, not work this job. I have graduated my training early and completed my first dispatch, while Goon is forced into retirement.

# 67

## AFTER

With no more intel than what they'd received from the call, Nena and Elin raced to the Baxters'. The neighborhood was quiet, but not for long. The moment a neighbor came out to walk their dog or a car drove by, they'd see the dead body lying on the lawn that Nena observed with growing dread as she cut her bike's engine. Parked in the driveway were Cortland's Chevelle and an F-150 that she remembered from the cookout was Mack's.

The house was dark, and the front door was cracked open. It was too quiet. Nena pulled her gun, sweeping the perimeter for anyone hanging around. She first checked the body. Mack. She felt his neck, hoping for a pulse. Nothing.

There was no more she could do for him, so she left him there and continued. Gun ready, she entered through the open front door.

She spotted Cort immediately. He was lying in the living room, unmoving, a puddle of blood beneath him. She ignored the sinking of her heart and contemplated not checking him at all. If she didn't check, then she could avoid the possibility that he was as dead as Mack a moment longer. She backed away from his still body, deciding to clear the house first.

Muzzle pointed to the floor, she swept the gun side to side. Moving carefully down the hall, she cleared the three bedrooms, the bathrooms, the kitchen, the dining room, and the garage. There was nothing else out of place in the home. Elin entered the house as Nena reemerged from the bedrooms. Elin was already dropping next to Cort's body, uttering an alarmed curse.

"The guy out there's dead," Elin huffed, as Nena knelt on Cort's other side. "Is he?"

Nena touched an artery. "He's alive."

"Georgia?"

"Not here," Nena said grimly.

Elin pulled her cell to call Network to get a team out. Nena balled a hand into a fist, pushing the knuckle of her pointer finger out. She pressed her fist into Cort's chest, grinding the knuckle into his flesh, until he gasped awake with Georgia's name on his lips. He looked around wildly, tried to sit up, grimaced when the pain hit him, and was back down. His hands went to the darkened area on his shirt. Nena lifted the shirt, making an initial assessment.

"Be still," she said gently. Her fingers tenderly traced his eyebrows. She ignored Elin staring at her.

"What happened?" Nena asked.

Cortland's response came in huffs. "Not sure? Some guy ambushed us when we came home."

Nena asked, "Who was he?"

"Never saw him before. We were at a movie, the three of us. I opened the door and came inside first. Mack was last. I heard shots. Oh God. Mack." His body jerked up. "Is he—?"

Elin dropped her eyes. "I'm sorry."

"Where is Georgia? What is your sister doing here?" Cort asked, still struggling beneath their hands.

"What happened next, Cort?" Nena pressed on in case he passed out again.

Cort took in a ragged breath. "When I heard the shot, I came around the corner and saw Mack outside. Peach was in the foyer, and the guy was pointing the gun at her and made her come in. I struggled with him, and he hit me with his gun. I pushed Peach out of the way, and he shot me. That's all I remember." He looked around, confused and terrified. "Peach? Where is she?"

"She's not here,"

"What do you mean, she's not here? Where is she?"

"I don't know. Yet," Nena assured him. "Can you describe him? Did he say anything?"

He concentrated. "No. He got me before I had a good look at him. And he had on a hat, black, like his clothes. Maybe he's about my height, fit, strong. I just didn't get a good enough look. Nena . . ."

"I know, Cort. We'll find her."

Elin had opened her mouth to speak when her phone rang in her hand, and Oliver's name appeared on the screen.

"Oliver, not the best time. I'm dealing with a situation," Elin rushed to say, watching with trepidation as Nena applied pressure to Cort's wound. "Can I get back to you?"

She paused as she listened to Oliver's response, her expression turning from worry to surprise, then confusion. She pulled the phone from her ear and pressed the speaker button.

"She can hear," Elin said. "But as I said, we're dealing with a situation here."

"Yes, and I believe I am that situation," Oliver said.

Nena and Elin froze. Oliver's tone was all wrong, not like how he'd sounded when Nena had met him the night of the dinner party. He sounded like his father.

Elin said, "What?"

"Shut up, Elin," he snapped, enunciating as if she were an imbecile. "I need to speak with Nena."

# 68

## BEFORE

When both Elin and I have graduated university with our respective degrees, we strike out from beneath the protective umbrella of Delphine and Noble Knight and are permitted to relocate to the States, to Florida to be exact, for a couple of reasons. And by "reasons," I mean me.

One, because Florida holds a special place in my heart because of the yearly excursions Dad and I make to the races. Two, because Florida can be hot and doesn't have cold weather like England does. We all know how much I detest the cold. Three, because Florida has Miami, which is a port city (something Dad loves) and is a melting pot of so many cultures I feel I am both back home and not, at the same time.

Elin chooses to live in the high-rise flat in Coconut Grove, which is beautiful and fitting of the type of woman Elin has become, chic and sophisticated. A true High Council member-to-be. But I choose to live somewhere subtler, more comfortable to me. It is in Freedom City, in a neighborhood called Citrus Grove, where I find my home. It is small, with chipped, faded yellow paint and shingles in need of work I will happily pay for. It sits on the corner, and I can imagine how it will look when I am done renovating it.

I also meet the man who will become one of my closest associates, Keigel, head of the 102s, the local band of merry gang members. Keigel acts tough at first but soon changes when he realizes I don't scare easily.

He appraises me as if I am a specimen. "And this ain't no gentrification-type shit?" he asks when I tell him I mean to be his neighbor—three doors down.

"Not in the least."

He twists his lips. "I ain't no superman, ya heard?" he warns. "You come across trouble here, I can't save you."

"I understand." Perfectly.

I enjoy Keigel's company because he's a softy under a gruff exterior. And he has impeccable taste in lemon-pepper wings from Wings and Such. However, if he asks, I will deny it.

# 69

## AFTER

Gently, Nena took the phone and switched off the speaker. She didn't want Cort to hear if the news about Georgia was bad. Knowing she had been right about Elin's now husband was devastating news enough for one of the people Nena cared about. She didn't know if she could handle destroying the hopes of someone else just yet. Beside her, Elin balled her trembling hands at her sides. Nena put the phone to her ear.

"What is it?"

"Did Elin share our good news?" Oliver said, as if he weren't waging war against them. Nena could hear wind whooshing in the background. Car. But how far had he gone? And was he alone?

"Where is she?"

"With me." He laughed, his words wreaking havoc on her system. "She's a spitfire and can hit like a motherfucker."

Nena weighed her words carefully, trying to keep her emotions in check as if she were on the job. But this wasn't any job. This was personal.

"What do you want?"

"You to come alone."

"This has nothing to do with you."

Oliver ignored her, rattling off an address Nena committed to memory.

"And come alone," he finished seriously. "No team. No Elin. No one but you, or—"

Dread squeezed the air from her throat. "Or?"

"Or history repeats itself. I'd say it's time for a little family reunion, don't you agree?"

The line went dead before she could get her question out. What did he mean, family reunion? Wordlessly, Nena returned the phone to Elin. She sat back on her haunches. Ice-cold tentacles of fear wound their way through every nerve in her body. Nena cursed herself for not knowing what to do next. It was her job to know. But everything was coming up blank.

Cort wheezed, "What about Peach?"

The question woke her up.

Nena wiped at her eyes and looked down at her fingers, surprised they came away damp. Now was not the time to sift through the tumult of feelings, not when there was work to do. "They have her," she said, getting to her feet.

Cort's eyes widened at seeing a gun in her hands. "Nena, what the hell?"

"I need to go after them before it's too late."

Elin tore her gaze away from the floor. Her face was riddled with guilt and shame, eyes rimmed with tears as infrequent to her as they were to Nena. "I am so sorry," Elin whispered, the enormity of the situation threatening to split her in two. "I should have known. I've failed."

"You haven't."

"I can't lead the Tribe if I can't trust my own instincts, my judgment of character. I can't. I fucked up." The tears pooling in her eyes spilled, failure consuming her.

Nena glanced at her watch. She looked away, thinking. Looked back at her sister, conflicted. What was the appropriate thing to do? For the second time that night, she chose to comfort someone else.

"We are a team," Nena said.

Cort interjected. "We need to call the cops."

"No cops," both women said automatically.

Elin tore her gaze away from him, her face wrought with worry and guilt and terror.

"I need to go." Nena turned to leave.

Elin scrambled to her feet, her outstretched hand stopping Nena. "Let me go with you. I can reason with Oliver. Maybe I can offer him whatever he wants."

Nena shook her head. "It's not about what Oliver wants. It's always been about what Paul wants, and it's nothing you can provide."

"Nena," Cort said again from the floor. He struggled to get up, but the wound in his side was too severe, had weakened him faster than they'd anticipated. The dark area of his shirt had grown larger. He crumpled back down, falling into unconsciousness.

Nena fought the urge to tend to him, to touch him. She thought of the night they'd spent dancing and being a normal couple. But she knew if she stopped a second to be the Nena he knew and not the Echo she needed to be, she wouldn't leave his side. And she had to, to save Georgia and end this thing with Paul.

To Elin, she whispered, "Get him medical attention. This time you actually do have to call the cops, if a neighbor hasn't already. Come up with a story for them. When I find Georgia, I'll bring her home."

Elin pointed at Cort. Leaning toward Nena, she asked, "And him? What do I tell him?"

"Tell him whatever it takes to get him on board. Tell him"—Nena looked down at him as well, wondering how he'd feel once he knew who she really was—"tell him he can ask me anything he wants, and I will answer when I return."

Elin's lips quivered. "If that little girl dies because of me . . ." She was unable to finish.

"Whatever happens will not be because of you." Nena hesitated. "And it will not be because of me either. Everything that's happened—is happening—is because of Paul."

# 70

## BEFORE

Several months after I purchase my little house, two things happen: my home is renovated and fitted to suit my needs, and my parents come to visit, meeting Keigel.

My house is a calming sea-blue color, reminding me of the oceans of the tropics. It has a security system fit for a bank, complete with motion sensors that could detect an ant traipsing over a blade of grass. There are hidden cameras everywhere. A privacy fence closes off my backyard, so I can sit out there in my oasis without the worry of spectators. The carport is now a fully enclosed garage.

In what I call my office or command center, there is a high-level communication setup and a hidden pantry-like room behind my closet wall, which houses my weapons arsenal, passports, and other accoutrements needed for my dispatch work. It slides open when activated by my palm print. The palm must be warm, with a beating pulse. The second room, my guest room, is for appearances only, because I don't intend to entertain overnight guests.

When my parents pull up in their black Escalade with their driver, Keigel is next to me on the sidewalk. He is there as a show of unity, to let the neighborhood know anyone who comes to my home is under his protection—laughable because he has no idea that he is under my protection now. He will know soon enough. When I introduce him to Delphine and Noble Knight, if they accept him, the options for Keigel will be limitless. He could have whatever his heart desires, and he'll have the support of me and the Tribe . . . *if* he plays his cards right and my parents accept him.

The driver, well armed, and another bodyguard exit the SUV. Behind them, another car, a silver Mustang, rolls to a stop, and more guards pile out. They all look around, no doubt wondering why a Knight daughter lives here.

Keigel whistles as the guards pile out. He begins searching the ground.

"What are you doing?" I say. The man has lost his senses.

"Looking for the rose petals and African drums." He grins. "I mean, the king of Zamunda has arrived, right?"

All I can do is look at him. Perhaps this meeting was not my best idea.

"Zamunda?" Keigel repeats slowly, his eyes incredulous that I have no idea what he's talking about. "*Coming to America*? Come on now, Eddie Murphy? Arsenio Hall?"

I shake my head as if clueless.

To increase my horror, Keigel breaks out in song. "Just let your soul-l-l glo-o-o." His voice cracks, but his smile is wide and proud.

"Is that a religious sect?" I ask. The nearest guard overhears us, and his shoulders shake from his laughter.

"Sexual chocolate!" Keigel blurts suddenly, startling me. I'm beginning to worry he is unwell.

I frown. "Is what? A new candy bar?" I say, pretending I don't understand.

The guard turns quickly, sneaking a peek at Keigel, whose face drains of all hope. It's official: Keigel is indeed unwell.

"Okay," Keigel says, taking a deep breath. "James Earl Jones was the king."

A light bulb. "Ah," I say, relieved we've gotten somewhere. "Yes, him I know."

He expels a breath of air, shaking his hand in victory. "Finally. Finally!"

"James Earl Jones was Mufasa in *The Lion King*."

Despair replaces Keigel's brief relief, and by now, more guards are laughing at his misery. The name "akata" is mingled with their muted comments. The name is one we call Black Americans when we feel they are beneath us, a name I've never approved of and one I am disappointed the guards thought was okay to say. No one is beneath anyone, especially Keigel.

In a sharp voice and in Ewe, I tell the chuckling guards, "If you value your life, never again let me hear you call him that name." I tilt my head toward Keigel, murmuring, "You know there is no country of Zamunda in Africa."

He rolls his eyes at me. "Shit, I know that, but one can hope, right?"

As Keigel's lanky body shrinks from disappointment, my nostrils flare as I try to remain serious. Later I'll tell him *Coming to America* is one of my favorite movies. *Lion King* as well.

Keigel says, more serious than I've seen him before, "You know what gets me by each day I see one of my boys dead or watch all this crazy political shit going on? Knowing there is a real place out there. Knowing that Africa, in its entirety, is an amalgamation of Zamunda and Wakanda, and I can always go there if I need it."

His words are the most profound and beautiful I have ever heard. They make me view those fictional idealizations of Africa in a new light, as well as Keigel, because he used the word *amalgamation*. And that is impressive.

When my parents complain that I live in a place they feel is unsafe, it is laughable, considering our line of business.

"This neighborhood and its people remind me of home," I explain.

"Del, my dear, let her be," Dad says. She sucks her teeth at him, and I know he will hear it during the car ride back to their flat. He follows Mum into their auto but calls over his shoulder to me. "Just make sure Network conducts several sweeps of this area, yes?"

Keigel stands with me, watching their caravan leave. Thankfully he has refrained from making any more stereotypical African jokes.

He lets out a huge breath and a curse. "Yo, Nena, your life's complicated. Your fam's fucking intense."

If only Keigel knew how complicated and intense life can really be.

Because here's the thing about the complexities of life, its cruelties and injustices, which permeate everything good and pure.

I can write a book about all of it.

# 71

## AFTER

In her lifetime, Nena had experienced terrible things. She'd been left to die. She'd suffered immeasurable loss. She'd killed without remorse. She'd lost a large piece of humanity, the part that made her soft and caring and able to have relationships beyond her immediate family. She wondered more times than not what she'd done to deserve her lot in life. She thought maybe she'd offended God somehow, made him abandon her to the likes of Paul and Monsieur.

But she had found the Knights. She'd been given a new mother, a father, and a sister. Nena had recently found something she'd never imagined having, love and a daughter in Georgia. Now, she stood to lose them all to the same man again.

Would God do that to her again? Surely there were consequences for all the killing she'd done. Maybe tonight was her reckoning.

Or maybe he had grace, she thought as she raced her bike past Keigel's home, ignoring his single wave from where he sat in his chair on the porch.

Maybe there would be a reprieve, she thought, maneuvering her roaring machine into her driveway and cutting the engine. She barely gave her property a once-over. It was dark, with no lights, normal. She hurried through the front door, not bothering to check the premises or draw her sidearm.

She walked quickly; there wasn't time to spare. She had one singular thought: to get Georgia.

She went to the hall. Everything was as she'd left it. The guest room door was open, and she ignored it, heading to her office-slash-command-center, where she conducted business if she wasn't in her backyard. She quickly keyed in the access code to the door.

Five steps took her to the closet. She pushed the clothes aside and stood before the large chest of drawers that from the outside looked like any typical piece of bedroom furniture. If someone pulled open a drawer, they'd see underwear and bras. But beneath the top drawer was a tiny hidden panel where she needed to hold her thumb on the bio-metrics scanner long enough for it to register her pulse and confirm her prints. She ignored the larger arsenal hidden within the closet, focusing on the bureau.

The level of urgency and anxiety she felt made her hands feel cold, and she balled them into fists, rubbing the fingers against each other to warm them, before placing her left thumb on the sensor.

The door popped open softly, revealing her assortment of weaponry—assault rifles, knives, garroting wire, handguns, explosive charges. From the bottom of the compartment, she popped out a box of ammunition.

She grabbed a black duffel from the corner of the closet, began stuffing it with what she might need. She didn't want to weigh herself down. But she wanted to make sure she was prepared for whatever Paul had waiting for her.

She heard a creak behind her and spun around with her gun locked and loaded.

Her muzzle came face to face with Keigel, his arms raised in the air. "What the fuck, Nena! Don't shoot. It's me."

It took a second for her to blink Echo away and bring Nena back.

She scowled at him. "What are you doing here? You're lucky I look before I shoot."

Arms still raised, Keigel asked, "Can I?"

She slipped her gun in her back holster, her silent permission for him to lower his hands. She resumed the business at hand. "Next time knock before entering."

"One of the homies told me you left your door wide open. And you blew past like hounds were on your ass. I came to check on you 'cause it ain't like you."

He watched her load up her bag and zip it. He noticed her arsenal for the first time. "You preparing for war?"

She turned to him. "Not your fight, Keigel."

He leaned against the doorframe, crossing his arms on his chest. "You been good to me since I've known you. We like family. Your fight is mine."

"This isn't lemon-pepper wings and gang turf wars, Keigel."

He looked at her. "I know it," he said somberly.

"I can't risk another important person being put in jeopardy."

He broke out in a grin. "So I'm important to you?" He chuckled. "I always knew it." He did a little dance, which any other time Nena would have found amusing.

When Keigel finally sobered, he said, "But seriously, I can't risk my protection getting killed 'cause she going into some war without backup. Let me and the homies be your backup."

"No homies," she reiterated, stopping her packing briefly to make her point clear. "No one goes."

"Then me. Whoever got you like this, you shouldn't go in by yourself."

"I can do this by myself."

"Doesn't mean you should," he said, unmoved. "It's okay to accept help once in a while, you know. You got people, girl. *I'm* your people."

They stared at each other. Him determined not to let her pass without his being right on her heels. Her trying to figure out why she was considering his offer and when he'd become her "people." She turned away from him, pulling open the drawer that contained the decoy bras and underwear. She shoved them aside and pulled out her two most cherished items.

She didn't care if Keigel thought her crazy as she squeezed a dime-size amount of her mother's scent and rubbed it on her face and neck. She took her father's cologne and spritzed it about her head and shoulders as if anointing herself. She inhaled deeply. Then inhaled again. Deeper, infusing herself with her parents, praying for them to give her strength and courage to see this thing with Paul to the bitter end.

"Fine," she sighed, closing up her closet and pushing past him. "You're driving."

"And you?"

"I'm going to figure out how not to get you killed."

# 72

## AFTER

Keigel sped down the interstate, following the directions Nena had typed into the GPS.

"This place is going to be out there in the boondocks," he warned.

"He wouldn't want witnesses."

Keigel shot her a glance. "Yeah, for the ambush he's probably set up for you." When she didn't answer, he continued, "So what's the plan again?"

She laid out the simple plan for him again. He didn't like it. Thought she was going in blind and wanted to call in his crew as backup.

"I didn't want you to come along, much less any of your people."

His nostrils flared in frustration, and he exited off Route 75 to Bumfuck, Florida, where they probably were going to die.

She'd procrastinated long enough. It was time to do what she should have weeks ago. Come clean to her mother. She enabled the secured line and dialed her mother's number, then listened as the phone rang on the other side. It was four in the morning in London, where her mother had taken her dad to finish recuperating two days prior.

"Darling."

Her mother's voice sent relief through her. She was safe. Nena hadn't been sure how far Paul had gone in his assault against her.

"Hey, Mum," she said. "How's Dad?"

"He's fine, his usual bossy self. I'm fine." She paused. "But how are you? Where are you?"

"On my way to make things right."

There was a weighty pause on her mother's end. Then finally, "So it is true. All Elin has just told me? You can't wait for reinforcements?"

"I can't wait. It has to be done now and for good this time. He's done too much, hurt too many. I can't have him hurt you or Elin—or Dad, more than he already has."

"And these Americans? The Baxters? You're protecting them too."

Nena stared out at the night sky, nearly pitch black along this narrow road to a secluded home. The car's headlights were barely enough to illuminate their way. "They're part of my family now." She swallowed, hoping her mother would understand. "I'm sorry I have to go against the Council on this."

"Darling?"

"Yes, Mum?" She was prepared to go against her mother, against the Tribe, and against whoever else stood in her way. She'd gladly end up like Goon, ignominiously retired, if it meant the people she loved were free of Paul forever.

"Kill the son of a bitch. Consider it a personal directive from High Council."

"Thank you, Mum." She released a deep breath, feeling as if every burden had suddenly been lifted from her shoulders. It was time for recompense.

# 73

## AFTER

The winding drive to Paul's estate, conveniently located away from curious eyes, did nothing to allay Nena's unease at going in without any intel. The house had only recently been bought, still had that new-house smell.

She had no time for intel on its layout or where in it they were holding Georgia. Nena had no idea what she was walking into and didn't care. She'd walk into hell for Georgia.

"Come on, Nena," Keigel argued. "You can't run up in there solo. That's suicide."

Against Keigel's better judgment, she wanted him waiting outside, near the car, and ready to leave the moment she freed Georgia. And Nena would free her, come hell or high water.

"I have to go alone if Georgia has any chance." She looked at him, assessing if he was ready for this important job. "You good?"

"I'm good, but you better be coming out here with this kid."

She grunted, not really answering, because that part she couldn't guarantee. She left Keigel standing there to stare after her, hoping he'd be safe and that she'd read Paul correctly and he wanted this meeting to be only for a party of one, her.

Nena entered the great hall. It was quiet, devoid of any security detail. She didn't focus on the lack of guards, deciding her guess Paul wanted no witnesses was correct. That way there would be no one to expose anything he planned to do to her.

She scanned her surroundings, her boots echoing in the sparsely furnished home. She strode through the archway, where the great hall split into a T. With a quick assessment, she could see the left was a hall with the kitchen at its end. The right led to the library. Ahead of her was a split-level staircase, where she spied Oliver descending. At the midpoint landing, he stopped and glowered down at her.

His father stood at the very top of the stairs, his hand wound tightly into Georgia's hair. Paul wore an amused expression, quite the opposite of Oliver's murderous one. Georgia's expression was plain terrified. She gripped Paul's hands to keep from having her hair ripped out.

Nena leveled her gaze once more at the immediate threat.

"Glad you could make it to our family reunion," Paul said solicitously.

Family reunion. His words were blasphemous. "Just because your son married Elin doesn't make you family," she said.

Paul was giddy, laughing gregariously. "Haven't figured it out yet?" He pointed a long finger at Oliver. "Has it been so long you don't recognize your own brother when he stands before you?"

It was now Oliver's turn to snap his head in shock toward his father, a move so sudden Nena was positive he got whiplash from it.

Nena's eyes narrowed in on him. Ofori? She scowled, looking back up at Paul. It wasn't possible. Ofori was dead. He'd died in N'nkakuwe.

"You're senile, old man." She scowled. "You killed Ofori years ago."

"Or perhaps I didn't."

"Father?" Oliver asked, confused.

Paul narrowed his eyes. "What are you two, nineteen months apart? Nearly twins, but not quite so. And you really did not recognize each other?"

"I don't understand." Oliver's confusion made him sound younger.

"Elin's sister is yours. By blood, you fucking idiot. That is Aninyeh."

Oliver reeled at his father's words. He grabbed at the railing as if to support himself. "That's not possible," he said. "Surely you mean by marriage."

Meanwhile Nena observed them, wary that this might be yet another of Paul's tricks. She didn't put it past him. She'd watched her family die. All of them—nearly all of them. She swallowed.

Ofori.

She'd only heard the shots fired. She'd never seen him die, not like she had with Papa and the twins.

"You said she died. You said the Frenchman killed her."

"Well, apparently she's a fucking cat with nine lives, dear son," Paul sneered. "She killed Attah, Bena. I suppose she fancies herself getting revenge, am I right, Aninyeh?"

Oliver looked back and forth, between his father and her. "How can it be? How could we have not known for all these years that she's alive?"

"Same as how she hasn't known we lived. She got fucking lucky and made it through just fine."

"I did," Nena said coldly. But not just fine. Not unscathed.

"Perhaps, Father, perhaps you are unwell."

Paul brought his hands to his face as if to keep himself calm. "Clearly, I picked the wrong child to mentor. Seems your little sister has the balls you've never quite grown. Maybe there's time yet to trade you in for the model I really wanted."

Even Nena felt the bite of Paul's words. She watched Oliver wilt visibly beneath the intensity of Paul's reaction. It was both moving and disgusting.

"Are you done?" she asked, watching Georgia squirm, willing the girl to keep silent.

Oliver reasoned with Paul. "Since she's alive, maybe we can use her to further solidify your position within the Tribe."

"Are you fucking mad, boy?" Paul bellowed. "You always have your head in the damn clouds, thinking about how things should be instead of how things are. You never think"—he tapped his finger to his head—"beyond two steps. I shielded you from the serious decisions, boy. I made you Ivy League, gave you a silver spoon, like Americans say, just so you wouldn't have to work like a dog and achieve nothing like your father, Michael."

Nena flinched at the mention of her father. Paul should never speak his name.

"She will never accept me, Oliver; she will never rally behind me."

"If I can get past what happened at N'nkakuwe—" Oliver reasoned, looking at her.

"I sold her," Paul spat. "I didn't sell you. That should tell you something."

She caught the flicker of satisfaction crossing Oliver's expression. It was like a slap in her face. She didn't want to believe Oliver was Ofori. No brother of hers would align himself with a man like Paul. Not after watching his brothers slain. And yet . . .

Her eyes narrowed as she looked, really looked, at the man Paul claimed was her brother. As she looked, it was as if his features began to take on those of her parents. She could see it now as she couldn't before when he'd sat across from her at Elin's table the night of the dinner party. His lips were her mother's lips, the heart-shaped ones that used to kiss her tenderly as their mother laid her down to sleep with her Olay scent wafting around her. His nose was her father's nose, with the structure of his cheekbones.

"It's not possible," she whispered, not wanting to believe.

Another step down the staircase. Now, Oliver—Ofori—stalked her like a lion with its prey. She had never dared dream anyone else had survived. She'd watched her village burn. Heard the shots she thought had taken his life. Now her brother was here, walking toward her. Her brother, alive this entire time. Her instincts screamed danger, but her heart wanted nothing but to take him in her arms.

Paul shook Georgia by her head, forcing a cry from her. "Stop your squirming, girl." He paused, regaining his composure. "Maybe my son has a point. Now that you two know each other, maybe you can be of value to me."

Ofori's hands tightened into fists, and he took another step down. He had one more step to go.

Nena spat, "You will never be our father." How could he believe she'd ever agree to work with him?

"No." Paul smiled mischievously. "I think you've had enough fathers, don't you? Think of the possibilities with you by my side. As my equal."

Ofori's head snapped toward the top of the stairs. "Father!"

Hurt flushed Ofori's face. She saw in him the son who thought he was never good enough for anyone, not their father, Michael, not even Paul. What a life he must have lived, always trying to be the everything son for a man who cared nothing for him.

She held out a hand to stop him. "Release the girl. She's got nothing to do with this. Nothing's gained from hurting her except to bring the American authorities on your head."

Paul snorted. "And yet you care for the girl and her father." An observation rather than a question. "Look how far you've come to retrieve her. You could have walked away. I tire of this."

He yanked Georgia slightly, making her yelp. Nena tensed, ready to fly up the stairs. "Put your sister in the holding room and watch her closely until I am ready." Paul turned on his heel, pushing Georgia in front of him as she fought to break free from his grasp.

Nena could hear Georgia fighting with him all the way down the hall as Ofori slowly approached her with deadened eyes, his hands flexing. She didn't want to fight. Surely she could reason with him. They were family. They had survived.

"Where is he taking her?"

He didn't answer.

"You could join us," she offered.

"Why would I want to?" He grabbed her upper arm.

"You married Elin. You're already family."

"I'll never be family like you. A son-in-law? Her parents only tolerated me for business's sake."

She couldn't object. He spoke the truth.

He pushed her toward the library. "My father gave me a chance. He chose me over you."

"Paul killed our father, Ofori."

She'd struck a chord, its vibration strumming through him until it finally snapped. Her brother looked at her with utter disdain. "That name is dead to me. Same as you are."

# 74

## AFTER

Ofori shoved Nena hard, causing her to stumble. She caught herself and turned to face him.

"Paul killed our brothers. Razed our village to the ground. He beheaded Papa."

She searched his eyes for recognition. She thought for a moment she had broken through when he stopped, becoming serene and unreadable.

Ofori was looking down at the portion of the floor covered in oriental carpeting. He looked back at the space Paul had just vacated at the top of the stairs.

After a moment, he looked away. "I don't give a fuck what he did to Papa or the lot of you." When he fixed his eyes back on Nena, she saw nothing but a black hate-filled void.

Same old selfish Ofori. Anger loosened her tongue. "Paul betrayed Papa, who he called brother. Imagine what he'll do to you when he betrays you," she said. "Because it's me he's always wanted. You were merely his consolation prize."

His face twisted into a rage, and he roared for her to shut up. He kept repeating those words—"Shut up"—spittle flying from his mouth.

It was as if all the pain of his years fighting for acceptance, his feelings of inadequacy, real or imagined, culminated in this one moment. The trapped sound he made was like that of a wounded animal. Reflexively, Nena increased the space between them.

He squeezed his eyes shut, lips forming a rigid line. He stilled, a stillness that was almost preternatural. She hadn't meant to anger him. She had only wanted to shock him into sensibility, but when he opened his eyes, Nena knew his decision.

"There can only be one of us, little sister." The chill in his voice sent all her danger sensors into hyperdrive.

"Only one," he repeated, his head bent as his eyes bored into her.

Nena let her shoulders slump, resigned to what was about to happen. She stared at Ofori, who was so much a blend of their parents. She refused to believe he could be anything but her brother.

"You are the only brother I have left," she said, trying to lull him enough to get close. She decided she'd only incapacitate him until she took out Paul. Then Mum and Dad would know how to help Ofori. Despite all he'd done, shooting Cort and kidnapping Georgia, he was as much a victim as she.

Her brother was a leopard, muscles coiled, eyes black as night, pupils dilated.

She took a step toward him. Closer. Maybe some doctor could help him.

Softly, she said, "You are Ofori."

She ducked when he hurled a nearby vase at her head. It sailed a hair above her before smashing against the wall.

"My. Name. Is. Fucking. Oliver!"

She put her hands up in appeasement.

"You were supposed to be dead, Aninyeh. All these years . . ." He choked back a sob, trailing off. "Why aren't you dead?"

He looked at her with such malice and hatred. What had she ever really done to him but survive?

Could either of them ever be well after what they had suffered at the hands of Paul?

"Ofori—"

He leaped and was on her, taking her by such surprise her reaction was delayed. She took the full brunt of the jab he launched at her side. She stumbled backward as pain flared through her. She touched the area, her hand coming away red with her blood. She stared at her brother, his legs now splayed in a fighting stance. In his left hand was the knife he'd used to cut her.

*We're more alike than we realize.* It was funny because she and her brother had both developed an affinity for knives. And shattering because just when the Asym children had reunited, one of them might have to die at the hands of the other.

# 75

## AFTER

He charged her again, his blade pointed at her. She pushed the pain away, wiping her blood on her jeans. She crouched, deflecting the one-two, jab-swipe combination he came at her with. She parried a thrust with an upper push to his chin, driving his head and the rest of him away from her.

She used her arm to shove the hand with the knife out so she could grab it with her other and twist his hand back. He grunted, and the knife dropped, skittering across the floor well beyond either of their reach. They continued to face off, him launching attacks at various parts of her body and her matching with defensive blocks and kicks. She didn't want him dead. She wanted him saved.

She landed a couple of punches to his abdomen. Her leg spun out, swiping his from beneath him. He fell hard, grabbing her ankle and bringing her down with him. Her knee took the impact, and she felt the crack of bone as pain ripped through her body.

He flipped around and was on her before she could recover. He punched her where he'd stabbed her, digging into the wound with his knuckles. She cried out. He grabbed her shoulders, bringing her forward, and slammed the back of her head against the floor.

The blinking motes swam in her vision, the pain threatening to split her head in two if it wasn't already so from the impact. She swallowed the bile rising in her throat.

As the stars cleared, her reality was becoming frighteningly clear. There was no working through anything with Ofori, was there? Her survival was a constant reminder to him of his choice to become Paul's son and give up his family. Nena was a reminder of his betrayal, of his weakness, of his failings. With her around, he couldn't shut away the memories of what he'd done in a drawer and lock it. He couldn't go through life pretending the first fifteen years of it had never existed. Finding Nena alive brought all that back. Keeping Nena alive would be a constant reminder. That could not happen.

"Ofori, wa—wait," she croaked, his hands wrapping around her throat, bashing her head against the floor as he choked her.

"My name is not Ofori!" he screamed, spittle flying in her face.

He was deranged, and she was running out of air.

She summoned her ebbing strength, gathering all of it as her hand scrabbled at the floor for something she could use to get him off her. She bucked up from beneath him, aiming for his face with a shard of broken vase she'd found. She sliced right below his eye, opening a wide wound, loosening his grip around her neck. His hands flew to his face. She rose to a sitting position, rearing her elbow back and connecting it hard with his ear.

He tumbled off her, howling, his equilibrium thrown off balance. She scampered away from him to distance herself.

"Do you know what I have suffered?" he asked, shaking his head to clear it, to balance himself.

If Nena weren't so exhausted and hurting, she would have laughed. "Shall we compare notes on who suffered worse? You could have had our village if it was power and prestige you wanted. No one would have fought you for it."

374

"Our village of jungles, dust, toil, and timber? Merchants and farmers? Who wants a lifetime of that?"

He sounded so, so much like Paul it made her sick.

She said, "I would give anything to have back the life we lived, the family we had."

"Then you're an idiot."

"Our father would have let you go if you wanted it so bad. He went off to university abroad. You could have done the same."

"He came back to be a chieftain of a dying tribe. He would have wanted the same for all of his sons." Ofori flexed his neck, looking coolly at her. "Paul didn't ask me to be his son."

She licked her bloody lips, fearful of what his response would be, although she believed she knew. "What did you do?"

"I asked Paul. I begged him to make me into his mold," Ofori answered so simply, so proudly, that it was worse than any punch he could deliver. "And he made it so."

# 76

## AFTER

They rolled onto their hands and knees, each trying to gather their bearings. Nena grabbed the edge of a cherrybark oak side table to help her get shakily to her feet, her side dripping blood. On the opposite end of the foyer, Ofori did the same, using a bench. He grunted through his pain. In her mind ran a mantra: Yes, Ofori had betrayed their legacy, but Ofori was not the cause. Ofori was merely the puppet.

"It's okay," she wheezed, a reassurance more to herself than to him. "Tell me where Georgia is, and you can live your life as you want."

He growled, "I'm going to send the little bitch off as I did you."

He started laughing at her, and it was a trigger, reminding her of when Paul laughed, when Attah laughed, when Robach laughed.

She didn't recognize the bloodcurdling scream coming from her. She forgot all her close-combat training. She no longer fought him for self-preservation. His disassociation from his actions, his hatred for their father, his threats against Georgia—there would be no salvation for Ofori because he did not want it. Ofori was gone, and in his place was this monster, Oliver.

He met her in a clash, grabbed her around her middle in a tackle. She used her elbow again, bringing it down hard and repeatedly at the back of his neck as he drove her into a table. She fought through the pain. He pushed her off, throwing a side kick to her hip. She stumbled, falling to her side, her wind gone and her strength right after it.

"Aninyeh, we are the last of our family. Is this what you want just when we've finally found one another?"

A trick. It was a trick, and he was taunting her. He didn't want to be a family any more than she wanted them to be enemies.

She wanted her brother. But he was the past.

She had a new life. Had the Knights, who'd taken her in and put her back together again. And she had Georgia and Cort, new and unexplored. They were her future.

"You know what, little sister? Do you want to know what I purchased with some of Father's profits from your sale to Robach? Sweets and a movie. It was glorious. You fetched quite a good price." Oliver stood, wiping the blood from his eyes.

He grabbed her hair, yanking it back to expose her throat, readying to punch her. She parried his hit, then kneed him in the groin. Bitch move for bitch move, his going after her hair.

"When you drove away from the village, I played football with Papa's head."

She swallowed a scream, trying not to fall for his bait. Instead, she delivered a roundhouse kick and jab of her own. He grunted, staggering back, shaking his head as if dizzied. She ran at him, using the fact he was dizzy, catching him in the midsection. They landed with a hard smack on the wood floors, rolling one over the other, crashing against a cabinet. It wobbled precariously but stayed upright.

He was on top of her again, wrapping his massive hands around her throat. She beat at his head with one hand while the other searched for anything to get him off. In his eyes, she only saw death and contempt, nothing but a bottomless pit.

"Say my name," he commanded, his hands once again wrapping around her throat.

She gagged.

"Say it."

"O—O—" she sputtered, her windpipe closing.

"Say my *name!*" he bellowed, blood dripping down his face. His lips curled into an ugly snarl, his thumb finding her Adam's apple. Her fingers stopped their searching.

If he pushed, he would end her right there, and that was his plan.

"Say it." He lifted his thumb, allowing her the briefest respite. "Say it."

# 77

## AFTER

He was still yelling at Nena to say his name as she searched the floor, weakened and desperate, for any weapon that would make him stop. She couldn't think about anything except the fact that her brother was going to kill her.

He was growling above her. "Say it." Venom dripped from his voice.

Her fingers found purchase, clawed at it—the handle of Ofori's knife.

"What. Is. My. Name?"

"OFORI KWAKU ASYM OF N'NKAKUWE!" She swung her arm upward, sinking his knife deeply into his neck. His hands loosened from around her, and she used that slack to release her own dagger from its sheath in her belt and then ram it into his side below the rib cage.

His eyes went wide, his mouth opening as blood spilled out. His hands felt along his neck to the knife protruding from it and then slid down his side to where her dagger was embedded in him. He looked down at her in astonishment.

His eyebrows puckered. He wheezed a phlegmy sound and began to list to the side, sliding off her. He fell on the floor, choking from his blood, wondering what had happened.

Nena sat up, painfully sucking in air. She turned to him. All the anger and rage seeped from her as her brother's blood seeped from him, leaving nothing but a void and regret.

He writhed on the floor, his hands flittering over his knife, trying to remove it. She held up a hand to stop him, knowing when he removed it, his life would run out much faster than it was. His eyes searched, not seeing. His mouth opened. Closed.

She whispered, "Ofori," hoping for a moment of clarity.

And finally, the cloud in his eyes cleared, and he looked at her.

Her remaining brother was the youngest son and looked the most like their mother but had so much of their father in him. His strong forehead with the same three deep wrinkles, deeper now than she remembered. Gazing at Ofori was like opening a time capsule.

Nena's throat constricted, allowing her emotions to take over as she watched her brother dying. She grieved for Ofori as she never had for the others.

"Me nua barima," she whispered. *My brother.*

His movement was beginning to slow. He was going to die, and acceptance was dawning on him. They looked at each other, tears streaming down their faces. He gave her a nod, his eyes telling her his death was okay. She tried to swallow the lump in her throat, pulled her hands away from his, allowing him to do what he must.

Slowly, he wrenched the first knife out, a sickening sucking sound accompanying it. The blood flowed. There were seconds remaining. His mouth moved, with only whispers coming from it. She leaned in closer.

"Say—it again," he whispered.

"Ofori Kwaku Asym. Your name is Ofori. Our papa loved you," she said. "I love you, nua barima." She chanted the lines over and over, determined he would understand, remember, and believe he was her brother. She was determined he know he was loved, even when she had had to kill him.

His eyes filled with tears and sorrow, as well as a deep remorse that death brought. He looked so young, as if he were aging backward.

"And I forgive you," she whispered, feeling his body release the guilt and self-loathing it had lived with for so long.

He nodded at that. They didn't have to speak of its meaning.

"Elin . . . I did . . . did love her."

The rock in her throat was so large. "I'll tell her."

His eyes swam. "Y-you smell. Like. Mama." He shivered. His strength siphoning out of him as the guilt and self-loathing had.

He struggled to take a breath. "I want. To see. Them."

She tightened her hold on him, fighting against the despair threatening to take over her. She would not turn from him, would stay with him to the end.

She nodded, saying, "You will." She'd say whatever he needed her to say.

"Elin." His voice wavered. And then, "Efie . . ." *Home.*

Ofori released Nena's hand, then grasped the handle of the other knife. She didn't stop him when he pulled it out of his neck, releasing the deluge of blood from the shorn artery.

She did not help him as his breath hitched and hitched, until there was no more breath in him.

Nena did not stop Ofori when he left her, the last of the Asyms.

# 78

## AFTER

Georgia's shout pierced the haze of Nena's grief. She gave a final, longing look at Ofori. How she wished they had had more time to pick their way through Paul's minefield of lies to be brother and sister again. It was all too late now. She summoned enough power to leave him and climb the stairs. Georgia was screaming, railing against Paul, who demanded she shut the hell up, fucking brat.

Nena followed their sound to the last room at the end of a dark hall, where a light shone beneath the door. She opened it.

Paul greeted her from the chair in which he sat. He was working through the realization that his Oliver was gone. Even with his gun trained on her, Nena thought she saw sadness, grief, even, in his expression. Propped up against his chair was a machete, one not dissimilar from her nightmares. Nena's eyes could not move from it.

Georgia sat in a chair between them. When she saw Nena, she called out, attempting to get up.

"Stay where you are," Paul commanded, moving his gun in Georgia's direction.

"Let her go." Nena started toward them, then stopped when Paul cocked the gun.

"You don't make demands here." He glared at her, eyes narrowed. "Is he dead?" When she didn't answer, he said, unaffected, "Doesn't matter. Oliver was weak and simpering."

She looked at him with contemptuous silence, disgusted at his lack of loyalty toward a man he called his son.

"Not like you." He cracked a wry smile, then cocked his head to the side. "You mourn him? He would have killed you."

"Because of you."

Annoyance sizzled through him. She could see the way it slid across his face. "He would have fucked you had I allowed it. Consider that as you mewl over him. Your brother would have raped you."

"Also," she said flatly, "because of you."

He paused, looking thoughtful. "I wonder what you would do to save the skin of your new father and your—what is this girl to you anyway? Your wannabe daughter."

He stood, using his free hand to straighten his suit, making his way around his desk to Georgia's seat. She sat ramrod straight, hands in her lap, her eyes never leaving Nena's face.

"Get up," he said.

Georgia listened, standing in the spot where Paul wanted her, as his shield.

Nena assessed the threat, scanning the room to see what she could use. She was too far away to disarm him without Georgia getting hurt in the process. It was why he kept her close to him, because he knew Georgia was his lifeline.

Paul caught her surveillance, a slow smile creeping across his face, and moved closer to Georgia, keeping his gun at her back, smug because he held all the cards.

"You are a resourceful woman," he said. "Kneel."

Nena balked, images of Papa on his knees flashing in her mind. "What?"

Paul raised the butt of his gun as if to hit the back of Georgia's head.

"Wait. Stop! Okay." She held her hands out, taking careful steps as she entered the room to sink onto the floor. Her voice was hoarse. "Don't hurt her." Slowly, she sank down, inhaling tiny breaths to ease the piercing pain.

"The boy worked you over good, eh?"

"What's next?"

Paul cocked his head to the side. "Now you choose."

She swayed a little, waiting, her side—hell, her whole body—throbbing.

"Over fifteen years ago, I made all the choices for you. I sent you to live a new life."

"You sold me as a slave."

Georgia struggled against Paul's hold. She tried to twist out of his grip, but he squeezed her shoulder and faced her forward.

"I gave you a new life," he corrected. "I helped you realize your potential. Look at you, wudini. Assassin. Killer. Lethal. Rich, now. Smart. Even beautiful. You should be thanking me."

She said nothing.

"Also, contrary to what you think, I did care for him, despite his failings." He regarded her. "Perhaps I chose wrong, eh. You are the survivor. The one. The queen among knights." He chuckled.

"I would have died first."

He shrugged, trailing the muzzle down the side of Georgia's face, her neck, her shoulders. She squirmed, trying to distance herself.

He swung the gun back to Nena.

"You get to choose now. I've got my seat on the Council. I'm untouchable now and can do what I want with their blessing because I can give them the territories they need. I can make things happen for them like they never could."

He didn't know he was ousted, that his dispatch was decreed. Whoever his benefactor was, whoever had helped him evade the Tribe fifteen years ago and worm his way in now, hadn't been able to outmaneuver Delphine Knight.

"You've got your seat at the table," she said. "Let the girl go."

His eyes sparkled. "I want *the* table."

"Let her go, and you can have it. My dad will give up High Council."

Paul pursed his lips. "You must think I'm stupid. Even if Noble abdicated his seat, it's not enough. This"—he poked the trembling girl with the muzzle of the gun—"is my safety net. You can have her back once you kill your dad."

Paul had presented that similar offer to her papa—kill his brother to save the rest.

"We don't have to kill him. He'll give it up, and then the Council will follow you."

"With Noble alive, there will always be questions, second guesses."

"I won't kill my dad."

"Then she dies." He chambered a bullet.

Georgia's body was so still Nena feared she was going to pass out.

"Paul."

"Make your choice. Or the girl joins her father."

# 79

## AFTER

Georgia's eyes welled with tears.

"He's not dead, Georgia," Nena said quickly, not wanting the girl to believe for even a second that her father was dead.

She held Georgia's gaze, shaking her head ever so slightly at the determined look in Georgia's eyes, the firm plant of her feet like she'd learned when they'd had their lessons. Her expression indicated she already understood what Nena wanted her to do next.

They were out of time.

"I don't have all day, Aninyeh," Paul snapped.

Georgia stepped back gently until the muzzle of the gun was flush against her back, just as Nena had shown her. She twisted suddenly, taking Paul by surprise and pushing his gun arm out and away from her. She jammed her fist into his solar plexus.

He staggered, grunting. Georgia's other arm snaked around his gun hand, keeping clear. She held on to his arm as she pulled the gun backward and snapped it out of his hand. It fell with a thud to the floor. Then she kicked him in the leg for good measure.

Nena didn't spare a moment to commend her prodigy for executing her disarming move so efficiently. She kicked the gun out of the way, then jumped to her feet, hurling herself at the disoriented Paul. They tumbled to the ground.

Nena struggled against the pain in her ribs to restrain Paul's writhing beneath her. His anger fueled him. He might have been older by thirty years, but he was a stone-cold killer in fantastic shape.

It was hard for Nena to breathe. Paul took advantage of it, landing a body punch to the very area that could tolerate it the least. Nena sucked in air long and hard, tears springing to her eyes. He grabbed her neck, rolling her until she was on her back on top of him. He tightened his forearm against her throat.

Georgia scooped up the gun and held it awkwardly on the two adults in a deadlock.

"Don't do it, girl," he growled. "I'll finish this one off; then I'll come for you."

"It's okay, Georgia. Get out of here," Nena eked out. "All the way out. Don't stop."

Georgia listened, and with one last, long look, she ran. Nena heard her feet pounding down the stairs.

When she was sure Georgia was clear, she lifted her head as much as she could and released it. The back of her head smashed into Paul's chin and nose. His head snapped back against the floor. Simultaneously, she pulled her remaining knife from its holster and slammed it into Paul's thigh like it was an epinephrine injector. He howled, loosening his noose enough for her to roll off him.

He grunted, breathing through the pain. She heard the knife clatter to the floor after he pulled it out.

She was out of weapons, her last having been firmly planted in Paul's flesh, and she was dizzy and trying to crawl away. She could hear a high-pitched sound, like metal against a sharpening stone. Her heartbeat raced. If only she could get enough distance between them to regroup.

She chanced a glance over her shoulder. Paul had limped to his feet. With one hand clamped over his wound, he had managed to grab the machete.

"You like knives?" he asked, spitting blood and approaching her. "Well, so do I."

She froze, staring at the machete as it scraped against the wood, making an awful, sickening sound. It wasn't the same machete from years ago, but its symbolism was as potent as the original.

"Bit of nostalgia, eh, wudini?" Paul grinned, favoring his injured leg.

She rolled over on the floor, exhausted. She could get out of the way. She could run. But her ribs slowed her down; the stab wound in her side hurt like a bitch. Her head swam. And she didn't trust her speed or her strength at the moment. She had no more time because Paul was coming at her, blade raised. But instead of running her through, he used the butt of its handle to strike her on the face.

He grabbed her shirt, hoisting her to her feet. With his forearm against her throat, he rammed her backward into the wall.

"Fuck a unified Africa. You think I'm the only one who feels this way? I'm going to dismantle everything Noble built. Eradicate the Knights like I did the Asyms," he whispered in her ear.

"One thing I've learned about you," Nena said, raising her arm and driving a palm strike right beneath his nose, "is that you've always talked too much."

His head snapped back. Her hand made a claw, and she pulled it across his face, grabbing his cheek in her nails and spinning him to the wall, where she kneed him twice in his stomach. He doubled over.

He used the machete to hold himself up. He began to lift it, but Nena kicked her foot out, stomping on the handle and his hand gripping it. She backhanded him in the face, the impact of it flinging him backward. The machete clanged to the ground. She bent down to pick up the heavy weapon. It felt alien to her. It felt wrong.

With the tip of the blade, she pushed him until he was against the wall. And then she pushed the blade in farther, leaning in closely, their foreheads nearly touching. She watched Paul's expression, how he winced in pain, the rounding of his eyes when shock hit him, the confusion at being bested. The blade's tip punctured his flesh, sinking in as she put her body weight into it. She didn't stop pushing until the wall stopped her.

Paul's knees buckled. He sank down, and her with him, the machete protruding from him. She refused to take her eyes from him. She grasped the hilt of the long blade and yanked it out. Paul's hands feebly reached for her, bloodied and weakened.

She shifted to the side of him, into position, curving her hands around the blade's handle like a batter readying to hit the ball.

"You . . . can't," he wheezed. "I'm Council!"

She raised the machete high above her shoulder. "And by the African Tribal Council, you are sanctioned for dispatch."

And with a whip through the air, she brought it down, separating Paul's head from his body.

# 80

## AFTER

Nena sat at the bottom of the staircase, battered, stabbed, bloody, and asking about Georgia, Cort, and Elin.

Witt replied through her phone, "At the hospital where the girl's father was admitted. Your neighbor took the girl there."

Her team member Alpha hovered nearby, keeping his eye on her and making sure every order was being followed per Witt's instructions. The Cleaners had already been called, and Network was doing its thing to keep the whole affair as low profile as possible.

"Keigel." She swallowed a spasm of pain where Ofori had drilled into her. She was thinking probably a broken rib, hopefully no damage to her kidney. "You'll put more security on Dad and Mum?"

"Already on it." She heard Witt's wry smile through the phone. "Not my first rodeo, my dear."

She didn't care. "And Elin?"

Witt answered her with silence.

She nodded her acknowledgment, though he couldn't see her. She needed to be stronger only a little while longer.

"His son?" one of the Cleaners asked as he approached. In his hands he held the tools of his trade: heavy plastic to wrap Paul's body and industrial-strength duct tape to keep it wrapped until they could place it in a barrel with lye for quicker decomposition. Ofori wouldn't suffer that fate. She had other plans for him.

"Take special care of the body," she said. "Put it on ice. I'll take care of it later." She ignored the dubious look he gave her.

He looked for confirmation at Alpha, who nodded. "Do as she says. Wrap him."

She was glad neither of them followed up with more questions. Right now, she needed a ride to the hospital to see Cort and Georgia.

From there, however it turned out with Cort, Keigel would take her home. And then she wouldn't have to be strong for anyone, if only for a little while.

———

In the late hour, the streets were thankfully deserted, so she and Alpha barreled toward Mercy Hospital, where Elin assured Nena that Cort was stable and resting in his room.

Elin was waiting for her in the hallway outside Cort's hospital room. Nena was anxious to see him, not because she worried over his health but because he now knew the truth about her. What would he do about it?

"He'll be okay. The bullet went in and out, and he has a pretty serious concussion from the blow to the head."

Nena processed the information. Elin was giving her fervent looks as if she wanted to say more. She wanted to ask after Oliver. How did Nena tell her what had happened to him? And more so, would Elin be able to forgive Nena for killing him?

She met Elin's questioning gaze. Delivering the news was the hardest thing she'd ever have to do. If she lost Elin, she couldn't fathom how she'd cope. Elin had been her rock. Would she believe Nena had no choice?

Elin took a breath. "He's dead, isn't he?" Her tone was dull. Her eyes held trepidation, but she'd clearly resolved to be the Tribe leader she was supposed to be.

"He is." Nena waited for a beat. "By my hands." She didn't usually explain her actions, but she owed Elin this.

"I learned . . . Oliver . . ." The expectant look, mixed with curiousness, on Elin made Nena falter. She hadn't even had the chance to reconcile who Oliver had been; how would Elin? Or anyone? She hoped Elin's questions would come later, not now, because she had no answers to give beyond her next words.

"Oliver was Ofori. My brother who I thought died with the rest of my family back in N'nkakuwe." The words rushed from her so fast Nena could barely understand them herself. But she pushed forth while Elin backed away from her, hand at her mouth, eyes wide and not understanding.

"How?" Elin managed to ask.

"I tried, very hard, for it to end differently. But Ofori—Oliver— Paul's brainwash was too great. I couldn't stop him," Nena tried to explain. "I am sorry."

She was with every fiber of her being. Elin hadn't deserved any of this.

"He loved you," Nena added. "You were one of the last things he spoke of. Before . . ." She ducked her head.

Elin's face was a mask of false stoicism. "Yeah, well, it was all a part of his plan? His and Paul's?" She didn't need a real answer, so Nena remained silent. "All of it was a ploy, and I'm quite over being a pawn." She rolled her eyes, laughing dryly. "The next man better watch the hell out."

Nena watched as her sister subconsciously twirled her new wedding ring on her finger.

Elin sniffled, shaking herself back to the present. "Anyway, you should get in there and sort things out."

Nena gestured toward the police milling around the hall. "What's the story?"

"They're going with an attempted abduction. Apparently, the detective Oliver killed was a friend of Cort's?"

Nena nodded. Mack.

"The police suspect retaliation for a case they were working on that Cort was going to try. They think the plan was to kidnap Georgia and blackmail Cort to not prosecute or something of that sort. It's the story Cort came up with."

Nena nodded again.

"They found Georgia's cell phone in someone's backyard, and she told them she ran from the assailant, was picked up by your neighbor who brought her here." Elin slipped her hands into her pockets, yawning.

"Did she tell you what happened to her?"

"Said she ran and Oliver chased her through the neighborhood. She thought she lost him by hiding in a doghouse."

"But he found her."

Elin's eyes were red rimmed. "He found her and brought her to Paul."

Nena inclined her head toward Cort's closed door. "How much does he know?"

"Everything. I know you said to explain things to him, but I couldn't bring myself to do it. So the kid did."

Nena waited a beat, unsure if she wanted the answer to the question she was afraid of asking.

Elin gave her a sympathetic look. "He's just angry right now. And in shock."

Nena mustered up a wry expression. It seemed her brother was not the only family she'd lost that night.

Her sister yawned again, and Nena suggested she head home and call their parents to let them know everything was fine. Nena was exhausted, too; the adrenaline was long gone. The pain from her injuries came at her like a truck. If they'd let her, she could lie on the hospital floor for a week. However, there was one more thing she had to do.

Nena limped to Cort's room, gingerly holding her stab wound. She waved away offers of assistance from the hospital staff who saw her. She would be fine, and she didn't want to answer questions. She stood in the doorway, waiting until Cort and Georgia noticed her, ignoring the officer assigned to protect them as he tried to tell her she couldn't be there.

"She's okay, Bill," Cort said, locking eyes with her. "Thanks."

She waited for Cort's next move, but he only stared at her, a storm gathering behind his eyes.

Georgia pointed the TV remote she'd been holding to turn the volume down, her eyes anxiously ping-ponging between Nena and her father.

# 81

## AFTER

Nena broke their three-way stare, hoping she could make it through the moment she'd have to pay the piper with Cort.

"You are unharmed?" she asked.

Georgia nodded vigorously while her father countered with, "What happened to the man who took Peach?"

"Dead."

They looked at her. Georgia already knew, having passed Ofori on her way out of the house; Cort looked as if he were about to be sick.

"This is like a fucking movie," he fumed, grimacing as he tried to adjust himself in the bed.

Nena said, "You two are no longer in danger."

"How big of you," he snapped, his face screwing into unrestrained anger. "Aren't you like an assassin or something? It's what Peach says. Hell, come to think of it, it's what you've been saying the entire time I've known you. And here I thought you were joking." His voice was gaining strength. "That's your job, for real? To go around killing people?"

"Not good people, Dad," Georgia quipped.

That wasn't true, Nena thought. They weren't always bad people. But she wasn't about to correct the girl now.

"Peach, be quiet."

"Something like that. Yes," Nena said carefully.

Cort narrowed his eyes. "And it's true you killed two guys the night you brought Peach home?"

"I told you, Dad, they were gang members who were trying to kill me. Nena saved my life."

Cort's nostrils flared. He turned slowly to his daughter. "Georgia."

Nena had never heard Cort speak to his daughter so sharply and full of barely restrained anger. Misdirected anger. It was her Cort was really angry with. Her who'd betrayed him. Georgia must have known not to push him, because she quickly snapped her mouth shut.

Nena said, "It's true."

Cort deflated, looking so hurt Nena's heart broke with him.

"I thought we connected," he said. "I thought you were opening up to me that night at the beach."

She stepped forward. She wanted to go to him so badly. She wanted to touch him. "We have. I did."

"I thought you trusted me."

Nena hesitated. "Trust is not why I didn't disclose that part of my life, Cort."

"Then what was it? Because my fourteen-year-old child knows more about you than I do. She may know *the* most important thing about you that I should have known."

"She only knows by chance. Only because she was there, not because I chose to tell her."

"Hey." Georgia spoke up softly, insulted.

They ignored her.

"What made you confide in her and not in me, even after sharing what happened in your past with your home and family?"

"Well, she didn't tell me that part." Georgia pouted, trying to lessen the blow. "Paul, the creep, did that. He was so creepy, like heebie-jeebies creepy."

Nena said, "Georgia, perhaps you can give your father and me a moment?"

Georgia hesitated, as if she didn't want to leave them alone, afraid the adults would screw things up without her there to mediate. In her face, Nena saw a discord of emotions, the want to be defiant and demand she stay, the awareness of her place as a child and that she should do as told. Begrudgingly, Georgia stood, casting an apprehensive glance at her dad.

"I didn't get hurt and I'm not scarred for life, so don't say anything stupid, Dad," she warned, heading toward the door.

As she passed Nena, Georgia suddenly threw her arms around her in a hug that lasted longer than Nena was accustomed to. Nena allowed it and found she liked it, even though Georgia hadn't asked. Eventually, she extricated herself from Georgia's grip and waited until Georgia left them alone.

Nena moved closer to the bed, assessing Cort's injuries. He looked so beautiful, despite his abrasions and swollen face. Her hand reached to touch him, but she managed to stop herself before she made contact.

"Why didn't you tell me everything?"

She balled her hand, bringing it back down to her side. "Because if you knew, then you would walk out of my life and take Georgia with you. I couldn't bear it."

He searched her eyes. "Do you understand that I am an agent of the justice system? I prosecute criminals, killers. You are a killer, Nena."

He was right.

"It doesn't matter if you're only killing other criminals for the benefit of your mobster family. It's still a crime."

She inclined her head. "The Tribe is not a mob—"

"You all are criminals."

She shook her head vigorously. "We are not. My team, when deployed, tries to right the wrongs our more problematic members inflict on others, wrongs that may fracture and weaken our organization. Any we feel impede the advancement of the African people, we handle."

He scoffed, "By taking the law into your own hands. Some kind of international vigilantes."

If that was what he wanted to call it. "I mete out justice for our own, by our own. It's how we do things." She thought for a moment. "Is it dissimilar to your Black Panthers? Malcolm X?"

He laughed dryly. "Who said how they went about things was the right way to do it every time? You can't speak about them. You're not even from here."

He made a point. "But their message, their goals, their intent to make strong Black Americans, to give you rights and freedoms, to give you safety from racists and others who sought to keep you under their thumbs. Was that not right? How different is it from the Tribe?"

He shook his head. "It's against the law, Nena. That's why we have laws, rules from which we govern to keep everyone in check."

"As do we. We have rules, and without them, there is chaos. I prevent chaos." If they'd already gone this far, Nena decided that Cort might as well know everything. "There's only been one time I've broken the rules."

He looked at her suspiciously before finally asking, "When?"

"When I shot Dennis Smith instead of you."

The monitors hooked up to Cort began a chorus of beeping as his pulse and heart rate quickened. Nena worried he was going to have a heart attack or the nurses would have to come in.

"What the hell are you talking about?" he whispered.

She told him.

Told him how she'd recognized him the night before when she'd brought Georgia home and how she'd chosen to shoot Attah instead of him two days later.

"You killed him because of what he did to you," Cort said. "If he wasn't there, would you have killed me?"

She shook her head. "No, because when I saw you the night before, I—" What was she supposed to say? Was this when she professed her feelings for him? "I felt something different about you."

"You felt what?" he pushed.

She was struggling. Professing love—emotions—was not her norm. The word *love* floated in her head, still so like a dream to her that she couldn't bring herself to say it aloud. She didn't say it to her family. They just knew and accepted it as her way. She wished Cort could do the same.

"Affection. I feel . . ." She licked her lips. "I care for you." It was the best she could do, but the way Cort's face fell told her it was not enough. Her choice of words was all wrong, and she didn't have the wherewithal to figure out the appropriate thing to say at this moment. Every fiber of her physical being hurt. And now, seeing the way Cort looked at her, as if she'd torn out his heart, her emotional being had nothing else to give either.

"You care for me," he repeated. "How fucking lucky of me."

The monitors began to slow, his pulse regulating. "And if you hadn't seen me the night before? Would you have killed me?"

"No, I would have killed Attah."

He shook his head at her response. It wasn't good enough. "But if Attah wasn't there? If it was just me and you hadn't seen me the night before or saved Peach from those assholes, would you have killed me?"

She waited a long beat. If there was any time to lie, it was now. But Cort didn't deserve lies. He had earned the truth.

"Yes," she whispered, forcing herself to hold his gaze. "It would have been business as usual."

She laid her hand lightly on his arm, the need to explain overwhelming. "But fate saw differently. Does that count for anything? You care for me, too, Cort. Can you get past my omissions of truth? Can you take me as I am? There will be no more secrets between us. You know it all."

It was an eternity before he answered. He considered her, and in his look, she saw what she'd seen on the beach. The space behind her eyes felt hot, and her vision blurred.

"Is that what you believe? That I only cared about you? The word's *love*, Nena. Love. As in I love you."

Her heart thundered in her chest, its beats tripling. For a second it looked like he might be able to see past it all. To see what she'd become, not what she used to be.

"But all of this," he continued. "What you nearly did to me . . . what you do . . . it's too much." The crestfallen expression on his face dammed her flow of happiness and hope. Cort wasn't like the dad in *Pet Sematary*. He wouldn't take Nena in whatever capacity he could have her. And the realization was crushing. Of all the things Nena had overcome, would this be what broke her?

"Please." It was the closest thing she could say aloud to the *I love you* playing on repeat in her mind. If only the words would come out. Then maybe he'd see how much he meant to her.

His face mirrored her heartbreak. "Your world and mine are too different. We believe in different things, Nena. How can I reconcile that? I'm bound to uphold the law. And you are the antithesis of everything I'm supposed to believe in. But you made me believe in you. And you made me . . ."

His eyes were glassy, though Nena couldn't really tell through her own. She willed herself to stand firm. She knew there could be no other outcome than this.

"You made me love you. Made me think I had another chance."

She held her breath.

"But I don't think I can do this," he finished.

Georgia was waiting for Nena when she left Cort's room, gently closing the door behind her. Georgia was a mess of tears and snot, looking a decade younger than her fourteen years. She was at Nena's side before Nena had a chance to move from the door. She grabbed Nena into a hug, burrowing her face in Nena's chest as she cried and tried to speak, but her words were muffled.

Nena gently stroked her hair, the hair she'd so lovingly fixed what seemed like eons ago. They'd been so happy then.

"It's okay. This is for the best." She extracted herself from Georgia's arms. "Be with your father, okay?" She took a few steps backward, distancing herself, though Georgia kept coming, kept pleading.

"He's just in pain. This is new to him, and he doesn't understand. We can make him understand."

"He's right," Nena whispered, spinning around so she didn't have to see Georgia's face. She began walking away.

"He's not right!" Georgia yelled behind her, her voice cracking. "Please don't go. Don't go, Nena, please."

Nena forced herself to continue walking, going against every molecule in her body. Georgia's pleas haunted her, would haunt her forever.

"Please, Nena! I need you!"

Nena's steps faltered. Her breath hitched. She rounded a corner, now out of Georgia's sight.

"*We* need you!"

And it was those words that broke her. The wudini. The woman of stone. Her hand reached out to anchor her against a wall as she stumbled beneath the weight of what she'd just lost.

# 82

## NOW

She returned to the home of her *before*. It was a merging of worlds so profound it weighed heavily on Nena's shoulders. She arrived in Accra, then drove the couple of hours to Chigali, now a bustling town at the base of Aburi Mountain that she didn't recognize. If memory served her correctly, N'nkakuwe was a bit farther up, a little less than an hour away.

She approached a small home where an older woman sold market items, rifled through the metal barrel of melting ice, and pulled out a sweating glass bottle of Pepsi. A rush of nostalgia took over, and she relished it. Her first thought went to Georgia—how she'd get a kick out of taking a swig from one of these old-school bottles. Then she was hit by the dull sadness that sneaked up on her more times a day than she cared to count.

When she asked about N'nkakuwe, the woman's eyes glazed over with a sadness Nena easily related to.

"There is no more N'nkakuwe, child," she said. "Has not been that way in a long, long time."

"I'm sorry to hear that, Auntie," Nena replied, sighing. "I was hoping that maybe it was still here." That no one had rebuilt the village was heart wrenching to hear.

Auntie shook her head slowly. "The land up there is haunted. Angry spirits of the murdered chief and his people roam the mountain. There is nothing but sadness and horror. All because their souls are in unrest." She moved her right hand in the sign of the cross.

She told Nena that she was better off heading back to Accra, Kumasi, or whichever way she'd come. "Best leave the unhappiness where it lies."

Nena appreciated the warning, knew well the superstitions of her people. She held those same beliefs, and it was one of the reasons why she'd returned. "I need to go," she said. "I'm not afraid of ghosts or sadness. I've lived with them half my life."

"Have you?" She gave Nena a closer assessment.

"N'nkakuwe used to be my home."

The woman's eyes grew large.

"Wo din de sɛn?" She asked Nena's name, squinting against the sunlight to get a better look at the strange, sad-looking woman dressed as if ready for safari, asking about a dead village in her British accent. "I think you may favor a man I once knew. Good man killed too young. Who are you, child?"

Nena pulled out money to pay for her drink. But the woman waved the cedis away, instead giving her a look that vacillated between suspicion and intrigue.

"Medaase," Nena said, thanking her.

As Nena began walking away, the woman called out, "Mema wo nante yie." *I wish you luck.* "N'nkakuwe ba baa." *Daughter of N'nkakuwe.*

Nena's eyes began to sting with hot tears at hearing the most beautiful words spoken to her in longer than she could remember.

On her way back to her Range Rover, Nena passed two other women. One of them was churning a long wooden spoon in a large cast-iron pot; the other sat in a chair, shelling a large bowl of black-eyed peas. Nena recognized the pungent smell of fermenting yeast and immediately knew they were cooking kenkey. Her stomach growled. Their slow stirring, shelling, having heard the auntie's words, all mixing Nena's worlds of then and now.

They saw her and said, "Akwaaba," as she passed. She waved. They watched her get back into her truck and drive off, rushing to guzzle her Pepsi before it became too warm and lost its fizz.

By the time she reached the indentation, the spot that marked the beginning of the path toward N'nkakuwe, it was late afternoon. Tall willowy grass, vines thick as a baby's arm, and leaves the size of bath towels had long overrun the roads she'd walked as a child, so she had to park her vehicle and hike the rest of the way. It wasn't long before she began to see the ruins. The burned and hollowed-out skeletal remains of buildings once inhabited by people she'd lived among. To an outsider, the village would resemble a lost civilization from thousands of years ago, instead of less than two decades. To Nena, it was the place of her birth and the burial grounds of a lifetime.

She was home again. And—she looked down at the glossy mahogany box she held in both hands—Ofori was home as well. Inside was all that was left of her brother. She looked around, trying to recall where things used to be—or where they should have been. So many memories invaded her mind. The weight of them was staggering, and her grief began to build momentum.

The years of despair and guilt were stacks upon her shoulders. She wanted to lie down in the dirt and cry, but she had to make her feet move. She was home, really home. *Home* home. Despite her memories of her last night in N'nkakuwe, Nena had had fourteen wonderfully blessed years with an incredible family to sweeten her memories. She had to remember that. Had to remember to think of the fourteen years before her *after* had begun.

Before she realized it, she was at the village center, where they used to gather. And there was the tree. The one Papa would stand beneath as he led his people. The tree was black and twisted, dead like the rest of the village and the people who'd lived in it. Nature had overrun the husk of the village, but it couldn't entirely hide the destruction or the ghosts that still roamed here.

She stopped at the base of the blackened tree. There she opened the box holding Ofori's ashes. She'd been robbed of the chance to bury Papa and the twins, Wisdom and Josiah. She'd never seen her auntie again after she'd left her in their kitchen. But Nena had brought the last male Asym home, where Ofori belonged.

She removed the bag and opened it. A light breeze began to rise. It was warm and dry, like a hug against her skin. The leaves of nearby trees started to rustle, sounding like rice cascading into an empty pan. The long, fingerlike grass swayed. She heard a soft beat. Then a distant thrumming. She thought maybe drummers in another village. She knelt, hesitating only a second before upending the bag and watching as Ofori's ashes tumbled out.

"Akwaaba, Ofori. Akwaaba, efie." She welcomed him back home.

The wind increased, catching the ashes and making them swirl. Her brother danced on the wind away from her. The thrumming she'd heard earlier increased, sounded closer now. The sun beat on her shoulders, through the thin cotton of her T-shirt, as the wind strengthened. She looked at the horizon spread before her. The sun's rays wavered like rising heat. All to the beat of thrumming.

She blinked, unsure if what she was seeing in the distance was truly there or if she was in the throes of heatstroke. Because as the wind increased and the heat shimmered and the sweat beaded on her forehead, Nena saw people standing before her. Rows and rows of them. Her people, as she last remembered them.

She sat back on her haunches, scared she'd lost her mind. But her fear eased into wonder when she saw they were smiling at her, waving. They were happy, not angry, not haunted or sad. And in front of them stood Papa. Wisdom. Josiah. And Mama. Nena swallowed a cry. She wiped at her face, and her hand came away wet.

It had to be a mirage. But she'd swear the wind carried the scents of Olay and Hugo Boss, and finally a sob did escape her. She watched as a man appeared from the edge of the clearing, walking toward her

410

family and the villagers behind them. He paused, glancing over his shoulder and nodding to her, and she saw he was Ofori as she'd known him the night he'd taken his last breath. He resumed approaching their family, and they looked at him with nothing but love in their eyes. They welcomed him, their arms open and accepting their son, their brother, back into the fold as if he had never left.

"Me ba barima. Me ba baa." *My son. My daughter,* Papa said, a whisper in the wind.

Ofori continued walking, and as he did, his height began to shorten. His chiseled muscles retracted and thinned. Nena watched the years shed from him, and his pace quickened until he was running toward them.

"Due. Due." He apologized over and over, nearing them with arms outstretched, becoming younger and younger until he was the child they last remembered. He ran into their arms, and they encircled him, obscuring him from Nena's vision. But she could hear him still begging for forgiveness.

His apologies were unnecessary. Ofori had been forgiven the moment Paul had forced him to choose between himself and his family. He had never been blamed, and Nena had eventually come to learn she'd never been blamed either. She'd realized her guilt was self-imposed and needless.

She got to her knees, tried to stand using the tree for support. She wanted that too. To be with them, with the family taken from her too soon. She, too, wanted to be fourteen again forever.

"Mereba!" she yelled, stretching her arm toward them. *I'm coming.* "Twɛn me." *Wait for me.*

Papa broke away from the group, stepping toward her, the distance still too wide.

"Aninyeh." His voice was as she remembered. "Yɛbɛhyia bio." *Until we meet again.*

She wanted to cry out, Daabi. *No.* Not to leave her behind. But as they looked at each other for what seemed like an eternity, she understood. It was not her time. Yes, this place was her home, would always be her home. But she had a new home, another family, and a life to live. And her work was not yet done.

Papa raised his hand. Then, two by two, they all did, waving at her. Ofori was the last, moving to stand with their father, looking so much like him that Nena's heart broke and swelled simultaneously.

Ofori said, "Medaase, me nua baa." *Thank you, my sister.* His body began to flicker in and out. "Medaase sɛ wode me aba efie." *Thank you for bringing me home.*

Nena raised her hand in farewell to her people. They began to fade out one by one. Papa and Ofori lingered last, taking one final look at their cherished daughter and sister, before they disappeared.

Once again, they were physically gone, but this time Nena was not alone, because she held them all in her heart. And she would keep each one of them there until she could finally join them.

———

Nena was making her way back to her truck, rucksack slung over her shoulder, when her satellite phone began to ring, sounding so weird when all she'd heard for hours were mountain noises. She paused to pull it from her sack and pressed the button to connect the call.

"So, funny thing." Elin's voice crackled through the line.

"What's that?" Nena asked, wondering what couldn't wait until her scheduled check-in once she'd made it back to the hotel.

"Turns out you're going to be an auntie."

Nena didn't answer. Both her steps and her voice were frozen.

Elin continued, "I'm okay with it, to be quite frank. I hope you'll be too."

Nena knew without question she was okay with it. She only wished she was there to hug her sister and shower her with all the love she now knew she was capable of . . . for her niece or nephew too.

"I was thinking to name the baby with your family's name. Asym. I'm still playing around with it all, and it's mad early, but I wanted your okay."

Nena had to stop and sit to catch her breath. What Elin was doing for her and her family had no words.

"Did the call drop? Damn sat phone. Hello?"

"I'm here. Still here."

"Are you good with it, sis?"

Nena could hear the worry in Elin's voice.

"Yeah," she managed to get out. "Of course I am."

The baby would be of her blood, a fusion of the lineage of Michael Asym and Noble Knight, the men who'd given Nena life two times over. Nena couldn't see through the thick, hot tears blurring her vision. She was unbelievably happy, despite the hint of sadness at the knowledge that she'd taken the life of this child's father, even if in self-defense. Her duty to the baby wouldn't just be as an aunt but as stand-in for the parent Ofori would have been. The responsibility she gave herself would be her cross to bear and her recompense. And she'd make sure to root out whoever had helped Paul infiltrate the Tribe, whoever had sought to destroy them, so that she could ensure this baby's legacy.

When N'nkakuwe had burned, her future had been unimaginable, bleak. But she'd fought for her life and survived. She'd suffered so much loss and gained more than she'd ever expected in Georgia and Cort— her breath caught. She couldn't think of them at the moment, couldn't think of them being lost to her, because they weren't. She'd try to find a way to have what she deserved back in her life again.

Because she was Nena Knight. She had shaped her *after*. She had made it her *now*. And most of all, she had learned to cherish every memory she had.

Both the gifts *and* the curses.

# End

# ACKNOWLEDGMENTS

First, my thanks to God, who stood by me and opened up windows when so many doors had closed.

And now for my Tribe . . .

To my mom, Evelyn Codjoe, for her love and dedication. She is the one person who keeps me grounded whether I want to be or not.

To the two most precious people in my life, my kids, Ethan and Ahmari Hunt, for their support, their laughs, and letting me hug on them almost whenever I want. It is for them that I had to make this writing thing work. I was determined to show them that giving up on your dreams is never an option despite life's adversities. I wanted to show them it is possible to pick yourself up after a fall (or many), start again, and do better than before. I hope they see all of that in me, and I know they will accomplish things in their lives that are beyond my imagination.

Thank you to my husband, Vincent McClinton I, who made it easy to dive into my imaginary world and write. Now, about getting a puppy . . .

My sister, Laura Bush (no, not the former first lady, but she's cool too), who is always the biggest supporter of my writing and my very first reader. Her insights and thoughtfulness were the calm in my storm. Derrick Angoe, my little brother bug, and Cecilia Angoe, the babe of our family: their sibbie group-chat messages keep me in much-needed stitches and in tears.

My found family, the Moores. Rhonda and Riccardo accepted me and my children into their family when we moved to South Carolina to begin a new life and knew not one single soul.

Melissa Edwards of Stonesong Literary, my literary agent extraordinaire, for helping to make my writing dreams come true and being a champion of my work. She answers my multitude of questions as if I've only asked one and is such a phenomenal agent that I'm always in awe of her agenting prowess. I am so excited for the many successful collaborations with her that will be coming up.

Megha Parekh, my editor at Thomas & Mercer, another great champion. Megha really understood Nena's story and her purpose. She recognized the importance of Nena's unapologetic voice and her rich culture and wanted to broadcast it to the world. I don't know how Megha keeps me all together, but she does. Caitlin Alexander, my developmental editor, for her grace, patience, and extraordinary ability to get more out of me than I knew was there. Laura Barrett, my production editor. I am missing more people from the team at Thomas & Mercer . . . but thank you!

To my writing friends—and now friends for life—Del Sandeen and Jane Igharo, who both read my book in its entirety and in its first draft. To read a writer's work is one of the best gifts you can give them, and these ladies did that for me. I cherish their invaluable feedback, our brainstorm sessions, and them just being some bomb-ass ladies. To Tina Ehsanipour and Stephanie Jones: Our text group chats are always filled with encouragement about writing and mothering. We saw each other through some dark days. To Kellye Garrett, who is talented, hilarious, and generous with her time and expertise. Kellye also connected me with Shawn S. A. Crosby (who Kellye warned was tough). He read Nena's earlier version and gave it his stamp of approval, confirming what I knew: Nena could keep up with the fellas. To Gia de Cadenet, who mentored me when I'd first landed on social media. She and her husband made sure the French in the book was as it should be. Whew!

To Sisters in Crime, for membership into their organization and for bestowing on me the honor of the Eleanor Taylor Bland Award for emerging authors of color. Winning that award sparked the lightning strike that is Nena, setting all of this in motion. To Crime Writers of Color, the best and most talented online group of crime writers one could surround oneself with.

And finally, to all those who have been a part of my getting here: Mom Maxine, a phenomenal mother-in-law, and my lovable stepsons, Vincent (Deuce) and Wilson; Christa Desir, who mentored me and taught me the editorial side of publishing, thus making me a better writer; members of the Twitter, Facebook, and Slack writing and author communities, who shared all things writing and gave an encouraging word or two—there are too many of you to name, but please know how much I truly appreciate you; my friends Catayah Clark and Jessica Ogburn, two of the best ladies I know both at the nine-to-five and after. They have been my biggest cheerleaders, provided the best words of wisdom, and pushed me to enjoy my accomplishments.

Lastly, many thanks and love to my fellow Ghanaians for allowing me grace to tell Nena's story, which celebrates our culture, and for forgiving any mistakes I may have made in my imagining of Nena's world. Good things are coming for Nena, and I can't wait to share more of her with all of you.

# ABOUT THE AUTHOR

*Photo © 2020 Tamika Williams of Creative Images Photography*

Hailing from Northern Virginia, Yasmin Angoe is a first-generation Ghanaian American who grew up in two cultural worlds. She taught English in middle and high schools for years, served as an instructional coach for virtual teachers, and spent time as a freelance copy editor.

Angoe recently received the Eleanor Taylor Bland Award for emerging writers of color from Sisters of Crime, of which she's a proud member. When she's not writing, she's in South Carolina with her beautiful blended family, trying new recipes and absorbed in an audiobook. *Her Name Is Knight* is Yasmin's debut novel.